THE WELCOME

The
WELCOME

Hubert Creekmore

Introduction by
Phillip Gordon

University Press of Mississippi / Jackson

BANNER BOOKS SERIES

The University Press of Mississippi is the scholarly publishing agency of the Mississippi Institutions of Higher Learning: Alcorn State University, Delta State University, Jackson State University, Mississippi State University, Mississippi University for Women, Mississippi Valley State University, University of Mississippi, and University of Southern Mississippi.

www.upress.state.ms.us

The University Press of Mississippi is a member of the Association of University Presses.

Library of Congress Cataloging-in-Publication Data

Names: Creekmore, Hubert, 1907–1966, author. | Gordon, Phillip, 1981– writer of introduction.
Title: The welcome / Hubert Creekmore; introduction by Phillip Gordon.
Description: Jackson : University Press of Mississippi, 2023. | Series: Banner books series
Identifiers: LCCN 2022045036 (print) | LCCN 2022045037 (ebook) | ISBN 9781496844859 (hardback) | ISBN 9781496844927 (epub) | ISBN 9781496844934 (epub) | ISBN 9781496844941 (pdf) | ISBN 9781496844958 (pdf)
Subjects: LCSH: Closeted gays—Mississippi—Fiction | Men—Mississippi—Relations with men—Fiction | LCGFT: Novels.
Classification: LCC PS3505.R398 W45 2023 (print) | LCC PS3505.R398 (ebook) | DDC 813/.52—dc23/eng/20221125
LC record available at https://lccn.loc.gov/2022045036
LC ebook record available at https://lccn.loc.gov/2022045037

British Library Cataloging-in-Publication Data available

To
Ted Rearick

CONTENTS

HUBERT CREEKMORE
Writing Letters Back Home

—Phillip "Pip" Gordon

In the spring of 1930, Hubert Creekmore, a young writer with his first manuscript and big dreams, left his native Mississippi for New York. On May 24, he stopped over at the Stevens Hotel in Chicago, where he took a moment to write a letter to a friend back home. The man he wrote to and the men he mentions may have names more famous than his, but beyond those names, one can also glimpse Creekmore's character, marked by the universal hope of any artist to conquer a little piece of the world:

> Dear Phil,
>   I meant to write to you just before I left to ask Bill Faulkner to send me the letter to Harrison Smith. But I got off in such a rush that I hadn't time. I have my book completed and typed and am now on my way to New York to storm the publishers. I'd never know how to thank both of you enough if you could help me with Mr. Smith.

William (Bill) Faulkner had submitted his manuscript for *As I Lay Dying* in January 1930 to his publisher, Harrison "Hal" Smith. By May he would have been working on page proofs for it or turning his attention to revisions for *Sanctuary* after Smith returned it to him with the famous exclamation, "Good God, I can't publish this. We'd both be in jail," because of its salacious content.

Smith was Faulkner's most important publisher, and in mid-1930, Faulkner's relationship with him was at its zenith.

"Phil" is Phil Stone, who is memorialized in biographies as Faulkner's first great muse for his role in introducing Faulkner to the early Modernists via literary magazines such as *The Dial* and *Poetry*. Creekmore, half a generation younger than his famous mentors, had a more complex connection to Stone, though in *The Welcome*, published nearly two decades later, Jim Furlow will recall how Don Mason also read these two magazines "that would have shocked the citizens of Ashton" (24), the fictional town in the novel modeled after Water Valley, Creekmore's hometown.

Creekmore's father was a lawyer in Water Valley; the Stone family had law firms in Oxford (twenty miles north of Water Valley) and Charleston (twenty miles west). Stone was an Oxford local connected to several North Mississippi authors in the 1920s and 1930s. Perhaps most importantly, Stone and Faulkner were members of Sigma Alpha Epsilon (SAE), a national fraternity with a chapter at the University of Mississippi (that often met off-campus at the Stone family home). Rufus and Wade Creekmore, Hubert's older brothers, were also members, as were most men in the Falkner, Stone, and Creekmore families save Hubert, who seemed interested in forging his own path. Not so his own, however, as to forgo these local and literary connections. Creekmore wanted to be an author; Stone and Faulkner apparently offered to help.

Creekmore wouldn't succeed, at least not in 1930. The manuscript, most likely *The Elephant's Trunk*, now housed with his papers at Boston University, never found a publisher. It would take more than a decade for Creekmore to perfect his prose enough to publish three novels in the late 1940s and early 1950s. The middle of those, *The Welcome*, published in 1948 though set in the late 1920s to the mid-1930s, is his most significant. In it, two young men, both from the fictional Ashton, were once best friends, but after college at the state university, they chart different paths in life. The first, Don Mason, eventually decides to leave Ashton for New York, only to return three years later to marry the local (wealthy) bohemian Isabel Lang. Jim Furlow never leaves; instead, he marries a coed, Doris, at the same time as Don's departure. Now, three years later, his marriage feels more like a trap than a promise of love and fulfillment. As the novel begins, Don's mother sends word to Jim asking that he meet Don at the train station upon his return. Thus turn the wheels of fortune to set in motion the tragic arc (though mercifully with no deaths, just heartache) of a forgotten literary masterpiece with a visionary commentary on the human heart and its universal, if too-often-denied, longings.

◆ ◆ ◆

Hiram Hubert Creekmore Jr. was born in Water Valley, Mississippi, on January 16, 1907, the third of four children to Hiram Sr. and Mittie Belle (Horton) Creekmore. He attended the local schools before matriculating at the nearby University of Mississippi, where he studied from 1924 to 1927. No individual photos of him appear in the yearbook for his freshman year, but his sophomore photo shows a bright smile in a youthful face, still more that of a teenager than a young man. His senior photo from 1927, on the other hand, is mired in shadow, with half his face obscured in brooding darkness like a Byronic figure in whom all the best of dark and bright meet in his aspect and in his eyes. His older brothers had attended the university as well. Rufus, the oldest, was a football star and popular socialite; he and Wade secretly rushed SAE despite a ban on fraternities issued that year by Gov. Lee Russell. Both Rufus and Wade would go on to study law. Hubert took a different path, joining the Scribblers, a campus literary fraternity that had rejected Faulkner a few years earlier, and the Marionettes, a campus theater troupe with which Faulkner was briefly affiliated in the early 1920s. In the 1927 yearbook, Creekmore also appears on a Who's Who page as the campus "literary vagabond" and seems to have crafted a persona on campus as a would-be author, a role previously occupied by Stark Young and William Faulkner, later by any number of hopeful writers in Oxford, that beautifully literary town.

According to John Bayne, a book collector with a special interest in Creekmore, the Creekmore family moved to Jackson, Mississippi, sometime in the late 1920s, possibly while Hubert was still enrolled at UM. In the late 1920s and early 1930s, Creekmore would come home to his parents' house on Pinehurst Street, not far from the home of Eudora Welty, two years Creekmore's junior. Creekmore's sister Mittie later married Welty's brother Walter, and, generally, biographies of Welty have served as a de facto location for the scant biographical details on her lesser-known friend. As to that friendship, it was bound by multiple shared interests: photography, gardening, and writing. Bayne suggests that Welty's first publications in the journal *Manuscript* in 1936 followed from Creekmore's recommendation of the journal to her after he published one of his own stories there in 1935.

Bayne's essay "Collecting Hubert Creekmore: A Bibliography," published online in proceedings from the 2013 Meeting of the Mississippi Philological Society, offers the best readily available biography of Creekmore in his own right, along with a resplendent bibliography that includes even the most esoteric of Creekmore's many publications. In his turn, Bayne drew heavily from a seven-page biographical entry on Creekmore published in 1971 by L. Moody Simms Jr., in a book titled *Notes on Mississippi Writers*. Simms fills in other data from after Creekmore's graduation from UM in 1927. He studied drama at the University of Colorado and playwriting at Yale University, sometime in the late 1920s. In the 1930s he worked for the Mississippi Highway Department in Jackson, then later in Washington, DC, for both the Veterans Administration and the Social Security Board. In the latter 1930s, he studied at Columbia University, where he completed a master's degree in American literature in 1940. Thanks to the aforementioned letter to Phil Stone, we can also place Creekmore in Oxford in the late 1920s, prior to his effort to publish his first novel in 1930. He must have at least still visited his old stomping grounds around UM in the mix of these other efforts to make a place for himself in the literary world.

He had his first major success not with a prose narrative but with poetry in 1940, with the publication of *Personal Sun*. He served as a yeoman and rose to lieutenant while stationed in the Pacific during World War II, though he continued writing and published another collection of poetry in 1943, *The Stone Ants*. This was followed by *The Long Reprieve* (1946), *Formula* (1947), and *No Harm to Lovers* (1950); the first two are collections of his poetry, the latter a translation from Latin of poems by Albius Tibullus. This period of his life also saw him begin the work for which he is, perhaps, best known, as a literary agent, editor, and translator. Finding his name listed as "editor" on various poetry collections is easier than finding works he authored himself. Beyond two boxes of his papers housed at the Howard Gottlieb Center at Boston University, letters and other ephemera from his life appear sporadically in archives for various agencies and publishers he worked for, including New Directions Press. He taught creative writing for a year at the University of Iowa (1948–49) and spent a season at Yaddo in 1951. None of this work elevated him to national prominence, but the breadth of his engagements as a man of letters has left a scattered if tangible paper trail.

He did manage eventually to publish three novels after the war, including *The Fingers of Night* (1946, later published in paperback as *Cotton Country*) and *The Chain in the Heart* (1952). Between these two novels, he published his most radically significant work, *The Welcome*. The original dust jacket for the novel subtitled it as *A Novel of Modern Marriage*, though its title page did not include this addition. It seems it was more novel than anyone knew.

◆ ◆ ◆

Somewhere around 2007, I took an independent study at the University of Mississippi with Jaime Harker. A transplant to Mississippi originally from California—with stops along the way in Provo, Utah, and Philadelphia—Harker was a newly tenured English professor, and she was well on her way to becoming a cornerstone of queer southern studies. She now serves as the director of the Sarah Isom Center for Women's and Gender Studies at UM, as well as the sole owner and proprietor of Violet Valley Bookstore, Mississippi's only queer feminist bookstore. She also calls Water Valley home.

Our topic was LGBTQ+ literature, at the time not a regular course at the university, graduate level or otherwise. Midway through the semester, she had me check out a book from the campus library by a writer named Hubert Creekmore. She explained that the book was from the 1940s, gay, and by a local author. She had heard about the book (and the author) from Annette Trefzer, another English professor at UM. Trefzer, a Welty scholar and Water Valley resident, had developed an interest in Creekmore and wanted to spread the word. This is how I first encountered the novel republished here.

The key detail that vexed all three of us was that Creekmore was completely out of print. Most notably, copies of *The Welcome* were exceedingly hard to find. According to Bayne, "*The Welcome* is a true rarity. An early novel dealing with same-sex relationships, it evidently has been bought up by collectors of books by gay authors or about gay themes. It is often cited but seldom discussed in books and papers about such works, most likely because who can find a copy?" The novel is, indeed, a fixture in bibliographic studies that attempt to identify all the gay-themed works from the pre-Stonewall era, a period notoriously rife with anti-gay sentiment and during which antisodomy laws and other legal proscriptions greatly curtailed visible gay life and representation.

John Howard's study of mid-century gay life in Mississippi, *Men like That: A Southern Queer History*, has previously offered the most extensive analysis of the novel, though even Howard's overview is minimal. Beyond Howard the most noteworthy comments on the novel come from two critics. First, Christopher Bram, in his book *Eminent Outlaws: The Gay Writers Who Changed America*, describes the novel as about "two men in love in a small Southern town. (It's striking how much gay fiction of this period is set in Dixie, as if the rest of the country could think about perversion only when it spoke a funny accent)." As a matter of fact, 1948 saw a sea change in the acceptance of same-sex desire, particularly in print and particularly in southern settings. Both Gore Vidal's *The City and the Pillar* and Truman Capote's *Other Voices, Other Rooms* were published in 1948, both by major publishing houses. Both fixate on the South: Vidal's novel begins in Virginia; Capote's is set in his own fictionalized version of Monroeville, Alabama, made more famous by Harper Lee. These novels are often credited as breaking through the proverbial (opaque) glass closet door that had limited previous depictions of same-sex desire in print. Notably, both are deeply pathological in their content. Vidal's novel ends in rape and murder, while Capote's includes a variety of southern gothic tropes that depict all modes of difference as deviant and perverse. *The Welcome* manages to tell a tragic story without the overdetermined pitfalls of either Vidal's or Capote's more famous works.

Second, Anthony Slides, in *Lost Gay Novels: A Reference Guide to Fifty Works of Fiction from the First Half of the Twentieth Century*, laments the dearth of knowledge about the novelist and his intentions: "There is no documentation on Hubert Creekmore. Neither is there any record of Ted Rearick, the man to whom he dedicated *The Welcome*." Slides also laments, "*The Welcome* will never be reprinted and never receive recognition for what it is." A notable tone of frustration pervades even these brief comments, a frustration shared by many scholars of queer literature who have struggled to explain why so many important works have disappeared into the ether of time. Thus, it is no small thing to have the opportunity to amend Slides's comment: "*The Welcome* [has not been] reprinted nor received recognition for what it is [until now]."

◆ ◆ ◆

In *The Welcome*, Creekmore subverts the conventions of a marriage plot, typically the purview of comedy, to craft a striking social critique, and he does so by structuring the narrative as a tragedy in the classical sense. As a reductive, though useful, way to differentiate comedy from tragedy, in the former everyone gets married, and in the latter, most everyone dies. (Think Shakespeare: in *A Midsummer Night's Dream* or *Much Ado about Nothing*, weddings are handed out like gifts on *Oprah*—"You get a wedding! And you get a wedding!"; in *Hamlet* or *Macbeth*, we count the dead bodies on the stage.) *The Welcome* is a novel about marriage, and it ends with everyone married and supposedly properly paired off. But if marriages are the stuff of comedies, at the end of this novel something is deeply amiss.

In a synopsis provided to his publisher while he worked on the novel, Creekmore explained, "The theme of the novel is the responsibilities of the man and the woman in a marriage, to each other and to their contract." That original synopsis identifies the novel under the working title *One to Another*; additional notes in Creekmore's papers allude to the manuscript under the title *Fulcrum* and suggests its setting was originally post–World War II. As he wrote it, Creekmore pushed its setting back to the 1930s, and began to explore these responsibilities by charting the trajectories of two couples: Jim and Doris, already married, whose marriage is disintegrating, and Don and Isabel, not yet married, who are determining they should marry each other because it is the normal thing to do. Jim married right out of college; Don left for New York. Now, a bit later than expected but still within reasonable bounds, Don has returned to marry and settled down in Ashton, as if his sojourn in New York had been a brief fancy on the road to the proper heterosexual union all citizens are destined toward. If Jim's marriage is any measure, we, as the audience, pity him for his folly in choosing a wife out of the inertia of expectation instead of love. Simultaneously, we fear Don might be making the same mistake in the final, devastating scene of the novel when he rebuffs Jim for Isabel, as if he and Isabel will somehow do better at this whole marriage thing. Jim, shattered, is left with Doris, who has, over the course of the novel, transformed into a grotesque caricature of a wife weighing down her husband.

Creekmore's depiction of Doris crosses over into misogyny (the novel is also given to the racial prejudices and blindness of its time, and the n-word makes two unwanted and jarring appearances). However, this depiction is meant as critique; Doris's transformation is a by-product of a social order that has given her no other way to understand herself. She is fully committed to being the wife of a successful, relatively upper-middle-class husband; when reality intrudes she cannot escape her programming and comes to embody all the faults of the institution.

But as with the best tragedies, this novel does not shoot its arrow down a generic storyline of marital dissatisfaction where all happy families are alike, but the unhappy ones make for more colorful drama. *The Welcome* becomes something more because Creekmore, as he revised it, added another element that pointed toward the possibility of a different outcome. Indeed, the best tragedy is not marked by heroes suffering from tragic "flaws" in their own characters. The majority of gay fiction prior to *The Welcome* structured tragedy as a natural outcome for being gay. Creekmore aimed higher and sought a narrative that does not show the same-sex lovers as flawed for their desires; rather, the problem is context. The best tragedy—of which I would rank *The Welcome*—follows the fate of characters who, in doing exactly what they are supposed to and must do, nonetheless miss the mark because something much larger than their lives shapes the outcome. In short, they are fated, despite their best intentions, to fail. The questions we should ask ourselves of this novel are: What is preventing a better future? Why does this love story go so terribly wrong?

After its publication Creekmore described his intention for the novel in an application for a Guggenheim Fellowship. After identifying that his goal was to question the usefulness of marriage in the modern world, he explained, "The problem is posed mainly on the negative side—the choice of not marrying, with emphasis on submerged homosexuality to dramatize the negative choice." He does not mean homosexuality is negative. Quite the contrary, he means that Don and Jim could have chosen not marrying women. They could have chosen each other instead, but they did not because the fates (or something much more powerful) prevented them.

Upon hearing of Don's return, Jim recalls a night from their youth when they drove into the countryside and came upon the remains of an abandoned church, where they drank and talked about the future but failed to say to each other what they both feel. Elsewhere they are described as going on double dates with women only to look forward to dropping their dates off at the end of the night so they can spend time with each other. In their youth Don loved Jim, and he knew it; but Jim would not admit he loved Don in return: "For in his jokes, his laughter, implications and horseplay, Jim betrayed restrained affection; but before Don could ever dare to speak the words, not with his eyes, but with his mouth, Jim had turned away from him" (59). Then Jim married Doris, so Don left town. Three years later, Jim hates Doris. Don returns, but he is no longer willing to acknowledge his feelings for Jim, even as Jim, all too late, can finally admit that he loves Don. They both love each other; they just can't see it and say it at the same time. When Don is willing to say it, Jim is not; when Jim is willing, Don is not. To paraphrase another gay author, they fail to connect, only connect. The fault, however, is not their own.

Creekmore begins the novel with a telling epigraph from Christopher Marlowe's *Faustus*, partially to suggest that marriage is like selling one's soul to the devil but partially to hint at something else—the fundamental tragedy these pages will unfold. In a world where one is told that the only option is heterosexual marriage, the other options, far more conducive to a person's happiness, slip away. When Creekmore wrote the novel in the late 1940s and when he chose to set it in the 1930s, he was writing in a world and of a world where saying the love that forms the fulcrum of the narrative was impermissible—it was still the love that dare not speak its name.

We are reading this novel now from a moment in time when that love can be visible, from a time when, even in Mississippi, that love can be celebrated by family, friends, and community in marriage ceremonies that are novel, for sure, but only in form, not content, because love is love is love. Thus, we can see and say the cause of the tragedy: the most important marriage in the novel is the one that is not allowed to take place. The expectation to marry a Doris or an Isabel is allowed, and it blinds Don and Jim to the one best thing they have in Ashton: each other. This is why the novel is a tragedy, brilliantly and brutally so.

◆ ◆ ◆

Creekmore's novel was too far ahead of its time to be recognized for what it is—a novel arguing for the value of same-sex love and fidelity, in Mississippi, no less. Luckily, in recent years people have started to pay attention to the writer and his works. In 2013 John Bayne, Elizabeth Crews, and I sat on the first conference panel devoted to Creekmore. In 2015 a historical marker was placed in front of Creekmore's childhood home. In 2019 Mary Knight, a student in southern studies at the University of Mississippi, released a short documentary film about Creekmore's life and legacy.

At that 2013 panel, I met Hubert's nephew Jimmy and his wife, Meredith, along with Hubert's niece Mary Alice Welty White and her husband, Donny. Later, I met Jimmy's brother Wade Jr. I was told Jimmy was more talkative, Wade Jr. less so, but that both had very fond memories of their uncle. When I met Wade Jr., he gave me a copy of a letter from May 15, 1966 from Hubert to Wade Sr., Hubert's older brother, Wade and Jimmy's father. Written from New York, it rambles on about plans for Wade's upcoming visit to the city and Hubert's upcoming trip to Spain. Hubert sent home a check for $500 for their mother with the letter, but it is mostly an unassuming missive documenting the general events of a life. He signed it "All best."

On May 23, Hubert Creekmore died of a heart attack in a taxi in New York on the way to the airport. His letter to his brother was his last letter home. He was buried in Jackson, Mississippi, a few days later. Several of his friends in New York held a dinner and reading in his honor. His agent arranged for his papers to be archived. Most of his books had only one printing; over time they became increasingly hard to find. For a while, Creekmore's literary accomplishments were effectively lost.

The past, however, is sometimes reparable in the present, and maybe we have reached a moment when we can, finally, welcome this native son of Mississippi home.

THE WELCOME

Mephistopheles: *Tut, Faustus,*
Marriage is but a ceremonial toy;
And if thou lovest me, think no more of it.
—MARLOWE

PART ONE

1

Between ten and eleven o'clock in the morning, the soda fountain of Herring's Drugstore always had a noticeable increase in business. Most of the customers were high-school and college students meeting casually to exchange comments on the past night or to plan the one to come. In these long hot days of late summer they were all weary of the unfruitful effort to make vacation seem exciting, anxious to return to the routine of classrooms, but feeling it treasonable to their group and the accepted opinion of their elders to admit it.

Singly or in pairs they pulled open the warped frames of the screen doors, whose bulging, ripped wire would have kept out only the most unresourceful of insects. By preference the young people settled around the two tables that stood in a bay window at the end of the soda fountain. They would order a coke or some intricate concoction such as a banana split, calling out to the soda-jerk, their schoolmate, who usually leaned over the counter to join in the chatter. The window tables were convenient because any passing friends could see them inside and join them, or, if the friends did not happen to look in, they could rap on the glass and motion to them. What else was there to do in the mornings during the summer in Ashton, Mississippi? Or in the winter, for that matter, if school had not given them its slight occupation?

Sometimes four of them would play bridge or even rummy; they might ride around town or into the country if one could wheedle the family car from father; they could go to the matinee at the Elite Theater, but that would leave them nothing to do in the evening, unless someone was having a party. They were too old to stay home and play, too important to help around the house, too young to be working (unless their families were poor), too innocent (with a few exceptions) to be interested in vices, too empty to find any amusement except in their own relationships.

Around the white tops of the parenthesis-legged tables they tilted in the wire-scrolled chairs, or leaned their elbows among crumpled sippers between clear spots of melted, spilled ice and dark, bubbly spots of spilled coke. The wide mahogany blades of the ceiling fans, slowly whirling above the door, wrapped them in frail billows of air scented with vanilla, milk and medicine. A few gnats vibrated above the rims of their glasses, and flies congregated at the corners of the window.

Watt Herring, who had just come through the deep red curtains that hung in front of the prescription closet, stood at the rear counter of patent medicines and looked through the dim interior. Two symbolic, glass apothecary jars of red and green liquids in two ornate niches rose at each side of his head, a bas-relief of "Swamp Root," "606," "Lydia E. Pinkham's Vegetable Compound," "Peru-na" and "Black Draught" spread behind him, and in front the display case crammed with small boxes of pills and capsules and stacked at each end with oversize advertising cartons of quick nostrums.

Two young women sat at a table in the center of the store, just behind a low case of men's toiletries. Mr. Herring remembered Anita Leffingwell and Alice Barnette when, only a few years before, they were in the crowd at the window tables—college girls wondering how to have a good time, wondering why there weren't as many "cute" boys in Ashton as there were at the University, wondering if they would really marry that young man who seemed to like them but never quite got beyond having routine dates; but now that they were somewhat beyond the young group, they had to bother about earning money rather than having a good time. They saw only the men who lived in Ashton, and they wondered now who might ask them merely for dates more than if anyone might marry them. As work and age and loneliness settled steadily over them, they became dependent on each other, and met for the movies once or twice a week, or for supper with either family, or simply to chat in their rooms and thumb magazines and sew on slips.

There in the dim light, with the sluggish fans stirring the air overhead, it was actually cooler than in the bright window at the front. But it was also a sort of retirement; the younger set, which included most of the single men in town, had retired them.

Alice, slowly sipping her drink through a straw, gazed around the store until she spotted Mr. Herring.

"Oh, Mr. Herring," she called in a low voice, "is Jake coming home at all this summer?"

He stuck his tongue between his lower lip and his teeth. "Nope, he won't be home. Said he's got to put in all the time he can interning and then go right back to classes."

"Gee, I'm sorry to hear that. I was hoping he'd get down for a week, anyhow."

"I was too," said Anita. "He'll make a fine doctor, though. He's so kind to people, so understanding."

Mr. Herring smiled obscurely. "I guess so," he said. Then he put both hands on the counter and leaned over toward them. "But I'll tell you who *is* coming home tonight." He waited a moment, but the young women controlled themselves and said nothing. They looked expectantly at him and forgot their drinks.

"Don Mason."

Together Anita and Alice incredulously repeated the name after Mr. Herring.

"Why, he's been gone for years!"

"Only three."

"I bet I wouldn't know him," said Anita. "How'd you find out, Mr. Herring?"

"Dr. Everett told me. Said he had to take a sedative out to Mrs. Mason, she was so excited."

"Well, he's all she's got," said Alice. "I don't suppose she ever gets out, does she?"

"She'll never be no different," said Mr. Herring. "It's just nerves." He picked up a box from the counter and vanished behind the curtains.

"Imagine seeing Don Mason again," said Alice. "I bet he's so New Yorkish you can't stand it."

"Well, I don't care one way or another. I never did like him much. He always talked about things you never heard of."

"Maybe you just weren't smart enough," said Alice.

"Well, I never dated him, anyway. He was older than my crowd."

"Was he as old as your date last night?" whispered Alice, with a grin.

"Oh, Alice," hissed Anita, "I could kill you for that. If you ever do that again, I don't know what I'll do. Suppose someone had seen us out with traveling men!"

"What's wrong with traveling men?"

Anita glanced around furtively to see if anyone could overhear them. "My mother has always told me about women in her day and time who went out with traveling men or ran away with them, and awful things happened. Traveling men have *ideas*."

"Well, have we got anything better?" asked Alice scornfully.

"Ssh! Here comes that Mrs. Furlow," warned Anita, and began to concentrate on the mass of shaved ice in her glass.

Mrs. Furlow had languidly opened the screen doors and was moving down the store with hardly a glance at the young people in front, although she did say good morning when Rosa Walker at the cosmetics counter raised her eyes from contemplation of Fredric March in her movie magazine. Once around the counter of shaving creams and lotions, Mrs. Furlow saw Anita and Alice.

"Well, goodness!" she exclaimed. "You were almost hidden. I thought for a minute I'd have to drink a coke by myself." She stood beside their table in a coquettish slouch. Her hair, a shade paler than lemon, hung in a medium bob of glistening waves below a small straw hat. The tiny flowers around the brim echoed the color of her hair and of her pale blue linen dress. In the subdued light, her face glowed with creamy pallor, the features regular and immobile as the features on a calendar picture, although a tentative smile would occasionally play over her perfect lips. One of these smiles now broke her usually reserved expression and she asked, "Have you already finished?"

"Oh, not really," said Anita. "Sit down. We're just eating our ice." She promptly raised the glass, soused the gob of ice against her lips and bit off a mouthful.

Mrs. Furlow dragged out a chair, piled up her handbag on the other two in the vacant seat and sat down to wait for the boy to come take her order. "I was just down at McGill's looking at some new fall outfits," she said.

"Oh, we were there too," cried Anita.

"I just haven't a stitch to wear," sighed Mrs. Furlow, gazing toward the fountain. "Sometimes I think I'll just have to run up to Memphis and shop there."

"Why, no one would ever know it, Mrs. Furlow," said Alice. "You always look so stylish."

"I can't imagine how," Mrs. Furlow murmured, with an ingratiating smile. "Anything you pick up is sky-high, and James simply can't afford it. He says if people don't have any money or property, they can't have any lawsuits, and the depression took most of what they had away. I don't understand those things, though. They're for the men to worry about."

"That's right," said Anita. "I just don't know a thing about money. When I go to normal school next summer I'm going to take a course in money and all that."

"Do you have to go to normal school next summer?" asked Mrs. Furlow. The fountain boy was beside her and she tilted her head to him and said, "Large coke and lots of ice."

"Oh yes, we schoolteachers have to go away ever so often and brush up on what we're teaching."

"That's real interesting, isn't it?" said Mrs. Furlow flatly.

"Well—not much," Anita mumbled, although for a moment she had thought it was going to be interesting, at least to talk about.

There was a moment's silence. The boy brought Mrs. Furlow's large coke packed with ice and she thanked him absent-mindedly. Anita took up her handbag and inspected her face in the dusty mirror in the top of her compact. Alice suddenly caught Mrs. Furlow's arm just as she was about to lift the drink to her mouth.

"Oh, I almost forgot," said Alice impulsively. "I have something to tell you."

Mrs. Furlow, slightly frowning, transferred the drink to her other hand, for Alice did not seem inclined to release her arm. "What is it?" She sucked on the two straws and the dark liquid in the tall glass dropped more than halfway.

"Don Mason's coming back tonight."

Mrs. Furlow looked completely blank. "Don Mason?"

"Sure. You know him, don't you? He's been gone about three years."

"Well, you see, I've only lived here since James and I were married." She sipped again at the drink. "That was back in 1933. He must have gone before I came."

"But you must have heard of him," said Anita, her lips drawn over her teeth while she stroked on lipstick. "He and your husband were best friends for years."

"I've probably heard his name but forgot it," said Mrs. Furlow. "James tells me so many things I can never remember. I don't know why it is, a woman can tell me something and I will remember it for weeks, but James can tell me something and it won't stick in my mind for two hours. I think it must be that lawyer's way of talking—so plain, or something." Her drink was now all gone and the straws burbled in the glass when she drew in on them. She stirred the ice about and began turning mouthfuls of it between her lips and chewing it.

"Oh, I remember now," said Alice. "Don left before you were married. Mr. Furlow told me he had wanted Don to be in the wedding, but this job with a newspaper or advertising company or something turned up and he couldn't stay. Jim must have been mighty sorry, because they always used to have double dates together and all that."

"Double dates," mused Mrs. Furlow, between shavings of ice. "I never liked them. Do you two have double dates?"

Both the young women flushed. Anita snickered and looked warningly at Alice.

"Well, we *have* had them once in a while," said Alice. "But we're lucky if we can find *one* and kind of pass him around between us."

Mrs. Furlow laughed and chewed ice. "Oh, it can't be as bad as that. There are lots of fellows around town who aren't married. There's . . ."

"You see, you can't think of any really good prospect," said Alice. "They've all married or gone away. I've always wondered why they go away. What are they looking for? But as far as we go, neither of us is much interested in getting married. It doesn't pay to think about it."

"Goodness, Alice, you're mighty wise for your age," said Mrs. Furlow, lifting her hairline eyebrows mockingly.

"For my age? Why, I'm older than you, Mrs. Furlow. You can't be *near* twenty-seven."

"Well, I'm pretty close to it," Mrs. Furlow simpered, as if she had been flattered on preserving a youthful appearance.

"You shouldn't be saying those things, Alice," pouted Anita.

"What things, for heaven's sake?"

"About not being interested in getting married," whispered Anita loudly. "It don't help a bit to act like we don't want to."

"Oh, I know," scoffed Alice. "The right man will come along someday, and all that rot."

"It's not all the fun you may think it is," said Mrs. Furlow in an attempt to be the wise matron. "It's not very important these days to get married, anyhow. I read somewhere something about girls who—didn't marry. They turn into something called career girls."

"Well, I'm the career girl of Ashton," boomed Alice heartily. She leaned toward Mrs. Furlow and lowered her voice confidentially. "Does that mean I can smoke my cigarette in the hotel office and anywhere in public?"

"Like Isabel Lang, you mean?" Mrs. Furlow asked with arched brows. Then she shook her head. "You couldn't afford to."

"Why not?"

"Isabel has enough money so she doesn't have to get married. She doesn't have to bother with what people say about her."

"And she sure doesn't!" exclaimed Anita enviously.

"But if she did want to marry, she'd stop all those peculiar habits she's got— smoking on the street, reading deep books, painting naked figures, wearing pants around town." Mrs. Furlow bobbed her head up and down sagely. "If you've got some craving like that, you keep it hidden till after you're married. Isabel is just a little— well, she tries to be bohemian, I guess."

For a moment the three of them thought how aptly Mrs. Furlow, a virtual stranger to the town, had analyzed one of its inhabitants. Then Anita's face lighted up suddenly, and with an excited gasp she began, "But didn't Jim—Mr. Furlow—I remember he used to date Isabel—" The words choked off as her eyes dilated in her blushing face. Mrs. Furlow smiled patiently.

"Oh, that," she said deprecatingly. "James would never like a woman who thought *thoughts*. No man would, as far as I can tell. They want a pretty, sweet woman they can admire and—worship."

"Everybody sure thought they were going to marry," said Alice, reflectively. "But I guess that was just college love. She wasn't—intellectual—then, you know."

"Oh, she wasn't?"

"No. Just a sweet, giddy"—in a whisper—"hell-raising girl."

"Oh, dear," sighed Mrs. Furlow with a tone of weariness that meant equally boredom at the turn of the conversation and concern about the state of her make-up. She began redoing her face with lipstick and a powder puff the size of a silver dollar while she peered into a small mirror. "I've just got to find some fall clothes. I simply can't go out anywhere in these same tacky things." She moistened the tip of her finger and drew it along her eyebrows.

"It sure is a problem," agreed Anita, admiring her prettiness. While she was tucking the cosmetics back inside her purse, Mrs. Furlow craned her head toward the front windows. "Isn't that James out there—on the other side of the street? I'm so near-sighted, I can't see."

Both the other women turned. "Why, yes, it is," said Anita. "I wonder if he knows about Don coming back?"

"Who's that with him?" asked Mrs. Furlow.

"Looks like Madge Dalton," said Alice. "Humph! Wouldn't think she'd be walking on the street with all the cars she's got."

"She's only got two cars, Alice," said Anita. "And her husband uses one of them."

"Heavens, I've got to run home and start dinner," said Mrs. Furlow. "I've wasted too much time already."

"We have to go too," said Alice, and Anita jumped up promptly.

Mrs. Furlow walked briskly ahead to the counter, where Miss Walker sat talking to Dr. Everett. "Good morning," she said to the large, tamale-shaped, graying doctor. He spoke in return and moved almost imperceptibly to allow her to approach the cash register. By the time Alice and Anita reached her, protesting that they must treat for the drinks, Mrs. Furlow had paid and was taking up her change. As she hurriedly turned to the door, saying good-by, the two girls thanked her and suggested rapidly that they get together again.

"Of course we will," Mrs. Furlow babbled thoughtlessly. "I'll have to run now. Maybe I can catch James and tell him about his friend coming back."

"Isn't she the prettiest thing?" sighed Anita as Mrs. Furlow passed through the door. "She always dresses so cute, too."

"Wonder if her hair is really that color," remarked Alice. "Like corn silk."

"Oh, Alice, you're so suspicious.... It's been that way ever since she came here."

"It's funny," mused Alice, "she always calls him 'James.'"

They walked out onto the street and glanced briefly in the direction Mrs. Furlow had taken. She was hurrying around the bend in the street.

2

As her high heels clicked along on the pavement, Doris Furlow envied Madge Dalton her huge house with all the expensive furnishings, and the two cars in which she could drive anywhere any time, and her trips to cities in the north and east. And against it all, she was seeing her own little rented house on Mulberry Street, furnished with wedding gifts and family pieces which only looked more shabby alongside the few new ones that James had bought.

He would not buy a place since the family home would someday be his. It looked as if they were both just waiting for his parents to die. He couldn't even afford a new car, and she, Doris, had to walk because like all the businessmen, he drove downtown every morning, parked in front of his office and let the car sit there all day—a token of his success. But what kind of success was it, she wanted to know, even if he had been practicing law only a few years, when she couldn't pay for a servant or another car or a new radio or what she needed most, some new clothes! Why, the women in town must be talking about her, saying James was "close" or was failing in business, if she didn't dress better!

About half a block ahead her husband was strolling leisurely beside Madge Dalton, as if he hadn't a problem in the world. Not wanting to catch up with them, in spite of her excuses in the drugstore, she sauntered along, watching the backs of the two heads. James's brown hair showed a rough half-moon under his panama and Mrs. Dalton's black straight hair hung much longer than was fashionable below a starched white crochet hat.

After a short walk, James stepped off the curb between the parked automobiles, opened the door to a shiny Buick and tipped his hat as Mrs. Dalton got in. While he was walking on toward his office and the car was backing out, Doris noticed that she had passed Mulberry Street and turned back. It would make her late getting dinner ready and James would be cross, mumbling, "We always seem to eat out of tin cans"—his way of saying she never cooked a roast or biscuits or fresh vegetables. Well, after all, what did he think she was? She had never cooked before she married, and her mother had expected her to marry some man who could afford a servant. Of course, the depression—she didn't understand that or why it had anything to do with her lack of essentials like cooks, houses, automobiles and clothes.

When she first met James, more than three years ago, he had been very different. A group of young men had driven to Oakville one Sunday in June to call on a girl who had been at Ole Miss with them, and the girl had invited several friends to meet them. And there she found herself with James. Somehow it had seemed to go exactly right from the beginning. When he had dates with her later on, he was as genteel as her mother could have required and didn't try to neck her all the time and muss her permanent and her make-up. They talked and held hands and rode around and went to dances. He was everything a girl could want in a husband.

He seemed to have such great possibilities for making a fine living for them. He used to drive from Ashton to her town and walk to the front door looking so neat, so unsmall-town in his college clothes. She always watched him from behind the lace curtains of her upstairs window, although it would be ten minutes before she came down. In addition to complying with custom, this delay suited her mother, because it gave her a chance to "size him up." Mother had inquired of close friends about his family and learned that he came from one of the best, as families went, in Ashton. Finally, three months later when they decided to announce their engagement, with the wedding to follow in October, his mother and father came over to meet hers. It was only after the honeymoon in Memphis that she went to Ashton, saw his home and got to know his friends.

He had not really settled down to work in his father's law office at that time—that is, he didn't seem to be doing much there, as far as she could tell. Even though his father and her own both explained that it took a long time to start making money in a profession like law, she had not expected her husband to be quite the sort of man he was.

In most ways he was still a gentleman, but the worst of it was he didn't make enough money to be a real gentleman. She remembered how kind he was the first night of their marriage; he did not act like a beast as her mother had tearfully told her many men did, but simply lay beside her and stroked her face and neck. She was not entirely devoid of curiosity, and eventually she was rather pleased that he became more possessive. When he first kissed her as if he meant to eat her up, she enjoyed it because it recalled certain scenes in movies that she had found fascinating. It was curious to discover that real people did act like movie characters. Here was her husband, kissing her eyelids and her throat, pressing his hands restlessly all over her body, murmuring speeches that might have been written for him in Hollywood. But it was really boring—messy and such a bother. Why didn't he just concentrate on what a nice pretty wife he had, as he used to when they were first married, and try to make more money so he could be proud of her when she was dressed up and all the people stared at her and said, "James Furlow's got the best-looking wife in town. He's a man I sure envy."

You never could tell what a man would turn out to be. Her mother had warned her that men got tired of their wives; then you had to be careful they didn't start playing around with loose women on the sly. You had to be patient and make them appreciate you, or they would wander off to greener pastures. Wherever did her mother get all those expressions she used—"greener pastures," "loose women," "the beast in men"? They seemed to flow out of her as if she never had to think them up at all, and yet they suited what she meant.

Of course, James was a rather handsome man, and it would be natural for other women to take a liking to him, even married women. But they didn't know him the way she did; they didn't know how moody he could be sometimes, really for nothing at all. Just a month ago when she told him her mother was sending them another bed so they could each have one, he sulked for two weeks. It was his pride, she supposed, because her mother was giving them one of her old beds. He agreed that it might be better in summer to sleep alone, but then he said something about "people will think we're separating." That, of course, was ridiculous, because she had no intention of ever leaving him. Unless he stopped supporting her. A wife's love could go just so far, and then she had to do something about it.

He was plainly selfish; she had long ago observed that. They were living in his home town and he didn't want her to show up better than he did. He was trying to hold her back, while she was trying to help him forward by being the best wife he could have found. On Sunday afternoons, when friends were most likely to drop in for a call, he would wander down to his office—business, he said; and many nights he would suddenly crush the newspaper in his chair, mumble something about having to work and drive away. If he had so much work to do, why wasn't he making more money? All the time, she just sat at home alone, listening to the broken-down radio, doing her nails over in a different color, plucking out straggling eyebrows, thumbing the fashion magazines for ideas, and trying to keep their home together, simply because she loved him and she had vowed at the altar . . .

Before she realized it she was at the gate of their rented house. With the vague feeling of vexation she always had when approaching it, she walked toward the narrow concrete porch with its oppressive brick pillars and brick parapet. Even though it had plenty of closets, electrical plugs and a modern kitchen, somehow she could not picture herself, like the women in the *Ladies' Home Journal*, being lyrical over the stove while fabricating the scraps of supper into a tasty luncheon dish. The yellow brick walls rose only one story, and the roof slanted at an acute angle to suggest an English cottage, she supposed, because there was a chimney on one side with an iron scroll halfway up that certainly was not in the southern tradition.

She propped the front door open with a painted iron dog so the breeze could blow through. Dropping her handbag on a heavily upholstered chair in the living room, she took off her hat and tossed it on another chair.

It was ten minutes to twelve. What in the world could she fix for dinner? She sank down on the sofa and turned on the radio that stood beside it. The music of a hillbilly band swelled up in the amplifier. She tuned it down and changed to another station with a dance orchestra. Her feet burned from the hot sidewalks; she wanted a cigarette. She pushed off her shoes, but the cigarettes were in her handbag on that chair across the room.

The clock chimed twelve. With a sigh, she got up and dug a cigarette out of her bag and lighted it. In her stocking feet, she went into the kitchen to see what was in the refrigerator. About a half-hour later she heard a car stop in front of the house and recognized the familiar long squeak of the door hinges as James got out. When he came into the living room, he did not call out to her; these days he never did, but now she paused with two plates in her hands and listened. His footsteps sounded softly, moving across the rug. Then there was a sound, something like a whining grunt and something like a scratching of claws. He must have found her straw hat on the chair. For some reason, he always seemed to hate to find her hat or purse or shoes in the living room. Mother never complained of it all her life; she simply picked them up or told the maid to. So Doris explained to James that a house was meant to be comfortable in, and if they didn't have a servant to pick up things, she couldn't run around all the time just to put everything in its right place. Once when he complained about her shoes being there, she jokingly set them with great neatness, the bows on the toes pertly facing outward, on the table by the door. He said he didn't think it was funny, but she laughed quite a bit, especially when he blushed and then began to sulk. Men were such children.

After she finished setting the table, she came into the living room. In his shirt sleeves, he was leaning over the radio, twisting the dial back and forth, trying to find one of those upsetting newscasts. He did not look up.

"Hello, James," she said, almost in a wheedling voice.

"Hello, Doris."

"The news doesn't come on till a quarter to one," she said.

"Oh . . ." He straightened up and glanced at the clock. "I must have got here a little early."

"Aren't you going to kiss me?" she asked.

After a moment's hesitation, he said blankly, "If you like." He touched her lips with his and turned away.

Why on earth did she ask him that? Their customary kiss, just as business-like as this one and certainly sufficient for her, occurred in the morning when he left for the office. She wondered, suddenly and with amusement, if she were falling in love with him all over again! Why, they hadn't been married long enough to have fallen out of love.

James sat down in his chair and quietly rippled his fingers on the velour-covered arms. As she turned back to the kitchen to bring in the platters of food, she began talking. "I was downtown shopping all morning and didn't have time to buy anything to eat. It's going to be just a cold lunch, but that's best in summer when it's so hot."

Shortly afterward she came to the wide arch that joined yet separated the living room from the dining room. "I guess it's ready now," she said. He rose with a stifled sigh, as if he were very tired, and moved toward the table.

"Mrs. Dalton's having a buffet supper Saturday night—for a business friend of Josh's from Chicago." James ate slowly, bringing forks full of tuna salad to his mouth between phrases. He didn't seem to be very hungry. "She said she'd call you about it."

"Oh? Did you see her this morning?" asked Doris.

"Met her on the street."

"She always looks so nice. She must buy all her clothes in Memphis or up North."

"Maybe."

"Why didn't she call *me* to invite us?" Doris asked.

"She said she'd call you," James repeated. "After all, you were out all the morning you said."

"Well, I guess she was too, if she was downtown with you."

"It's not important which of us she told," said James impatiently. "It's nice she asked us at all."

"Oh . . ." Doris thought for a minute, holding a tomato sandwich in midair before her face. Then she bit into it. "I don't see why you think we should kow-tow to her. Our families are twice as good as hers."

"I don't think we have to do anything to her. And I don't think she cares what we do."

They were silent for a short while. That was just like men, she thought, never concerned about keeping up standards of living and family; they let everything fall into the gutter because it was too much trouble to bother about anything except their own pleasures. They would defend someone like Mrs. Dalton, who was really a nobody, with no background, simply because she and her husband now had money. You couldn't expect much more from the people of a railroad-shop town. No one here had any respect for tradition, because they hadn't ever had any. Men always left it to women, anyhow, to uphold the manners of society; but how could she do anything about it with James acting the way he did and hiding all his money and not letting her spend enough to show her superiority to people like Mrs. Dalton?

She poked about in her salad with a fork, spearing pieces of celery out of the fish and crunching them meditatively.

"Oh," she said, as a preliminary to announcement. "Do you remember a boy here named Don Manning, or something?"

He put down his fork but his hand hovered near it, the fingers moving as if to take it up again. "Don Mason, you mean?" He looked at her. "Sure."

"Well, why didn't you ever tell me? I felt like a fool when they mentioned him as if I ought to know you were friends."

"Who mentioned him?" asked James.

"Anita Leffingwell and Alice Barnette," she answered in a tone that implied he ought to have known. "They were very surprised that I never heard of him. They said you were such *good* friends. Seems like you would have talked about somebody who was as close as that to you."

"School friends, that's all," said James. He pushed away his plate. "People drift apart when they grow up. I hadn't thought of him in months, I guess."

"You want some canned peaches for dessert?" she asked.

"No, thanks." He lighted a cigarette and dropped the match on his plate.

"Aren't you going to offer me one?" said Doris.

"I didn't know you were finished."

She swallowed quickly when he held them out to her. Leaning forward, she closed her lips around the cigarette and pulled it out of the package. He struck a match.

"Why were those girls talking about Don?" he asked.

"He's coming back to town tonight. That's what Mr. Herring told them."

"What's he coming back here for?" he asked irritably. "I thought he was doing pretty well in New York."

"Well, don't get sore about it," said Doris. "He won't cut into your law practice, will he?"

"No, he's not a lawyer." James blew out a fat stream of smoke.

"What's he like? The girls seemed terribly interested. Of course, they're both old maids—almost."

"I don't know what he's like now. New York life and all that . . . I wonder if he's coming just for a visit or what."

"They just said he's coming, that's all."

She didn't know anything to ask or say about the home-town boy who was returning from the north. James sat in thought for a few minutes. For a change, he had not talked in his usual crabbed way after she mentioned his friend. She would have to talk to him more about his friends, even about their acquaintances such as Mrs. Dalton, but without being catty about it. She would let him take out his fussiness and criticism on them rather than on her.

Then, without another word, James got up and walked into the living room. He stood for a moment in the center of the room, looking slowly around at the walls and the furniture, and blowing out smoke clouds. He moved to the window and leaned between the net curtains.

"Are you going back to the office already?" she asked.

"I guess so," he answered wearily and began pulling on his coat. "Lots of work to do." He crossed the floor and took his panama hat from the table by the door. "Why don't you put your shoes in the bedroom, Doris?" he called as he opened the screen door.

3

As Jim stepped off the dim, dusty porch into the sunlight, the heat tingled through his suit and over his skin. The hot, turgid air felt unaccountably freer and better than the cool but suffocating dimness of his living room. He walked down the concrete flagstones to his car.

When he opened the door, it gave its prolonged squeak. Sitting at the steering wheel, he glanced toward the yellow-brick cottage and thought he saw Doris between pushed-back net curtains under the shadow of the porch. Still in her stocking feet, he supposed, with the uneaten food and the dishes on the table, the radio tuned loud on a jazz program, a cigarette between her fingers, wondering how to spend the long afternoon.

She would not read. All his own books were there, and the old library sets of Dickens, Thackeray and Balzac he had brought from his father's house to fill up the shelves on each side of the fireplace; but Doris, even in her utmost boredom, never had opened one of the glass doors, he was sure, merely to take out a book and turn the pages, to stare idly at the brown engravings in the sets or at the naughty illustrations in the *Decameron*, *Aphrodite* and *The Golden Ass*.

Once he showed her a few Beardsley drawings in *Salome* and she refused to look at more. They were repulsive and indecent, she said, and no one with a clean mind would have them around. That night, after they had gone to bed and he tried to kiss her, she angrily blamed his passion on those "filthy pictures" and said she would throw them in the garbage can. He was puzzled, angry too, for a while; but then he warned her not to destroy them because, he lied to her, leaving out any consideration of their merit, they could be sold for quite a lot of money. She said nothing at all, but relaxed slowly; and after a long time, while he lay quietly beside her, she kissed him several times, said "Good night, James." And he got up and slept on the sofa in the living room. The next morning she said that she was practically asleep when he got up and

21

didn't know; he mustn't sleep out there on that uncomfortable sofa. A few days afterward she informed him that her mother was sending them another bed, which crowded the house in Oakville.

Jim pressed the starter and pulled away from the curb. Instead of turning around toward town, he continued up Mulberry Street, driving slowly, dreamily, hardly noticing the cars which passed, seeing none of the people who waved at him, and began the steep ascent of the ridge of hills on the west of town. His mind, focusing on an inner landscape, plagued and softened by memory, ignored the street's old gingerbread houses and squatty bungalows. Along the top of the hill, the street was built up with residences on only one side, for the opposite side sloped away very sharply. Here, beside a barbed wire fence overlooking the town of Ashton, he stopped the car.

A few cattle grazed on the steep hillside below him. Beyond, under a quivering, heated atmosphere, houses showed between clumps of spongelike trees, spreading down to the valley and up again on the eastern ridge to the pale, blue, sun-stricken sky. In Ashton there was no courthouse square, so typical of a southern county seat, to serve as the focus of the business of the town. The stores, cafés hotels and garages were aligned on the town's main highway, which imperceptibly crossed and recrossed on wide bridges the stream that drained the valley. From this channel of commerce, residential streets for the four thousand inhabitants swept up the hills to east and west, lined with late-Victorian, Swiss chalet and bungalow homes coolly sheltered by big oak and elm trees and sometimes perched high on a bluff where the road had been cut down. Up the valley, chuffing, it seemed, right through the stores, moved a spout of dark smoke from the afternoon train creeping, town by town, to Memphis. At a few points, he could see the cars between the trees or the buildings. The flat, corrugated metal or tar-paper roofs reflected streamers of hot air that warped the landscape behind them like a defective windowpane. Toward the north rose two church spires, the black water tank, and a mist of blue smoke from the railroad shops.

Sometimes, when he thought of the town in comparison with Memphis or New Orleans or the exciting cities in movies, it seemed the dreariest of human settlements. A farm, with its sensible cows and hogs and chickens, its routine variations of activity, its logical elemental calm, would be more natural for a man. And now, as at other times, when an intangible, unexplainable satisfaction came over him, his town became an endearing and warm society, fascinating in its waywardness, but with all its faults and deficiencies, more alive than any city.

It would not seem so to Don, after the excitement of New York. This town to which he was returning, his home town, unchanged in three years in look or attitude, the town for which a few country people abandoned their farms to work in the shops, and from which each year some young men would go to larger communities in search of more money, more pleasures, would now be tiresome and unstimulating. Its pattern of life was too calm, too ordinary, for anyone who had once forsaken it. Growing slowly from the late 1700's when it was an Indian trading post, through the early phases of settling and liquor-swilling, it received great impetus toward expansion with the coming of the railroad shops. At its peak, about the time Mississippi passed a law in 1907 to prohibit the sale of liquor, Ashton maintained its position for many years. But hardly any new people moved in, except occasional preachers and wives, such as Doris, who were brought in by their husbands. The young women, if they were fortunate, married the young men who went through high school with them; the men, if they went to college, might marry some girl from another town; if the girls went, they might have the same luck and move away from Ashton. The population continued to dwindle. More and more young men drifted to larger places—Jackson, Memphis, or Greenwood in the rapidly developing Delta; and young women were left alone, like Alice and Anita, who did not know, as they grew older, where they might find a suitable man. Or most revealing of all, like Isabel Lang, who was certainly the catch of the town; but he had never asked her to marry him after all their dates (why had he been such a numbskull?), nor had any other man, as far as he knew, proposed to her.

Yet in Ashton, in all such towns, you married, you worked; and then what? What did they all think they were marrying and working for? Surely not just to go to the movies twice a week. Not just so the wives could make formal calls on each other twice a month, leaving a card in the door or on the hall table as if they had met only shortly before. Not so their children could grow up and live exactly the same way their parents had lived. Not so they could gossip about each other at night around the winter fires and on the summer porches. But what else did they have, do, or offer themselves? What purpose did they feel, beyond these slight essentials of existence? Did anyone else in Ashton ever dream of something beyond, something richer in life—not the fake richness of religion—something that would enrich their world, small as it was, and make sense of their efforts to earn money?

Since his own dreams were safely laid away in a deposit box, he could easily hear the obvious answer: you work to make your family happy and your own happiness lies there. But did men really accomplish that? Was Doris happy because of his work? Was any wife, any daughter, happy simply because a man was working and paying the bills for her clothes and food and home? There was surely something else—something inarticulate or smothered, perhaps starved out, in all of them; the something that made the men restless, made them move away, made the women who stayed cross and fastidious and envious, made their children do unpredictable things and get into trouble. Years ago, during college days, he understood more clearly what the need was; he could almost have put it into words. He did almost, a few times, when he and Don talked seriously.

Or perhaps it was an illusion, because Don was always reading magazines and books that would have shocked the citizens of Ashton. There was one called *The New Republic*, and a literary one, *The Dial*, and *Poetry* and other strange and wild publications. Their minds were stimulated by what they read, sometimes angered, but they had an illusion of movement, or purpose, it might have been, and progress away from their cramping surroundings. Obviously, what he felt now was only nostalgia for college life. For he was a married man with all of marriage's responsibilities, and his duties as a citizen and a lawyer; there was no place for useless, speculative things in this mature life. No one else in town could join him in discussing or appreciating them.

He realized suddenly that the thought of Don's return awakened the warmth and tolerance he had just felt toward the town. It was Don's friendship—the assurance that he would always give his knowledge, his loyalty, his love or anything that Jim might ask for—which had added the now vanished richness to his life in this complacent community. But even while the prospect of those gifts—so generously, happily but cautiously laid before him if he only controlled Don—swelled with pleasant anticipation, he was conscious that their residue set him to the strange questionings of the emptiness around him. For there was one point at which Don withdrew; he would not follow Jim through marriage. And though Jim knew that he himself was the one who first deserted—or because he knew?—he was now angry that Don was coming back.

That was it, really; that must be it. He did not want Don, who would be so filled with new ideas, new experiences, new manners, to find him completely dull and to see the woman he had married. And yet, in spite of cringing at the thought, he was not ashamed for Don to see her. She was beautiful, ingratiating to people and she wasn't stupid. Of course she wasn't, he said to himself. Then what was it? Nothing of any importance, after all: he and Don had talked many times about the kind of wives that would suit them; there had been descriptions of physical charms, mental charms, personal charms, and so on until their catalogue was wiped out in wild, drunken laughter. For they were usually drinking when they talked about such things—riding from a dance, riding across country on a trip, or just riding around the gloomy streets of Ashton at night—and Don always ended by saying he would never be able to find the kind of woman he would like to marry. Then Jim would make his joke about how it's the woman who lands the husband, not vice versa.

One night, after buying their whiskey from the bootlegger's cabin about a mile west of town, they had continued driving into the country. It was a warm night, the dirt road was smooth, dry and silent, and the moon shone with a light that seemed to chill the sky and clouds. They swerved into a country churchyard for a drink, chased quickly by a cigarette and the bottled coke they had brought. The moonlight poured down coldly on the white walls of the church, making it unnatural. The doors and windows ate blackly, like water through thin snow, through the walls. The spire reared a short, pointed shadow against the sky.

"Let's go inside," said Don.

"Why?" Jim corked the bottle and put it on the seat, knowing that they would go in.

"To see, of course," answered Don, sliding out of the car and slamming the door. He swayed a little as he stood in the dimness. "It's an old church, alone in the moonlight," he went on, while Jim followed him across the tangled yard. "It's like something left over from the Victorians . . . church steeple, moonlight, dark trees. . . . But we need an owl, some ivy and scudding clouds."

They mounted the four steps to a tiny platform. When Don put his hand on the knob, it fell away from the door. He let it drop from his fingers and pushed the door with his shoulder. It dragged slowly over the floor and opened on a vault of unpainted, raftered emptiness. For a moment they stood just inside; then Don walked forward a few steps.

"Is there anything as empty as an empty church?" Don murmured. Unsteadily, he turned about as he surveyed the room, echoing with the prisoned silence of years. "A place that even without people should still be crowded with color, and form—the singing of music or design—and most of all, even in a little country church, with meaning. But here, no altar for sacrifice, no pulpit for the preacher, no bench for the worshipers." He circled slowly about the hall, his white linen trousers shining when he crossed the milky light that fell through the arched windows and lay in phallic patterns on the floor.

"Probably filled with rats and fleas," said Jim. He didn't like the way their low voices pulsed through the close emptiness.

"Probably is. It's our heritage—from the Puritans, the Victorians, the feminists—and their opposites—and this is us." Don had completed his circle, and standing before Jim, he peered at the face, vague against the brightness outside the door. "And mostly it's women. Nobody has remembered that women are animals, too, like us. Or they haven't remembered that they ought to be more than fine pieces of interior decoration. Women, or somebody, ought to remember that they're human. They've made themselves"—turning with a drunken, dramatic gesture about the church—"this."

Jim hesitated and swallowed with difficulty. "I don't follow you," he said. "Let's get back to the car." He took Don's arm and pulled him out of the church.

"No, you can't follow it," Don went on as they lurched across the yard. "Some day you'll marry one of those women. The real women are hard to find—if there are any. Your wife, when she chooses you, will be like that church."

So at last it had come out clearly! Though Jim had paid little attention at the time, he knew now it had been haunting him for months. It had hovered just under the surface, like a sodden piece of refuse floating in water, and had nipped and broken on his thoughts only to sink down before he could catch it. The remark, probably, had long ago been forgotten by Don; but just the same, he hated having Don come back to find that what he had said was now true.

An empty church in moonlight—a place of worship with no place for the worshiper or the sermon, only a cold white dimness beating through the tall, arched windows. Could it be his fault because he had not loved her strongly enough at first; because he had been patient with her; because he had not been brutal? He could not imagine that she would change, since she became more and more like that church as time went on. He could not refurnish it; someone had taken all its furniture away. On the other hand, did he himself really bring enough to their marriage? Was it he, rather than Doris, who was at fault?

Living in Ashton he had been able to feel no freedom, no separate life, no life at all, actually, except what he had with Don, for his other friends were getting married. The stimulation and pleasure which Don brought him in a mass of ill-defined, unrelated and varied ideas from books and in discussions of what their lives meant in the world—discussions which seemed so perceptive when they first rushed down the by-paths of philosophizing—were so much a part of school that he felt bound to scoff gently at them. College was over; and now he must set his mind, not to reading and thinking, but to the adult activities of making money, a home and a place in the community. As a young unmarried man, he had no place there, was in fact looked upon as shirking his duties to society. Vague allusions, direct questions and occasional innuendo from his family and friends made him forcefully aware of the isolation, the social quarantine, which was slowly closing around him.

He began to break away from Don, first inside himself with rationalizations that became convincing proofs, and then with open excuses. No, he couldn't go to the movies; no, he couldn't go swimming; he couldn't do any of the things he used to do, because he must read up on a law case, he must work at home. And finally when for the first time he did tell the truth it was even more wounding to Don because Don quietly understood the excuses. When he said, "I'm going out with Gus Traywick and Bea on a double date," it was meant to hurt; but he discovered that Don passed it off casually, just as he seemed to ignore several later occurrences. Only when he told Don he was driving to

Oakville with three young men to call on a girl from the University did Don show the first tinge of the wound that Jim had been slowly cutting into him. He could see it in Don's eyes and the sudden constriction of his movements, and hear it in the tone of his voice.

But it must be done, he told himself, it must be, but I don't want it to hurt too much. It will have to hurt some, because it hurts me too, and I can't let myself show it. But I want us still to be friends. And I think we will be, because Don likes me so much; he'd never go completely from me, and it will be best for him, too, because then he'll have a chance to fit himself properly into the life of Ashton. It never occurred to him that in return Don would desert him.

More and more frequently he drove with Gus Traywick to Oakville and talked to Doris and danced at the little parties in her town. Don was left to himself, and Jim never wondered what he was doing through those summer months, until the day when they met casually on the street and Don announced that he was going to New York soon.

At first Jim felt unexpected relief, but as he echoed the words "New York?" an annoyance writhed inside him and he began to frown. While they talked, he twisted nervously from side to side as if turning to speak to passers-by. Suddenly he interrupted Don to ask if he was on his way home. "My car's right up here. I can take you." They walked in silence to the car. As soon as they drove off from the curb, Jim inquired haltingly, "Why are you—going to New York?" He did not turn toward Don's home, but headed leisurely down the main street.

"I've got a job up there," answered Don.

"How could you have a job there with things as bad as they are?"

"Well, I think I have." Don's face was tense and stern.

"But do you?" insisted Jim.

"Never mind about that. I'll know when I get there."

Don made no comment on their driving out of town instead of home. They had always, by unspoken agreement and custom, made the trip home by a circuitous route; this was to be expected. For a while they rode without talking.

Finally Jim asked, "Why are you going?"

"To get a job."

Jim's voice sank to a softer tone, and he was afraid his hesitating would suggest disappointment. "Why not get one in Ashton?"

"I don't want to stay in Ashton."

"Since when?"

"I don't remember the exact date. Maybe you do."

Jim clenched his jaws in anger, but his anger faded suddenly into guilty pleasure in the knowledge that his actions had brought about Don's decision. He did not answer at once. Then he said, "I don't know why I should remember."

"Well," Don began in a clear voice, but then his words dropped slowly to a low, unsteady level. "I'll be more honest with you than you've been with me. I—just can't take any more."

"Any more what, Don?"

"Pretense . . . indecision . . ."

"I don't know what you mean."

"I think you do. But let it go . . . I try to figure things out and see what's going to happen. Anyone with sense should do the same. What I see now is that I'm all alone—"

"How can you say such things, Don?"

"In Ashton, it's true, especially now. Now that you're planning to get married."

"I'm not planning any such thing."

"I think you are. And I'm planning to make a place for myself somewhere. It won't be in Ashton."

"There's no reason why not."

"No, none—except that Ashton just doesn't provide it. It was fine with you here; I'd never have asked more than that. But you know unmarried people in small towns are left out of whatever society there is for adults. The single ones are supposed to bother about finding someone to marry so they can qualify for the group. Most of them marry just so they can qualify."

For a long time Jim said nothing. He drove along the country road automatically, seeing no precise image of the fields and trees and wagons he passed. "Aren't you thinking of ever marrying?" he asked at last.

"I'm thinking more of happiness than of marriage," answered Don. "You're thinking only of marriage. And you'll marry that girl over in Oakville."

With a half-hearted laugh, Jim said, "Yes, I think I'm going to. I didn't want to let anyone know yet because . . . well, anyway, I wanted you to be in the wedding."

"I'll be gone."

"Couldn't you wait till afterward?"

"No."

Probably he should make some kind of apology, but for the life of him, he could not decide what it was for. "Will you write me, Don? I'll want to hear how things turn out." They were coming back into town. The houses were ranged along the streets like pigeonholes for filing away the people.

It was the last time he talked to Don. Now he realized that once more Don had been incisive in telling him what he would do—how he would feel. But it was not true, Jim insisted to himself, that he had married to "qualify" in Ashton. He had loved Doris with a tender and dependent love. If their love had bumped here and there against rocks, that was to be expected. And what had he loved in her? (Had Don invaded his mind now, that he asked himself the

same kind of questions that Don might?) Her beauty, her sweet personality . . .
her beauty . . . Don would have asked, *And what did you talk about?* Damned
if I know; you don't remember what you talk about when you're in love. *You
don't?* Don is asking sarcastically. A man doesn't like to live lonely, Jim says by
way of excuse. And Don: *A man is lonely unless he's married, isn't he? In a small
town he gets married. Because* . . . Because he's in love, Jim breaks in, because
he wants his own friends around him, because he wants to get away from his
family, all kinds of becauses but the one you think!

And all the while that Jim was thrusting Don back into the past, he heard,
spreading like a tarpaulin over his thoughts, in dragging syllables, *Qualify.*

He hurriedly took out a cigarette and lighted it. In front of his car three
boys, barefoot, in knee pants, were climbing through the barbed wire strands
around the hillside meadow. A woman was shrilly calling someone from a
house across the road. He started the motor and drove away.

Downtown, he pulled up to the curb in front of Floyd's Grocery Store. An
oppressive quietness, filled with longing and frustration, crowded in with the
heat and lay like a sultry pall over the town. The weak stirring of the afternoon
wind from the south only emphasized it.

He climbed the narrow stairway between the grocery store and the café.
The aging worn steps rose in gloom toward the strip of light that fell from the
open office door. A fuzz of dust hung over the walls at each side; no one ever
cleaned them.

The stenographer, Miss McKinney, sat at her desk wiping her eyes with
a handkerchief as if she had been dozing. On the floor in the corner, an old
bumbling electric fan droned with a drowsy hum, hypnotically sapping away
any impulse to activity.

The offices were originally two large rooms, one for his father and the other
for the stenographer and clients. Now the reception room was partitioned
down the middle to make an office for Jim. Nearly every wall in the suite was
stacked with cases of law books. With the exception of several calendars and
his father's framed composite of photos of the Mississippi Bar Association,
there were no decorations.

Miss McKinney was about forty years old, and while she had earned the
admiration of the town for her earnestness and ability, she had won little friendship from any of its people. She had grown up in poverty and the backwash of
family scandal. Now, lonely and industrious, she was never seen at night except
at the movies in company with the accountant at Traywick's auto supply store,
a woman also single, forty and lonely.

"Hasn't Mr. Furlow come back from dinner?" asked Jim.

"Oh, yes, some time ago," she said in her sharp voice. "He's gone over to the courthouse."

As Jim crossed the room toward his office door, Miss McKinney's voice cut again through the stuffy room. "And your wife called twice. I think she wants to talk to you."

"Thanks." Jim sat down in the swivel chair at his desk and muttered to himself, "No doubt she does." Miss McKinney sounded as if she disliked the idea of anyone's having a wife. And Jim disliked the idea of Doris's trying to check up on him. He picked up the phone and called his home. After several rings, Doris answered.

"Did you call me?" he asked.

"Yes. I thought you were going straight to the office," she said acidly.

"I said I had some work to do," he answered. "I had to look up a deed at the courthouse." Why did he have to explain where he had been? "What did you want?"

"A woman called you here soon after you left," said Doris. "She said it was important." There was a short pause, as if both were waiting to see which would trap the other. Suddenly, Jim became very angry, with a kind of deep burning anger that would not come out, but seemed to thrash about in a little box inside of him.

"Well, who was it?" he asked.

"A Mrs. Mason," she said. "Who is she, James?"

"Don Mason's mother. She's an invalid," he said. "What did she say?"

"It was something about meeting Don," said Doris.

"Well, I better call her. Good-by."

But he did not pick up the phone again. He certainly was not going to meet Don at the train. He did not even want very much to see him, and would make no effort to do so. Don could come by to see him, if he wanted to. He took up a sheet of a brief on the desk and held it before his face.

Heat poured in the west window, rising from the metal roof of the grocery which extended behind the offices. The two windows, looking down on a side street, admitted drafts of the south wind. Soon Jim found himself gazing, not at his unfinished brief, but at the brick wall across the street, painted with a large, faded advertisement.

He was aroused by a chuckling grunt. Gus Traywick stood in the door, grinning at him. "I didn't think you could possibly be busy," said Tray.

"Hello, Tray," said Jim as he let the sheet of paper slide down to the top of the desk.

"Where've you been all afternoon?" asked Tray. He tipped the wide oak chair back and put his crossed feet on the desk.

"Has everybody been on a search for me? Why didn't you get out the bloodhounds?"

"Well, Doris said you'd come down here, but you weren't in and nobody knew where you were." Tray's voice rolled out deeply and slovenly, syllables and words joining, dropping out or toppling over each other. He had a wide, full mouth and his cheeks, even when smooth-shaven, were heavy and dark. His huge figure, once the principal support of the university football line, seemed to crowd the small office. "You know Don Mason's coming in tonight?"

"Sure. Is that why you walked all the way down here to see me?"

"Walk those five blocks? Not in this heat. I drove." Tray flicked his cigarette with a finger. Though the unpainted, gray floorboards where the ashes fell were imbedded with grit and dust, Jim pushed an ashtray toward him. Tray smeared his cigarette across the bottom of it and left the butt thinly smoking. "You talk to Mrs. Mason?"

"No. Why?"

"Well, for one thing, because she called you and she's a sick old lady." Tray put his feet on the floor and twisted the chair about. Crossing his legs, he sprawled from the partition where one shoe braced, across the chair to the desk where a shoulder and an arm leaned, with the hand cupped at his temple. "It's the kind thing to do, I think."

Ignoring him, Jim hummed a vague long note of agreement and busied himself with lighting a cigarette.

"She called me to see if she could find you," Tray continued. "She wanted you to meet Don at the train tonight."

"Why does she want someone to meet him?" Jim asked crabbedly. "This is his home town. He knows where he lives."

"It's not a matter of life and death. Sure, he knows. She just wanted him to be met. She thought you being his closest friend—"

"That's a long time ago," Jim interrupted testily. He would have gone on, but a puzzled light flowed over Tray's eyes and Jim realized that no one knew how he felt about Don. After a brief silence, Tray began slowly to smile.

"That's just her reason for asking you," he explained patiently. "She thought it would be nice, after three years, if Don found someone at the station he knew."

"Well, I can't do it anyway," said Jim in a kinder tone. "I told Doris I'd take her to that movie tonight."

"Oh, balls, the movie is out by the time the train comes in. You can take Doris along with you."

"She doesn't know Don. She probably wouldn't go." Jim turned around toward Tray and asked, "Why are you so interested? Maybe you should go yourself."

Tray's mouth was half-open, in boyish thoughtfulness, and his tongue pushed slightly between his teeth. "Guess I will," he said at last. He pulled his long bulky figure up from its sprawl and reached for the telephone. "Mind if I call her? "

"Go ahead."

Now he would have to ask Doris if she wanted to see the movie tonight. She would, because she never minded what the picture was about; even at westerns, she could comment on what cute clothes the rancher's daughter wore.

"Yes, Mrs. Mason," Tray was saying into the receiver, "I talked to Jim and we fixed it up. . . . Yes, I know you'll be glad, . . . Yes, Jim said he would. . . . We'll all try to. . . ." He went on with his broken, mumbled answers and finally said good-by and hung up.

"Old octopus," he muttered.

"Why do you say that?" asked Jim.

"You know she'll try to keep him here now," said Tray. "She won't let him get away again."

"Well, why shouldn't he stay? Is there anything wrong with staying in Ashton?"

"Why are you so grouchy today? Nothing wrong with Ashton for you and me, but Don's for something better. He needs a bigger place—somewhere to expand in. You know that better than I do, Jim. Are you turning Rotarian just because you've got a wife?"

"You belong to the Rotarians, Tray," said Jim, with an uneasy laugh.

"Yeah, but I know why. I know what I can do and how and why. That kind of thing is O.K. for me, but not for Don or you."

"For Christ's sake, did you come down here to talk Don to me?" exclaimed Jim. "All day long I've heard Don, Don, Don." As, with this lie, he attributed his inner and hidden impressions to other people's speech, a strange prickling swept over his body. He was disturbed at considering his motive for such lying. It was all on account of Doris, the way he felt about her, the way she treated him, the way Don would think of her. . . .

"Well, I was coming down to see you anyway," said Tray soothingly. "I wanted to talk to you about a hunting trip."

"In weather like this?"

"The season will open in a couple of months or so. This is just the last hot spell. We can rent Cy Baudry's shack over in the Delta for two or three days and shoot ducks."

"Oh, I'm no good as a hunter. You know that," said Jim. "Doris would be alone and—"

"Good God, man, has she got you hog-tied so you can't do anything? Every time I mention doing something, you say Doris can't be left alone."

"Well, you know how women are. They don't like to stay several days by themselves."

"My wife don't mind if I want to go somewhere. If I'm having a good time where Bea can't go, it suits her."

"That's what you think."

"Hell, Doris can go stay with your mother. Women are always happy together. Spend all their time together anyhow. Men never get a chance to see each other for fun. That's one big reason for going. We can get away from the womenfolks."

Jim laughed. "You sound like a confirmed bachelor instead of a married man."

"Marriage's got nothing to do with such things," said Tray. "Women have their clubs and teas and bridge games and shopping trips all day long. Then at night they want the men to take them out and show them off to other women. A man never gets a chance to see another man for pleasure. He's so busy being a showcase for his wife he can't have a friend. He joins the Rotarians, the Elks, the Masons, he goes to conventions, homecoming games, anything to make him feel he's got a friend as well as a wife. But it don't work out the way it should."

"Want a soapbox?" asked Jim.

"To hell with you," snapped Tray cheerfully. "We'll get five or six of us—maybe Don, if he's here. It'll be—"

"No reason to ask him," Jim interrupted. "He can't shoot."

"He can learn. It'd do him good to go."

"Well, he won't be here. He'll be going to back to New York." No matter how he tried, he couldn't disguise the bitterness from Tray.

"You don't want him to go, do you?" asked Tray.

"Why the devil should I care?" Jim demanded with sulky irritation.

"Don't get your dander up. You're sure touchy today. What's the matter?"

"Nothing, I guess. I just feel restless, sort of."

"Yeah," said Tray. He clapped one of his huge hands on Jim's where they lay folded together on the unfinished brief. "Too much wife and too much work. That hunt is just what you need."

"Maybe so." Jim lowered his voice. A timid intimacy came over it. "But sometimes I feel like it's more than a trip I need. Maybe I need to move away from Ashton for good."

"Move away!"

Jim motioned to quiet his excitement and pointed to the outer office. Tray looked in surprise at the partition and then grimaced in understanding.

"But where could you move to any better?" Tray asked. "I'm not being Rotarian now. But do you know any place, any chance for you?"

"Oh, I'm not too serious about it," said Jim with a sad laugh. "I just think once in a while I'd like to move, say, to Jackson or Memphis. They're bigger towns, more there, more business."

Tray did not answer him. Their eyes met, Jim's dark gray ones holding steady against Tray's black boring stare, and then Jim turned his head toward the window.

"I live on Dad's practice here," Jim said moodily. "I want to stand on my own feet."

"A sucker for the great American dream," scoffed Tray.

"Well, I don't know." When he leaned his elbows on the desk, he found that Tray was still looking intently at him. "I just feel depressed sometimes when I look around town—the people, the way they live and work, what they enjoy, what they miss—what we all miss, I suppose. I wonder if it's not—well, poisoning itself in some way, dying happily in its own poison. And I begin to think some other place might be different."

"You wouldn't be any happier," said Tray slowly and solemnly.

With a mixture of faint guilt for what he imagined was behind Tray's words and of calm gladness for knowing that the knowledge of his guilt was shared, Jim laced his fingers tightly together. How could Tray, or anyone, know how he felt? He had concealed his shame and hurt in every way he could. Possibly in the first few months of his marriage some perceptive person might have noticed his tension and moodiness. But since then he had been careful to let people see his affection for Doris. He was always attentive, he held her hand when they sat in public, he put his arm around her in the movies, he talked to her as if they were old friends reunited and inexhaustible with news. Neither he nor Tray had said anything for a long time.

An impulse to discuss his marriage—at least part of it—with Tray, without going into details that were painful, throbbed inside him. Probably it sprang from a suspicion that Tray already knew and understood; but it was a familiar impulse. For a long time he had wanted to talk to someone—his father came first to mind, then his mother—but with them he was ashamed. They would probably tell him he was imagining things.

"I guess you're right," said Jim in a low, thoughtful voice. "I wouldn't be any happier."

Suddenly Tray chuckled. He stood up and clutched the back of Jim's neck between his big fingers. "What you need is a trip to a whorehouse in Memphis," he whispered, so that Miss McKinney would not hear.

"Fine thing for one married man to suggest to another," said Jim, wriggling out of Tray's grip and flushing over his forehead. "What would Bea say to that?"

"It'd be all right with her as long as I didn't throw it in her face. Sometimes I think she wishes she could have a change herself for a few weeks."

"Good God!" Jim exclaimed. "It—it—well, I don't think—"

Tray shoved his chair against the partition and laughed. "Don't choke, Jim," he said. "Maybe a drink would help. Got any liquor here?"

"You know I don't keep whiskey in the office," Jim said sternly and pointed to the locked bottom drawer of his desk. "Anyway, it's too hot to drink."

"Come on down to my place," said Tray. "Got some beer in the ice chest."

"Nope, can't do it today. I got to finish this brief."

"All right, slave away and see what it gets you." Tray walked to the door. "Better be on my way," he said, going out. "I'll see you."

4

T ray clumped noisily down the steps and, outside the stair slit, stopped to peer through the café window. None of his friends were there for afternoon coffee—only a mechanic at the counter and a Negro paying for a bottled soda that he would drink on the sidewalk. He strolled on up the street.

Every time he talked to him, he was struck with the strange wrenching of Jim's personality—the lack of authority and confidence, the unsureness which changed him from a familiar into an unknown person. Certainly Jim was not working this afternoon, but his reason for not leaving the office was hidden, a part of his deepening reticence, as if he were afraid people would discover a secret. Tray himself hadn't the slightest intention of working. It was hot, a brilliant day, he didn't like to work, he wanted to be outdoors breathing or indoors drinking; he wanted to laugh and talk with friends.

Damn it, Jim hadn't been like that before he married Doris. If he had been, he never would have met her, because it was Tray who took him to Oakville that Sunday. In those days, Jim had always been ready to go anywhere that promised a good time. But he wouldn't do anything now; his excuse was Doris every time—"Doris can't . . . Doris won't . . . Doris isn't . . ."

A momentary sense of frustration swirled about him. Why the hell couldn't he find out what was wrong with Jim? Something had got hold of him by the short hairs. If he'd only let it out, just talk it out to him as a friend.

Not long ago, over a highball after work, he tried to persuade Jim to open up a little.

"You look like you're worried," he said. "Anything wrong?"

"Why?" Jim's face clouded with anxiety. "I'm not worried."

"I just thought . . ." Tray hesitated and then closed his hand around Jim's arm. "We're good enough friends, don't you think?" he stammered painfully. "I'd like to—help."

36

Jim's voice became tight and thin. "There's nothing wrong. I'm not worried."

There it was again—the distrust, the recoiling, the solitary wound—and poorly shielded by a transparent lie. They were silent for a while.

"Men can't talk," said Tray musingly, at last. "I guess women have taken that away from us. We can't talk to each other any more."

"What do you mean?"

"Well, we tell each other our sex life—or invent some to tell—or we talk business. But we won't let our best friends know what we are—what we feel. That goes to some stranger, maybe, because he can't ever hold over us what he knows. I guess we're ashamed we even have feelings. What kind of people are we?"

"I don't talk about my sex life to you, do I?" asked Jim.

"Not any more. That's just it. It's got so we can't talk at all—seriously. That's why I thought—"

"I'd better get on home," said Jim. He hurriedly drank the rest of his drink. "Doris didn't know I was stopping by."

But after all, he was not close enough to Jim for confidences. If Jim shared his secret with anyone, he would more naturally share it with Don. Still, it might be something he would tell nobody, because nobody could do anything about it except Jim. It might be something—someone—only Jim could suffer from, only Jim could understand, only Jim could reach.

He turned back down the street. A bottle of beer at his auto company would taste good, if those niggers hadn't raided the ice chest. When he got into his car, he growled, "Damn it!" aloud as he slammed the door. What the devil were wives for, if not to help out in such a case? He backed from the curb and drove slowly down the street.

The sun had dropped low in the western sky, and the shadows of the buildings fell half across the pavements. Boys and girls whirred past in their family cars, or strolled toward the drugstores. In front of the hotel the first of the evening's traveling men was getting out of his car to register for the night.

At his Ford agency, Tray parked the car alongside the building where it would not interfere with customers and walked through the wide central entrance flanked with racks of tires and shelves of motor parts. On the right, in a glassed-in room, worked three accountants and stenographers. On his left, a similar but smaller room had been fitted up as his office.

He opened the frosted-glass door. His wife looked up from behind the desk, smiling as if she knew who was coming in, and threw a trade journal aside. "God, that's dull reading," she said.

Her hair was almost as black as Tray's, but now, as during every summer, there were coppery gleams of sunburn in it. Her mouth was small and her eyes, dark violet under the heavy lids, were accented by the pallor of her skin. The short nose, with a tendency toward the aquiline, did not relieve the roundness of her thin face. She was not the beauty that Doris was, but then, thought Tray, he didn't want ever to sleep with Doris.

"Where have you been all afternoon?" she asked.

"Are all the wives checking on their husbands today?" he exclaimed. After turning the electric fan a speed faster, he dragged off his coat and flung it carelessly on a hook beside the washbowl.

"Oh, never mind," she said. "I just wanted to get away from home. I saw Mrs. Hodge—she was making calls leaving Mrs. Thornton's—and I just felt like she was coming to see me next. So I jumped in the car and came down here."

"You don't have to explain," said Tray, falling loosely into a straight chair. "But I wish you'd do some work when you come."

"Sure. What'll I do?"

"Go out to the ice chest and bring in two of those bottles under the orange soda in the back left-hand corner."

She mumbled over his words.

"And don't bring back soda," Tray added. Then he stirred himself to an upright position. "Now get going. I want my easy chair."

He moved toward her and she scampered out the door. When she returned, carrying two dripping bottles of beer, he was leaning far back in the swivel chair, blowing smoke at his feet crossed on the desk. She handed him a bottle and jerked a paper towel from the rack over the lavatory. They set both bottles on the towel and Bea slid up on the glass-topped desk beside them.

"You sure it's not too early in the day?" she asked.

"Early? I drink it in the morning if I want to."

"What will your stomach think?"

Instead of answering he took a drink. They smoked in silence and from time to time raised the bottles to their lips.

Around three sides of the office, arranged in slapdash fashion, were calendars, advertisements of automobiles, accessories, charts for tires, oils and fixtures, two coat racks and three file cabinets. The third side, at Tray's back, was a large, steel-framed section of glass panes looking out on the service station. The lower row was painted green and a wide green window shade hung part way down from the ceiling. The two big panes that opened for ventilation were propped wide on metal levers. Outside a car was being filled with gasoline and water.

"Reckon we better pull the shade?" asked Bea. "Some angel of the gospel might drive up."

"To hell with them," muttered Tray. "They'll think we're drinking cokes."

"Never can tell," warned Bea. She got off the desk and walked toward the windows.

"Leave it up," said Tray stubbornly. "If we pull it down they'll think we're screwing in a place of business and there'll be all kinds of talk."

"Aw, Tray," said Bea reproachfully, and came back to the desk.

"Well, it's no sin to drink beer," he said. "It's even legal if you happen to be a citizen of the United States."

"Now don't start talking politics," Bea said, patting him on the jaw as she passed behind him. "You know you're not a thinker, so don't try to be."

"Maybe I'm not deep, but a guy can't help thinking, sometimes. I don't like to just soak up what the damn newspapers print." He drained the last beer from the bottle, tossed it into the wastebasket and got up. "I'll find those other bottles," he said on his way to the door. Outside, he rummaged around in the icy water of the soft-drink cooler.

Bea would drink another one, or two or three; in fact, she'd drink beer or whiskey just as long as he would and always stay on her feet so she could get him home in case he passed out. That was a problem in Ashton, where morals were not basic social tenets, but incidental, personal tastes. Only a small group of the women approved drinking whiskey, and that approval was secret, not to be expressed to the older, established arbiters of society.

Even though Bea now made slight concessions to the local "society" pattern, because she felt it was good politics, she would never go all the way. To him she scoffed at the ladies and the standards of the arts club she had joined, but she couldn't openly do so and tended more and more to arrange their household so that it would conform to the accepted mold. She knew as well as he the fortuitous line between the social groups, and how most of those at the top clung desperately to their position by making use of the little customs, the trivial actions, the careless word, that could rule others out. There was no outstanding difference, no moral difference to anyone who knew all about the majority of the families. Once Bea and Tray were both identified with the "wrong side of the tracks"; but she was accepted now because she had married him, and he was accepted because he had gone to college and had been a great football player.

He pulled five bottles of beer from the icy water of the chest. Spreading his fingers between and around the necks, he carried them into the office. Clattering them on the glass-covered desk, he began rolling up his sleeves. "Let's get down to business, now, huh?" he said.

"Umm," Bea agreed, picking up a fresh drink. "Opener?"

Tray tossed her the bottle opener. She pried off the cap and flipped it into the wastebasket.

"What are you worried about, Tray?" she asked, as he returned to the swivel chair.

"Worried? What makes you think so?" How like himself and Jim he and Bea were now! Couldn't anyone be honest about his own sentiments?

"Well, first thing you always do is try to think," she said. "Then you sort of flounder around, like a cat with something stuck to his feet, trying one time to shake it off and next time ignore it."

He laughed mournfully and drank. "I guess I'm not subtle, am I?"

"Being a man, you don't have to deceive people—well, not unless you want to make money. But if you were a woman—my!"

"If I was, it wouldn't be any fun," he said. "How can women have fun, anyway?"

"Mainly by subtle deception, dear."

"Is that fun?"

"Most of them think so."

"And you?"

When she answered, "I think women stink," she banged the bottle on the desk in disgust. The sheet of glass cracked in an irregular arc around the corner. Both of them were startled at the sharp sound in the sultry afternoon.

"Ouch!" cried Tray, and began to laugh at her amazement.

"Well, it didn't break the bottle," she muttered. "I'm sorry, Tray. I just get angry at some things."

"Like what?"

"Like what's making you angry."

He looked steadily at her for a moment and then opened his lips slowly to form words that were not spoken.

"Women can see more of each other's inside workings than men can," Bea went on. "They can see more of a man's mind, too, if they've got sense enough."

"Looks like we haven't got a chance," he said lightly, hoping to avoid the subject which she was approaching.

"You haven't," she said.

He did not respond, but sat quietly smoking and drinking. His wide eyes looked vacant but disturbed. But Bea did not say any more, and he sighed resignedly. There was no reason why he shouldn't talk about it to her—just some silly notion that women never understood men—and after all, she had shown she was on his side.

"How did you know it was Jim?" he asked at last.

"I know he's the only man in Ashton that you care about," she said. "It could only be me or him. He's not strong enough, some way, to protect himself, Tray. From what women will do to him—to any man."

"Didn't know you hated women so much."

"Why, all women hate each other," she exclaimed.

"Bea," he said in amused surprise, "are you getting drunk?"

She laughed. "Nope, but I guess I sound like it. I just feel so sorry for men."

"Because of me, I reckon." He straightened in his chair to open another beer. The sun, hanging just above the tops of the western houses, shone through the wide windows straight across the room.

"Well, what about Jim? And Doris?" asked Bea.

He tilted back in the chair, swiveled slightly from her and considered what he should say. After a moment's thought, he hedged. "I don't quite know. A man picks the woman he thinks suits him."

"Yes," drawled Bea in a sustained tone. "And if she turns out not to be the right one?"

"Then you're supposed to act like a gentleman, I guess."

"Not divorce her, huh? How long do you think Jim can act like a gentleman?"

He confronted her with a flash of resentment in his eyes. "He is a gentleman. Always. It's not a matter of 'how long' with him." Stiff with uncomfortable conflicting urges, he watched her teasing smile with rising annoyance.

"How long before she'll wreck him?" she insisted. "You know without me telling you what the wrong woman can do to a man, especially when the law and God have tied them together."

"Jim wouldn't stand for divorce. He's too—sensitive."

Bea laughed quietly. "It's Doris who wouldn't stand for it. She couldn't."

"Why are we talking about them divorcing?" he asked unhappily. "What do we know about them anyway?" He tipped the beer to his mouth.

"Don't ask me," she said matter-of-factly. "What has he told you?"

"Nothing," he replied. "It's just a feeling." He flopped his hand through the air and let it fall on the arm of his chair. "Seems like I can't say anything to him, and he can't to me. Anything really important, I mean." He lifted his face to her for help and confidence. She was waiting quietly to hear more. "I've tried," he said defensively. "But I don't know how." He got up and began pounding back and forth across the room from the windows to the rear wall. "I feel like it's all because of Doris—something she's done to him, something she's taken from him. She's got no feeling but for herself, has she, Bea?" He stopped in front of her, hoping for some agreement or encouragement in her eyes. She nodded thoughtfully. "And she's married a man who needs lots of love given to him. Most of all he needs to give a lot himself, and he—can't, I guess. He deserves a better break than that."

"Men asked for the dirty end of the stick long ago," said Bea. "Back when they let women out of the home."

"Why the hell didn't he marry Isabel Lang?" growled Tray. "She'd have been a good wife for him."

"Too late now. Poor guy."

"Pity doesn't do any good," said Tray in harsh annoyance.

"Maybe not. And there's no use crying your eyes out over him," she answered with a faint smile. "Let him work it out or crack up."

"I won't do it," he muttered. "If you like a fellow, you can't just sit around—"

"Well, for God's sake, Tray," she interrupted, "don't stick your big foot in it."

He stood moodily in front of the windows facing the street. The sun had dropped behind the trees and housetops, and the west was beginning to glow and redden. Frail shaggy clouds that had been barely visible during the day caught a yellow and pink tinge and behind them the sky seemed a deeper blue. A car rumbled on a flat tire up the concrete ramp and through the passage into the garage. Bea was as silent as he was now; she didn't care about Jim very much one way or the other. Maybe he was wrong, though, and would better forget the whole thing. At least for the time. At least until something definite, something he couldn't tolerate, developed.

He turned back toward her and said, "I guess I ought to get out some work, Bea."

She got up, surprised. "Oh, Tray, why didn't you say you had work to do? I'll run on home. Now, don't bother anymore about Jim."

"All right." He sat at the desk and fumbled in a drawer for paper. "It's just that—well—I respect what he is." He twisted the paper around the platen of the typewriter.

Bea clanked the last beer bottle into the basket, quickly wiped the glass top with paper towels, picked up her handbag and turned to the door. "See you at home," she said briskly, and went out.

"O.K., Bea." And he began pecking at the keys.

5

As Bea stepped into the passage, a musty little woman came from the accountant's office and, without slowing her pace, nodded and smiled to her. Above the clangor of the garage, Bea said, "Hello, Miss Julia," and continued to the side street where she had parked the car.

The long, melancholy summer twilight wrapped the enervated town, as if trying to soothe it after the bright sweltering day. Against the colored west everything seemed to be a silhouetted darkness.

Funny old Tray, she thought while she drove home; still the Boy Scout, stirred by impulses of teamwork, fraternity, friendship, pulling together, helping. . . . A big clumsy guy who wanted to show his affection and wanted a little in return; he went on loving people in a lumbering doglike way.

He never had hated, as she used to, the prominent families in town. Most of the people of the North End worked in the railroad shop. Some worked there for only a few years; some had come with the opening of the shops and had been there ever since. But they never quite got in with the merchant and professional families who made up what was considered society. They felt little love for the ladies with their formal calls and clubs and seated teas. The children mixed in school and church, but that was the end of it. Few of them ever sensed the distinction until they were grown up, and by that time they were thoroughly settled in their own class and did not bother.

She herself had not envied them so much as scorned them for what they pretended to have. Most of them had nothing but a small bank account and that intangible mutual something called acceptance. But it had influenced her feeling about some of them—Don, in particular, and (because of her worship of Tray) also Jim, who had Tray's friendship and could not show himself worthy of it.

When she was a child, she used to wonder why Tray did not get angry with Jim, why he ever had anything to do with him at all. They could play together

43

only at school, when they were in the lower grades. Even though Tray later on was usually busy with football or baseball practice, Jim was never allowed to go to his house or to invite Tray over. Jim had to play with friends on his side of town—Don Mason and the others who would eventually take over the social regime.

Why should Tray—so trusting and uncomplicated, so honest in trying to do the right thing and think straight, so unconcerned about the "right" people, so casual about his business—why should he worry about a friend's marriage? Jim was always going to do the "proper" thing, no matter what it did to him inside. If he, even as a child, weren't already imprisoned by his family's ideas and way of thinking, why wouldn't he have run away to play with Tray?

But of course, she knew that people changed with maturity; she herself had undergone a few changes. When she went to work in Jackson, she gradually forgot her resentment of Ashton society, since she was fortunate enough to like someone from whom its social categories couldn't bar her. After that successful evening of the Thanksgiving football game—an evening which she had virtually forced on Tray ("But Beatrice," he argued, "I told Zack and Moon I'd take them to this girl's house I know . . .")—she decided the thing to do was return to Ashton where she would be near him. She brought back with her enough experience to smooth the rough edges of her poise, and she was able to meet any of the Ashton ladies not only without embarrassment, but, because of her familiarity with a larger town, with a disturbing aura of superiority.

She turned into the concrete driveway leading to the double garage behind their house and left the car at one side. With a short glance at the clothes she had hung out, she went through the back porch into the house.

In the bedroom, she put her handbag away in a dresser drawer and after a casual adjustment of her hair, hurried back to the kitchen to start supper. With an apron tied around her waist, she took vegetables and the left-over roast from the icebox to make a beef stew. A fluffy spoon bread would go nicely with it. Thank heavens, she enjoyed eating as much as Tray did, or cooking would be a chore.

She suddenly left off peeling and chopping the vegetables and went into the living room to turn on the radio. In the deepening twilight, everything was noticeably hushed. She heard no dogs, no cars, no calling voices. A special isolation such as she had never felt before encircled her now, even though there were neighbors close on each side, and the telephone might ring any moment and she knew Tray would come in soon. And yet it was like this every night—the stores began to close, the businessmen went home, the wives and children waited for supper, night closed over each family in its house, confined with relatives until after breakfast.

Was it loneliness she felt in this particular twilight—the loneliness of a night in a small town, of having no world outside your home except the movie theater, and no world inside except each other? Maybe it was not having a child, the feeling of some other human being in the house with her. Maybe it was Tray's disturbance about Jim, transferred to herself.

The image of Jim's house at this moment, with Doris puttering around the kitchen, Jim taking refuge in the Jackson evening paper—an image that wavered, hazed and flowed like dissolving scenes in movies—flickered in her mind. Though she made an ineffectual mental effort not to control the action in these rippling images, she knew that Jim would not dash his paper to the floor, as she imagined him, stamp into the kitchen and thrash Doris thoroughly. She knew that Doris would not grab the carving knife and slice Jim up and down from groin to stomach. They were quietly moving about the house; Doris rattled pans and moaned kittenishly about the cooking, and Jim rustled the paper and turned up the news on the radio. And that—the silence, the choking back of speech, the absence of contact—was why they were so far away and inaccessible.

There seemed always about them a chilly isolation, even from each other, as if they were quite separate objects, legally and morally joined, but never, in spite of all their displays of affection and intimacy, merging in the slightest degree. It seemed ridiculous, but she could not say exactly how. Perhaps in the sense that a child could love a doll, a woman her house, or a man—well, just what could a man love besides some woman; what else, in the same way that she was thinking of, the selfless way that a child loved a doll, a woman her house, giving it her attention, her warmth, her work, and demanding nothing because it could give back nothing. Could it be his guns, his pipes, his machines, his job? A man would feel a deep need to have his affection returned. A dog, a horse, returned it; but a man could never hate a dog or a horse because it rejected his love, as he could a woman or a friend.

How fortunate she had been to find that her early longing for Tray, that period of puppy love which amused middle-aged couples, had developed, almost unwaveringly, through later courtship into this strong attachment to him, loving him physically and enjoying him companionably, and yielding to him unselfishly, because giving to him gave her an almost sexual pleasure, whether it was the sacrifice of a dress, or a trip, or of her body which he had taken calmly and gently from her months before their marriage. And now, although his heavy pressure between her limbs was familiar, not with the thrill of unknown excitement but with the expected union of a loved understanding, she had no fear of his looking toward some other woman, even of his taking another to bed somewhere out of her sight. Most men would do that, and Tray certainly would, and she must pretend not to suspect. It would be no more than another sacrifice that she could make to him. They would always be together, would always be faithful in a sense beyond such a simple thing as sleeping together.

She had barely got the table set when she heard Tray's car drive into the garage. By the time he entered the kitchen, she was pouring spoon bread into a buttered casserole.

"Something smells good," he said, looking inquisitively at the stove.

"It's tarragon in the stew," she told him. "Now get away while I put this in the oven."

"I know—get out of my kitchen, don't touch that, stop eating the nuts off that cake," he grumbled, and paused to pick up a quarter of tomato which he salted and tossed into his mouth.

"And don't shake the floor, either, you ox," she cautioned. "That's spoon bread. Go read the paper or do something quiet."

"All right. Quiet as a mouse." And he went into the living room on exaggerated tiptoes. The prisms of the crystal candlesticks on the buffet tinkled at his jarring passage through the dining room.

While they were eating supper, the telephone rang and Bea got up to answer. "Oh, hello, Mrs. Dalton," she said. "Why, no, we just finished. I was clearing away the dishes." Tray was piling more yellow spoon bread on his plate and covering it with stew. "Oh, that sounds wonderful. Let me ask Tray."

She covered the mouthpiece with her palm and moved as far inside the dining room as the wire would allow. "Tray, are we doing anything Saturday night? Mrs. Dalton's having a buffet supper for some Chicago friends."

"Sure, let's go," he said boisterously. "Free meal!"

"Sh!" she warned, and took her hand from the mouthpiece. "We'd love to, Mrs. Dalton. . . . It's so nice of you to ask us. . . . At six-thirty. . . . Yes. . . . Thank you so much. . . . Good-by."

"Buffet suppers are a nuisance, though," Tray grumbled when she returned to the table.

"It'll probably be quite an affair," said Bea. "They're connected with a chain of textile plants like the one Mr. Dalton owns."

"Oh, they'll put on the dog, all right. All the most prominent married people in town, boring each other and scared they'll hurt their business if they don't pretend they're enjoying it. . . . Let's drag Don to the party with us," he suggested mischievously. "Might liven up some of the dopes."

"Don? You mean . . ."

"Oh, I forgot to tell you. We're meeting Don Mason at the train tonight."

"He's coming back?"

"Now, don't be silly. Why else would we be meeting him?"

"Well, why are we?"

"Mrs. Mason wanted someone to. Jim wouldn't—rather he couldn't do it. Doris . . ."

"Oh," she said blankly. "How nice of us."

"Now, Bea, don't start acting like that. Don's a good fellow."

"All right, all right. I won't hold grudges. But I wouldn't take him to Madge's party."

"Why not? He'd do fine with those city people."

"Oh, Tray!" she burst out in exasperation. "We're all married people, settled down—at least, so they say. He wouldn't want to be with us."

"Maybe it's the other way around. We don't want to be with single people. We're jealous of them, aren't we?"

"Not if they're women." She put her crumpled napkin on the table and began to collect the dishes. "The main thing, you stupid lunk, is that Doris and Jim are probably invited too."

"So what? All the better."

"So if Jim won't meet him at the train tonight, he won't want to meet him at the party next week."

Tray looked searchingly at her. He seemed to demand an explanation, but she could not give a better one than Tray had given for his own anxiety over Jim that afternoon. "That's just woman's intuition," she said glibly and rising, began to put the dishes on a tray.

"I'll ask Madge tomorrow," said Tray with the stubbornness she knew so well. "I don't like mysterious peeves." He was hunched over his plate with a moody air. "And I don't like stupid people."

"What I like about you is you don't have any vanity," she whispered as she leaned over and kissed him.

Then she took his plate with the others into the kitchen.

"Want to go to the movies before the train?" he called.

"What is it—something terrible?"

"Oh, Katherine Hepburn in something. Name of a girl, I think. Something about a small town."

She brought in the dessert and coffee. Tray was smoking and flipping the ashes into the flower bowl.

"Just as soon go," she answered, and shoved an ashtray under his hand.

As they rode toward the theater, the night streets looked forsaken without their daytime variety of color, plants and painted boards in the sun. The shades were drawn close over the few lighted windows, like blind eyes in the trees, and stray beams broke through the crevices. At the corner of each block, a dim yellow bulb at the top of a lamppost fuzzed out into a sphere of light revolving with insects. There was no one on the sidewalks, no car on the street. Far ahead at the main intersection, the oil flares of a PWA paving project smoked somberly.

In front of the theater, cheerful and gaudy with arcs of naked electric bulbs and colored posters of beauty and drama, a few people still loitered. Since they could hear popular music bursting out of the amplifiers inside, they knew that the show had not begun.

When Tray had bought their tickets, he asked, "Popcorn?" The smell of it—a hot, buttery, thirsty smell—flooded out from the tiny booth built in one corner of the open lobby.

"Not on top of supper," she said, although she knew that it was almost a ritual to eat a bag of popcorn before the show. She went on toward the door.

The green baize curtains billowed out in the draft from big fans flanking the proscenium. In the small dim auditorium, the chattering audience almost filled the plywood seats. The crackle of popcorn bags, the shuffling of feet, the high piping of children up front, the louder tone of friends calling across the rows, broke lightly through the loud, undeveloped jazz tunes. While looking for seats, they waved to acquaintances, nodded their heads or motioned with their arms in silent communication. They moved into a row and sat down.

Then the unfiltered lights overhead went out and only the four wildly colored wall brackets gleamed in the darkness. The jazz continued through several typewritten advertisements and faded as the more expensive ads with their own music and insistent voices were screened. Shots of disembodied hands reaching for perfect food in refrigerators, simpering men and women in dinner clothes admiring an engagement ring, dreamlike automobiles rushing down model highways, flashed before them.

By the time the ads, the newsreel and the short-subject were finished, the audience had relaxed in the dark vault of the movie house. Each person retired from the nightly social exchange that preceded the program into his own isolation, his own intercourse with the unapproachable shadows. Bea began to understand now that strange intuition she had had about Jim and Doris, and about the whole town. They all went through certain formal motions, they signaled to each other from house to house, from seat to seat, from eye to eye, but they were really absorbed in an ideal contact, which they could not possibly attain and, worse still, could not even work toward.

With the unfolding of the movie, everyone found himself in a nice small town—their own town—with sweet people who had good sentiments like their own, who acted just as they would have wished to act, who were really themselves. Tomorrow, some of them would try to look more like the identity which they now watched; they would do what they had seen themselves do. But only in their minds; they could not afford to betray by any overt action the dangerous goodness in themselves. They would not reach toward their neighbors because obviously their neighbors were not in this film, and not in that ideal film which was the accretion of all of themselves they could absorb from all the films.

When the movie had wound out to its conclusion, the lights overhead came on and the audience sidled into the aisles and out the doors. Bea took hold of Tray's arm so she would not be separated from him in the swaying crush of people. Outside in the fresh air, she took a deep breath and they turned toward their car.

A couple of autos were already waiting at the railroad station when Tray and Bea got there. The fading lights under the eaves of the roof were on, indicating that the train would arrive any minute. Tray headed in against a curb of old railroad ties around a crushed limestone areaway. A few travelers wandered about the waiting room door, an occasional employee walked to or from the baggage room, one or two loiterers leaned against the walls, a group of Negroes huddled near the entrance of their waiting room.

They could already hear the train blowing for the crossings to the north, and in a short while the lights shone along the roadbed. The noise of the engine roared increasingly louder. Tray opened the door.

"Want to get out?" he asked.

"I'll wait here," said Bea.

He strolled down the crushed stone area while the train ground and squeaked sootily to a stop. Through the row of coach windows a line of passengers was visible waiting in the aisle. The vestibule of the coach for whites was directly in front of Bea. From the little crowd around it, she could hear the soft excitement of voices as visitors greeted their relatives or friends.

In a way she had gratified her feeling of dim dislike for Don by staying in the car. And in some other peculiar way, she had gratified Tray by staying behind so he could meet Don alone. She watched him now, waiting for someone who meant little to him, because that person meant something to someone else who in turn meant a great deal to Tray. Good Lord, how complicated she could get when she tried to figure out a simple man like Tray! How could she ever understand anyone like Don, with his unpredictable moods and intellectual interests, his solitary ways? It was easy enough to drop him into that disdainful category where she had always kept him; but it was not enough when she considered what must be in him to cause Jim and even Tray to like him. Men and women certainly must not see the same things in each other.

Tray was calling out, "Don! Hey, Don!" He moved swiftly around the group at the vestibule toward a halted figure. Putting down his suitcase, Don shook hands. Tray slapped him on the back as if he were a teammate after a hard-won football game. Their words came to her over the short distance, sometimes clearly, sometimes obliterated by a spew of steam from the train.

"Come on, I'll drive you home," said Tray.

"Why . . . don't bother, Tray. Thanks, but I can walk," said Don. "It's not far."

"Oh, shut up. That's what I came down here for."

"What do you mean?"

Tray laughed, and then the noise smothered both voices. In a moment she could hear Tray again. "We were up anyway. Come on, the car's right over here."

As they started away, Tray with boyish insistence pried Don's hand from the suitcase. "Go on, I'll take it. You're company tonight!"

Bea suspected that Don was embarrassed. He seemed bewildered, almost annoyed, as if he had wanted to come back to town unseen and quietly. The light-brown hair with a tendency to wave and the thin figure that she remembered were not changed, nor was his voice, rather light, pronouncing words too carefully for the townspeople. But in the light of a car wheeling from the station, his face seemed more grave; his eyes, always tender, were quite sorrowful, and his mouth drawn with unhappiness.

With a routine of cries and signals from the flagman and tooting and puffing from the engine, the train was pulling out of the station. When the two men walked up to the car, Tray asked, "You know Bea, don't you?" He opened the door to the back and tossed in the suitcase.

"Hello, Bea, how are you?" said Don. "Seems like a long time."

They shook hands through the open window. Then Tray reached down between to turn the door handle, and urged Don into the front seat. "Get in, get in."

"I'll ride in the back," said Don uncertainly.

"Go on, get in." Tray pushed him in beside her and closed the door. He ran around the back of the car and slid under the steering wheel. "I'm not jealous," he said.

6

As they drove away from the station, Don peered out curiously at the buildings of Ashton. They seemed different, but doubtless they were not really changed at all. During his absence he had reconstructed them in imagination and his surprise now was that of first recognition. The car passed down the dim main street, past the dark store fronts and deserted curbs. A few laggard figures strolled home, obscure in the shadow of metal canopies and then momentarily outlined in the feeble light of a corner lamppost. Two soda fountains stayed open to catch the last summer-night customers, and two lunch counters waited for anyone who wanted sandwiches or pie or coffee. Now that the few remaining cars at the station had whirled away into darkness, there was virtually no traffic, no life, at all.

"You want to go straight home?" Tray asked.

"Well—I think I'd better," Don said hesitantly, wondering where else Tray thought he might go.

"We got a bottle in the compartment there," said Tray. "Didn't know but what you'd like a drink after that long trip."

"Oh, I don't know," Don murmured. He was puzzled somehow at being in a car with Tray and his wife suddenly after stepping off the train in his home town. Not only the strangeness of the situation, even if it had been accidental, but the explanation which Tray had given seemed to bounce dizzily in his head.

"I guess I better not," said Don. "I'll have to see Mother when I go in and she'd think I'd been drinking ever since I left here."

"Well, you're right, I expect," said Tray. "Want to ride around a while? It's not really late."

"I ought to go on home, I think. Mother will know the train's in and there'll be all kinds of questions. It wouldn't look right."

"Whatever you think best," said Tray, turning the car off the main street toward Mrs. Mason's house.

Why was Tray so intent on keeping him from going home? It was surely not what a person would do or invite anyone to do after being away for three years. What could be subconsciously moving Tray to ask him to have a drink, to go for a late ride? And with Bea, the plain little girl who always mooned after Tray in high school, sitting between them and, though not definitely urging him to join them, at least supporting her husband by her silence.

"Let's get together, though," Don suggested in conciliation, but phlegmatically, "and have a party some night."

"Sure will," said Tray enthusiastically. "Got lots to talk to you about." He was pulling up at the walk leading to the Mason house. "Stop in to see me at the garage, Don. Sure good to have you back."

Don ducked his head and stepped out of the car. Two squares of subdued light filled the glass front door and a window of his home.

"Many thanks for meeting me, Tray," he said, reaching for his bag. "It would have been a hot walk up here tonight."

"I see your mother is up, like you said," Bea remarked.

"Oh sure, I knew she would be," he said. "Well, good night, Bea. See both of you soon. 'Night."

He turned quickly, swinging the suitcase, and walked toward the steps. In the shadows, the house and its thin columns looked like a giant gray spider reared on its legs. It was an old cottage, one of the earliest in the town, with a low porch across the front supported by square wooden pillars. The original frame was a log cabin in the trading-post days, but the logs had been covered over with clapboard, and the roof lifted so that two extra rooms with dormer windows could be built underneath. Extending from each rear corner, wings of two additional rooms had been added in fairly recent times.

At the doorstep he paused. Now he faced the ending of the freedom he had sought by running away from Ashton, and his mother. The dark anxiety of night fell around him, just as in his adolescence, but now it demanded a reconciliation that left no hope.

Softly he stepped across the piqué-ed seams of the old planks on the porch and softly and slowly opened the front door. Against the lacy-etched pane of glass forming the upper half of this door he had leaned his forehead many times as a child, gazing out at the bright empty street. The milky design on the glass edged with the diffused frills of some heartless Valentine framed his search into a world of unknown longings. He could never discover what he looked for during those sweet and lonely moments—perhaps for some great adventure to move implacably up the walk and engulf him; perhaps for some wild stranger to say to him: *You are to come with me; you have a special gift for me, and for the world*; perhaps for some embodiment of escape and protection to bear him away from all that gave him security. Through it all he never conceived of love. And nothing had ever come up the walk that seemed to be the shapeless goal he had tried to materialize from behind his eyes.

Inside the wide hall running through the older part of the house, he set down his suitcase. A large frosted globe, painted in red with sprays and tendrils of vines, lighted the passage dimly. The musty smell which had lingered there a decade, and the silent familiar arrangement of the scene around him, brought upon him the massed, jostling memories of his early years.

The pottery cylinder, decorated in commonplace Chinese style, that held umbrellas; the splash-shaped coatstand with a chest that smelled of cold rubber shoes; the hall runner, its pile worn thin, whose pattern he had examined for hours; the tall, carved oak chairs on which no one could sit long; the two awkward portraits of his mother's ancestors which she had brought from Natchez—they all hung before his eyes so loaded with unimportant recollections that he was momentarily paralyzed by the shock of what he had discarded from his consciousness.

While he stood there, low voices murmured in the room on his right, and then his mother raised her plaintive voice. "Donald! Donald! Aren't you out there, Donald?" The door opened then and his Aunt Marny, robust and neat, appeared, spreading her arms for an embrace. He kissed her quickly, for his mother was calling more loudly from the bed, "Come to your mother, Donald! Oh, my baby boy!" And he went quickly and reluctantly to the bed and leaned over her white puffed face.

She kissed him again and again, and hugged him to her so often that he was pulled onto the mattress beside her. "My baby, my Donny-boy . . . I've waited so long for you to come back. Oh, you look so tired. You haven't been taking care of yourself. Oh, Donald." When finally she released him from her close embrace, he sank down on the edge of the bed and held her hand. Helplessly he faced Aunt Marny, sitting in a rocker and smiling with benign approval at the reunion.

Almost nothing in this room was changed, either. The bed, the dresser, the bureau, the massive wardrobe banked the brown walls. The line of medicine bottles still stood on the bureau; the old hair container, pin trays, powder boxes and brushes still were arranged on the dresser; the framed photographs of himself and his father still on the round center table beside the catch-all bowl; the clock and the water pitcher in a thicket of more bottles filled one bedside table, and the telephone and the radio the other.

"I'm so glad Jim went down to meet you," said Mrs. Mason. "I would've gone myself if I'd had the strength. But I had to ask Jim, because I didn't want you to come back home and feel all alone when you got off the train."

"But it wasn't Jim," said Don. "It was Gus Traywick."

"Gus Traywick?" Mrs. Mason looked as if she had been insulted. "Why, I only called him to find out where Jim was. What does he mean, going to meet you? Of all people! Do you suppose he didn't tell Jim?"

"Oh, it doesn't matter, Mother. The main thing is I'm here, regardless of who met me." It was strange that Tray had told his mother Jim would meet him and had said nothing about Jim at the depot. But he could not think of that now, nor of the impending unease at seeing Jim again—not even of the aging pain that he had drowned in the anonymity of New York—because his mother kept talking and talking. She always talked on and on, telling again the incidents he already knew—recalling now his childhood and college days, the preparations for his trip, her excitement while she awaited his return; and then she would repeat her reminiscences. There was so little life in her waking world that she had to squeeze out in speech again and again the vitality of the few moments that touched her.

While her words trickled out, alternately cheerful and mournful, the clock struck eleven. She did not seem to hear. Even though she had grown noticeably older, he could not have said that her appearance or health were better or worse. Her reddish-gray hair curved from a center part over her temples and shortened her face even more than fatness did. Her skin had a doughy texture; she seldom bothered to inspect her face in a mirror. Her toilet, as long as he could remember clearly, had always been quick and careless. No doubt she had used cosmetics when she was young, and in other ways made the most of the beauty that was apparent in her early photographs. Her hands, useless except for bathing and eating, since she rarely sewed, embroidered or even read, smoothed and pulled and folded back the sheet time and again.

The mournful tone in her voice sounded more and more frequently, like a deep bell in a carillon drowning out the lighter ones, and Don sensed that the worst moment of his return was about to descend upon him. He had expected that sooner or later she would force him to live with her through the death which he had avoided witnessing. And although her repeated experience of it would never be completely done, once he had shared it this time he could more or less ignore the later recurrences.

"I knew you wouldn't leave your poor old mother lying here with no one to help her," Mrs. Mason began with mingled relief and reproach. "When your father died, I just didn't know what I would do. You were gone and no one here to do anything. None of his own blood even to follow him to his grave."

Guilty of default in family honor, Don turned his eyes away to keep from showing how glad he was that he had not been present for the funeral. If he had liked his father or his father had liked him, it might have been different. But he had been tolerated because of his sick mother. He had been allowed to go to college instead of made to go to work, because she wanted it so; he had been allowed to buy books and read during the summer, because she liked him to read; he had managed to go to New York, because she got the money for him in spite of his father. But now, because of her, he was forced to come back and take his father's place in the house.

"Why didn't you come home when he died?" asked his mother. "Donald, why didn't you come to be with me?"

"I couldn't, Mother. I didn't have any money," he explained wearily. "I told you all that in my letters."

"You could have borrowed. You know your employers would have helped you get to your own father's funeral. You should have come weeks before he passed on, when I wrote you how sick he was. You knew I needed you." Her voice became more plaintive. Tears might roll from her eyes any minute. There was nothing he could say. "He wanted so badly to talk to you, Donald," she went on. From references to the death, she now derived the satisfaction she would have had if Don had been with her. "He kept talking about you before he died. There were things he wanted to tell you . . . our only child. But you didn't come back."

"It just wasn't possible, Mother," he managed to say. With a pat on her arm, which he hoped would indicate his affection and understanding, he rose hastily and walked to the dresser. "I better go to bed, Mother. It's late and I'm worn out from the train. Almost two nights and a day."

"Oh, Donald! I wanted to talk to you. It's been so long since we talked."

On the dresser scarf lay her heavy, encrusted silver comb and brushes and hand mirror. He opened the hand-painted, whorled powder box that had sat unused on the oblong painted tray for so many years. It still had a small quantity of pinkish powder on the bottom.

"I think it's time we all went to sleep," said Aunt Marny. Don was grateful to her, although he knew she had not meant her suggestion to be more in his favor than in her own. "You mustn't upset yourself too much, Mathilda. It's been bad enough today, already."

After some whimpering objections, Mrs. Mason agreed and called Don to kiss her good night. Aunt Marny offered to go up to his room and see if there was anything he wanted. "I'll be back in a minute," she said to his mother.

"Good night, Donald," said Mrs. Mason in a thin trailing voice as the door closed on them.

They went up the stairs to Don's old room, where Aunt Marny switched on the light. He immediately dropped his glance toward the floor. Everything was too redolent of the tenderness of his past; every familiar object fairly dripped memories, smirking, grinning, gloating over his acquiescent return.

"I opened the window late this afternoon so it would cool off," said Aunt Marny.

Following the rug so as not to see anything in the room, he crossed to the four-poster bed and opened out his suitcase on it.

"Your mother is right, Donald," she said. "I was here, too, when your father died."

In annoyance he shifted piles of clothing from the suitcase to the bed and back again, trying to seem busy, but he kept stooping over and did not move toward the bureau to put away his clothes. Obviously Aunt Marny's main idea in coming up was to get in her own words on his father's death.

"He did talk about you all the time," she went on officiously, as if he would not believe it; "never about Mathilda. That struck me as odd, but then you can't expect much consideration for a wife from a man— Well, he *was* your father, but I must say none of us Wyndhams ever thought he was her *equal*."

With some innate quirk of loyalty, Don suddenly wanted to curse her. He wished he had not hated his father, so he could shout angrily at Aunt Marny that she couldn't say such things, that he loved his father, that he was as good a man as any of her family ever saw. But the feeling was not in him; he said nothing and continued to sort handkerchiefs and socks on the bedspread and put shirts in one pile after another. He didn't want to see anything or hear anything; he wanted silence and darkness.

"But he did love you, Donald. I know that now, though I never thought so before his last week. He talked about how he had never been kind to you, and had tried to make you just like he was. Of course, he was delirious; but all the same, that's when the truth comes out. You never know what a person thinks until he doesn't know what he's saying."

She paused, but Don neither looked around, stopped fumbling with the clothes nor responded. He couldn't imagine why these two women, in the guise of love and family, should want to bruise him with their accusations, and lock him in the handcuffs of penitence simply because he had been free when his father died. Aunt Marny started again:

"He worried all the time about how you'd get along—never about how your mother would. And I must say he left precious little insurance or anything else. You can always tell good family by something like that; and your father . . . Well, I *must* say we Wyndham girls didn't make as good choices as we deserved."

Once more she paused, possibly for breath or for an answer. But he was prepared this time and said, "Well, good night, Aunt Marny. I'll see you in the morning." With a sharp look which conveyed all her scorn for the ungallant, unsympathetic blood of the Masons that flowed in him, she said good night. Her heavy footsteps thumped laboriously down the stairs.

Then he stood upright and went swiftly to shut the door and put out the lights. He waited until his sight was adjusted to the reflection of the moonless sky through the dormer windows. From the door he couldn't see the window frames, but gradually his eyes distinguished furniture. He moved slowly toward the nearest dormer and, rounding the corner it cut into the room, faced the pale windows. The sill was about two feet from the floor, and he sat down with the deliberation of a man drinking poison, and leaned his arms on it and looked out into the night.

The treetops at each side of the roof furled up around his view like dark, restless lace framing the perspective of dim, unpeopled shapes opposite. The lawn stretched flat and unbroken to the black street where two round, clipped lygustrum bushes guarded the walk. On the pavement, at the left, a wriggling mottle of shadows fell through the branches of a tree crowding around a street-light. Nothing had life but these shadows and the reminiscent wind that gave them life. The houses across the way were vacant shells, solidly impenetrable in their heavy obscurity, an occasional column, banister rail, iron fence or cornice touched pallidly by the distant light. This was the development of the childhood dream-vision he had stared into, waiting and wondering; and it had all darkened and deadened, and in its barrenness and hunger had dragged him back to stare in its scornful face the rest of his days.

His father had loved him. How was he to know, thinking of things he could not objectify, that a father's love could take such a strange and unmanifest form? It had had the brooding and unyielding quality of this scene out his window; but it had died without fulfilling itself to the one object, probably, of its aim. With this new conviction, suddenly he could no longer imagine that his father had loved his mother during his later years. Of course, his father would not worry about her on his deathbed; Aunt Marny had her own Wyndham standards of the proper concern toward a woman.

When, years ago, his father through rash speculation in cotton lost finally the last thread of the credit which supported them, they had to forfeit his mother's inheritance—the Natchez mansion, the plantation and most of the furnishings. She was able to carry away only the few personal articles in her room and the old portraits of two ancestors which a traveling artist had painted in the days of their unrestricted wealth.

Of those early days, Don could recall only indistinct, meaningless scenes with no relation to each other. And what his parents might have said to each other about their misfortune, what his proud Wyndham mother might have thought, he never knew. Neither talked about it in his presence, and the only references to such a period in their lives were to the beautiful days before they went bankrupt. These references emerged as decorative vignettes in sad monologues from his mother, when they seemed mainly examples directed at his father of a girl's folly in marrying beneath her station. Obviously, it wrecked her life.

For the first few years in Ashton, she struggled to keep house and manage on the income of a public servant; but then she broke down. She complained of dizziness, called a doctor, crept into bed, and never again did she have to bother with the house or their lives. Everything must be done for her. She never left the bed except to totter to the bathroom, and Don knew now, just as the doctors had always known, that she was not and had not been ill. She had her memories of the big house in Natchez in which she grew up in wealthy comfort and spent her early married life. Lying constantly in her bed, she could rediscover the servants who had vanished with that house.

Now it was too plain. It was as if his father's death, removing the active pole of his dislike from his world, allowed him to see through what he had known for years but had been content to distort. His mother had retreated from responsibility, womanhood and motherhood. Out of her traditions, she had made herself a cancer on his father and on himself.

And he, sucked back into the smothering void of his town, was now to suffer under this burden, abandon his will and go on and on tending his mother, for it was expected of a son, as of a husband or any man, that he should be kind to unfortunate women. And she would not die and release him. She will not die, he said to himself again; my mother will not die, she will live and live and live, and I, like my father, will be the one to die. I will die as others in this town have died, but still go to their work and their meals and their homes. Somewhere they have died so that some woman may live in the way she prefers.

In how many houses were these dead men rolling on their sultry mattresses, puzzled at what had happened to the dreams of their youth, the vigor that had surged in their minds? Maturity, they said; it's getting old that does it.

He couldn't visualize many of the families around him now; the few years he had been away pushed many things into the back of his mind. His mother, having slight contact with the town, seldom wrote him any news of the people. But he thought at once of Tray and his wife, lying in their bed, enjoying with animal-like nonchalance each other's bodies. No ideas in their heads, no background to hinder them, only a material future ahead; Tray, a big good-natured handsome boy with so little sense he would have to be successful; and Bea, a stupid girl who chased him down and married him.

And Jim—Jim Furlow—with his wife, in their little house, in their bedroom, happily married, settled down into family life. . . . When he thought of their companionship now, it was lighted with frank sentimentality; it seemed only natural that it should be so. Perhaps far under Jim's love for Doris, the same sentimental light flooded over his recollections of days spent with him. Jim's presence had been an ordering principle of each day, a focus in which the jumble and drabness of small-town life acquired a purpose and a symmetry, a magic instrument by which the commonplace changed to beauty. He was never ashamed of his willful transformation of Jim's qualities into powers of a higher degree; that too was as natural as the sentimentality with which he looked back on it. For in his jokes, his laughter, implications and horseplay, Jim betrayed a restrained affection; but before Don could ever dare to speak the words, not with his eyes, but with his mouth, Jim had turned away from him. And in marrying Jim, Doris preserved for them both the finer part of their relationship and saved Jim from experiences born of desperation. Don no longer trusted himself to feel the sting of seeing Jim's happiness, to face the jealousy he had run away from or to tempt the resurgence of emotions he had sealed away.

He would have no friends in Ashton; they were all married, all gone away from him in one way or another. He would be alone, wandering about the streets, looking out his window into the sky, reading, reading, reading, in the shadow of his mother. And waiting and waiting until she would die.

All around his horizon, the houses he no longer felt close to, the houses that must already have shut him away, lifted their roofs above the trees along the two ridges of Ashton. They secretly guarded their inhabitants and held them silent in their walls and made those mysterious in the night who in the day were trivial. The warm breeze brushed over the town, like an ineffectual blessing; in the east the deep yellow arc of the moon had thrust above the hills. But only he saw it tonight. And only he saw the houses imprisoning the people, the people imprisoning each other and each person imprisoning his own heart in the dark silent fear of community.

Footsteps clacked regularly along the sidewalk near his house. A thin shadow stretched and moved from below the streetlamp swallowed in the tree. A man walked before the gate.

He might have been coming from some shabby adventure, from the door of a Negro's house, from the back door of a white man's house, from a poker game in a store loft. . . . Or, he might be me, any night, wondering how not to have to go home.

PART TWO

1

ulcy was calling again. The flat but resonant sound, like some sort of vocal guitar, approached closer to the door. "Miss Isabel! Ain't you ever goin' to get out of that bathroom? You'll wash all your skin away."

"I'm coming, Dulcy," she said. "With all my skin, too." She smiled into the mirror at her face, shining with highlights on the cheeks, scrubbed like a school girl's, and then went into her bedroom.

The yellow glow of the late summer afternoon filtered through the organdy curtains looped across the windows. It shone warmly in the dark stain of the floor and stretched in diffused streaks across the gray rug to the bed. Against its brightness, the rest of the big pleasant room was obscured. The staggered clumps of green foliage rising diagonally on the wallpaper looked black; the prints of Marie Laurencin showed no design or color; the huge wardrobe lifted like an ominous shadow. The only light came from outside; it was fading rapidly—she could almost see the shades dissolve on the white bedspread—but lingering like a shy, unsatisfied child.

"I'm so tickled you're going to a party," said Dulcy. "Been a long time since you been to one with men there."

"Oh, Dulcy!" scolded Isabel. "I go to as many as anyone else."

Dulcy sniffed. "Hen parties! ... Here's your slip, Miss Isabel. I just pressed it."

"But it was already pressed!" She stared uncomprehendingly at Dulcy. "It was in the drawer with all the others."

"I just wanted to press out the creases where it's been lying so long." She held up the slip for approval. "See? Now you'll look fit to kill."

Isabel chuckled and took it from her. "Thank you, Dulcy. But do you think anyone is going to see it?"

"It ain't what people sees that counts, it's what's underneath." Dulcy turned slowly toward the door. "I'll go get your dress now."

Isabel untied her robe, drew it from her shoulders and tossed it on the bed. Loosely gathering the slip endwise into a circle over her wrists, she raised her arms and let the silk fall about her hips and legs. The windows had now lost their color, the thin curtains glowed with a neutral light and the room was darkening. She switched on the lamp on her dressing table and sat down before it to rouge her cheeks.

"It ain't what you see that counts . . ." But most of the time that actually was what counted. People were like a theater in reverse. They raised the curtain only on a pastoral scene and lovely costumes—calm, customary, harmless—but it was behind the scene that the real drama went on. The actors never appeared to their audience; they would be hissed off the stage if they dared remove the painted drops and flats that protected them.

And so it was with her, if she ventured a step out on the stage. Hardly any of her friends were likely to think of her as unfortunate or unhappy. Most of them were married, but she, though single, at least had an income of her own. They might think her lonely, perhaps, but they surely envied the money which her father had left and which, in their minds, kept piling up mountains of cash in the bank. Occasionally she had been told this, almost scornfully, because she suggested that she was not the wildly happy creature they liked to imagine her and liked her to pretend to be. How else could one account for unhappiness except through lack of money?

According to them, she ought to be traveling around all the resorts of the world, just as she had run around over the state when she was a giddy young girl trying to be popular with the boys. The people she had grown up with, had entertained in her home, had gone to college with, now considered her odd and unconventional because she no longer sought popularity, had intimate friends or definite purpose. They could not know the loneliness that reeled slowly through her heart, nor could they understand its nature. No more could they understand that those things to which she had turned for solace in her first loneliness, as she grew older, with her mother and father both dead, gave her now more pleasure than she got from her increasingly rare dates; until, with the gap between herself and the friends of her youth spread wide, she realized that she could not have been happy married to any of the men.

Except possibly Jim Furlow; she always felt drawn toward him—drawn by a challenge, a dangerous, impossible conquest. Why she failed she did not know. She wanted to be in love with him, and for a short time imagined she was. But when their affair dwindled to an obvious stalemate she didn't fret about it, but went on in her usual gaiety, saying that after all Jim was a bore with his intellectual talk to Don Mason, and it was more fun to go around with someone else.

How stupid of her not to have been able to interest Jim then, to have moved him enough, so that they could have shared a deepening life that would have led to marriage. But they found their common interests at different times; and now she wondered how genuine his seriousness had been. It might have been merely a reflection of Don; for Jim had forsaken all intellectual curiosity and, since his marriage, become bored, silent and complacent.

Dulcy returned, as Isabel finished her make-up, and crossed the room with the pale ultramarine dress floating behind her from a hanger held at arm's length. "Here it is, all fresh-pressed," she said, flourishing the dress in a cautious whirl before she laid it across the four-poster bed.

"It looks wonderful, Dulcy, but you shouldn't have gone to the trouble. You should rest when you can." Isabel considered whether she could do something interesting to her hair. She spread her fingers around her forehead, pushing the strands back tightly until she held it all in her hands at the back of her head, and examined the effect.

Dulcy hovered over her shoulders, inspecting her face in the mirror. "You don't look good that way, honey."

In the mirror, she glanced at Dulcy's head shaking back and forth in disapproval. She released the coil of hair and let it fall about her neck. There really wasn't much to be done once it was cut. "All right," she said, taking up a comb to arrange the long bob. "You don't have to help me, Dulcy. You know I always dress myself."

"Yes, I know." Dulcy turned away and moved slowly across the room. "But this is party night. We don't have many these days, like when I used to help your mama. Such goings-on in them days! My, my, when I used to get her dressed for the big Eastern Star meetings! And for Mrs. Furlow's wedding—*big* Mrs. Furlow, not that new one—it took her all the morning." Dulcy put a hand on her knee when she bent down toward the rack on the closet door. "You dress so quick I don't hardly get to feel like I'm in on the party myself. Which shoes does you want? These here red ones is mighty cute."

As Dulcy twisted to look back, her thin face, ashy with age in the dim light, was reflected in the mirror. "The red ones are for picnics," explained Isabel. "Bring the silver ones." While she rouged her lips, she watched Dulcy trudging back toward the bed with one fragile shoe in each hand. "When I get married, Dulcy, you're going to be at the party."

"You don't mean *at* the party. You mean in the kitchen."

"No, I mean *at* it. You're going to be a guest." She spoke light-heartedly, watching with pleasure the way a freshness and calmness—she hoped it was to others some degree of beauty—began to show in her features.

"Now, Miss Isabel," chided Dulcy. "There you go again with your harebrained ideas. No wonder you're the talk of Ashton. But you ain't going to make a monkey out of me, and get me kicked out of town, to boot."

"Oh, don't be silly, Dulcy. You've lived with me nearly all my life. If I say you're to be there, you will be." She rose from the dressing table and went to put on her shoes. "It'll be a long time, though, I'm afraid."

"Ain't you interested in marrying, Miss Isabel?" Dulcy removed the wire hanger from the dress and with her arms run through its neck, raised and shook them so that the bodice and skirt shrank in folds against her shoulders and bosom.

"Of course I'm interested. But I'm getting a bit old to have too many hopes."

"You ain't old, Miss Isabel," said Dulcy, holding the dress ready. "You just scare all the young men with your deep thoughts and the crazy things you do. No wonder you don't have no—uh—"

"No what, Dulcy?"

The woman wiggled her fingers at the hem of the dress and lowered her eyes to the waves of cool cloth that spread below her chin. "Well . . . it wouldn't surprise me at all if *some* of the ladies in town aren't just plain scared for their boys to go out with you."

"Oh, Dulcy, you've been listening to gossip again. I'm too old for most of the single men around this town, anyway." She held out her arms and bent forward while Dulcy slipped the dress over her head. Then she stood up and worked her shoulders to make the sleeves set easily.

"Maybe you'll meet some nice widower tonight," said Dulcy hopefully. She brushed down the folds of the dress and began to fasten it at the side.

"Who, for instance? Judge Dorn?" Isabel burst into a laugh.

"No, for pity's sake! That man from Chicago, now . . ."

"He's married—his wife is with him. They'll all be married. I don't even know why I'm invited."

"Anyhow, it's nice you're going—like back in the old days, when the young people were always at married folks' houses. Then they could see all the married folks being sweet to each other and saying pretty speeches. And if any man or lady showed the least sign of interest in each other, the mothers was on the lookout to make a love match."

"That hasn't gone out of fashion, Dulcy." She walked away from Dulcy's final fluffing of the skirts and put on a touch of light perfume at the dressing table. "The women around town still work at making matches as hard as they can. But nobody made one for me." After a final survey of her appearance, she hung around her neck a heavily engraved locket that had belonged to her mother.

"Oh, but you're different, Miss Isabel," said Dulcy with mixed admiration and disapproval. "You ought to been the first in your crowd to marry. Some man ought to 'ave snatched you right up. When I think about all them nice gentlemen that used to come here. . . . And now you got all the ladies talking about you 'cause you wear them men's pants downtown and smoke cigarettes on the street, and—" She put her hands on her hips. "Why do you *do* them things?" she demanded in exasperation.

"I guess I'm a little bored. But it's not really shocking, Dulcy. If we only knew, they probably do much worse things."

"Whyn't you *tell* Miz Dalton you wanted a man to call for you tonight? That's the way you are—you don't act like you need a man."

"I just try to act natural, Dulcy. I'd rather go to the party alone and have a little fun than spoil the whole evening for some young man."

"You ain't got the sense your mama had, even if you do read more. You're just a scandal, Miss Isabel." Dulcy gazed reprovingly at her. "I wish I hadn't inherited you."

Isabel shoved aside the clothes in the closet and drew out a white piqué jacket. Dulcy hastened to hold it for her, tottering behind her and pulling the shoulders straight while she took an evening bag from the top bureau drawer.

"You don't wish any such thing, Dulcy. What would we do without each other?"

"Ah, Miss Isabel—"

"How do I look?" She stood poised at the door, with a hand on her hip, imitating a fashion model.

"Mighty pretty, mighty pretty," murmured Dulcy. "Men are such fools. Now you be careful," she went on, as she followed her through the house. "You know what can happen to young ladies at night."

"All right, I will." It was always like this when she went out—cautions, worries, commands—just as if Dulcy were her own mother. "Why don't you go to the movies, Dulcy? It'll be my treat."

"Sit in that colored folks' gallery on a night like this? Not me!"

"Well, go get yourself some ice cream, and relax." She stepped off the back porch and crossed the yard.

"I'll just sit here and fan myself, Miss Isabel." From the screen door, Dulcy called, "I'll put out some lemonade and cookies for you and your young man."

"You always say that, Dulcy," answered Isabel, looking back through the dusk. "Don't you ever give up?"

"Plenty of time to give up when you're dead."

"Good night, Dulcy," Isabel called softly as she turned about the clump of shrubbery and into the driveway. She backed the car into the street and drove down the hill.

2

Madge Dalton's living room differed little now from Don's childhood recollection of it. Here and there small modern tables and chairs, no less ugly than the original furnishings Mr. Dalton bought with the house, had been added. Along the high walls the dismal engravings of Roman ruins still hung, foxed and brown in carved gilt frames. The naked bulbs of the tarnished wall candelabra between the pictures blurred his sight. A chandelier of dark, mottled glass with bead fringe hovered low over the massive center table and was reflected oppressively in a mirror above the false marble mantelpiece. The atmosphere of dry smothering was heightened by heavy fringed curtains reaching to the floor at doors and windows. Of the whole room, Don remembered with pleasure only the two figures of female water carriers painted greenish brown with plaster draperies swirling about their limbs, which stood in corner niches on each side of the dining-room door.

With a slight nudge, Madge urged him beyond the entrance. "I think you'll know everybody," she said as she led him forward, "except the Chicago couple—the Victors."

About a dozen people, mostly women, sat about on the late Victorian sofas beneath the Roman ruins. The women wore dinner dresses, and their voices dominated the room with a high, wavering sound. He could distinguish no resonance of men's voices; from the way the men looked, they were listening, but saying nothing at all.

Although Madge hurried him on toward the guests of honor, they made a formal round of the room. Mrs. Everett, forcing vivacity above her troubled years, said, "Why, hello, Don. Now we have the Beau Brummel of New York back with us!" And Judge Dorn, a widower hovering at her side, added, "I guess you're a real Yankee now." The others continued the monotonous chorus: "How'd you like

New York?" "Glad to get back to home folks, I bet." The Chicago visitors, Mr. and Mrs. Victor, were not so impressed with his travels and merely remarked that New York, too, was a wonderful town. Standing beside them, Horace Saxon, publisher of Ashton's weekly newspaper, shook hands. "Glad to see you, Don," he grumbled. Then Madge abandoned him in front of Bea Traywick and Evalyn McGill.

"I think it's simply wonderful to have you back home," gushed Evalyn. She held on to his hand and giggled and pulled him down to sit on the sofa. Obviously marriage had not calmed her habit of automatic flirtation. "I want you to tell me all the exciting things you did up there," she said, moving as she always did with a man slightly closer than necessary.

"Nothing exciting," said Don casually. He raised his hand, from which hers reluctantly slid away, to the pocket of his linen jacket, "Would you like a cigarette?"

"I would, Don." Bea held out her hand for it. "I'm glad you came."

He held a light for her.

"Parties can be so awful with no young men around," sighed Evalyn. "Madge was simply too cute to ask you."

"Was it Madge's idea?"

"I just love to have young men around," Evalyn babbled; "especially when they aren't married, like I am. They always say such cute things—really daring, if you let them."

"Doesn't Andy get jealous?" he asked mechanically.

"Oh, Andy—" Evalyn began deprecatingly. Then she squeaked, "Tray! You've come back to us."

Tray grinned above them and, leaning over, caught him by the arm. "Yes, I came to rescue Don. He deserves a drink."

A sigh of chagrin rose behind him as, with mounting discomfort at the prospect of the supper party, he followed stiffly behind Tray. They passed through the double doors into the hall.

A young woman in a light-green dress was coming down the stairs. She hesitated a moment, standing tall and at ease with her hand on the stair rail. A smile broke on her lips and a light of gratitude flooded from her eyes. Then, when he faltered without recognition, she moved quickly, almost surging down the remaining steps.

"How nice to see you, Don," she said, intercepting them. "Hello, Tray." It was Isabel Lang.

"Why, I'd hardly have known you, Isabel," he said. "You're—well, you look so different. Like the product of a designer."

"Thank you, Don."

They faced each other, briefly silent. With the past clamoring in his mind, he could hardly reconcile this self-possessed, serene woman with the absurdly coquettish girl he used to know.

"I'm glad to find someone else here who's not married," she said.

"So am I," replied Don. Damn it, somehow she made him feel uncouth.

"Were you—going somewhere?" she asked Tray.

"To get a drink," said Tray.

"Oh, can I have one too?" she whispered eagerly, turning to Don.

"Why—" He stopped, not quite sure of current local custom.

"Madge says it's only for the men," Tray observed. "You know—lots of older people here, and all."

"Well, I'm damned if I'll drink tomato juice before supper," Isabel retorted. "Sneak me one out, will you, Don?"

"I'll try," he promised.

Then she moved gracefully from them without hesitating for company, as if she always went her way alone.

"I'd have thought she'd be married by now," Don remarked.

"Me, too." Tray proceeded toward the study. "I don't think she cares."

"She seems almost—"

But Tray was knocking on the door. "Like at lodge meetings," he explained. "You know how Josh is."

A crack of the door opened and exposed the bulging middle of Josh Dalton's spare frame pressed against the gap. "Give the password," he croaked.

Tray answered seriously. "Are you the man from Nantucket?"

Roaring with laughter, Josh flung open the door. "Am I?" he exploded. "Are you?"

As soon as they were inside the smoky room, Josh in swift succession closed the door, shook hands and began mixing drinks while he intoned, "There was once a young man from Nantucket . . ."

Stuffed fish and heads of animals decorated the walls of the study. The square Mission-oak furniture was sturdy enough for its purposes—to survive Josh's drinking bouts. Andy McGill sprawled in one of the chairs and giggled words at no one in particular.

Josh handed out their drinks. "Another snort, Andy?" he asked.

"Don't care if I do!" Andy responded with theatrical abandon, and joined Josh at the whiskey table. Shaking with laughter, one hand on Andy's shoulder and the other gesturing, Josh chanted, "Don't care if I do die, do die . . ."

Don slumped into a chair and leaned against the leather cushions. On the edge of the library table beside him, Tray perched expectantly.

"Adolescence certainly fascinates Josh, doesn't it?" Don murmured after a big drink.

Tray glanced toward Josh but said nothing. Cigarette smoke drifted in blue whorls before Don's face; then Tray blew out a puff that smeared them in the air. "Jim is coming tonight," he said quietly.

Don lifted his eyes coldly. "I imagined he would be."

"Be quite a surprise for him, I guess," Tray went on; "unless you've already seen him."

"No, I haven't," he said doggedly, and swirled the ice in his glass.

"I'd like to talk to you about Jim sometime. He doesn't—" Tray began earnestly.

"Are you the reason I was invited tonight, Tray?" he interrupted.

Tray made a disparaging movement and grinned down at him. "Sure. Why not?"

"The point is *why?*"

"Oh . . . I thought it would—sort of get you back in the swing of things."

"Like meeting me at the train when Jim refused?"

An expression of wounded innocence spread over Tray's face. "Well, Don . . ." He emptied his glass with a big swallow and drooped his head in embarrassment. "I don't know why, exactly. Your mother wanted—"

"Oh, to hell with that."

"All right, then." Glaring angrily, Tray banged his glass on the table. "*I* wanted . . . I wanted to meet you. I was glad you were coming back. I wanted you to talk to Jim, and be with him." Tray rested an arm across the back of his chair and, leaning down, spoke in a low, troubled tone. "I wanted something in Jim to—change back to what it used to be, when he was himself, when—we liked him. I thought maybe you could help, maybe understand what it is. I can't. I never can."

Don laughed with a soft, throaty sound. He drank the rest of his drink and looked dreamily across the room where Andy was going out the door. But, except for a light touch on his consciousness, he was not reacting to the sight of Andy, or of Josh in the doorway talking noisily to someone in the hall. He was thinking of the irony of Tray's notion that he could possibly help Jim, who had always had the stronger will and now had a wife to encourage and help him, understand and comfort him in whatever sufferings might come.

Then his thoughts were scattered and submerged as the tall figure moved through the door. Vaguely he was conscious of Josh chortling over the liquor, of Tray speaking and his replying, and of sitting rigid in his chair while Tray's figure crossed between him and his vision of Jim, as if at the end, near but seemingly distant, of a kaleidoscope. He had expected this meeting, but not the kind of paralysis it produced in him. He saw, but through a smoky cloud inside his eyes; and he heard, but faintly under a thin buzzing inside his ears. His hand was clenched on the empty glass; its sweat trickled between his fingers. His sight focused only on Jim, whose voice he could hardly understand; around Jim, visible objects faded off into darkness as if all other areas of sensibility had been drugged and only that one point of reality remained.

The figure turned, the profile silhouetted by the table lamp, and the dark shape of Josh moved across the background. Jim was coming toward him. The head of crisp hair, shaded between brown and red, swayed closer and closer in an exaggerated duration of time. The dark gray-green eyes blinked mischievously, the cheeks like sandstone drew up in young creases and the smile broke over the lips in a way that had always moved him with despair and delight. They were in college and Jim was bringing him a shot of whiskey before a dance. The glass in his hand suddenly glittered in the light.

"Hello, Don."

Jim's voice now sounded clearly and the buzzing died away. The dark nimbus surrounding Jim also vanished, and he could see the whole room again, and Jim taking a step in the center, holding out his hand. But Jim's smile was gone, too, with the darkness; something mechanical, which wasn't quite a smile, momentarily stretched his lips. The gaiety and youthfulness which he had just visualized were merely a picture in the camera of his brain. He stood up and went toward him.

"How are you, Jim?"

Their hands closed together, and Jim quickly withdrew his. Don raised his glass to drink, but noticing that it was empty, let his arm sink halfway down.

"Where did Josh go?"

"To get some of the other men, I think."

"Guess I'll make a drink for myself, then." He wondered if Jim could notice his nervousness. He would probably fumble the ice and bottles as badly as he was fumbling his speech.

Jim followed him to the table. Don stirred his drink and picked it up. Turning, he came again face to face with Jim, who stood before him almost in a challenge.

"How long you going to be here?" asked Jim casually, looking straight into his eyes.

"For good."

"Oh? Not going back to New York?" There was a trace of sarcastic antagonism in the tone.

He shook his head and moved toward a chair. "Mother needs me here now. Anyway, the job—" His words trailed off to a mumble and then quick silence.

"What about the job?" asked Jim, sitting near him.

In its unqualified starkness, the question irritated him. If Jim had added another question to it, probably he could believe Jim was sincerely interested. He did not have to apologize for or prove anything, least of all now to Jim. But because it was Jim who asked, he couldn't be anything but frank, and he described the miserable work he had done and the small salary he had received.

"I wouldn't have lasted much longer anyway," he concluded. "People are being laid off all the time."

"Yes, it's getting that way everywhere," agreed Jim wearily.

How pathetically like the conversation of two slight acquaintances their talk was; how obstinately they both avoided any suggestion of former friendship. Jim did not smile when he spoke and his behavior was that of a man performing a polite duty.

"I guess you're glad to be back."

Challenging again; not sympathetic. . . . Jim probably would like to hear that he was unhappy about it.

"Yes," he lied, out of annoyance. "Very glad."

Jim moodily scratched a fingernail along the crease of his tan linen trousers, and stirred restlessly in his chair.

"You never met my wife, did you?" he asked abruptly. "Let's drink up and go find her."

"Good. I'd like to meet her."

"A wife's a wonderful thing for a man to have." The sudden heartiness, after Jim's reserve, came almost with a jolt.

Before they finished the drinks, Josh barged in with the Chicago manufacturer and Judge Dorn. "Had to save them from the women," he shouted needlessly.

"Come on, let's go," said Jim quietly, and the sound of it echoed far back to the days when Jim was urging him to share some personal adventure and not, as now, to show his resentment of Don's peacefulness or his own pride in being a married man.

Without disturbing the other men, they left the study. In the living room, Jim walked directly to a sofa where a young woman sat with a glass of tomato juice in her hand.

"Doris, this is Don Mason," said Jim.

She got up hastily. "Why, James has just told me so much about you," she said. "I've been dying to meet you."

"We've been inside having a drink," Jim went on.

"Oh, that's all right," Doris sang out cheerfully. "Tray told me where you were and I wasn't bothered."

As far as physical qualities went, Jim's wife was undeniably beautiful. The corn-silk hair, the clear skin and the crystal eyes were certain to dazzle anyone's first glance. What Don missed was the intangible, deeper beauty—the beauty he had seen in a few plain women and old portraits; painted on canvas, Doris would be no different from the women on the dozens of Christmas calendars sent out by local merchants. After all, Jim never demanded anything of women—or men, for that matter—except physical attractiveness. Why he had put up with Don's speculations and reading for so long was something of a mystery. Obviously, Doris was now the ultimate fulfillment of his happiness—the beauty, reflecting beauty back on him, which Jim had always wanted.

"I'm going over to talk to Mrs. Victor," said Jim, moving around them.

Doris reached after him. "Oh, stay and talk to us," she begged.

"I think we ought to mix around a little."

"If she wants to talk to us she can come over. Don't you think so, Don?" She pouted coyly and then smiled.

"But she's a visitor. You stay and talk to Don," suggested Jim.

"No." She spoke almost angrily, and turned half away from Don. A flush of resentment rose over Jim's face. "I'll go, if you think one of us must. *You* stay with Don. You both want to talk about old times, don't you, Don?"

Jim gave him no chance to reply. "Her husband's right there. I hope you're not—jealous."

Doris laughed theatrically and clutched Don's arm. "For heaven's sake," she said. "How ridiculous!" Then, while Jim stood indecisively, she whispered to Don, "You take care of him." And she went rapidly across the room.

"Let's go talk to Isabel and Mrs. Everett," suggested Don, hoping to escape the tension of their scene.

With his expression still clouded with irritation, Jim moodily agreed and they joined the two women on a sofa near the door.

"I was just telling Isabel," said Mrs. Everett, when they sat down, "how I wished we could get her into our Seven Arts Club. She would be so stimulating. But you have to be married to belong."

"I'd shock the members, Mrs. Everett," answered Isabel, giving an appealing glance at Don. "You know how bohemian people think I am. I paint pictures of nude bodies."

"What imagination!" exclaimed Don. "People haven't seen those in centuries, have they?"

"Oh, Don, you still talk the way you used to, when we all— It's like our double dates, you and Jim, and me and—except Mrs. Everett will have to substitute for Corinne."

"I'm pretty old for dates with young men," Mrs. Everett said with aged vivacity. "And of course, Isabel, Jim isn't quite as eligible as he was."

"Now, Mrs. Everett, you know there was never anything serious between us. Was there, Jim?"

"No. Not a thing."

At the harshness of Jim's voice and his angry fixed stare, a sad emptiness spread in Don. For no meeting with Jim ever had so inexpressible and charmed an air as the final minutes of their double dates, when after hours of postponement, they gradually freed themselves for each other, seeing first one girl home and then saying good night to the other girl, until finally he and Jim were alone in the car in the night of the silent town.

"Boys and girls are so different these days," Mrs. Everett said. "I sometimes think . . ." And she was off on one of her interminable monologues.

Hardly listening, Jim leaned on the sofa arm and frowned crossly. Then he got up, mumbled that he wanted to find Josh and, excused with a nod from Mrs. Everett but no suspension of her words, he left them.

"Of course, you young people," she continued, "you get around and you're not fooled. But some people need to learn that life isn't what they read in romantic novels. It might help, when their own life—" she hesitated a little and her voice became lower and more serious "—bursts in their faces."

A silence followed, in which neither he nor Isabel seemed to find any reply to her stream of words. Isabel began to fumble for her handbag when Mrs. Everett leaned toward her.

"You can see it all around you, if you look," the old woman resumed confidentially. "I sometimes wonder . . ."

Isabel suddenly put her hand on his arm and said, "Don, we must . . . Will you excuse us, Mrs. Everett?" She rose at once, almost pulling him with her, and led him toward the hall. "What did you do that for?" he asked. In Ashton you couldn't simply walk away from people because they bored you.

"She always wants to talk about it, but she never dares to say it right out," sighed Isabel. "Anyway, I wanted that drink."

"Oh, I see." He stopped in the hall, and examined her face curiously. "You said you were sort of bohemian, didn't you? Well, just come on inside." He indicated the study door.

She laughed and turned aside to the foot of the stairs. "I'm not really bohemian; it's what others think of me. I'll just sit right here till you bring it out."

"Have it your way, then."

Inside Josh's study where the men, in the thickening fog of tobacco smoke, were talking around the table, he managed to get two glasses of straight whiskey and disappear out the door without being questioned. When he rejoined Isabel, she surveyed the living room suspiciously.

"We'd better go to the dark end of the hall," she suggested. "Just in case—"

Seated on an ancient tufted-leather sofa that was shadowed under the flight of stairs, they sipped the burning liquor.

"Now, what about Mrs. Everett?" he asked.

"Oh, it's really nothing—nothing definite. There's always gossip, you know. Even I am supposed to be terribly wild, not at all what a southern lady should be. Why, I drive to parties alone at night! But it does look bad."

"Your driving alone?"

"No. Dr. Everett and Miss Rosa."

"Do you think it's true—whatever it is?"

"It's always the same thing," said Isabel with amused disdain. "Whatever else could it be?" He merely laughed softly, and in a moment she went on. "There's a lot of pretending on all sides, except for the ones who talk."

"But isn't that rather—well, courageous—if the result is good? After all, people always pretend about something."

"For Mrs. Everett it *might* be courageous. For Miss Rosa, it is."

"What makes the difference?"

"There's always so much no one knows about other people, even close friends. A woman like Miss Rosa might be glad of a chance at . . . What I mean is, it might be the only pleasure she's ever had with a man, even if it's nothing more than riding in a car with him, and a kiss now and then. I couldn't really blame her much if she didn't bother about the moral consequences."

"Not even if it were your own husband?"

"You mean I should be jealous?"

"Partly. You wouldn't like to think your husband—"

"I think it's better to be jealous of your home rather than your husband."

"No wonder they think you're bohemian. Don't you know a home to a wife means responsibilities she must live up to? But a husband means someone who's responsible to a wife."

"Right. Don't sandbag me. But a—an old maid has personal responsibilities too, a sort of ingrown duty to her emotional nature. It's a moral issue, too, with Miss Rosa. But then she has to choose. She wants, I'd say, to be loved, at least one time, at least in make-believe, even if it's not the real thing. And when she gets a chance, she's got to decide whether to take it or not. She knows what's expected of her. But do others know what they failed to do for her?"

By the time she finished her defense of Miss Rosa, he was smiling and when she abruptly faced him as if rather astonished at herself, she was disconcerted by his amusement. But he did not try to conceal it. He wanted to ask her what she would do, but it was too delicate a question.

"I hope I didn't sound like a communist or a free-love advocate," she said, abashed. "I just feel that one point of view isn't enough for the whole story. No one knows—no one outside ever does know—the secrets until it's too late to help."

"Nobody dares trust secrets to anybody."

"I must sound pretty silly," she said, and lifted her glass to drink the last swallow.

"You sound like you didn't use to sound, I'll say that. . . . Want another?"

As he reached toward her glass, a shadow slid along the carpet at their feet, and they leaned forward to look down the hall. Horace Saxon was moving deliberately toward them. With the light behind the thin figure, a kind of aura glowed around the sparse, graying hair which stretched in three peninsulas above his forehead.

"I heard your voices," said Mr. Saxon.

Don got up. "We were just—"

"Wouldn't you rather go where it's lighter?" Isabel asked hastily.

Mr. Saxon glanced down the hall. "Back in there? No." He pressed Don back down on the sofa. "Sit down, sit down. I wanted to talk to you before I go. I'm leaving as soon as I get fed."

"Well, Mr. Saxon, I really did nothing up there that could make any kind of interesting story," stammered Don.

"I don't want a story on a little squirt like you in New York," Mr. Saxon said testily. "Plenty of other news around. Charlie Ann Davis has written you up already."

"Oh. I—just thought—"

"That's rather mean of you, Mr. Saxon," said Isabel. "Saying sarcastic things like that about Don. After all, he's not just a grocery boy, without any sense."

"What makes you think grocery boys don't have sense?"

"I don't mean that. I mean Don has got some and has read and traveled and knows something. I think Ashton needs to be made to respect people like that instead of people who simply count money out and watch it pile up."

"Of course I agree, Isabel." Mr. Saxon took the glass from Don's limp fingers and smelled it. Then he tossed off the remaining swallow. "It wasn't meant as sarcasm, exactly. I ought to have the privilege of abusing him as much as anyone in town. I was the one who lent him books when he was in high school—books he'd never heard of, or wasn't supposed to read."

"That's true, Isabel," said Don. "I was—too concentrated on myself, I guess. Mr. Saxon was always telling me things to read, ever since I tried to get him to buy a poem I had written."

"Did he print it?" she asked.

"Of course not," snapped Mr. Saxon.

"I'm glad to say," Don finished. "It was pretty bad, but I was too young to know. I made it up out of my own head, and I thought it must be good, simply because of that. I even tried to make him print it free."

"I thought you ought to be protected," said Mr. Saxon. "A man's best protection is from himself. I saved your ego and your reputation, Don. Think what might have happened if I'd printed that poem."

"What?" asked Isabel.

"I would've written more and brought them in," he said.

"Exactly." Mr. Saxon handed the glass back as if he were bored with it. "That was one of my more noble deeds. I gave him good books to read instead of encouraging him to write bad ones."

"I can't imagine why," said Isabel. "He might have become one of our best poets."

"Who can tell? I might have destroyed a poet." Mr. Saxon's eyes, as always, were devoid of sympathy. "We have lots of poets. But I kept Don from putting silly thoughts on paper and disgusting other people with them. I think he has gained in other ways."

"Well, I hope so," said Isabel.

"But maybe he hasn't," Mr. Saxon continued. "Maybe he has come back to Ashton to be a poet again—but a better one, I'm sure."

Don grinned self-consciously. "No, I haven't written a poem in a long time. I don't think there'll be any more."

"Good. We all stop sooner or later. Maybe that's too bad. But why did you come back?" Mr. Saxon folded his arms and rocked on his feet like a genial family inquisitor.

"I couldn't buck New York."

"I don't believe it," Mr. Saxon said. "Any man can buck New York if he wants to, and doesn't care how he does it."

"I don't believe it either," said Isabel.

"Mother needed me here," said Don. "That's the truth. I felt obligated to take care of her."

"Ah, rats!" snorted Mr. Saxon. "You wanted to be with her, I'll bet, so you wouldn't have to take care of yourself. Where's your independence?"

"It was in the poems I stopped writing," said Don lightly.

Mr. Saxon grunted and unfolded his arms. Then with a change of tone he said, "That liquor was pretty good. Think I'll get myself one." And he walked away with his hands clasped behind his back.

3

The party was beginning to break up. Madge hovered near the front door to tell them good night and Josh kept inviting the men to have another drink. Jim stood uncertainly with Doris by the center table while the guests drifted past. As the room was gradually emptied, it assumed the musty, stolid air of a relic, not old enough for charm nor fine enough for care. Only Mr. and Mrs. Victor, edging Judge Dorn toward the hall, and Don and Isabel, engrossed in talk in a window seat, remained.

"Hurry up, you two," said Tray, as he passed Jim.

"We'll drive ahead and put on the lights," said Bea.

Doris plucked at Jim's sleeve. "I don't want to go to the Traywicks," she said. "I don't feel well."

"But we promised. We can't get out of it now." He waited stubbornly, without knowing why he did not go into the hall.

"You never consider me when you make plans," Doris sighed. Then, after a moment's hesitation, she started out. "I'll get my wrap and meet you on the porch." She wound between the huddled guests.

All during the evening, Jim had been disturbed by Don's silent appeal, the look that seemed to accuse, yet ask for pity and renewal of friendship. Balancing his supper plate on his knees, he was morosely, acutely conscious of Don and Isabel in lively conversation, joking, laughing in the window seat. They hadn't left that withdrawn spot since the buffet was served. He repressed several impulses to join them out of spite, because Don would obviously like him to do just that. Don's eyes constantly wandered toward him, and meeting his, seemed devoid of interest—though that very emptiness professed a deeper concern, just as his gaiety spoke out the lonely plea it concealed from others. Don was pretending to be a brave martyr to his mother because he couldn't bear to be separated from him, because he wanted things to revert to the way they used to be.

But of course, Don couldn't revive in him what was now dead. There was Doris, a barrier beyond which Don could never reach, no matter how intense his appeal, even if Jim, unable to bear it any longer, out of pity . . .

In the hall, Doris was gesticulating to catch his attention, and pressing between the lingering guests toward the door. As he went to overtake her, his eyes were drawn aside and his muscles felt a drag. Without consciously wanting to, he moved in an arc and slowed before the seat where Don and Isabel were talking. Don did not notice him immediately; and when he did, his face colored with surprise and his words trailed away. Isabel too looked up inquisitively.

"We're leaving." It sounded blunt and unimportant. Jim halted in front of Don. "Good night," he said gloomily and impersonally, with a glance that included Isabel. As if against his will, his hand moved out to Don, and with the same unwillingness the name "Don" came from his mouth.

For a second he met the entreating stare, those brown eyes that meant to bore with their supplication, their anguish, through to his very last defense. . . . Surely, Don couldn't think that Doris was nothing to him. . . . He left them hurriedly, said good night to Madge and joined Doris on the porch.

With cautious sliding steps they descended the long dark flight of stairs to the street. Doris slid into the seat of the car.

There was a long silence while he twisted the wheels from the curb and rolled down the steep hill from the Dalton house. Doris sat motionless, her pretty face drawn with chagrin, her hands gripping an evening bag, her eyes fixed beyond the windshield. When she finally spoke, her voice trembled. It was low and halting, as if she were talking only to herself.

"You certainly don't have much consideration for me, James. Planning a party at the Traywicks'—common people like the Daltons. You know I wanted to go home, but you never think of me. . . . You don't care how I look. Whether I have old ragged clothes or not, or a decent car to drive in. . . . If I didn't try to save on housekeeping, I'd never even have money to get a permanent. Have to charge everything at the beauty parlor till I can get the money out of you. You sure fooled me and my family, letting us think what we did about you. . . . Letting me throw my love away on you when you don't appreciate it."

While the sentences fell muttering from her lips, Jim clasped the steering wheel tightly. He sighed in resignation, for he seemed to have heard these words before, although it was actually the first time. As she went on with her complaint, he drew in deep breaths in frustrated anger. His defense clamored to be spoken; but he tried to hold back. Finally, thinking there would be no end to her charges, he answered her last words.

"You've never showed much appreciation for being loved. You always refused to give me any real, honest-to-goodness love. What do you think love is? You don't want to sleep with me. You won't have a baby. What do you expect me to do?"

"I don't expect you to go around flirting with all the other women in town."

"For heaven's sake, Doris—just because I put my arm around Madge? I've already explained that we were simply excited over Mr. Victor's offer."

"It wasn't an offer."

"Well, you heard the way he talked. It was encouraging. And Madge was just telling me she hoped it would work out."

"Mr. Victor wasn't serious," Doris replied. "You know perfectly well a huge firm like Premium Products wouldn't take you into their legal offices."

"They're taking Josh in—absorbing him and his plant here. And they're absorbing lots of other southern plants too. They need southern lawyers. And I'd jump at the chance."

"Personally, I think it's Madge needs a lawyer and she's jumped at you."

"Oh, hell, why hash it over? I've known her longer than I've known you. She may be common to you, but by God, she's got feeling."

"Of course," said Doris primly. "Feeling for other women's husbands. One isn't good enough for a woman like her. With so much trash like her in this town, it's no wonder all the men act like you. If it weren't for decent women . . ."

"Too bad you didn't marry some aristocratic pansy," said Jim. "That might have kept your family blood untainted."

"I don't know what you mean by that," she said after a moment's consideration. "James, I don't want to go to the Traywicks'. Take me home."

"We're here now, and we've got to go in." He slowed the car and veered toward the curb.

"You and Bea shouldn't have planned this. You did it just to spite me, because you knew I wanted to go home."

"Bea and I didn't plan it. Tray did, and I thought he had already talked to you, Doris."

He switched off the motor and got out. Doris sat firmly in her seat until he opened the door at her side.

"Come on, and try to be pleasant," he said.

As she reluctantly got out, her bag fell to the ground and she spoke harshly again. "Why don't you hold my arm, James? I nearly turned my ankle."

Without answering, he picked up her bag and led her to the open front door, through which a broad streak of light fell onto the lawn.

4

"Heard you coming," Tray rumbled exuberantly, unlatching the screen door to let them in. "Gosh, it'll be nice to have some private fun." He rustled Jim and Doris like two sheep into the living room.

Bea had furnished it, not altogether successfully, according to a picture of a New England farmhouse in a decorator's magazine; but the result was a pleasant enough imitation, with chintz and colored lithographs and brass lamps. A wide arch opened into the dining room where Bea was setting out glasses and a bowl of ice on the table.

"It's all ready," she called. "You can dive in, if Tray'll produce the whiskey."

"No trouble about that," he said. What the hell was wrong with Doris? She looked like a thundercloud. So did Jim, for that matter, but then he always looked glum.

"Want to powder your nose, Doris?" asked Bea. "Come on, I'll go too."

When they had vanished down the hall, Tray led Jim into the dining room where he squatted on his haunches before the sideboard. "Parties with no drinks are awful," he grunted as he rummaged in the cabinet. "Bea nearly went crazy with thirst—and envy." He handed a bottle up to Jim, and then a second one.

"That's cruel," Jim responded, cradling a bottle in each arm. A smile crept over his lips. "Madge should have given the girls a shot in the kitchen, or where they powder their noses."

Tray began to tear at the seal on the neck of a bottle. "Line up the glasses," he ordered. "Thank God for Josh's little room," he said while he poured the whiskey. And thank God too that Jim could squeeze out a stubborn smile! "Some of those people are too much to take sober. Old Judge Dorn puttering around like an aged tomcat."

"And old Gus Traywick sneaking a pinch from all the young ladies," added Jim in a suddenly light tone.

"Oh, Tray's a horny old bastard," broke in Bea's casual voice. She was puffing up the cushions of the living-room chairs. "Where's my drink?"

"Where's Doris?" asked Tray. He lifted his glass toward Jim in a silent toast.

"Oh, she drowned." Bea picked up a drink from the table. "I knew I'd have to come for it."

"Can't you wait?" he circled her with his arm.

"For you, any time. For Doris—no. Anyway, she says she's not well and won't have a drink."

Then from the hall, Doris called in a soaring voice, "Where is everybody?" She sounded lively enough for someone who was sick.

"Let's go inside," said Doris, leading Jim away.

Tray followed, and offered Doris a drink just to see if she'd take it. She accepted the glass, thanked him and sipped from it.

"Shall we tear the party to pieces?" suggested Bea.

"Yes, let's do," Doris agreed brightly. "I've got loads to tell."

"No, let's don't," said Jim.

"Why not?" Doris turned defiantly toward him.

"We've torn enough to pieces already. Something very good might happen because of this party."

"Oh, you mean Mr. Victor's talk about giving you a job," she said scornfully.

"With Premium Products Mills?" Tray exploded.

Before he could get any more out, Bea had joined him in an excited confusion of questions. When they finally subsided, they got the whole story from Jim, bit by bit, along with Doris's dubious opinion of the proposition.

"And that's all I know," Jim said at last. "It probably means moving away from Ashton."

"We'd sure hate to see you leave," said Tray; "but it's a chance you can't afford to miss."

"Sure, you might get to be a big, big man and have a picture in *Time*," agreed Bea. "Our Man of the Year!" With a flourish she raised her glass to Jim.

"Now don't be sarcastic, Bea," warned Tray.

"I wasn't being sarcastic—just silly. I was only dreaming, and all dreams are silly, but sometimes they come true."

"Well, it's silly to dream of leaving here," Doris broke in. "We've got everything here, and in another town we'd have nothing."

"I can't see that, Doris." Tray spread his arms wide in one of his pointless gestures. "You're at the end of the road here. There's nowhere to start unless you do leave."

"It's perfectly stupid to think of going to some strange city, swarming with all kinds of—dirty people, foreigners and so on, when we've got our place and our own kind of friends right here."

"But Doris, it's a chance to expand—to grow," Bea argued. "You'd be able to give more to your children and to yourselves."

"Well, I don't feel socially cramped here," she said loftily. "Not if we had a little more money to keep up our standing. But I can't think of giving this up to be a little fish in a big pond."

"If the water was better, I wouldn't mind," said Tray. He noticed the bite in Doris's voice and the determined fire springing up in her eyes. Jim's stubborn, downcast expression brightened hopefully every time Bea rose to his defense.

"Of course," Doris retorted, "if you don't have any real social standing, I guess it wouldn't matter about moving away."

What a little fool Doris was to think that either of them cared about social position. The remarks she meant to wound merely betrayed her fear of competition and her insecurity. She had to depend always on her family and now, even in a neighboring town, on her husband's to guarantee the acceptance which her life demanded.

"Well, I guess Jim will decide what's best to do," murmured Bea.

"Umm," said Doris, but made no other comment.

You are a wicked girl, thought Tray; Bea, you are sweetly wicked the way women are when they unintentionally hurt a man, meaning to hurt his woman. But you're wickedly sweet, too, and Doris isn't that. She doesn't have any sweetness, mixed with anything, inside; it's all on the surface.

With a long, grating sigh, he twisted on the sofa and stretched out with his head in her lap. She reached up toward his glass, hoisted askew, and cried, "Don't spill that, Tray! Damn it, if you'd watch what you're doing." She pried the glass away and set it on the floor. With his face against her stomach, he mumbled "Thanks" and began to bite her gently. While she wriggled and squealed lightly for him to stop, his arms fumbled around her waist and held her tighter.

"Bea!" gasped Doris. "You both look—revolting. Like those pictures in James's filthy books."

Bea stopped struggling and began to push herself out of his sprawling grasp. As she did so, she kicked over the glass, cried "Oh!" and left him laughing, spread-eagled on his back, his shoulders and head hanging over the edge of the sofa cushions.

"My!" said Jim, with warm envy tingeing his voice. "Does this go on all the time?"

"Every night," said Tray.

"It does not," said Bea, pulling her dress straight and going out.

"Only some nights it's worse," gurgled Tray. "How about another drink, Jim?"

"Think I will." Jim got up and started toward the dining table.

"Mix one for me, too," said Tray, "as long as you're at it."

"James, we have to go home," Doris called insistently. "I'm feeling sick again."

"Mix one for Doris, too," chanted Tray mischievously. "What's the matter, Doris? Why don't you relax a little. Like me."

"Well, I'm sick and James won't take me home. He never thinks of anyone but himself, you know."

Bea returned with a soiled towel and knelt beside the broken glass and spilt liquor. "Why don't you sit up, you fool?" she whispered into his face.

"Too comfortable."

While she picked up the slivers and put them into a wastebasket, she gazed into his dark eyes, upside down, blinking just below her chin. "Crazy," she said.

"I'm sorry, Bea," he said with no suggestion of regret.

"James has a selfish streak, I think," Doris began in a loud voice. "I don't know what he does with his money, but I do think he could give me a little to buy a few fall clothes."

She's making sure Jim can hear, he thought; making sure we don't forget she's here and really start screwing. Let her rattle—I don't care. Bea was paying no attention to her, either. She gave a final swipe to the rug and leaned over to kiss him.

"Your nose tickles my chin," he said dreamily.

"Now sit up," she commanded, as she flopped on the sofa by his head. "You nearly knocked over the lamp with your big feet."

Jim brought three drinks clutched in both hands, and gave one to Bea.

"We've been talking about getting a new car, Tray," Doris was saying. "I thought maybe we could get one like Madge Dalton's or maybe even better-looking."

He struggled upright and took the drink which Jim was vaguely shoving toward him while frowning in astonishment at Doris. After the first gulp, Tray sighed with noisy satisfaction.

"What do you think, Tray?" persisted Doris. "Would that cost too much? We wouldn't have to pay it all at once, would we?"

"What's that, Doris?" he asked.

"A car like Madge's," she said. "James could pay for it by installments, couldn't he?"

"Oh, sure. Anything for Jim." He waved his glass extravagantly. "Take two years if he wants to."

"Do you have any cars now, or how long would it take?"

"Well, Madge's got a Buick," he said. "But I could get a Lincoln in no time."

"Oh, that would be wonderful. A Lincoln!"

"We can't afford another car," Jim said sternly.

Well, it's about time, old boy. Get in there and speak up. He grinned dourly at Jim's sullen defense. The spark of fun that had flickered when they were alone was now gone.

"We've got to have one, James," retorted Doris. "Don't be a stupid fool. You can pay on as easy terms as you want."

"That's not business."

"It *is* business; it's good business," snapped Doris. "And I intend to have one. I won't have people saying my husband isn't even able to keep up with his—his inferiors. Even if I have to ask my father for the money."

No one said anything. Tray drank uneasily. What a filthy thing to do—actually blackmailing Jim into buying a car. Absent-mindedly he pressed Bea's hand.

"What about something to eat?" Bea asked, smothering a quiet laugh. "Plenty in the kitchen."

"No, thanks," said Doris. "I'm sick, you know. Really, we'd better go home."

"Ah, don't go now," Tray urged. "Let's have a good time. Come on, get drunk. Come on, Doris, have another drink." Impetuously, he rose and approached her, with his hands stretched out before him. He caught her wrists to pull her up. "Come on, now. Let's have some fun."

She cringed against the back of the chair and her mouth fell open in a faint snarl. "Take your hands—" she began fiercely, but abruptly halted, as she leaped up. Backing away, she spoke in a calmer, forcibly controlled voice. "No, Tray. Not tonight. I'm not well. We've got to go."

For a few seconds he clung to her wrists, startled, never thinking to release them. Now they twisted in his grasp, and when he let go, his fingers spread wide as if they had touched something repulsive. With hurt and apology in his eyes, he turned to Jim, and then suddenly retreated to Bea.

"Yes, it's time we left, I guess," Jim mumbled, abashed. "Getting late."

"Well, if you have to go . . ." said Bea. "I'm sorry you aren't feeling well, Doris."

Then they were saying good night and Bea was chattering to cover Tray's confused silence. Doris's outburst was now becoming funny and revealing to him, and he smiled without effort. When the door had closed on the Furlows, he looked at Bea for a moment before they both started to laugh softly.

"Calls for another, doesn't it?" he said, and they had a fresh drink.

On the sofa, they murmured to each other much as if each were rehearsing his own private thoughts.

"She was upset over something all night," said Bea.

"You'd'ave thought I was a nigger trying to rape her," he said.

"Or a white man."

"What's the difference? To her, anyway?"

"Just being touched set her off."

"Do you suppose she's like that with Jim? How could she be?"

"Just like I told you—a real bitch."

Bea wandered about the room, pulling chairs into position and dumping ashes into the wastebasket. She switched off two of the brass lamps.

"Ah, leave that piddling alone," he exclaimed. "We can do it tomorrow instead of trying to go to church."

"Which we never do." With a decisive shrug, she returned to his side. Tucking her knees up on the cushions, she began to brush her fingers through the hair at the back of his neck.

"You know," she said, "you probably shocked her when you started nuzzling my belly. After all, she used to be shocked when we kissed before we were married."

He snickered gleefully. "Well, I just couldn't help it. I saw her acting so stinking, and thought about Jim being tied to her, and I had to show how glad I was. I had to prove to myself, too, how lucky I am. Tonight, they both sort of—oh, drained the life away from everybody, killed everything like a plague of locusts. I'm glad they're gone, damn 'em."

For the first time, he realized the prisoned hunger in Jim's marriage. Jim could do nothing about it. Neither he nor Don would ever be able to help except with friendship, for Jim was determined, apparently, to fight it out in silence and solitude.

"Poor old Jim," he murmured.

Bea drew his head down and reaching up, kissed him. "Stop thinking about Jim," she said. "You worry about him all the time."

"I guess I've got a mother instinct," he said in light despair. "Comes from being big enough to protect other people." But he couldn't remember ever protecting Jim from anything; only once, protecting Don from a couple of toughs after a football game in New Orleans. He stretched out his long legs and slid further down on the sofa. Bea took his glass and put it with hers on the end table.

"Let's go crawl in," he said with a yawn.

"All right, let's go."

She tugged at his arms to lift him—a thing she obviously could never do; and he, of course, pretended that she must do it. In the end, he pulled her flat on top of him, enclosed her in his arms with her body lying between his legs, and his lips and beard brushing the edge of her mouth.

When they got up from the sofa and went into the bedroom, they leisurely took off their clothes. He dropped his coat on a chair, his shirt on the floor beside it and his trousers on the bedpost for Bea to pick up. And, mumbling her exasperated and kindly disapproval, she always did, between hanging her dress in the closet and turning down the bedclothes. From a hook in the closet, she took his blue pajamas and tossed them to him as he stood in his drawers.

"Pajamas tonight?" he asked incredulously.

"Sure. Don't be silly." She stepped out of her pale, tea-colored slip.

"But it's too hot, Bea. Even—"

"Well, you've got to wear the bottoms anyway." Having turned off the ceiling light and left only the tiny lamp beside the bed, she slipped off her brassiere and panties and reached for her nightgown.

He wouldn't let her wear the pajamas that were becoming popular with young women; the delay and difficulty of rolling up a nightgown was too much pleasure to sacrifice. He sat on the edge of the bed in the pajama trousers. In the dim light her arms raised the white silk above her head, lifting her small breasts a trifle as if they vibrated in response to his glance. The lace-edged hem descended over the rounding pale stomach with its reddish line from elastic pressure around the waist, and over the dark groin and small white heavy thighs and tapering legs, until it was a rippling curtain, above which had emerged her round plain sweet face and her arms fluffing up her hair.

"Well, go on and get in bed," she said, peremptorily.

He rolled back and stretched out on top of the sheets. She got in on the other side of him and switched out the bed lamp. When she turned toward him, his right arm skillfully slipped under her head and around her shoulders; and with her left arm crushed between their bodies, her cheek against his shoulder, she spread her hand on his breast. Both breathed heavily and contentedly. Her leg lay across his, and his left arm drew her closer.

Tilting her face, she kissed him under the jaw. "I'm glad we're like this," she said. She rubbed her nose gently against the bristles of his beard.

Then he kissed her on the mouth, and they both lay for a long time in silence. At length, his arm relaxed and his hand drooped from her side; he was almost snoring. Bea quietly rolled away from him and lay prone on the other side of the bed.

5

Isabel drove the car up the long hill to her house. "You didn't really have to see me home," she said. "I go to parties alone and come back alone whenever I want to. That shocks the town, like lots of other things I do, but I can't see why. Dulcy always waits up for me."

"I wanted to come," Don replied. "After all, I could have got out when you passed my house. But it's early, and—and I wanted to come."

She guided the car skillfully up the cindered drive and stopped on the level plot halfway from the street. "I'll leave it outside. I do most of the time." She switched off the motor and the lights and got out. "Can you see?" she asked.

When she rounded the car and came next to him, he took her arm, more for his own guidance than hers. "It's supposed not to be good for the paint," he cautioned. "The dew, and then the sun . . ."

Wavering in the darkness alongside the tumbling shrubbery about the porch, they crossed the lawn toward the front steps.

"Oh, I know. But down here we're all careless. You must have forgotten, Don." In the faint light that spilled through two glass panels in the door, she mounted the steps. "We're so careless we trust everybody because we think they're all nice. We don't lock our houses or our cars." She pushed open the door and preceded him into the hall. "There might be a murderer here right now. We leave our purses in stores, our bills unpaid—nobody bothers anybody."

Tossing her piqué jacket on a chair, Isabel led the way into the living room. She circled about it and turned on the table lamps. "You'd think nobody ever felt anything, or anything ever happened inside them. The surface is too cozy, too unemotional. It's deceptive."

The room was brightening with areas of light. It was quite different from the way Mrs. Lang used to keep it. Isabel had thrown out all the ugly bric-a-brac and souvenirs of travels her mother would never surrender. Only the best pieces of the old furniture had been retained and now there was an air of inviting simplicity in the house. The thin curtains, now bright as they billowed in the glow of the lamps, now dark against the screens at the open windows, the huge cases of old books and new ones with gaudy covers, the big bowls of flowers and the water colors on the walls, created a cheerful atmosphere in which he felt entirely relaxed.

"What we need in Ashton is a villainous stranger," he said. He strolled around the room, smoking a cigarette and examining the pictures. "The tent-show kind that used to seduce the women and fleece the men."

"But we don't have any villains that obvious. We've got only ourselves—our gossip, and malice and isolation. We know each other too well."

"Is that dangerous?" he asked.

"No, but it makes us complacent. And it's deceptive, too, because we don't know each other at all and we don't really try."

"Who did the water colors? These are local scenes, aren't they?"

"Yes; I did them around town."

"Mississippi looks much more charming in a picture than in reality. They're very good, though."

"They're romanticized. Like all of us. We think of ourselves in healthy, glowing colors, but we're really sick and won't admit it. We have the sickness of—fear, of littleness."

"But that's not confined to small towns, Isabel. People in New York suffer from it too, trying to compensate for the huge buildings and crowds, trying to equal the lavishness and wealth they see around them."

"Maybe so—but they can get release from it by revolt, all the way from public arguments and insults up to depravity, petty crimes, rackets and murder. Here in Ashton, we can't do that. We can't cure ourselves. We depend on the violence in the papers, the radio programs, the movies, like a bunch of dogs munching that medicinal grass they eat. If we were all more strangers to each other, instead of pals infested with the idea that we know everybody's heart, nature, social place and so on, we'd feel more of a challenge to be ourselves—to compete with life, instead of with shadows. Just look at us now. I can't talk this way to anyone in town, you know. They would call it wicked—in fact, they have. But I can say what I think to you, because now you're almost like a stranger after all these years."

"So are you. Or rather, like an acquaintance I never got to know very well."

She smiled with apparent pleasure at the notion. "And now," she said whimsically, "we have met again on the Panama Limited. You recall that we were introduced long ago on the Gulf Coast, and I say 'Let's have a drink in the club car and talk over old—' Why not have a drink? Just for realism, of course." She rose and moved toward the door without waiting for a reply. "You wait here. Find some music over there, if you like." With a wave toward the phonograph, she went out and he heard her footsteps die away in the long hall.

He scanned the titles in the record cabinet. Basically, Isabel's little pretense of having met him only briefly was true. Their old selves, once friendly, now after a long separation seemed mere acquaintances. This was the time they would get to know each other with more understanding. A strange, rather pleasant excitement, almost the thrill of exploration, hung over the prospect of the next few minutes. When Isabel returned, he was sitting cross-legged on the floor with an album opened on his knees. She left the glasses on the low table before the sofa and opened the phonograph.

"What do you want to hear?" she asked. "It's a little wacky, so I'll have to operate it."

"Do this Haydn symphony." He handed the black discs to her in order, one by one, and she arranged them on the machine.

For a while they sat together, drinking and listening and smoking. In the quiet after each side was finished, the records clicked as they slid onto the turntable and the needle whirred briefly before the music leaped out again. When all the first sides were played, she reversed the records without a word and came back to the sofa. From time to time he glanced at her, apparently absorbed in something in a far corner of the room, and he wondered if she too stole glances at him, curious to know what the new basis of their relationship would be. Toward the end of the symphony, he spoke softly.

"Do you find it lonely living by yourself—I mean, sickeningly lonely?"

She looked cautiously at him, much as if she expected him to injure her suddenly. "Sometimes it's tedious and trying. But it can be that with someone around. Dulcy is here all the time, and she's company."

Don made no further comment. After a pause in which she seemed to reassure herself, Isabel continued. "My sister comes down from Missouri sometimes. She's worse than Dulcy. I can't enjoy talking to her at all."

The swirling music of the orchestra filled the air around them. Though she seemed to be listening to it, he suspected that she was not. "It isn't just having no people around," she resumed shortly, and her eyes drifted slowly toward him. "You know that, I imagine . . . from New York. It's an—aloneness, inside. Yes, a sickness."

The symphony ended. She removed the records and without asking his choice, put on another set.

"I would have thought you'd be married, Isabel," he said reflectively.

"You're the only man I know brave enough to say that," she answered with a short laugh.

"Maybe that's because I don't know why you're not."

"I don't know either, Don. Unless the old romance about 'the girl next door' is a fraud. That girl's a little too familiar to be enticing to the boy."

"Most of them tonight were 'girls next door,'" said Don. "Everybody used to say you were going to marry Andy McGill."

"At least I escaped that," she sighed. "Whatever made me think of such a thing I don't know. Desperation, I suppose; or boredom. All my friends were marrying. . . . I did all the proper things. You know that. I was popular, I made the most of my looks, I was never serious with a man. . . ." She laughed self-consciously. "I've never talked about this with a man before. I suppose I shouldn't be so confidential. What about you? Why didn't you bring a wife back from the East?"

"Do you think I could make a woman happy?" he asked with a smile.

"That's an unselfish way to put it. I didn't think men ever considered it from that angle. A man can go on looking for years, one place or another. A woman simply has to wait."

"Why don't you take a job here?" he asked. "You would get about more."

"Work in Ashton? I don't need to work, even to occupy my time. I don't get restless as I did when I expected a date every night. I read a lot and listen to music. I paint sometimes—travel sometimes. It's pleasant, now that I don't expect any more."

"But there can be more, even without marriage," Don said with sudden earnestness. "There can be the argument and agreement of friends—exchanging ideas—a sort of freedom and a bond at the same time, when you—like someone."

"You're thinking of your own good luck; but there's no one I can have that with," she said with a grateful smile. "My—friends—think I'm a little eccentric because I haven't conformed to their standards. But you—you've always had Jim."

A chill of sadness breathed through him. Though the memory of Jim had beat strongly beneath his words, he wasn't aware of it until Isabel spoke his name. Feeling that there was no need for constraint with her, he could almost hope she would understand. But he could not be as candid as he wished to be.

"There was that much," he murmured. "I miss it."

"When I think about it now, I envy you and Jim those days. You were always so completely in agreement, it seemed; always had such a good time together." She seemed to search in his mind, perhaps in her own, for some lost dream—the dream that for him almost came true and then became a dream again. "When both of you used to leave me here after those double dates, I was always furiously jealous. I rather hated you, Don. I seemed to be the one who was put aside, while you two were the ones who really—said good night to each other. . . . I've always been very fond of Jim."

"Yes," he said, uncomfortably. "I suppose he's happy now?"

"I don't know; but maybe I'm prejudiced. I don't see how he could be. Doris is pretty but she just—well, she emanates. I get a feeling that she thinks I'm still trying to catch Jim."

"Why should she worry? She's got him. You might say she owns him, by marriage."

"That's a legal way of looking at it. But I'd say she felt insecure about holding him. She doesn't show any of the stimulation, the common interests, that you and Jim had. She's a pretty fixture for the house, and that's all."

"Well, isn't that what most men want when they marry?"

"You're a man. Is it?"

"But I'm not married. How would I know? What men want and what they get don't always coincide." He stood up and walked aimlessly toward the center of the room.

Long ago they had finished their drinks. The melting ice in the glasses clicked as it settled toward the bottom. The phonograph had automatically shut off.

"Let me fix another drink." Isabel reached out to the glasses.

"If I can help," he said.

"Come along. I want to hear about the new plays."

While they refilled their glasses in the kitchen and returned to the living room, he recounted his impressions of the shows he could afford to see in New York. She inquired about the settings, the acting, the directors, with such familiarity that he finally asked, "How do you know about all those people?"

She pointed to a stack of periodicals on a table. "I get lots of magazines and papers," she said. "Ones that most people here have never seen. Did you see the ballet? I've never seen one. What was it like?"

He went on talking, more expansively than he could recall having done in years, about the music he had heard, the gallery seats at the opera, the paintings at the new Frick museum, and she urged him on with a question now and then. No one else in Ashton had been interested in hearing these things; all were satisfied with a general comment which tended to condemn the city by contrast with their home town. His story wandered from art to anecdotes of the human spectacle in New York streets and parks, the knots of argumentative men in the drab squares, the subway crushes; and then to his personal life in the shabby roominghouse with its curious inhabitants, the Italian restaurants with wine-stained cloths where he ate, the tawdry artistic life of Greenwich Village, until he realized that he must be delivering a tedious monologue.

"I think I'd better start home," he said abashedly. "I'll talk your ears off at this rate."

"But I'm not bored at all, if that's what you're thinking."

But he insisted and she walked to the door with him and offered to drive him home.

"Oh no, Isabel. Thanks," he said, both amused and flattered. "It's not a long walk."

"Well, don't refuse just because it's not usually done," she said.

"It'll do me good to walk." He hesitated, silhouetted against the screen door, and held out his hand. "Some other time."

"Will you come to supper some night?" she asked. "I don't like eating alone, with no one but Dulcy to talk to. I have women over sometimes, but very few."

"I'd like to," he said. "Just us two?"

"Yes, unless you want some others. . . . Jim and Doris?"

"No. I couldn't talk to them, I'm afraid." A delicate irritation crinkled the corners of his eyes. "Just us. I'll call you during the week."

They said good night, and while Isabel held the door open to light his way, he walked down the steps to the sidewalk. He turned to wave to her, partly as a final good night and partly as a signal that she might close the door, and strode down the dark hill from her house. In the valley, he followed the lifeless and silent main street for a few blocks and turned up a street on the western slope of town.

He never imagined that he would meet anyone at Madge's whom he'd truly want to know; least of all would he have supposed it could be Isabel. It was odd that she had admitted her attraction to Jim. How much better it would have been if Jim had married her; but how many of her present qualities might never have developed if they had married? Disturbing and wild as the notion seemed, he couldn't help believing that today marriage sapped the life from both man and woman, much as if the institution were a parasite on the hearts and minds of those who kept it alive. In spite of its compensations, it had lost some very definite quality, probably the decisive factor, that used to make it durable and valuable. What was it—where had it gone?

In the shadows of the neighboring trees, he saw the squat yellow-brick house where Jim and Doris lived. A light seemed to shine from one of the back windows. He pictured Jim lying in bed with Doris, gently touching her body with the tips of his fingers; and for no apparent reason he suddenly, in his mind, married Jim to Isabel instead of Doris, and saw them lying together for a moment. At least, Jim and Doris were not lonely like him; at least they had, in spite of Isabel's suspicions, the compensations of marriage—warm companionship, comforting understanding and the drug of passion, desperately fleeting, to shield them from the tottering world. Now, in the loneliness that had fallen over him since he left Isabel, he didn't want to think about them any longer. He couldn't understand Jim; he hoped he was happy.

6

From Doris's room, through the narrow connecting passage and Jim's open door, the sounds filtered teasingly. The clatter of her shoes dropping to the floor, the click of the closet latch, the jangle of wire clothes hangers, twinged in his ears. She would be changing from her dress into a negligee. He could visualize her smooth, pale, almost-naked body, distantly remembered, crossing the room and pulling the lacy silk folds about her and then lying indolently on the bed. And distantly remembered, too, was his awareness that this body was the supreme gift of a woman he wanted to love—a delicate gift that he must touch most tenderly and not bruise, least of all in its sensitive reaction to him; for that reaction must be molded slowly, with care and gentleness, into an offering of love, a union of love, a salvation by love for him, which would bring order to his life and hers, and create the meaning they both sought. But so distant now was that conception that the guidance was merely a gesture of his mind and the goal dreamlike; the order and the creation had never been achieved. The chance slipped through his too-gentle fingers, and the love he failed to mold had hardened like clay. Doris was equally conscious of his failure, and had closed herself tightly behind defenses which mocked his ineffectual approach. He stood alone, unprotected, outside the barrier.

Uncertain of each movement, feeling his muscles catch and quiver, he undressed and pulled on his pajamas. The cold, sterile emptiness of his room oppressed him. Details of its furnishings which he had hardly noticed before eddied up through his consciousness and crystalized into the sharp impersonality of a middle-class hotel room. There was no life or meaning in the polished bureau, the dark carpet, the neutral pictures, lamps and curtains. What were they there for—a solace for his loneliness, a reflection of his barren masculine existence?

Into this complacent exile, the scrape of the bench in front of Doris's vanity table intruded tauntingly. A bottle clanked against the glass top, where rows of lotions and perfumes were lined before the mirrors. In the center mirror and its two side panels, her face was reflected, soft and warm in the tinted light of the small, pink-shaded lamps. She would be brushing her hair. It was falling sleek and yellow, whispering the most minute crackles under her strokes, and dropping from the bristles, when she raised the brush, like long shreds of down.

Abruptly he strode to his door and pushed it shut. Then he pressed the light switch to blot out the room. He walked a few steps hesitantly and wavered, angry with confusion, in the darkness of his miserable dilemma.

As he stood there, his closing of the door, assuming an importance it didn't really have, became the permanent closing of the door between his love and Doris. And now that he seemed to have shut it finally before him, just as he shut one before Don, an itching anxiety spread through him. All doors couldn't always be closed. He waited, facing his last barrier, as Don waited now once more outside a door, and knew he must fully cross over the threshold of Doris's life. For Don had to know that their life could not include him, certainly not as Don had formerly belonged to him. Doris belonged to him now; she was his other self, making him whole, reflecting back into his emptiness the fullness of his body, the answer to his hidden needs, the answer to Don's tacit invitation.

Desperately he walked to the door, swung it open and went into her room. Doris's back was turned, and she was stepping out of her slip, with one hand holding for balance to a chair. He spoke her name softly.

She whirled around, snatched up the chiffon gown that lay on the chair and clutched it against her body. "James!" she cried. "What do you mean coming into my room? With me undressed!" Impulsively she jumped into the bed and pulled up the sheet, tucking it snugly across her breast and under her arms.

How pathetic it was; and yet how comic it would appear to anyone else. He went cautiously toward the bed.

"Doris," he said, "I just wanted to talk to you a while. I didn't mean to frighten you." His quiet hesitancy betrayed his turmoil.

"You know you should knock before coming in," she said angrily. "It's the decent thing to do."

"I know. I forget those things. I get to thinking about—other things."

"Yes, you're always thinking of something besides me."

"I think of you every time I think of myself. I think of both of us at the same time. But tonight I couldn't understand you. You were in a nasty mood. You've never been like that before." Edging closer to the bed, he studied her face, fresh and milky and natural now, lying in a nest of yellow hair on the pillow, and the blue eyes coldly following each move he made. "I thought—maybe we could smooth things over—for each other."

"Oh, is that why you came in?" she asked in a bored voice. "Well, I wouldn't worry about it."

"No, that's not really why I came. It's something more important," he said, sinking onto the mattress.

"Now don't sit on my bed, James," she interrupted irritably. "You make it hot and wrinkle the sheets."

He rose, but with the slowness of resistance. "I'm talking about us, Doris. The things we should give each other—the love and—closeness—that would help us know each other, and belong."

A wave of aversion flashed over her eyes. "I'm not a common woman, James. I won't be pawed over, like Gus Traywick was trying to do tonight."

"I'm not talking about Tray," he said. "I'm talking about us—you and me."

"You were talking about giving to each other. I try to give you a home and the respect of the town. But I can't do it unless you give me something to do it with. We live like—like shopworkers. Cheap house, cheap furniture, no servants, no cars, nothing equal to our position in town. And people like Madge on top where we deserve to be."

"No one can have everything he wants, Doris. You can't have anything in this world unless you give something for it. I give you everything I have."

"The little you give me isn't enough to make the impression we need," she said sarcastically.

"We're young, Doris. Money isn't the main thing. That will come and you'll have what you want with it. But there are other things too that count while we're young." Again he sat on the bed; she seemed to cringe from the nearness of his hands.

"James—"

"I've offered you my love," he went on plaintively. Extending a hand along the sheet, he leaned on his arm and looked into her taut and apprehensive face. "Can't you offer me yours? When we married, I thought we had a chance for happiness. But now I'm afraid it's slipping away from us. Unless we do something—to save each other—we'll never have it."

"Why, that's not true, James." The tension of anger in her voice was suddenly replaced by the quiet, sing-song inflections of a southern coquette. Her eyes softened with a warm gleam. "What on earth could we save each other from? We're safe and happy right now, just like we've always been."

Filled with an intense fear, he twisted shamefully from her. "I've never told you this plain out," he said slowly. "I couldn't ever say it, but I've got to now. I haven't been happy. I kept saying it was ahead—in time I'd have it. Instead,

I've been miserable and ashamed." He turned back to her, entreating with the pinch of anguish in his expression. "I'm full of shame for the life I lead, Doris; my life in our house, alone in that room every night. I'm ashamed to be with other men and talk with them. I'm afraid of women's eyes, afraid they're whispering about me."

"You're just worrying about your work," she said sympathetically. "Everybody knows you're working hard. They won't criticize you for not making more money at a time like this."

The convulsion of a laugh or a sob gushed up in his throat. He pitched forward on the bed, face down. Conscious that she shrank away in astonishment, he pressed the pillow to both sides of his head. He must shut out the sound of defeat, the monotonous defeat of words that were powerless against action.

"Get up, James, and go to bed. It's late," she said with suppressed fright.

After a moment, Jim turned his head and looked abjectly above the white mound of the pillow. Doris's profile was silhouetted against the gauzy silk and lace of the bed lamp.

"Can't I make you understand?" he whispered indistinctly. "I keep telling you over and over. . . . It's not money; it's us. It's not being really married. Not having anything to give each other—that no one else could give."

"I don't know what you mean, James."

"I mean, just loving each other. Being able to touch each other and enjoy it—feel that loving belongs to us, is right, is our own joy and no one else's. Something no one else could give us. We never sleep together. We never have—never really. Only those few times when we first were married."

For a while she was silent. Then she said, "But we're above things like that. We're not common trash."

Threads of ideas darted through his mind, each seeming to bind up the core of his dread or unravel its problem, but they all finally left him helpless and bewildered. One idea, desperately recurrent, hung in his thoughts until he mumbled it aloud. "Men can divorce—a woman—for not—" He couldn't bear to finish it; the solution must be somewhere else. In his own ineffectual urging, perhaps; in his failure to arouse her love . . .

Doris drew in a short horrified breath. "James," she gasped, "you wouldn't . . . you wouldn't make me a divorced woman!"

"No, no," he answered sadly.

"I'd kill myself first. I couldn't bear the shame. I couldn't ever hold my head up again. The scandal, the loneliness, disgrace . . ."

"I wouldn't do it, Doris. But I can't go on this way. I can't stand this either—this loneliness around us."

"But, James, we have a home. We don't want to wreck it."

The shock of his drastic suggestion seemed to have released them momentarily from their conflict. Jim felt a surge of rational calmness and spoke more soberly. "We don't have much of a home this way. We don't have any children."

She stirred under the sheet, settling herself more comfortably. "Now, James . . . We want to enjoy life while we're young, don't we? We don't want children to spoil our marriage."

"I do want children, Doris. I've told you so lots of times. I want a child."

"Well, James, there are lots of things we can't have. You've been telling me that, too. I want a new auto, but you say I can't have it."

"An auto costs money; it's something you buy—anybody can buy. A child is our own. It's us, something we make and shape and feel is a sign of our love."

"A child costs money, too," she said caustically. "And women get fat afterward. They look awful while they're pregnant. I couldn't stand it. I know I couldn't."

All his cool reasoning vanished before the returning desolation and despair. He pounded his fists into the pillow and raised his body. "Damn it," he said hoarsely, "if you loved me, you'd want one. At least, you'd want me to sleep with you. You'd like it."

"If you loved me you'd do things for me, too," she retorted. "You never bother about my comfort or my feelings. You simply want to paw over me, and lie on top of me and hurt me. All those nasty things you men think of—filthy, horrible things."

"Oh, Doris—Doris," he moaned, drooping his head. He wanted to close his eyes, to cry, to hide somewhere. "Can't you be kind to me. Won't you help me? Can't you understand?" He lay close, breathing against her, and stretched his arm across her breasts and trembled as he held her body.

She squirmed to free herself, partly sitting up in bed and then falling back against the headboard in a higher position so that the pressure of his arm now circled her waist. "Stop, James," she cried. "Stop being foolish."

He did not answer. Almost embracing her, almost in an act of love, he lay and shook with fear that even this pleasure would end immediately.

"You ought to go to bed, James. You're drunk, I know, or you wouldn't be acting this way. . . . James, get up and go to your room."

"Please, Doris," he whispered. "Please help me. Please love me. Be my wife, my real wife."

Gripping his arm, she tried to push it away. But he clung to her and, with his head just below her breast, murmured his pleas over and over. Through the sheet the warmth of her flesh rose against his mouth.

"You don't even consider me," she said tearfully. "You make me feel like—a prostitute."

"No, Doris, don't say that. I want you to be someone I love more—more than anyone I can think of. I want you to help me forget everyone else in the world. I want you to be everything in the world I love. I need you, Doris, I need to have you love me." With a quick movement, he rose and drew her body completely down onto the bed, clasped his arms around her and kissed her twisting face.

"Stop this, James. Stop it," she cried. Her hands pushed with all her strength against him, but he did not release his hold. "Why do you treat me this way? Oh, James, why don't you be good to me? Why don't you make me happy?"

"I'll do anything I can, just tell me, Doris," he whispered. "If you'll be good to me. Love me, Doris. What will make you happy?"

Her struggles gradually subsided, but she did not reply. She gazed thoughtfully around the room and then down her cheek at him. "You never let me have any nice clothes, or a nice house. You won't buy a car for me. You won't do anything for me. You just want to use me—this way."

Something cold passed over him, something ghastly swirled inside him and drew all his body into a tortured knot. His mind insistently keened, as if unwilling to hear itself, *there will be no more; this is all; no more, no more.* He had to force the words from his lips, but when they came they were suffused with resignation. "Do you want that Lincoln?"

"Oh, James," she sighed.

"I don't know how, but I'll get it for you."

She stroked his hair and smiled. "People will think you're rich and that'll be good for you, James." She spoke dreamily, holding his head between her fingers as if it were a genie's lamp.

He closed his eyes. A shudder wrenched his limbs. "Doris," he said, "I want a child."

There was a long silence. If only she would wind herself closer to him and say she wanted a child too. If only she would say she didn't need a new car, or clothes, or anything but him lying beside her at night and working with her in the day. If only he hadn't blindly, foolishly maneuvered both of them into this situation, this cavern of degradation. . . . He could have gone on, unprotesting, suffering, through the rest of their married life. But to turn away now was cowardice. He despised himself and her; he almost hated her for always being stronger than he was. If only she would refuse to answer.

"You're crazy, James," she said. "It would kill me to have a baby."

"That's not so. You're lying and you know it."

"It's true," she replied heatedly. My father's a doctor and he should know. He told me I couldn't ever have a baby."

"He'd have told me before we married if that were true." He waited for her to answer, but she said nothing. "Wouldn't he?"

For several minutes she lay silent in his unresponsive arms. He didn't urge her any further. Perhaps the whole conflict could rest unresolved with this trivial impasse, and no change would come into their lives.

"Will you promise to give me the car," she asked hesitantly, "if I . . . if . . ."

Now it was all gone, the last trace of hope he might have kept was dissipated. She was no longer a wife; she was no longer even a woman. She was a thing for which he knew no name, and to which he had dedicated his life.

"You want that car," he said with difficulty. "I'll give it to you." He closed his eyes. How could he look at her now? "I want a child."

She began to whimper.

He got up, filled with loathing for her and himself, and without ever opening his eyes, moved slowly along the foot of the bed. Doris spoke then, through her tears, as if she thought he might be leaving her.

"All right, James." The words were gasped out in a whisper.

Still blinding himself, he reached the door and found the light switch. He clicked it off and waited. The chain on the frilled bed lamp tinkled delicately.

Though the room must now be dark, he dared not look. He could no longer think clearly. He drove himself on toward the destruction he had so stupidly invited; it would be a penance for his weakness. He fumbled toward the bed.

So many nights in their three years of marriage he had yearned to hold her body to him, soft and yielding. Those few times when he was granted his desire seemed unbelievably beautiful, in spite of her detachment from any pleasure in them. For in her reticence he found pleasure, as if such beauty should not, by its very nature, participate in his actions, but remain the distant ideal which he struggled toward and tried to encompass. In the darkness, in his despair, he revived the delight of those explorations of her body; and the memory of that bright, selfish happiness, flowing up through him again to make him tremble in anticipation, clashed now with the thought of the wreck of his pride and the woman who inhabited this beautiful body. The body which he would never again possess; for now it was as if there were no body before him. What he touched sickened him. He fixed his mind stubbornly on the picture of loveliness he had longed for, the excitement he had known with her, the memory—always the memory, for the actuality had dissolved—of his first touch of her breasts, her thighs, her whole dizzying flesh against him.

There were no words. No sounds except Doris's weeping. Her limbs were lax and heavy. This was the cold, empty church which Don pointed out to him years ago; the house of worship with no place for the worshipers. He was a fool to try to prove to Don something that Don would never have been able to know.

For now Jim was alone, in the most distressing aloneness the world can provide.

PART THREE

1

On Sunday morning Jim opened his eyes to the brilliant sunny windows and the dusty, rough, white-plaster walls of his room. The nightmare was over, yet was just beginning.

The door, a tall brown rectangle against the neutral wall, was closed. No sounds outside the room, no noises from the kitchen, no voices near or far. The hands of his watch showed ten-twenty.

Why did he have to wake up at all? Why couldn't he have slept all day, rather than open his eyes to the emotional shambles about him? Last night, while he rolled desperately about his bed, trying to sink into the oblivion of sleep, a bottomless world yawned under him. He was the prisoner of the chasm of his bewildered and shameful life, falling and falling through it, grasping frantically for support, hiding his eyes from the wreckage, unwilling to explain or repair or know it more clearly than he did now. If he could only have continued to sleep and never know that life, which forced alternatives on him, can be worse than any involuntary dream.

He got out of bed and moved awkwardly to the door. After pausing to listen, he opened it quietly. The door to her room was shut. Barefoot on the cool floors, thinking what a tiny unimportant pleasure this was to seem so gratifying now, he walked through the hall and into the kitchen. He had opened a cabinet and taken out the percolator before he realized that if he made breakfast, or even coffee, she would hear him. She would come out of her room; she would want a tray brought to her bed. Leaving the percolator on the table, he turned back to his room, padding along in a daze, and once inside, carefully closed the door again.

What he wanted most was to hide, to disappear from everybody, but he did not know how to do it. He could go out of town, he reasoned, pacing slowly and unsteadily around the room; he could get into the car and drive and drive and then stop somewhere for the night and go on again. But then he would have to make explanations, not only to her but to his family. Listlessly he put on the clothes he had worn the night before, searching in his mind one distant point of refuge after another, and disconsolately returning to the fact that he must go on living in that same house with that same woman because society expected them to stay together. When he finished dressing, he went as silently as possible out of the house to the garage.

The noise of the car's motor grated on his nerves. He hoped it wouldn't wake her. The trees and houses gliding past the windows as he drove to town seemed artificial in the glaring sunlight. They hurt his eyes with their brightness and new unfamiliarity. He was glad to reach the main street and park at Callahan's Café.

Seated at a table in the dingy dimness, he ordered breakfast. Beyond the covered sidewalk outside, cars passed with children returning from Sunday school and grown-ups going to church. In their best clothes, people strolled idly before the café. The waitress set his food on the table. Automatically he took up a fork and broke the yolk of an egg, and then put the fork down on the plate. The yellow ran slowly out and over the edges of the eggs. He drank the coffee.

Walking swiftly toward the door, he slapped the correct change on the counter before Callahan and rushed out the screen door. He would go see his mother.

On the hillside before the rambling frame house, he parked. Its clapboard walls and gingerbread cornices were now weatherbeaten and flaking their paint. Like so many homes of its period, it thrust a useless tower with a bell-shaped top above the main part of the roof. Several rooms flaunted windows of colored panes. The building might have been mistaken for a boardinghouse, except that the porch, with its thin, fancy pillars and banisters, was buried, unlike public lodgings, under a thick growth of moonvines. There, in the cool shade, he found his parents rocking in hickory chairs.

"Why, Jim!" his mother exclaimed. "Come in."

She hadn't cut her hair short according to the fashion. It was brushed back loosely from her forehead and wound in a large knot at the base of her skull. Her skin was fair, though with a few small blemishes, and she used only powder on it and a tinge of color on her thin lips.

His father, gray too, in the ring of hair around his bald crown, closed a newspaper across his knees and took off his reading glasses. From him, Jim inherited the long nose, the dark gray-green eyes, the sandstone complexion. Even the expression in the eyes, the look of patient sadness, had been passed on to him.

"Where's Doris?" they both asked.

"I—uh—dropped her off at church."

"You ought to go with her," said Mrs. Furlow. "People will think it funny if you don't."

"That's right, Jim," said his father. "You make fine business connections in church. Besides the spiritual benefits."

"Doris is such a sweet, fine girl," murmured Mrs. Furlow. "I know she's a good influence on you. Did she go by herself?"

"No—with the McGills," he explained. "I didn't feel like going. That party at the Daltons' last night . . ."

"Oh," said Mrs. Furlow, "what was it like? Who was there?"

He sank down wearily in the porch swing and began to describe the party. One by one he named the guests until he finished with Isabel Lang.

"Oh? I hope she wore a dress," remarked his mother.

"Of course, she wore a dress."

"I mean, I hope she didn't wear overalls or pants, like she does when she paints downtown."

"She looked very pretty," said Jim. "She talked to Don nearly all the time." He picked up a section of the paper from his father's lap and turned the pages.

"Don who?"

"Don Mason. I told you he was there," he said crossly.

"No, you didn't. You didn't mention him at all." She rocked back and forth in smug meditation. "Him and your old girl . . . hmm, what did you think of that?"

"Nothing. What should I think?" He raised the paper higher in front of his face.

"Well, *you* couldn't manage to catch her," his mother teased.

"I don't think Don's trying any more than I did."

"You tell Don when you see him to come by and tell me about New York," Mrs. Furlow said.

"Why don't you call him?" He rattled the pages as he turned them disinterestedly. "I won't be seeing him soon."

"I don't want to call him. Why won't you be seeing him? You'll both be downtown."

"Oh . . . I don't know."

After muttering answers to her insistent questions and ignoring others as often as he could, Jim fell finally into silence. He examined the paper slowly, section by section, but knew nothing he read. His father, erect and tall in his chair, said little but contemplated him seriously from time to time. Why should Dad look at me like that? he fretted, shifting the papers more. Why do they ask so many questions? He dropped the papers and walked to the porch steps to gaze down the street. Conscious of their rising curiosity, he returned to the swing and pretended to read again.

"You're so restless today, Jim," his mother remarked. "Can't you sit still?"

"Do I seem restless?" he asked. "I just can't concentrate, I guess."

"Too much drinking's not good," said his father. "I've an idea Josh Dalton rather overdoes it."

"Jim," said his mother, "when you pick up Doris, why don't both of you come over here to dinner? We've got plenty and I'd love to see her."

"Those—friends are going to take her home. We'd better eat there. It's all ready." Before he knew it, he was up again and walking down the porch.

"You're not going so soon?" asked his mother.

"Just wandering around," he mumbled and entered the front door into the hall.

There was a kind of consolation in being back where he had grown up. Along the walls inside the door were the stacked bookcases he knew so well from childhood explorations. He read the familiar titles through the glass doors, each book carrying with it some node of faraway secure happiness, now so irretrievable. But soon the memories depressed him and he proceeded through the hall. Hardly anything in the house was changed. Even the wallpaper was the same as when he was in his teens. Every corner, hallway, door and window was in its expected place. At the back porch, he strolled outdoors and around the yard, garish with late summer flowers. Almost hidden behind a huge wave of forsythia stood the tool shed adjoining the garage. Many years ago it had been a workshop for his youthful carpentry and secret experiments and inventions.

He re-entered the house by the back door and climbed the rear stairs to the second floor, drawn by a yearning for some narcotic to still the rebellion and despair in him. In his old room he sat stiffly in a rocking chair while the cold desertion of the furniture and walls came down all around him. Like the rest of the house, it too was little changed, except in atmosphere; the room was really ugly, but it had never seemed so until this intrusion. Here he grew up and studied and dreamed his young dreams, surrounded by a succession of toys, tops and cowboy suits; of B.B. guns, baseball bats and Tarzan books; of photos of friends and movie actresses lining the mirror, intimate letters piled in a drawer, reproductions of great paintings tacked to the walls, books that Don had given or lent him, and even the four college pennants that had finally provoked Don to protest, "For God's sake, take those things down! Are you going to fall in love with an institution?"

And as he sat today, not rocking because the noise would drown the faint tinkle of summer leaves and birds and announce his own presence, he knew that the room contained above all Don. Not only by what he had taken from it, such as the pennants, or what he had added in the way of their favorite pictures and books. The life of the room, now impersonal to everyone else, was Don; and now he felt the ghost of that life return to set the stage—himself stretched on the bed and Don leaning out the window, talking, arguing on spring nights, winter afternoons, making out of words (and what else besides?) a nearly tangible, nearly visible existence for the room itself. It breathed and glowed with a magic vitality. But today it was no more than the grave of that existence; he could see the ghost. He sat there a long time to watch it live its shadowy life again, and to rest in the calm sweetness of the nostalgia that crept over him.

His mother called that it was nearly dinnertime, and he'd better go meet Doris. He went downstairs and told them good-by.

In the hot noon sun, he drove to his office and climbed the dark tunnel of stairs. When he opened the door, the smell of dusty air and calfbound lawbooks filled his nostrils. Once inside, he locked the door and went into the cubicle that was his own. From the bottom drawer of his desk, he lifted a bottle of whiskey and took a drink. Then he pulled off his coat and opened the windows. The breeze raised a sheet of paper from a file tray and blew it to the floor. He looked at it coldly.

How had he expected his parents to help him unless he were able to tell them of his monstrous night with Doris? And if he had, wouldn't they have told him he was wrong? He'd never be able to make them understand at all, because he couldn't tell it all—the feelings, the reactions, the faint flickering of relationship—to anyone; and he himself couldn't know what was hidden underneath. Somehow, somewhere, he must grow strong enough to face this world in which he had closed himself, and make it over again the way it should be. He drank and wondered and drank.

Late in the afternoon, hoping no one had seen him come out of the office, he staggered down to Callahan's Café for sandwiches and cigarettes. He brought them back upstairs and ate, washing the food down with more liquor, and watched the sunset changing the colors of the clouds above the slanting roofs of the town.

Sometimes, he would suddenly become aware that the pressure of the previous night had gone away, washed away in whiskey—only to realize that after an absence it was merely returning to him again, and his quick hope was nothing more than the knowledge that for a while he hadn't felt his anguish. Gradually the skies darkened with night, and the office was filled with a deep gray gloom of smoke and shadow. He heard the croaking of frogs in the boggy creek, and the dim screeching of katydids. Lonely evening sounds filtered through the windows. Someone, someone, he said to himself, squeezing the glass in his fingers, someone who could know and could understand. Someone who could help. Someone . . .

When the scene outside the window had vanished in the night and only the storetops lifted visible shapes, acquiring dimension from the distant streetlamps,

Jim turned on the light above him. From the green-glass shade, it glared down over the plain furniture, the bread crusts and sandwich wrappers still scattered on the desk, the bottle of hot whiskey, sickening and stinging, and the glass of tepid water with which he chased it. It was like a pallid, feeble spotlight on a stage of loneliness. His stomach convulsed and he took a long breath. Sweeping the paper and crusts together, he pressed them into a tight ball which he threw into the wastebasket.

He got up and lurched to the outer office. Chairs scraped aside and thumped on the floor when he knocked against them. Swaying hard against a doorjamb, he leaned there for a long time and stared at the unresponsive, repellent forms around him. Someone, someone . . . He raked his scalp and his face with his fingers. He was forbidden; he was forbidden everything. Someone . . . someone . . .

As he turned to go back to his office, he lost his balance and crashed to the floor. He wanted to lie there, but after a few minutes he cursed and got up. When he sat again in front of his desk, he began to drink the rest of the whiskey. His throat tried to close as he forced it down. He shuddered and drew deep on a cigarette. How long had he been here? What time was it? What the hell—who cared? But his father would come in on Monday morning; he must be out before then. He must go—he must go—but where? He couldn't bear to go home. Finally, he finished off the bottle and threw it out the window. At the sound of the breaking glass, he gave a cackling, hiccoughing laugh.

Exhausted, seeing only fuzzy shapes in the aching light, he leaned his elbows on the desk and stretched out his arms before him. The black telephone seemed to move from one spot to another. Reaching out, he knocked the receiver down. With both hands, he grasped it and brought it to his ear. Someone . . . someone . . .

A voice rasped in the instrument. He could hardly pronounce the words he wanted to speak.

2

It was not until late in the afternoon, when boredom was settling relentlessly over her, that Doris began to wonder where James had gone. For an hour or so after she waked, she lay in bed, fearing to see him after that detestable night; but when she finally arose, reassured by the silence of the house, she was relieved to find that he had left. She read the Sunday papers and listened to the radio and thought about cooking dinner. She waited restlessly, growing more miserable and a little frightened at the quiet and the solitude.

Worst of all, he had left her stranded without the car. She didn't really want to visit any friends—she was in no mood to chat—but she would have liked to ride around the country in the warm sunshine. She could do nothing but sit and listen to the religious voices droning on the radio programs. At last she fled the choirs and sermons and made some iced tea and sandwiches.

After eating with no appetite, but simply because it killed time, she turned once more to the papers and read all the ads for clothes and accessories in Memphis and Jackson stores. She tried new stations on the radio to escape the pious sounds. Toward evening the programs began to improve and she was able to stop reading about the presidential election. She listened to the music eagerly now, for it helped her to escape from her distasteful thoughts.

When night came she felt both vexed that she didn't know where he was and glad that he wasn't near her. At length she found herself worrying that if he returned before she went to bed, she would have to face him, speak to him. What could she say? How could she ever talk to him again with any patience? She retreated early to her bedroom and locked the door. Every night now she would lock her door and there would be no changing her attitude.

On Monday morning James came in about seven o'clock. The noise of the front door startled her, and she leaped from the bed and rushed out, almost, she thought, to prevent him from entering. But she stopped abruptly in the narrow hallway. Unshaven, nervous and haggard, James walked toward her, looking at her with lifeless eyes, and passed into his bedroom without saying a word. When he had bathed and put on fresh clothes, he went out.

After that first meeting, the tension gradually relaxed, but conversation was still tedious. Neither of them spoke more than the few words necessary to their daily civilities. James never commented on her locked door or, as far as she knew, even looked into her bedroom when she was in it. He seemed to move in a blind, mechanical way; whatever he observed in their house produced no reaction. Often he prepared his own breakfast, since she lingered in bed for him to leave the house; he seldom came for dinner at noon, and even ate supper downtown many nights, explaining that he was working late at the office. When he did come home, he retired to his room after they had eaten and left her to enjoy the radio alone.

She tried little by little to lighten the strain of their relations. She told one or two feeble jokes which were received in glum silence; she related chit-chat heard in the drugstore and the market, but he barely answered her. It was ridiculous for them to act this way, and she finally told him so.

"We're behaving like children, James," she said meekly. "We can't go on this way. Our life with each other is—well, it's something we have to make look right."

"Pretend, you mean?" he asked.

"Everybody has to pretend a little. What I mean is, people are going to think we've had a quarrel if we keep on. Your family must think something is strange. We can't act this way in front of them."

His eyes flickered. "Yes, I suppose you're right."

"We have to get over little—oh, little disagreements like this. We have our place in town . . ."

He paced about the room moodily. "Yes, Doris. We'll pretend. We'll be the prominent young couple, the leaders of society, if you wish."

Shortly afterward, they went to a movie together, the first time in weeks, and he put his arm around her while they sat watching the film. They had both reached an even course of behavior. In spite of her physical loathing of him, she was able to seem affectionate when there were witnesses, she could kiss him in public with convincing warmth. And he managed to pretend equally well, even though in privacy he was likely to be sharp or sullen.

Only when she asked him whether he had put in an order for the Lincoln, did he waver toward anger. The more she tried to find out about the car, the more furious he seemed to get. "It's ordered," he said sternly. "It'll be delivered when I know you're pregnant."

His crudeness shocked her, and it also brought with panic the thought of how horrible it would be if she weren't pregnant. Turning toward the asylum of her bedroom with a shudder, she murmured, "Please, God, let it be a baby. . . . Don't let that have to happen again." Then finally she thought her prayers had been answered. She had a slight queasiness in the mornings; she missed her usual period. An examination would prove the truth, and she would have her Lincoln.

"Dr. Everett says it's so," she told James that night. "I'm going to have a baby."

"When did you see him?" he asked.

"This morning. I went down to his office." For a moment a flash of enthusiasm overcame his usual apathy. "Has the car been sent down yet?"

"Oh, for Christ's sake, shut up and leave me alone!" he shouted.

"James! What in the world . . ."

"You're always dinning, dinning about that car!"

"Why, I've only mentioned it once or twice."

"No! Every day—every day—" Suddenly the loud, trembling fury guttered out. He bowed his head on his hands and spoke in a low, bewildered tone. "I hear you all the time asking, 'Has the car come? Where is the car?' Every time I look at you, I hear you."

"Ah . . . you're just imagining that," she said cautiously. "You told me it would be here when you knew I was pregnant."

He sat erect again. "How can you be sure you are?" he asked with cold obstinacy. "It's only a month or so."

"Dr. Everett told me it was true. Don't you believe me?"

"Did he examine you?"

"James! I don't intend to— Are you calling me a liar?"

"You said you couldn't have one."

"You're a low, vicious brute, James. A filthy, stingy, hateful—man!" The words were squeezed out in a slow, quiet voice, but on him they were ineffectual.

He stared into a far corner of the room. Then he spoke without turning to her. "You'll have the car when I know there's a baby coming."

"Well, if you can't take my word . . ."

"I'll talk to Dr. Everett tomorrow," he said.

So he really thought she had lied! He meant to insult her by his doubts. For a long time they sat in constricted silence. She couldn't bring together the words to express her hatred. By degrees she began to weep, snuffling and gasping, with her eyes fixed hypnotically on his face, but she did not lift her hands to wipe away the tears. Her fingers clutched around the arm of the chair.

"I wish . . ." she sobbed. The brine of tears trickled into her mouth. She meant to say, "I wish I . . ."; but loathing was stronger than self-pity, and she continued: "I wish—you were dead. Dead. Dead." Then she covered her face with her hands and rushed into her bedroom.

Two days later, at noon, James drove the new Lincoln, gleaming like a young girl in a debutante dress, up to the house. When she saw it parked on the street, and James walking toward the porch, she almost forgot the revolting impasse between them. All of a sudden she felt an impulsive urge toward him, as if she might have wanted to kiss him.

"There it is," he said coldly.

She went straight out in her house dress, slid into the seat and drove away. Far out on a country road she rode, rubbing her hands over the steering wheel, touching the faces of the dials on the dashboard, blowing the horn incessantly at every car or wagon, reveling in the wild sound that drowned out all of James's words and all her longings and chagrin, until she stopped on a deserted hilltop. There she got out and walked around the car, opening the doors, stretching on the back cushions, stroking the radiator cap, the fenders, the upholstery, and then, peaceful and spent, she drove back to town. She would have liked to pass Madge Dalton's house, in hopes of letting her be the first to see the car, but she didn't dare do so wearing only a plain house dress. When she reached her house, James had gone without bothering to serve his dinner. She ate a little very quickly, changed clothes and called Bea to get dressed and wait for her at once.

It was wonderful to see Bea's expression when the car loomed before her. It was wonderful, too, to know that every head turned toward her when she drove down the street, and to dream what awed remarks were made. Her delight in the car almost wiped out her antagonism for the child which was growing, which would make her ugly in a short time.

About a month later, James told her a letter had come from the Chicago manufacturer he met at Madge's party. Mr. Victor enclosed another letter from the legal department of his firm which expressed interest in adding James to the staff. Mr. Victor wanted to know if he would accept a position in their Atlanta office.

"Of course you wrote him you couldn't take it," she said.

"No, I didn't. I'm going to accept."

"But you can't, James. We can't leave Ashton—it's our home."

"I want to go away from Ashton," he replied in the dead and cruel voice he now had.

"That's ridiculous. I thought it was all settled long ago. We don't know anyone in Atlanta. We'd be lost."

"We can't afford to let a chance like this go by. It means a lot of money."

"No, James. No. We're not leaving Ashton."

"Then I'll leave by myself."

She caught her breath sharply. His face was set in a dogged, morose heaviness which, coupled with his statement, alarmed her. No matter how hard she tried to mold their lives into a solid, enduring home, James always threatened it with his childish notions. And now in his threat of desertion, he struck again at the foundations. Filled with dread of what might happen if she were left alone, she couldn't answer him for some time. When she did speak, her voice was strained to a whisper.

"You—wouldn't—do that, James."

"Yes, I would. I've got to get away from Ashton."

"Be reasonable, James. Please." She could talk with more force now that her first surprise was over. "We can't go moving about the country, hunting houses, shipping furniture and all that, with me—in this condition. I'm not able to. It would injure me."

"I've got to get away!" he said with sudden vigor, and slapped his hands flat on the table.

"But your father—have you talked to him about it? He'd hate for you to leave him alone in the office here."

He sat before the table, trembling with a sort of restrained frenzy.

"Our lives are here in Ashton, with our friends and our family," she went on eagerly, hoping he was beginning to understand the folly of leaving. "We've been through all this before, James, and you know I'm right. Ask your father and see."

He lurched up from the table and stalked erratically about the room. "I can't stand it," he cried, but the words were muffled by his hands pressing on his face. "I can't stand it, Doris. I've got to do something. I'll go crazy. Get a divorce and let me be free. Let me go away alone, please, Doris. Divorce me."

"No, no, don't say that," she whispered rapidly as she ran to his side. She put her arms fearfully around him. "Don't say such things. Oh James, please don't act like this. I—I don't know what I'd do if—if I were left alone. If I didn't have—a husband. I'd rather die than go through a divorce."

"I want to be free. I can't stand this," he muttered.

"But the child," she gasped. "You wanted a child."

"I did. But I didn't want—to—"

Tears came into her eyes. "We must stay together, we mustn't have any scandal," she said softly. "We can't think of divorce. We owe it to our child. I could never bring it up alone. We must make a home for it here, where we can give it a good background, all the things that families can give, all they stand for. That's why we mustn't move away and sacrifice everything our mothers and fathers worked to build up for us. Don't you see, James? We can't move to a strange city where we won't mean a thing."

She couldn't be sure her argument had affected his decision, but at least he was calm again, though sullen. Her arms dropped slowly from around him and she moved back.

"After all," she said, "it's not a definite offer. It's just asking if you *would* take the job. Later on, maybe, something better will come along and you can take that."

He whirled around and for a minute seemed to fight to put words together. "I can't wait," he groaned. "It's something that can't be put off." He walked dazedly up and down before her. "When things like this are put off, they die away; they shrivel up inside you. And they're never done, because you never get the same chance again."

Then from his obstinate expression she realized that her words had not moved him. The only other way to keep him from destroying their home was to appeal to his parents. Although she had never felt very intimate with them, she suspected that if she told them about the baby they—at least his mother— would be sympathetic to her wishes. Mrs. Furlow would want her grandchild here with her, where she could enjoy the knowledge that the family was going on, building itself in the town's social structure.

"Why don't you stall Mr. Victor for a while?" she asked. "Find out more about the job and living in Atlanta. Maybe he could let you work for them here."

"The thing I want is to get away from here," he said dully.

"Promise me you won't do anything foolish right away," she urged with all the gentleness and warmth she could summon. "We'll talk to your father. I'll do whatever he thinks best, James."

But it was to his mother that she went the next morning. With an almost demure countenance and a shy smile, she confessed that she was about to have a baby and needed the comfort of an older woman—someone who could take the place of her own mother in counseling and guiding her. Mrs. Furlow, as she had expected, was overjoyed and they leaned into each other's arms in a warm, understanding embrace.

"I'm so happy," murmured Mrs. Furlow with a quick sniffle into her hand-kerchief. "Now I feel you really do belong to us. We've both, Mr. Furlow and I, wanted a grandchild here in Ashton with us."

The increasing intimacy of their conversation aroused in Doris a feeling of dependence on the older woman. Now, in this unexpected way, she had justified herself in the lives of all the Furlows. A sense of the rightness of her actions, reflected in the mother's happiness, pleased her; and even more, a sense of her absorption into the bosom of the family made her peaceful. She hated to have to tell James's mother that he wanted to move away, but it was better that she know now what he was planning.

"I simply can't get over it," Mrs. Furlow was sighing. "It'll be so wonderful for you both. Children really make a home—they bring people closer together. I think it's so terrible, the way lots of these young people don't want to make a real family."

Doris's face was troubled. She reached out and patted Mrs. Furlow's hand. "I—I don't know how to say it, Mrs. Furlow. I—"

"What is it, Doris?" asked Mrs. Furlow in alarm. "Is something wrong?"

"Not really," she said. "It's just that James wants to move to Atlanta. He's offered a job there."

"Why, you can't think of moving now, Doris. You'd be all alone there. Jim would be heartless to leave Ashton."

"I'm sure he thinks it's for the best, Mrs. Furlow." She smiled forbearingly. "I try to see it his way, but I just can't stand to think of leaving here."

"He shouldn't worry you with such things at a time like this," said Mrs. Furlow. "I'll just have to talk with that young man. And his father will, too. He'll put his ideas straight in his head. Of all foolishness!"

During the October days that followed this, the argument went on between James and his father. When they occurred in the office, Mrs. Furlow relayed her husband's account of them to Doris. But often in the evenings, Doris and Mrs. Furlow, entrenched at one end of the living room, could overhear the two men at the other end.

"You must consider carefully," warned Mr. Furlow, "what you'll lose if you go away. I think you'll be happier here where you have old friends, in spite of the much bigger salary. You'll learn to stand on your own feet here. And eventually our firm will be in your hands. That's a great responsibility, Jim, whether you realize it or not. In a town like Ashton, a good lawyer is as important an influence as a preacher. You can mean something here."

"That's about what Doris says," James murmured, looking sadly into the low fire on the hearth.

"Well, Doris is a smart girl, Jim. You should pay more attention to her."

As the days passed, Doris could see the doubt taking hold on James. His defense and his support of the Atlanta job slowly weakened until he hardly answered anyone who spoke of it. Both his parents mentioned the expected child so frequently that finally he burst out, "Children aren't the ones to decide!"

"Of course not," answered his father mildly. "But neither should grown-ups act like children. If you don't have a child, there are many things you can do. But when you have one, all your life—your duties—are changed."

"Yes, they are," James muttered.

But he fought on against them, gradually conceding one point after another until one evening he sighed. "Yes, yes, I suppose it is foolish. We belong here. . . ."

Poor James! He was unhappy, certainly, to have his whim defeated, but anyway, at her instigation, they had all saved him from making a great mistake. Someday he would realize it. She listened to Mrs. Furlow's quiet gossip and smiled tolerantly at James, who was poking disinterestedly at the coals in the fireplace.

3

During his first weeks after returning to Ashton, Don consoled himself with a vague notion that in some as yet undefined manner he would be released from the town and set free to go away. But as the days wore on, he became more and more reconciled to the fact that such a dream would not come true. His conjuring it up was simply evidence that he wished vainly against the reality of his confinement.

There was almost nothing he could do during the daytime to escape his mother. If he stayed home to read or write, she sent Aunt Marny to interrupt him with a whimsical reason to come down to her. He would rush downtown and hang around the drugstore, drinking coffee or cokes. In the afternoon he could go to the matinee at the Elite Theater or stroll about the streets. None of it was rewarding or amusing except insofar as it killed time.

That, unfortunately, was the trouble with the whole place. All activity was directed toward killing time, and that meant killing yourself because when time is dead so are you. Even making money was basically killing time; give any of these people a fortune and they couldn't use it to any benefit. Perhaps some would try to attract lots of friends by spending the money. But most of them hadn't enough depth or warmth to make a friend and in the end they merely made debts. Yet there had been Jim in the old days; there were Tray's unselfish, open, brusque gestures of affection. And there was Isabel, who with plenty of money had come up from the shallowness of her schoolmates into the sincere, independent world of her own character.

By contrast, his mother's world, restricted to her blowsy bedroom, her gossip about people she rarely saw, her constant yearning for attention, exasperated him so that he hated to go home in the evening. He lingered in the entrances of stores, talking with idle clerks about weather and politics; he drank more soda pop, he walked up the street again pretending to be busy—anything to keep from having to go home, anything to make living seem a conscious thing. But eventually he must go back. Aunt Marny was away, visiting her family in Green Springs, and his mother would want her supper.

At the sound of the door latch, Mrs. Mason opened her eyes. She had been dozing, propped on the pillows. The window curtains were drawn and the shade on the bed lamp turned to keep the brightness out of her face.

"Oh, Donald," she murmured, "you've been out all afternoon. It's after six." She rubbed her hands up both cheeks, across the temples and over her thin hair. "I've been alone ever since Marny left. I get so tired being by myself all the time."

He lighted the lamp on the center table and sat in a chair near the fireplace with his back half turned to her.

"I'd think Uncle Wallace would get tired of her staying down here so much," he said. "Doesn't she like to keep house for her family?"

Mrs. Mason made a despairing gesture which he could see without turning his head directly toward her. Her arms dropped heavily on the quilts. "Oh, Donald, you don't seem to understand. The children are almost grown now and they take care of Wallace. They don't need Marny there."

"I wasn't thinking about needing her there; I was thinking about didn't she *want* to be there." It was foolish to bicker this way with his mother; if Aunt Marny weren't here to help, they would have to hire a companion-housekeeper. But always a tendency to oppose her ideas, to argue with her, to overcome her, rose up more strongly in him.

"Why should she?" asked Mrs. Mason incredulously. "There's not a thing in the world for her in Green Springs. You know as well as I do what kind of a place it is. Not even a movie for her to go to. And practically all her neighbors nothing more than hill farmers." She began to fumble among the bottles which Aunt Marny had transferred from the bureau to her bedside table.

Don pretended not to notice. "What about Uncle Wallace, though? Doesn't he matter?"

Mrs. Mason looked away from the little forest of bottles. "Uncle Wallace?" she echoed. Then her hand overturned a bottle. "Oh, Donald, you'll have to come help me. I'm just too weak to reach it."

He rose slowly, leaving the cigarette between his lips, streaming smoke about his nose and eyes, and walked around the foot of the bed. His mother continued her plaintive explanation.

"Wallace's always down at the office during the day and at night he sits with a bunch of his cronies on the porch of the general store. You know that. He only comes home for meals. Marny doesn't like being turned into just a cook. And I don't blame her."

Don chose a bottle of medicine at random. Barely glancing at it, she flicked her fingers and said querulously, "Pour me out a teaspoonful in a little water. I'm afraid I'm late. I usually time myself by when you come home in the evening."

He measured the dark fluid, added water from the pitcher and gave it to her. As she drank it with her hand shaking slightly and the glass clicking against her teeth, he righted the lamp shade and arranged the objects on her table. Then she handed the glass back and he set it down.

She wouldn't want him to go out tonight, with Aunt Marny away; he'd have to sit there for several hours and try to read. She might even want him to read to her. He couldn't go to his room without offending her, much less to a movie or to Isabel's.

Ordinarily he would have dropped in at Isabel's house as he did many afternoons and evenings since meeting at Madge Dalton's party. At Isabel's supper a few days later, he had come to realize that they depended on each other for companionship. She seemed to welcome his visits and always encouraged him to come back. As she suggested one day, each felt the other to be a fellow countryman met in a foreign land. "As far as most of the people here are concerned," she went on, "we might as well be talking Greek." If there were an interesting movie in town, they went together, with a casual air, although Don was conscious now that their neighbors attributed to these appearances at the theater the quiet formal meaning of a "steady date."

But pleasant as it was, he couldn't spend all his time with Isabel. He had to think about a direction for his life; he must find some more lucrative way of killing time. His mother hadn't money enough for him to loiter on the streets and amuse himself with Isabel without his earning something on his own. When he finally acknowledged his sure imprisonment, he knew then that he had avoided thinking of a job because it would be a further chain on him. After that admission, it took no survey of possibilities to see that Mr. Saxon could offer the only logical work. At least this one morning as he walked up the main street he had a definite objective.

Two concrete steps on the sidewalk led directly through the open door into the confusion of the Ashton *Herald* office. A composition-board partition rose halfway to the ceiling in the fore part of the large room and screened off the sprawling, animal-greedy presses. The rumbling of the machinery poured over the wall and filled the air with a pulsing noise. Against the partition stood a long bank of shelves stacked with back issues of the paper, syndicated mat pages, ready-printed insert sheets of pictures and feature stories, and boxes of office supplies. At one of the three littered desks sat a young girl who was faintly familiar. At the other desk, Mr. Saxon was bending over some sheets of yellow paper.

The girl's eyes flashed eagerly when she looked up at him. "Oh, it's Don Mason, isn't it?" she said excitedly, rising with a sudden motion that toppled her chair. "I don't guess you remember me. I'm Charlie Ann Davis."

Mr. Saxon turned his head while they were shaking hands. "Good morning, Don," he said casually. "What's your trouble?"

"Does it have to be trouble?" asked Don.

"Sit down." The editor pushed a cane-bottomed chair toward him. "Most people seem to have trouble. We hear it every day."

"Well, maybe it is trouble. I want a job. I mean on your paper."

"Here? What makes you think I could pay you? This is a county newspaper."

"Well, you do make money, don't you? I can't say I've got much to offer, but I could be of some use. At least, more use to you than to anybody else in town. You know what I can do—I don't have to tell you."

"Oh, you're right about that," said Mr. Saxon. "But you're wrong if you think I make money."

"I won't worry too much about what you pay me," Don said. "I want some work, that's all."

"Got to occupy your time, huh? Can't keep your mind on a book or making love?"

"Certainly. But I need to make some money. I don't live on air."

"There's not much to do on a paper like this—no reporting to speak of, or none you *can* speak of. I do that, and Charlie Ann does the society, the telephone, the bills and the community news letters. What could you do?"

"I don't know. I want you to tell me."

"You want me to offer you a job?"

"I want you to give me one. What can I do?"

"Almost anything you want to. Right now I'd say you could go to hell."

Don's laugh had none of the ease of amusement in it. "Let's be sensible, Mr. Saxon," he said. "I see you working here at night lots of times. If you have to do that, you do need someone else, don't you?"

"If I didn't work nights, what would I do? What else is there for me to do?"

"Enjoy yourself. Get your mind on a book. Make love."

Mr. Saxon snorted as if to ignore the biting tone in Don's voice. "Not possible. . . . And don't get fresh with me."

Certain now that he wouldn't be hired, but also doubtful whether he'd want to work for such a perverse, unpredictable man, Don got up. "Who works at this desk?" He pointed to the third desk, piled high with papers against the opposite wall.

"Nobody. That's work for us," said Mr. Saxon severely.

"Who did work there?"

"None of your business."

"Well," said Don, "if you haven't got a job, I guess you haven't." As he held out his hand, he caught a glimpse of Charlie Ann leaning forward anxiously. Saxon did not move.

"Aren't you going to beg me?" asked Mr. Saxon.

"Why should I?"

"So I could enjoy refusing you."

The old selfish bastard—to have encouraged him in his youth, and now to have become so crabbed and peculiar—vengeful, possibly—that he wouldn't even be sympathetic to a man trying to start work. "I'll send you my new poem," said Don crisply. Mr. Saxon's blink at this reference to their past relationship pleased him.

But except for the flicker, Mr. Saxon paid no attention to the remark. "There aren't many good newspapermen in the world," he said. "Their day is past; they call themselves journalists, but they're pretty sad imitations of—well, ignorant, egomaniac garbage-sorters. Why should you want to join them?"

"I don't want to. I want to be a poet," said Don, stubbornly pursuing his own petty teasing. "But I want to make a living."

"You're getting pretty thick with that Lang girl, aren't you?"

"Why?"

"Nice girl. Good for the town to have somebody like her here."

Cynical old goat, thought Don. What in hell is he trying to do with his meandering talk and his curiosity about gossip he picked up from women? "Well, I'll be seeing you," he said and turned toward the door.

"Monday morning, nine o'clock," Mr. Saxon called.

He stopped abruptly, with a tingling along his back and heard a gasp of delight break from Charlie Ann. Mr. Saxon was returning to work and peeping slyly from the corner of his eyes as if pleased with the little game.

"I'll leave all that for you to clear up," said the editor, with a wave toward the heaped desk. "You played me a dirty trick, Don."

"How, Mr. Saxon? I—" He moved toward him, apologetically.

"Stirring up my sentimentality. Now don't try to explain. Go on off." Mr. Saxon suddenly raised his shoulders and turned in his chair. "And stop flirting, Charlie Ann. You've already got a boy-friend."

His work was varied—almost inclusive—but mainly it was the advertising and some editing of regular news releases. Mr. Saxon promised to let him handle more of the editorial work later on, when he learned something.

Charlie Ann began to ask him for suggestions on her short pieces of society news, and for definitions of words and uses of grammar. At the beginning of each week, she copied out piles of assorted papers, scrawled in awkward, tedious country handwriting, on her typewriter for the page of community news.

"Mr. And Mrs. Jacob Trumbull of Hebron Crossing spent Sunday with her parents Mr. and Mrs. Henry Crump." "Several members of the Glenwood community are low with the flu and church services last Sunday were not well attended." "Mr. Whitcomb McNeese has married Miss Esta Tolliver and is moving from our community. We are sorry to lose him but know he will be welcomed by his new neighbors in Slate Springs."

He had forgotten about these items and now wondered whether seeing their names in a paper of fifteen hundred subscribers gave those people a flush of pleasure, a release from the isolation of their circle of hills and farms. Did they think it a forging of their link with the larger world—their personal imprint on the pattern of society—just as the people in Ashton justified themselves in a broader sphere of seated teas, receptions and artistic clubs; and the people of all the New Yorks felt the cosmopolitan bond, not through mutual love and sorrow and parting, but through the new book, the art gallery, the concert platform, the proscenium arch? But there were first causes in them all: "has married and is moving from our community . . . We are sorry to lose him . . ." Surely, in some omniscient equation, the longest, most complex link would reduce to Whitcomb McNeese and Esta Tolliver. Stripped of all our gadgetry, even of art, they were the primal forces—the lover, the wanderer—who together produced a child, the discoverer. Why couldn't they all, here in Ashton and everywhere, strip off the gadgets, both mechanical and mental, and move, lovers, wanderers, discoverers, to a new community? Perhaps these people who sent Charlie Ann their modest records were the ones—the most uncluttered ones—who could see first the newness of that imaginary community he would like everybody to reach.

By the time summer was dying out in the warm, glowing days of September, Don was at ease in his job. Happily, it earned him money of his own and at the same time kept him from home most of the day. Although his mother continued to complain of loneliness, in spite of Aunt Marny's company, he paid little attention. Most of his nights at home were spent reading in his room after she had gone to sleep.

He and Isabel continued their occasional suppers at her house and their weekly visits to the movies. Being together so often somehow seemed to bring both more into conformity with the ideals of the townspeople. He noticed it first in an ill-defined camaraderie which colored the small talk of friends on the street. It was as if they shared knowledge of a secret plot. Then, the Traywicks, for no particular reason, invited them over for a Saturday night supper.

Feeling some inner tension now mysteriously released, he began to discover that the Traywicks were rather an enjoyable couple. Before them, he and Isabel could address remarks about what Tray called the "deeper" subjects to each other with no fear of objections or sarcasm. On the contrary, they often expressed a kind of fascinated interest which he fed with tiny bits of information, as if he were giving drops of water to a desert-parched traveler. He had come to enjoy their casual banter and jokes and to regard their attitude as a down-to-earth way of facing life in a small town. The four of them met more and more regularly, sometimes just for drinks and sometimes for a meal and the whole evening.

Late in September, Bea suggested that they have a picnic before the warm weather was over, and they went out to Pine Hill in Tray's car. As they walked through the tall straight trees, their dark boughs whining softly above them and the air scented with resin, Isabel caught his hand and swung it childishly between them. They followed along the ridge of the hill ahead of Bea and Tray. They watched in the leaf mold for arrowheads left from ancient Indian battles or villages. On each side the trees slid down below them along the steep slopes and beyond their tops, shivering like a choppy green sea, the sky shone with bright clouds over the lower land.

"This is the loveliest spot around Ashton," said Isabel; "but no one except children on picnics ever comes here."

"Children like us," said Don.

"Yes." She glanced at him. "Like us."

Suddenly she veered over the side of the crest, dragging Don along. He let out a yell. "Hey! What're you doing?"

"The spring's down here." Then her feet scooted from underneath and she plunked to the ground.

While Tray and Bea jeered at them from a distance, Isabel laughed so hard she couldn't get up. He put down the lunch basket and tried to lift her, but every time her feet skidded on the steep veneer of pine needles. Her shoe-soles had caught the smoothness of the incline and there was nothing to do about it. Just as Bea and Tray arrived at the edge of the crest above them, Don's feet shot out too, and he collapsed beside Isabel.

"Well, of all things!" exclaimed Bea. "So this is what happens to the intelligentsia when a little fresh air strikes them!"

"It's the only way to get to the bottom and you know it," gasped Isabel between laughs and the jog of skidding feet.

The slope seemed almost vertical, falling so far that branches of the lower trees hid the bottom. The surface was spotted golden with sun and brown with shadow.

"Don't break the speed limit," called Tray, "and watch out for passing trees."

Don almost got Isabel to her feet. Like amateur ice skaters, they huddled against each other, half-stooped, bracing against the sleek descent, and giggled at the encouraging cheers behind them. But it was no use; they plopped again and Isabel slid and rolled, and Don tumbled and slid on his pants and finally simply relaxed until he came to a halt with a foot against a tree.

"Oh, hell!" he shouted to Isabel who clung panting to a root below him. "Why bother? Here I come!" He flung himself out on the slope, skidded into her and both, clutching and shrieking, slipped and rolled down to the bottom of the hill.

"Poor Tray has to manage both baskets," he chuckled, peering up the slope.

"We'll end up with pressed sandwiches under bell, I guess," she said.

They gathered berries from clumps below the spring—the last tiny berries of the season—and warned each other, "Look out for rattlers. Snakes love blackberry bushes." They spread their lunch near the spring, on a shady spot of chill clover and sweet grass and afterward climbed another arm of the hill, holding to outjutting corners of red sandstone which, in the late summer heat, really smelled like red sandstone. And with the challenge of the slope won, they slid down again on fresh pine boughs over the dry brown mattress of needles and lay on their stomachs at the spring to dip their noses and lips to the water.

About his whole life with Isabel—the picnics, the long evening conversations, the suppers, the movies, the lazy rides in her car—there was a calm but buoyant air of pleasure and inevitability. He was conscious of no straining away, no boredom and no desire beyond the present. Sometimes, when they sat alone in the night or walked across the fields and woods, now turning brilliant with ruddy autumn colors, and talked about new poetry and new novels and new ideas, with jokes suddenly materializing to shatter their seriousness or one of them gently spoofing the other, he felt with a strange sense of identification that his earlier days with Jim were a mirror of these—a reflection, long past, of the actuality of a future which was now.

As he walked home from work, a sharp wind blew from the north and died away. The temperature had dropped noticeably during the day; there would probably be sleet that night. It would click and tap insistently on the roofs, and hiss in the bare trees. It would pierce with its stinging barbs the longing of all those lying wakeful and lonely in the winter night. Falling sleet was the saddest sound of all.

Inside the house, he hung his topcoat on the hall tree and entered his mother's room. The bed of embers in the grate looked as if it had recently been banked with coal; the half-burned lumps were still black on top and spewed jets of smoke from cracks in their sides.

Mrs. Mason stretched up her arms and smiled with delight. "Now kiss your mother, Donald, and go help Aunt Marny fix something for supper," she said.

Holding his cigarette away from the bed, he put his mouth to hers lightly and drew back. "I won't be home for supper. I just came to change clothes."

"Change?" she echoed, with her watery eyes searching toward his. "Are you going out tonight?"

"I've got a date."

"A date? Again?" Her hands lifted protestingly and then fell heavily on the covers. "Not with Isabel Lang?"

"Yes, with Isabel."

"Oh, Donald." She brushed back the bands of gray hair that looped about her ears. The fingers trailed haltingly down her face and came to rest almost in prayer beneath her chin. "Do you *have* to see so much of her? She's such a strange girl—so—so unconventional. If she didn't come of a good family, she simply wouldn't be tolerated for all those outrageous things she does."

"What things, Mother?"

"Oh, you know as well as I do. I hear about them—the way she dresses, the things she talks about, those pictures she paints—" He didn't answer her and in a moment she went on. "I get so lonely here at night with you out courting that—girl. Don't you ever think to stay home with me sometime?"

"I'm home with you lots of times, Mother. You just don't remember them."

"She'll try to rope you in, Donald. She's missed her chances to get married and now she's—well, desperate." Mrs. Mason spoke urgently and imploringly. "She'd just as soon try to take you away from me. . . . Sometimes, Donald, I think you don't appreciate all I've done for you."

He couldn't say the things that came into his mind. His lips drew into a tight line. He couldn't look at her. "I'd better hurry," he said; "Isabel will be here in a little while."

Mrs. Mason was astounded. "You mean *she's* calling for *you*? Why, Donald, that's indecent!"

"It's just common sense, Mother," he said, chuckling to himself as he rushed upstairs to dress.

When he was ready, he clattered back down, stuck his head in the door and said, "Good night, Mother."

"I didn't hear the bell—the horn, Donald," she complained.

But he was outside now. Of course she hadn't heard anything. He simply didn't want to wait in the house. It was damp and cold on the porch, but he liked it. In the darkness, the weather which most people would have called bitter he felt to be a momentary independence. Probably it was his old yearning toward freedom from obligations—family, friends, town—all except himself.

There was, somewhere deep in him, a strange trust in the security of living anonymously among masses of people in cities. But that modern vagabondage couldn't be satisfied now. Not as long as his mother lived.

How much longer would she keep him tied down to Ashton? So long, no doubt, that his desire to wander in unknown places would have died away and he would be an old man, mired in the town, fidgeting in his mind and pouring his disappointment on all acquaintances—an old man like Horace Saxon, a town character. Probably he would inherit Saxon's role, Saxon's cynical, solitary way of life while waiting for his mother to die and free him. The editor would grow old, and would let him buy in portions of the business, bit by bit, until Saxon died and Don owned the *Herald* and Mrs. Mason lived on, waiting for him to come home at night and cook her supper and talk to her and read aloud from a romantic novel.

They had finished supper at the Traywicks' and were sitting in the living room with their first highballs when the doorbell rang. Tray opened the door. Under the porch light stood Jim, blinking sheepishly and stuttering that he didn't know there was company.

"I—I thought that was your car, Tray. Honest." Jim hesitated, but it took little urging to get him inside. He actually seemed afraid more of not being urged than of intruding.

"Are you sure it's all right, Tray?" he asked, almost creeping into the room.

"Where's Doris?" inquired Tray. "Did you run off and leave her?"

A grin clung persistently to Jim's lips. "She's at home, I think. I've been working at the office." He spoke to Bea, then to Don and Isabel as he crossed the room and sat down in a chair slightly removed from the group. "As a matter of fact," he said solemnly, "I thought she might be over here. That's why I came."

"Would you like another drink?"

"Another—? You're a dog to put it that way, Tray," answered Jim. "Sure, why not?" He got up quickly, his whole body wavering, and took two steps toward Tray.

"I'll bring it," said Tray. "Sit down and talk to the folks."

While Jim hesitated, the grin drooped away to a sad look of meditation. One hand moved vaguely toward Don and Isabel but fell back against his thigh. Then he sat down again. Apparently he was unable to keep his attention from them. Between a brief glance at the vase of yellow chrysanthemums, at the line of dampness around his shoes, at Tray in the dining room, his eyes returned guiltily to where they sat on the sofa. He began some small talk with Isabel, but abandoned it when Tray handed him a drink. He asked Bea a question and dreamily let the matter drop when she replied. Gazing at them over the rim of his glass, he drank slowly, and when he lowered the drink, the grin spread again over his face.

Don was uncomfortable before this disconcerting performance. Here was the clearest evidence of the change Tray had tried to explain to him at the Dalton party. He sensed, behind the smile that pulled tiresomely at Jim's lips, an accusation whose nature he couldn't guess.

"You're looking pretty spry these days, Don," said Jim. A tone of mild derision nullified the compliment of the words. "I thought you didn't want to come back?"

"Maybe looks don't tell the whole story."

"You and Isabel are getting about together quite a lot, I hear."

"Yes," said Isabel with an almost visible leap. "Bea and Tray are our chaperons."

"And we'll swap any day with you and Doris," added Tray boisterously. "I can't take their arty talk, but you're used to it, Jim."

"Oh . . . I always just . . ." Jim let the sentence hang, and with a frown lifted his glass.

No one wanted to continue the subject, least of all Don, and they sat in a strained silence. Finally Isabel spoke up.

"That's a wonderful new car you've got."

"It's Doris's car," Jim said disinterestedly. His voice grew gradually sad and muffled. "Hers alone. I don't even ride in it." He drank quickly, sloshing a few drops on his shirt.

An indistinct tension began to oppress them. Tray was staring pensively at Jim and chewing on a fingernail as if it were a tremendous problem.

"Oh God damn," said Bea softly.

Tray smiled foolishly and patted her arm. "O.K.," he said. Then he leaned to Don and began to tell about the hunting trip he had planned for January.

"So far, there'll just be you and Jim and me and Josh. But you can't ever tell. Josh wants Andy to go." He described the hunting lodge in the Delta swampland, and the plans for the journey. "Don't know what the women-folks are going to do while we're away," he said.

"Be glad to get rid of you," exclaimed Bea. "Won't we, Isabel?"

"Oh, sure," Isabel agreed faintly.

"Tray, it's silly for me to go," said Don. "I'm not a hunter and won't know what to do."

"Well, it's time you learned. You're going, if I have to tie you hand and foot and carry you over my shoulder."

"I guess that settles you," Isabel laughed.

"How's the world of art and literature, Don?" Jim asked abruptly, still with his insane smile. The question jarred everyone. "I haven't seen one of those little magazines in a long time now," Jim continued; "in fact not since you left here—and I'm a little out of touch. What's going on these days?"

"Oh, about the same as usual, Jim," he answered with a light expiration of breath. "Proletarian literature's the big thing, you know."

"No, I don't," said Jim. "This is a hick town, you know. Is proletarian better than Gertrude Stein?"

"Probably not," said Don with a tremor of his mouth. "The—stimulus is different."

"That's getting pretty deep for us folks down here, don't you think?" Jim suggested in mock seriousness.

"It depends."

"I'd say that maybe what this town needs most is a good course in reading Gertie Stein. Over microphones from the hotel balcony."

"I don't think our politicians would allow it," broke in Isabel. "They wouldn't know which one of their rivals it was."

"What rivals?" asked Tray.

"Isabel—" Jim began, and then stared at her as if his thought had vanished. He rubbed the arm of his chair and drew his eyebrows together. She prompted him and he went on. "Isabel—doesn't he run you crazy with all his talk about books and pictures? And poems?" Jim smirked and cocked his head cunningly at her. But there was a mournful quality in his voice. "And his social problems? And music?"

Isabel didn't answer. In the quietness, Don breathed so heavily from the excitement of Jim's attack that he was afraid he could be heard.

"Always bored the living daylights out of me," Jim resumed. "One good thing about marriage—" He sighed noisily. "Glad I don't have to listen to him now— unless—" On his face was a look of gleeful nostalgia and self-torture, as if he meant to transfer to Don his torture for being the source of it. His voice was frivolous, but spiteful. "Well, unless I happen to run across him, like tonight. That's the sort of thing I'm not—I feel like belongs to a certain kind of—"

"Oh, Jim," broke in Bea impatiently. "What are you trying to do?"

A shadow of chagrin fell over Jim's countenance when, suddenly conscious of some strangeness in his behavior, he looked at Bea, and then slowly, one by one, at each of the others. His lips parted and moved, but the words did not form.

"Jim's always kidded me, Bea," said Don. "Don't pay any attention to it."

And when a soft, drunken gratefulness flooded Jim's eyes as he raised them toward him, Don was glad he had lied. Jim had let something break through the shell to say *I remember it all; I miss it; but I must pretend. . . .*

4

I n the sunny October morning, farmers crossed back and forth from their tethered wagons to the grocery stores. Under burdens of pumpkins and bas-kets of squash, purple turnips and yams, they waddled awkwardly through the spare traffic, trailed as likely as not by a wife with a basket of eggs in a checkered cloth or several frying-size chickens tied at the feet. A good scene to paint, thought Isabel, as she paused at the curb—the mud-tan wagons, the brown teams, the variegated quilts on the spring seat, the vegetables, the man in his fading blue jeans, the woman in her dark gingham dress, shapeless sweater and sunbonnet.

"What's so fascinating, Isabel?" said a voice at her shoulder.

With a start, she turned about. "Oh—Mrs. Furlow!" Jim's mother, outfitted in matching dress, hat and handbag, smiled and glanced roguishly, not too discreetly, at her bare head. "You surprised me a little," she explained. "I was just wondering how those wagons and farmers would do to paint."

"*Those*?" Mrs. Furlow scowled delicately. "Really, Isabel, I know you're tal-ented—but why can't you paint beautiful things?"

"I try to make them beautiful, Mrs. Furlow," she answered with an uneasy laugh.

"I don't know how anyone could make those ugly, dirty things beautiful." In accord, they moved from the curb and strolled down the street. "I see enough things like that around me every day. I certainly wouldn't want a picture of it on my dining-room walls. Are you going shopping?"

"Well, I'm pretending to," Isabel said. "I really don't have to buy a thing. It's such a nice day not to be outdoors."

Mrs. Furlow cast her eyes up again to Isabel's head. "Aren't you afraid the sun will dry out your hair without a hat? My mother always told me—"

"No, I've found just the opposite," she said hastily. Mrs. Furlow, like all genteel women, wouldn't dare say what she really was thinking—that it wasn't decent for a girl not to wear a hat. "Jim told me not long ago he might move away. Is that true?"

"Oh, no," laughed Mrs. Furlow. "He has been offered a very good place, but it's sort of secret. He wasn't to mention it because he thinks it's best in the long run to stay here, you know."

"He seemed quite keen on it when he was at the house," she said.

"Well, he's so changeable." Mrs. Furlow, with a warning pat on her arm, darted to the show window of a store, as if to distract the conversation from Jim; for she returned almost at once with a new topic. "I just saw Don up the street," she said with a teasing twinkle, "going to have coffee with Charlie Ann. He's doing very well, isn't he? I mean on the paper."

"Yes, I think so," Isabel said grudgingly. "Mr. Saxon seems well pleased."

"I imagine he gets a very good salary."

Isabel ignored the hint and walked on in silence.

"He's such a bright boy," Mrs. Furlow continued. "He ought to make a nice living."

"Well, there's his mother to care for," she answered. "They aren't wealthy, I suppose, even for Ashton."

"I've heard some talk about him and Charlie Ann," said Mrs. Furlow off-handedly. "They say she's simply crazy about him. . . ."

"Oh, Mrs. Furlow, you know how people make up things. She's engaged already, isn't she?"

"Well, yes," Mrs. Furlow admitted. "And after all, she's not the sort he'd marry. I know Don too well." She nodded her head sagaciously and consolingly, it seemed, for bringing up a possible rival. "I'd say, just as an example, that you'd be the type he'd choose, Isabel."

She hoped her laughter was deceptive; and yet it sprang from a mixture of delight and fear which roused a brief, almost intolerable anxiety for assurance of Don's love, for escape from the loneliness. But she knew Mrs. Furlow's matronly game. "That's the farthest thing from his mind, I'd think," she said, and hoped she was wrong.

"Come on in here with me," suggested Mrs. Furlow, indicating a small shop. "I want to look at some gloves. Then we can go have a coke."

Isabel made the excuse that she had an appointment for a fitting with Miss Turner in McGill's and she'd better get on. Though Mrs. Furlow's sly remarks were quite normal for the women in town—one of their methods of "pumping" some new tid-bit of news from you—she wouldn't willingly subject herself to more of it now. Perhaps it was faint annoyance at having her stroll in the crisp morning interrupted by such prattle, or perhaps disturbance at the idea of another woman with Don, which Mrs. Furlow had injected into her prying talk.

At any rate, as she parted from the woman, she had to assure herself that it was too soon to hope that any enduring attachment had grown up between Don and herself. They had, of course, their dependence on each other for understanding companionship in the desert of Ashton—the meetings when they could talk honestly about what interested them, with no fear of shock, intimidation or superiority. But she wasn't fool enough to confuse such a dependence with love; even less with a desire to marry. For its needs could be satisfied quite easily without marriage.

And yet, obviously, everyone expected them to marry. She could spot in speech and looks the sly implication that it was all arranged and she had only to admit the secret and confirm their knowledge. In past years, she had watched the same suggestive attitudes directed at other couples and, in spite of some wrong assumptions, this sort of communal conjury had most often proved effective and true. To herself, she couldn't pretend she wasn't pleased by the frequent indications that Don had been allocated to her, much as a plot of ground is staked out by a homesteader. After all, he would be as fine a husband as she could ask for—except she couldn't ask for him. And all these neighborly innuendoes and suggestions were so lacking in actual support that she was concerned over their interference with Don's attitude to her. The town's too-quick, too-public acceptance of his courtship might balk the unfolding of his love.

She entered McGill's Department Store—wide and drafty—and walked reflectively down one of the aisles. Across the piles of dress goods, Alice Barnette called to her, waving gaily and hastening to the end of the table to intercept her.

"I'm so glad I ran across you," said Alice exuberantly. "I've been wanting to ask you, why don't you play cards some night with me and Anita? You know Anita Leffingwell, don't you?"

"Oh yes, of course." She gazed from Alice's eager face to the dim shelves of dry goods. "Cards?" she echoed weakly.

"Three-handed bridge. Or rummy," said Alice. "But mostly rummy, because usually it's just me and Anita. It'll be fun this winter, now that the nights are getting cold. We have the fire going, and apples and ginger snaps and raisins, and other things too. There's so little to do, you know."

No plainer suggestion of her solitary, hopeless state had ever come to Isabel. If Alice hadn't yet heard rumors of Don's "courting"—which seemed incredible—then she was inviting Isabel into the company of girls who despaired of marriage. But since Alice must have heard, must have seen them together at least in the movie theater, she seemed to hint that there was no hope, even with Don. Though Alice meant, no doubt, to be kind, she had wounded Isabel more strangely than anything in her life.

The procession of Ashton's old maids, and their progress, piled up in her mind while she tried to construct a polite refusal. She saw Miss Frances McKinney riding with Miss Julia Taylor in their new car down the Sunday afternoon streets, and heard a bystander snicker, "Well, I guess they're much happier now." She imagined herself, forced to find a woman friend out of unendurable solitude, going to the movies together, and playing rummy, and making tea in the afternoons and finally taking up some kind of social work to enlarge her world.

"Well," she said hesitantly, "maybe I can play some night. Don comes up to the house a lot, you know—and, oh, we play records and—" She broke off the stammering words; they must sound cruelly boastful. They were scornful of Alice's dependence on girl-friends for entertainment. She was guilty of that cheap, selfish air of girls toward their dates, which she deplored—flaunting a man, not as someone they loved, but as someone other women would like to take from them, as a decorative possession, like a tawdry jewel, not beautiful but rare enough to arouse envy. Conscious of the cheapness of her involuntary pride, she suffered momentarily and at the same time urged herself to justify it by admitting more strongly her affection for Don. From the conflict of the two, emerged the fear of admitting her love, because she might be hurt.

"I've seen you at the movies several times," said Alice pensively, "and Bea Traywick told me about that picnic you all had together. Don is such an attractive boy." She retreated falteringly from Isabel, as if each of them had understood too perfectly the impulse behind the other's words.

"I'll try to come some night," Isabel called after her, hastily and cheerily, hoping to repair the clumsy offense. "I'll phone you."

With a disappointed smile, Alice moved down the aisles of merchandise, and Isabel knew she had delicately bruised her good nature. And she was aware, also, of a growing, depressing suspicion—the reverse of her fear of admitting her love—that someday she might have to come to Alice and out of loneliness beg for the invitation to play rummy. Unless Don . . .

While she gazed down the cavern of the store, a tenderness, almost of passion, came in a wild rush that seemed to pour through her with stinging, yearning pain and flow out, leaving her empty and sad. Unless Don . . . if only Don . . . She remembered it now—just as it rushed through her at night when he wasn't with her, and when he walked down her steps going home from a quiet, pleasant evening, and sometimes while he looked at her, saying a harmless sentence, but with a combined twinkle and melancholy in his eyes—and remembered that she had tried to repress it, not daring its hidden threat, but remembering it had strengthened its roots in her. If only Don would . . .

The air was chilly and damp on the autumn day they rode through the little hill towns of north Mississippi toward Memphis. The slate-gray clouds, threatening a slow drizzle, didn't completely hide the sun, but writhed restlessly across its face, reducing the blaze to a white disc. On the shiny pavement at each intersecting farm road flared a bouquet of muddy wagon tracks. Isabel watched the country people working about their cottages, with lazily smoking chimneys, and their outbuildings, where the cattle clustered close as twilight came on: a woman slopping muddy hogs or milking a cow; a man unharnessing a team or hauling hay into the barn; a boy chopping wood, a girl pulling up collard greens. Through the brown woods, where soggy leaves paved the ground under almost bare trees, and over the frost-bitten meadows and weed clumps, the fallow slanting farmlands of dried corn and cotton stalks, the pale filtered light spread with complacent melancholy.

But Isabel felt not so much melancholy as sweet discontent. Outside the car window, the quiet landscape unreeling its panorama of the elemental challenge of nature—man's simple, long chores of provisioning for food, warmth and shelter through the winter—touched her pleasantly. It suggested a natural time for recapitulation of hoarded hopes and the prospects of fulfillment when the seasons had come round to another spring and renewal, rebirth. Yet under her relaxation, as she sat on the back seat beside Don, she was tense with longing to press herself close to him—even to touch him without the subterfuge of asking for a light to her cigarette. It wasn't that Bea, half turned in the front seat, or Tray, in his rear-view mirror, could see her, but that she was afraid Don would resent the intimacy and think it cheap.

The sun, setting red and early over the dark fields, brought the comfort of dusk in which she might touch him, unembarrassed. But every time she sensed his hand near hers, she withdrew. She couldn't make the slight move toward him. The intensity of her feeling, and the uncertainty of its goal neutralized her power for forthright action. She could do nothing toward Don without entangling herself in a paralyzing web of cautions.

Tray drove swiftly along the highway, now thicker with traffic since they were approaching the suburbs of Memphis. "What's this thing we're supposed to see tonight?" he called banteringly to Don.

"Supposed!" said Bea. "We're *going* to, if you just quit wanting to have a snort at every pigstand."

"It's *Carmen*," said Don. "Bizet's opera."

"Italian stuff, huh?" said Tray. "I won't know a thing that goes on."

"French," said Isabel. "Of course you'll understand most of it. You've seen it in the movies."

"And you used to march to the Toreador song in high school," added Bea.

"Oh, yeah! Tor-e-a-dor-a, don't spit on the floor-a!" he sang.

"It's a cinch we'll have you on the right side of the footlights," said Don.

"Say, Don." Tray turned his head slightly and assumed a mock confidential tone. "What you say we ditch the girls—let 'em go to the opera by themselves. Then we'll go out on a tear. I know a swell place."

"Now, Tray," said Bea ominously, though she was fully aware of his joke. "No cat houses while we're around."

"Why, Bea, what are you saying?"

Isabel's heart fluttered briefly. The kidding was all right between Tray and Bea—they were married; but Don wasn't. And though he made no answer to Tray's suggestion, Isabel suddenly found herself in that ridiculous dilemma of single women. What if Don wanted sex with her but, out of diffidence or respect, dared not ask? But that was too old-fashioned. That was the simpler dilemma of their mothers, when it was assumed that nice women were virgin until married, while men sought a lower class for their low pleasures. In these days, so many girls didn't wait, men were easy to fool about virginity, and it was easier to get a husband if you slept with him beforehand. And even if he didn't marry you, you'd had some fun, if you were careful. Who cared about virginity, anyway? That was prudish women's protection against the others, and now that they all were—ugh! She turned to the window to watch the almost hidden landscape.

Night had closed all around them and the car was now riding down the lighted, neon-splashed city streets. Tray wove about the unfamiliar blocks, finding his way toward the center of town, hilariously forgetting to watch the red traffic signals, and at length pulled up in front of the Peabody Hotel.

They registered and took the elevator. Tray joked about which room they'd take, and finally in the corridor assigned them: "Girls in 723, boys in 724!" with a joyous concession to morality. Meeting shortly afterward in 724 where Tray had ordered ice and soda, they had drinks before dinner. To Isabel, it was increasing happiness, freedom and escape from Ashton, but moving toward its sure ending—the return, which would throw her back into the familiar life which she must always adjust somewhat to the custom of the town.

During the performance of the opera, she sat rigidly beside Don in the double pleasure of experiencing the excitement of the theater and for the first time with him. Constantly, she tried to wipe out the image of Tray, patiently attentive on Don's other side, gravely kidding him and muttering from time to time, "I want a drink." After the final curtain, the four went dancing on the roof garden of the hotel.

Moving close with Don's guidance over the gleaming floor, with his arm around her, his legs brushing hers (but himself so far away, so untouched, so sufficient) she liked to believe that by the intimacy of this contact she bound him a little more firmly to her. But after each dance, the contact was sharply broken, the intimacy dissipated into mere friendliness and they returned to the table. Tray danced with her a few times, and once he whispered in her ear, "Happy?"

"Yes, Tray. You're a beautiful dancer."

He blushed and grinned. "I didn't mean that. I wasn't fishing for compliments."

Retreating slightly within his arm, she gazed at him in gentle dismay that she couldn't hide a secret. The simple music swept across the big room—a soft trumpet calling "More Than You Know"—and the couples revolved about each other in the subdued light. She lowered her eyes and nodded shyly.

He laughed and drew her again into the rhythm of the dance. "Good," he said gruffly; and she thought tears would burst into her eyes.

When the roof garden closed they took the elevator down to their floor. As she told the two men good night, and turned with Bea into their room, she knew that the height of her excitement was passed and the rest of the excursion would be anticlimax.

"Bea, do you suppose they might really go out—somewhere?" she asked with timid anxiety.

"Are you thinking about Tray's stupid joke in the car?" Bea was undressing and hanging her clothes in the closet. "Don't pay any attention to what he says."

"Oh, I wasn't worried," she hastened to say. "I just thought—if—"

"Are you jealous of Don?" asked Bea bluntly.

"Why should I be? We're not engaged." But her casual air didn't quite come off. If everyone else noticed her concern, surely during the night Don must have noticed it too.

Bea sat beside her on the bed. "You wish you were, though, don't you?" she asked gently.

"We're just friends," answered Isabel, ashamed she couldn't confide more easily in Bea. "We simply have a lot of interests in common." But how much of an obstacle were they? she wondered. Always now, through their hours of companionship, she longed for something more—something to annihilate their unpassionate interest in art or focus in both of them a joint meaning of art and life. "It's such fun coming up here with all of you," she said lightly to distract attention from herself. "Not having everybody in town ready to jump on you."

"Yes, it has been fun," replied Bea. She put her arm around Isabel's shoulders. "But don't get hurt in the fun, Isabel."

"Why do you say that so seriously?"

"Because I mean it. Don't get too interested in Don. I can see his good points now, where I couldn't years ago. And I like him. But you two see a lot of each other and . . . well, I just don't think Don's the marrying kind. You'll be disappointed."

"Oh, Bea," she chided, "how can you say such things? I'm not trying to marry him."

Lies—lies to protect the tender, exposed quick of love, to avoid the scorn of knowledge, to soothe the fear of defeat. She rose quickly from the bed, with Bea's arm trailing off at the movement, and began to put on her nightgown.

No more was said about Don, and when they were both in bed, Isabel lay wondering what strange state she was in. Perhaps all men, not only Don, had become not the marrying kind, because there was so little reason to marry. That was why they fled the small towns, where the women developed so little out of their teen age, and came to the cities where a man could find at least the adventure of many new women's bodies. They found readily the same excitement she had found tonight—the theater, the night club, the freedom from parochial criticism. For some such reasons Don must have gone to New York, and he would return at last unless she could supply the adventure lacking in his life.

A few times he seemed so close to a gesture of love that she imagined it was her own fault that he never touched her as if unable to resist putting out his hand, unable to deny his hunger the enjoyment of her flesh. But she couldn't expect of him the brash, experimental caresses of their youth, when no one thought anything of a hug and a kiss. And she really wanted more than just that. His seriousness appealed to her, fastened on her mind all the more since it apparently kept him from her. He would never make a frivolous move like a curious child; but when he did, if he ever did, take her in his arms, it would be with honesty and assurance.

As the chill days of autumn changed into winter, the first excitement of discovering her interest in Don, then her affection and finally her frank love for him, began to discolor in static friendship and frightening uncertainty. She might be no more able to win him over to loving her than in the past she had been in winning a man merely to marry her. Those earlier failures were no great disappointments, for she hadn't been touched deeply; but failure with Don promised a long ache of suffering and loneliness.

Puzzled and unhappy, she decided to investigate the lonely climate of the other women who had not yet married. There was no point in approaching Miss McKinney and Miss Julia, for they no longer had any hope and their lives were crystallized into one, like a monstrous double scarab. But she remembered Alice

Barnette's invitation and phoned to make an engagement with her and Anita. In them she could observe the compensations for the failure and deficiency of their lives, while they still had flickering confidence that some man moved through the world somewhere looking for the idea that was really one of them.

They met in Alice's house, where a card table was set up in the parlor, and after commenting on each other's clothes, they sat down to a game of hearts. Although Anita squealed in delight throughout the game and Alice laughed at her in tolerant amusement, Isabel found the atmosphere discouraging and forced. As she watched them warily while they studied their cards, she imagined they had already forfeited the qualities that would attract men; and with no men at hand, even the vestiges of those qualities would fade away and they would enter slowly and inevitably into the realm inhabited by the Miss Julias and Miss McKinneys of the world. Then, realizing that she was herself older than either of them, her mind fought back the idea that the same stamp was indelibly marked on her and she could see it no more than these two frivolous girls could see their own.

She was angry that they should seem so ridiculous over their game, their bowl of cracked pecans and their expected "refreshment course," while men seemed to fit so neatly into bachelorhood and remain so apparently happy. Groups of men in clubs, out hunting, on the street, anywhere talking and laughing together, seemed so much more logical and appropriate than groups of women. We always need men, she thought, to make us something in the world, to make us proud, beautiful and kind, to keep us fresh from the staleness of our hungers and the dryness of our female lives together. Then why were there so many women like Doris who had their men and destroyed them? Why were women, in their spiritual proddings and moral support, on which men used to depend, so ineffectual today? Why was the small town, which used to be the choicest of habitations, now the acme of dullness? It took only primer-grade answers for all: progress in man supplanted by progress in machines. Women had degraded social life to the point where men couldn't tolerate it—the rituals of death and marriage, silly groups like Madge's party, the banalities of the culture clubs, the gossipy coke parties—until now they inherited this dreary game of hearts where no one could really win.

At last, when Alice suggested that they have some tea, Isabel hoped she would be able to leave soon. Anita pushed back her chair to go to the kitchen and Isabel offered to help her.

"Oh, never mind," said Alice with a wave of dismissal. "Anita always makes the refreshments. It's our arrangement. She makes the food and I clean up the dishes."

"It's much nicer that way," chirped Anita going across the room. "We each have our little duties."

Isabel shuddered faintly. It was as if one were the husband and the other the wife, each with the expected functions and yet completely a mockery, for there was no real function for them. They unconsciously imitated their throttled desires, falling deeper and deeper, as the genuine desires decayed, into a substitution that would be their only recompense for having lived. The bands of their common isolation from the world of love were winding closer about them with a repulsive aura of invoked hermaphroditism which would have horrified each of them. She saw no escape for them from each other. She had never liked the company of women too well, and she vowed that she would never seek a close woman friend. If necessary, she would always be alone, a hermit, but with her own personality, which she wanted to sacrifice to a man, still her own and untainted. Her mind would have to be her mate; she would grow old with it alone.

But something rebelled against this sterility. She refused to rot away in solitude and longing when she might with definite action gain at least the formal structure that would shape and give reality to her desires. No matter what man, if he were good, she intended to satisfy and enlarge her life with him, as a husband, as a—yes, as a lover. In Ashton, all the men except Don were married. They had sought out a woman whose personality was unfamiliar, a mystery to them; or out of frustration they chose the unadventurous girl next door; or they went away from the still, complacent town and would never return. She, too, could go away from Ashton to a city where there would be many men. In New Orleans—crowded with strangers who didn't care what you did—she could live, but not quite on the lowest animal level, as a woman with a man. Though she probably couldn't achieve the richness of fullness of her real desires, at least she could, without disgrace, escape the enforced spiritual onanism of her life in Ashton. Bound to no such reticences as at present, her physical urges, if nothing else, would in some degree be satisfied. She could openly seek and offer herself, not sordidly, transiently, in parked cars or hotel rooms, but as a lover to a lover. Even this, she realized, would be shadowed always by the cynical acceptance of eventual separation.

And yet, this compromise simply for sex, aside from corroding her self-respect, reduced her to a status comparable with the mockery of the pairs of old maids. Her brash questing, her initiative, her emphasis on sex, would be actually masculine and would usurp man's prerogative. It would destroy her purpose—to be possessed by a man—and would end by endowing her with a special kind of old-maidishness. By imitation she would be the man seeking adventure, like Don in New York. But if there were to be no Don for her, no man to offer anything similar, she might as well make the best of the pattern the world had created. But there was still time, still a chance, still hope. Wait—despairingly, maddeningly—wait. Still hope.

5

The last light behind the roof of clouds had dwindled away and against the dull, massive heaving lobes the features of the landscape were silhouetted indistinctly. Trees and hills were black, the road a shining streak of gray, and gray points of mist spread on the windshield of Tray's car.

On the left meandered the wide, willow-bordered creek between the wooded hills and pasture land at the outskirts of Ashton. On the right stood a few Negro shacks, the shops of a blacksmith and a dealer in wagons and feed. Then, on the flatter bottom land near the river, the tiny points of red and green lights on the Three Points Inn shone with frenzied desolation. Tray pulled in on the thinly graveled expanse before the garish front and parked. Almost before he had pressed the horn, Mac came trotting out the door to take the order.

"Two cokes and two setups," said Tray.

Mumbling the order to himself, Mac ran to the shack.

"On your toes, Don!" said Tray, fussing with his pack of cigarettes. "Get the bottle."

"In the usual place?" Don asked, as he punched the button on the glove compartment. He drew out a bottle of whiskey.

"Do you miss New York much, Don?" Now that he had Don in the privacy of the car, Tray couldn't think how to approach the subject on his mind. He took the bottle and, pulling out the cork, nursed it in his lap.

"A little," Don answered. "I miss all the things like music and shows. But the people, deep down, aren't any different from people down here. They just seem so on the surface."

"Everybody thought you'd be a lot different when you got back."

"Maybe I seem different to some of them. But that's just a sort of veneer, again—like clothes you put on."

"I think you're different from when you got back," said Tray. "You're not moody and strange like you used to be. Maybe it's Isabel's influence."

"Good God, you sound like all the old ladies around town. I'm just the same as ever. People don't change much inside. Motives—excuses change. Maybe their understanding deepens or dries up."

Mac arrived with glasses, ice and cokes on a small waiter which he attached to the window of the car, and then returned to the Inn.

"We're not much different now from a few years ago," Tray said, as he mixed the drinks. "That's certain. I'm married and so's Jim. But here we are, still parking in cars, ordering setups, getting drunk together. Why is all our life that's fun spent in cars?"

"That was you and Jim," said Don. "It never included me when you were around."

Tray took a long drink and said, "Brrr!" He stirred restlessly in his seat. "Hell—it was Jim, actually," he faltered. "Just like his attitude on our hunting trip."

"Oh, I understand all that, Tray. It's not important now."

"Well, I wish you'd explain it to me."

"I can't explain what it is now," said Don thoughtfully. "Not what you really want to know about Jim. I thought I knew when I first came back, but now . . ."

"What did you think it was?"

Don swirled the liquid in his glass. "I was wrong."

Tray could feel the alcohol tingling through his body. He finished his drink nervously and quickly began mixing another. Raising it to his mouth, he emptied half of it. Then he turned seriously to Don. "It doesn't matter to me, Don, what you say. I'm not bright in some ways, but I'm not a fool either. I would've been glad to've had you along lots of those times me and Jim were out together. Somehow I—I couldn't figure out what we could say to each other. I was embarrassed, I guess, because I thought you were so much smarter. Anyway, you and Jim always had double dates and then it was me and Jim, and I never heard of triple-dating, did you?"

"Kind of crowded as a regular thing, I imagine," said Don with a chuckle.

Tray laughed too, and reaching over, he pressed Don's thigh. "It's a hell of a thing," he said, "when one person likes another. It makes one or both of them feel guilty. I guess that's why they invented marriage—to absorb the guilt."

Don held out his glass. "How about another?" he asked. "You're getting way ahead of me."

While he poured the drink, Tray said, "It's not you, Don—not right now. It started a long time ago with Jim. It's something in him, or Doris, or both of them. It's something that's wrong and I want to know what it is. Because I like Jim, and I don't like the way I see him. I was hoping maybe you could help some way." How easy it was to say it all now, suddenly, after a little talking, a couple of drinks, a curling back of the old leaves that covered their past and letting an older light filter over it. He felt again that wild urge to protect, not so much Jim, for whom he had a different affection, but Don, who was practically a stranger in spite of the years they had known each other.

"There's no way I can help, Tray. I couldn't mess into a married couple's affairs. From all I can see, they may be happy. Except sometimes Jim . . ." He broke off and took a drink. "I hope he's happy."

"I know he's not," said Tray almost angrily. "He's not. And I don't know what to do."

"How can you tell he's not?"

"The night after Madge's party, he called me on the phone. About twelve o'clock, roaring drunk. 'Hello, you ol' bastard,' he said. I asked him what the hell he was doing and where he was. 'In a whorehouse,' he yelled. And then I could hear him crying. And I kept asking him where he was and said I was coming to get him, and he kept on crying and put up the receiver. Put it up slow, like he didn't want to. I could hear it. But he wasn't in any whorehouse."

"Well, where was he?" asked Don.

"He was in his office," Tray answered. "All day and night Sunday."

After a silence, in which Don seemed to meditate on this information, he spoke casually. "I wonder why."

"Can't you find out, Don? You're closer to him than anybody else, except Doris. If we just knew, if he'd just tell us, we might be able to do something for him. You're the only one I could depend on and I tried to ask you when you first came back home. But you didn't like me butting in. Well—O.K. But now Jim's getting worse. Anybody can see it. It's—"

"No, I won't do it," Don interrupted coldly.

"But when someone—when—How can you say no, Don? How can you let him go on this way?"

"It's not my affair. I've got no right to do anything about it."

"You mean you don't care what happens to him? He doesn't mean anything to you anymore?"

"I don't mean anything to him, is more to the point." Don's voice was growing tense. He rubbed the glass on his knee and stared fixedly out of the car.

"Well, for Christ's sake, does friendship have to be paid back and forth equally, like a loan and a debt?"

Instead of answering, Don drank the remainder of his drink. Tray watched him closely, hopefully, but no sign of relenting showed on his face. A stubborn resistance to his helplessness and failure rose steadily inside him. He was thinking hard, pressing the butt of his palm on the steering wheel. Then he spoke, urgently beneath the softness and the sadness of his tones, and tenderly hopeful.

"How can you be friends like you both were for all those years and then just cut it off dead? You don't really want it that way, I know. Do you, Don? . . . You still like Jim, don't you?"

Don whirled toward him, dropping the empty glass to the floor, bracing his hands on the dashboard and the seat back, and glared across the short dim space between them. His words burst out in loud anger. "God damn it, do you want me to tell you everything?" Then, at the sound of his strident voice, he relaxed from his strained position, slowly dropping his arms, and leaned back in the seat once more. Through the dark, Tray could watch the frightened surprise wavering over his face until it settled in a mask of guilt. There was a long silence. At length he threw his glass through the lowered window. It splintered and tinkled on the rough gravel.

"I guess you don't have to now, Don," said Tray softly and wonderingly.

Neither of them moved for some time. Their faint breath stirred slight sounds in the misty night.

So that was the story, that was what explained Don's reluctance to help Jim. Well, under the circumstances, he wouldn't be much help anyway. In the first surprise of realization, Tray was a little dumbfounded, a little inclined to assume such things didn't happen here in Ashton, to friends. Don had been going around with Isabel; people expected them to marry soon. No one would ever think, unless Isabel . . . Did Isabel understand what she was involved in? Then, after a moment's reflection, he saw that his only surprise was one of acknowledgement. He had really known all the time, but didn't want to admit it. So why bother now? There are worse things less frowned upon. People were too silly about their feelings. After all, they'd glorify their affection for dogs and the dog's devotion to them, but any such emotion between two men they would degrade in every way. And deny, and wipe out.

"I oughtn't to have asked, Don," he murmured. "Maybe I am a fool. Anyhow, I don't take back anything . . . anything I just said to you. I mean that." When Don didn't move, Tray dropped an arm over his shoulders and shook him gently several times. "Forget it, Don," he said. "I will too. Let's have a drink."

He opened the bottle and looked for his glass. "My glass seems to have got broke," he remarked lightly.

"Mine's got dirty on the floor," Don answered stiffly.

"Oh, well." Tray waved the bottle under Don's nose. "There's still some chaser."

Don smiled bashfully, took the bottle and drank. Exchanging it for the chaser, he gurgled down a couple of swallows.

"We better get back home, hadn't we?" Don asked.

"Sure had. Bea will snatch me baldheaded."

At the sound of the horn, Mac loped out to the car. "Another round?" he asked.

"Nope," answered Tray. "Got to be moving on. Better clean up that broken glass where my drink fell off the waiter." He pointed toward the slivers on the gravel.

"You mean it fell all the way over there?"

"Well, to tell the truth, Mac," said Tray, sonorously playful, "Don threw it at me, but I ducked." He grinned at Don, as he pressed the starter. "I guess we're all fixed up now, aren't we?"

6

Driving the new Lincoln across the side streets to pick up Bea Traywick, Doris hummed with satisfaction. How smart she was with her soft fur scarf nestling luxuriously around her shoulders and her cocoa-brown tailored suit harmonizing with the paint on the car!

Two little Negro boys on the sidewalk stopped in their tracks to goggle and slapped their thighs in awe. Of course, everyone stopped to admire her car. It was the insignia of her station in life and, just as she told James, it made the right impression. Men on the street told each other, "That Furlow boy sure is getting along. Ever see such a car?" "Depression can't be hitting him very hard." "Yep, he must be one good lawyer—better'n his pa." She was certain that people readily acknowledged the young Furlows as the most prominent couple in town. It might be years, naturally, before anyone realized her part in securing them such a position; but it would be immodest for her to mention it. Now they wouldn't decline into poor aristocracy. When a man looked prosperous, people wanted to give him business. Eventually, gradually, her share of credit for achieving their success would be granted. "If he hadn't had a wife like her," people would say, "he'd never have gone as far as he has. Just goes to show what the right wife can do for a man."

Pulling up before Bea's house, she blew the horn. It sounded rich and sullen in the November afternoon. The sky was heavy with cold, sluggish clouds massed so thickly that no sun broke through. In the gray and fading light, the trees, some bare and others tattered with clinging brown leaves, stood sadly around the shadowy houses.

There was Bea coming out now, wearing a plain black dress and a tweed coat with a flat fur collar. Clutching the coat together, she walked quickly toward the car. Something casual and unpremeditated about Bea's clothes made Doris wonder if she ever considered their effect on other women. Surely no woman

145

who hoped to impress her friends would wear such an outfit as she had on. But now that Bea had a husband, she probably didn't bother any longer about her appearance. On the other hand, Bea must be very confident that no one would try to take Tray away from her. In fact, Bea's solid assurance about everything made Doris, not without a touch of envy, almost hate her. She seemed to suffer none of the indecisions, the longings, the doubts that Doris had; above all, she shared none of the enthusiasms. She didn't say much about the new car, never suggested that they use it together, and today even hesitated at the invitation to go to the Seven Arts Club in it. It was obviously jealousy, for Bea wouldn't naturally act that way. Doris didn't intend to let her pretend she was just as happy without a new car, and spoil her own pleasure in it. She meant to force her to ride in it, to admire it; in fact, to be obligated to it as if it were a personal friend.

Bea opened the car door and got in. "We're going to be late, I'm afraid," she said.

"Oh, those women are always late," scoffed Doris. "We won't miss anything."

The car moved away in a sumptuous purring of machinery. It rushed swiftly along the narrow streets and passed any vehicle that loomed ahead of them, as if it were offensive to the motor.

"You're looking well, Doris. Aren't you putting on a little weight?" asked Bea.

A slight flush rose to Doris's face, and she craned her neck at the rear-view mirror. "Why, not that I know of. Do I look stout, Bea?" she smiled wryly, while biting her lip delicately.

"Not really, I suppose. It's these low seats, I guess."

"That's a darling dress you have on, Bea," said Doris.

She had a momentary surge of rebellion at the thought of showing signs of pregnancy. When it became too noticeable, she would hide in the house, as all good women used to, and never let anyone see her ridiculous figure, never let people joke behind her back, never let anyone know there was to be a child until after it was born. She couldn't stay in Ashton much longer. She'd go visit her mother. James was actually forcing her out of their own home. Worst of all, in a few more months she wouldn't be able to drive her car. It wasn't right that a baby should take so long, should ruin so many months of her life and deprive her of her pleasures.

"Doris!" cried Bea in alarm.

They crashed joltingly over two steep scoops in the roadway where the gravel street crossed a paved one. The springs pounded together and bumped the chassis, a sharp crack as of breaking glass sounded, and the whole automobile see-sawed wildly a few times. Bea put a hand to the back of her neck and said, "Goodness, you'll wreck the car in no time at that rate! Didn't you see it?"

Doris was smiling blandly. "Why no," she answered. "I guess I'm not a very good driver. It didn't hurt anything."

But I wish to God it had, she thought; I wish to God it would be as easy as that to kill the damn thing. Maybe it will; maybe it will later, if not this time. There's always another time. And there are other things too—what was it that girl in Oakville took? Turpentine, wasn't it? But she was deathly sick and everyone knew what had happened. I couldn't risk that on account of James. But if he thought there was a miscarriage—if he thought I was really right when I said I couldn't have a baby—wouldn't he feel sorry for me then and treat me better? There's something besides turpentine—quinine, that's it. But it doesn't always work. And could she trust a man like James to have any sympathy for a wife who couldn't bear children? She couldn't expect him to be tender or to understand her feelings or what she wanted out of life.

In front of Mrs. Everett's home, she pulled up behind the line of cars and parked. With Bea, she walked to the broad front door where the doctor's wife let them in. "You're just in time," said Mrs. Everett. "We're about to begin."

In the living room, five short semicircles of chairs were arranged facing a table where the president of the Seven Arts Club waited for the ladies to be seated. The fall hats bobbed and shook as they chatted and shuffled among the chairs. At last they came to order facing the president's table and the background of a mantelpiece banked with autumn leaves. The syrupy, elocutionary voice rose and fell as the president announced that she would open the meeting with a prayer which one of their members had written as a poem.

"Dear Lord," *she read*, "as we are gathered here,
We wish that you our humble prayer would hear.
Grant that all who live according to your word
Shouldst thereby reap their just awards."

Doris gazed critically at the new hat that Madge Dalton was wearing. She was unable to examine it carefully on their arrival, since Madge had turned away almost at once after speaking to her. No doubt she was concerned over Doris's relation to her, now that the new car had been delivered.

The president sang on at the prayer:

"And when we have done our daily work
Let us not our holy duties to Thee shirk.
And help us to cultivate this holy ground
That is our bodies to enrich with artistic thought."

And help us in our Seven Arts Club
To take our parts without a rub. Amen."

When she finished, the members were uncertain whether to applaud or maintain reverent silence. Finally, from the front row, Mrs. Everett said, "Oh, that was lovely! But you didn't tell us who wrote it." And a soft chorus of voices sprang up: "Yes, tell us who wrote it. Tell us."

The president shook her head with a sad smile. "No," she said, "I can't. I was asked by the lady who contributed it"—she scanned the room with a teasing glance—"not to reveal her name." A rustle of disappointed sighs fluttered up. "But I do think that we have a real talent there."

Hearing Madge whisper to her neighbor, "I bet she wrote it herself," Doris grunted inside, "Jealous cat! You couldn't do it." The neighbor whispered back, "She did."

"And," continued the president with a rising inflection, "I am sure we have other talents hidden in our little group of art lovers. So I would like to suggest that each of us write a little poem for next meeting. We can all choose the same subject, something like 'Desire' or 'Passion' or 'Nature,' so that no one will lack inspiration. That way, too, we'll have a basis for comparison of the poems."

A woman raised her hand. "I would like to put that in the form of a motion, Madame President."

"Do I hear a second?" asked the president.

"I think we're out of order, Madame President," said the secretary of the club. The president looked indignantly at her. "We haven't yet had the roll call," the secretary explained.

"Oh." The president shuffled some papers on the table. "Then let us have the roll call, Madame Secretary, and proceed to the business on our agenda and then to the program. As you all know, in accordance with our custom of answering not 'Present' but by phrases, the response for today is 'Beautiful Words.' I do hope you have all thought up some beautiful words for us."

The secretary then called the names of the members and they answered in turn: "Moonlight." "Sunset." "Twilight." "Roses." "Children." "God." "Nature." And when she called, "Mrs. James Furlow," Doris said demurely, "Mother love," and did not listen any more.

But the words brought her sharply back to the baby. She certainly wasn't projecting her own feelings toward that minute bit of life, but rather her reciprocated feelings for her mother, who should be beside her now to counsel and console her. Her mother, who in her indirect way had taught her, with all the warmth of maternal love, her responsibility to the society she represented, to the man she was expected to marry, to the parents who would make it possible for her to find in a husband a proxy for their support, and to her own inherited, cherished and precious beauty—her mother would know how to solve her confusion and soothe her growing distress. She would know how to deal with James, who with his bestiality wrecked everything that she and decent people stood for. Those faraway, warm afternoons, lying on the bed beside her mother, talking in whispers as balmy as the summer breezes—"Women are the sacred vessels of the Lord's will and men are the vandals who wish to destroy it. The beast in men is like the beast in the Apocalypse, insensitive and slobbering over the ruin of nobility and purity. You are too lovely, Doris, ever to be despoiled."—gone, now; irretrievable. But when she grew older, her mother's words waned more distant and melancholy, more suspicious and cryptic, while young men called at the house, and she was invited to dances; until finally, in the empty lag before James met her, she overheard her parents arguing one night: "But I'd be so lonely," her mother moaned, "if she were to marry. I don't care if young men don't come around." "Yes, you will be lonely," her father retorted, "but who will support her when we're both dead, and she is completely alone? I think she has a right—" "But no man has a right," cried her mother. "No man is good or gentle enough to have the right. No man—" Her father almost shouted a trembling expletive. "Sometimes I wonder what made you this way," he said more quietly. "How can it happen and I, a doctor, not know?" And then, getting up from her sleepless bed and closing the door on the terrifying words, she thought of the beast in man, the beast in her father, the beast that would always be threatening her beauty. And now had corrupted her so that only her mother could save her.

But she was ashamed to tell her mother all the truth; she would never find the strength, the candid words, the mood in which to speak to her as she had done in childhood, stretched in their underclothes on the cool afternoon bed, whispering so that the empty house wouldn't hear their confidences. Her mother would hate James, of course, more than she did before the marriage, more than Doris did at the moment. Doris couldn't bear to make her more unhappy.

A crash of piano notes aroused her to the progressing program of the Seven Arts Club. She recalled vaguely the last soaring words of Madame President: ". . . will favor us with a rendition of a classical song—'I Love Life.'" Then the strident voice of the soprano from the Methodist Church choir battled vigorously against the chords played by the pianist.

How she hated Jim, Doris mused comfortably, hated him for his caution, his niggardliness, his lust, his cruelty, his stubbornness, his friends, his silence. ". . . and I want to live!" tremoloed the singer, while the piano jangled and boomed.

After the song ended with three blasts of sound, the sudden silence and then the enthusiastic applause startled her. She beat her hands together and looked appreciatively toward Bea who smirked back. The president shuffled her papers and announced that Mrs. McDougall would now read a paper entitled "Maud Muller in Mississippi." Mrs. McDougall rose from her chair, and with a furtive pressure of one hand against her stomach, began to read from trembling sheets, "John Greenleaf Whittier had never been in Mississippi when he wrote . . ."

7

When the bell rang, Isabel frowned and closed the album of records. "Now who in the world?" she muttered fretfully.

"Who do you think?" asked Don.

"Oh . . ." The bell rang again, and she got up from the floor impatiently. "You put them on, Don."

Brushing down her skirt, she went into the hall and opened the door. "Hello, Jim," she said, and added the automatic phrase she didn't really mean. "Come in."

He smiled timidly. "Are you busy tonight, Isabel?"

"Don's here," she said. "We're playing records. That's about all."

He hesitated, as if he were conscious that he had no right to intrude, and stammered an apology.

"Don't you want to come in?" Isabel asked, not too warmly. "I mustn't keep the door open. These fireplaces, you know."

Jim came inside nervously. "Thanks, Isabel," he said as she closed the door. "I just felt like—seeing people. I thought maybe—listening to some music might help."

"Well—" she answered irresolutely, "if your and Don's tastes are still the same . . ."

"I guess I oughtn't to stay if Don's here," he suggested meekly. Tediously he removed his coat and hung it on the hall rack. "But I won't stay long."

No one but Jim would ever come at this hour of the night without phoning; no one but Jim ever did. Still something in his manner touched her. He sounded almost like a pleading boy, uncertain of his authority and fearful of refusal. But now that he was in the full light of the hall rather than the shadowed porch, he appeared more like a dejected man carrying the failure of his business on his conscience. The rims of his eyes were bloodshot, probably from lack of sleep, for he wasn't drunk as she had at first suspected. He seemed to have grown old—the change that haggardness works in the young—but it could have been merely the need of a shave. His hair was disarranged, perhaps from plowing his fingers through it. He glanced self-consciously in the mirror and furtively adjusted his necktie.

"Do you mind?" he asked humbly.

"Don't be silly, Jim," she said contritely. "We're old friends. Come on in to the fire."

Inside the living room he grinned sheepishly at Don, who was just closing the phonograph, and waved a hand. "It's nice to see you here, Don." Crossing the room, with almost pointed disregard of the sofa, he sat in a wide green chair. "Don't mind me," he said, as the music began to play. "I'll just sit a while and smoke."

Isabel smiled tolerantly and sympathetically back at Don's questioning stare. Don poked at the fire, sending a shower of sparks up the chimney, and joined her on the sofa. Occasionally she wondered if they should make some effort at conversation with Jim. It might have been only chance that Jim appeared so often at the door when Don was with her; for though he didn't come every time, just the same, he never rang when Don wasn't there.

Jim lay back in his chair with his eyes closed, as if trying to erase himself from the room, and with a drawn smile on his lips, as if he were secretly enjoying the music and their infrequent talk. Sometimes he stirred, opening his eyes, and tapped ashes into the tray beside him, but most of the time the ash fell on the carpet. Smoke floated slowly from his mouth. It was even worse than if he were talking to them.

Isabel let the phonograph switch off mechanically. "See what Don brought me?" she said, holding up a book to Jim. "Some new poems . . . by Robert Fitzgerald."

Jim blinked and straightened in his chair.

"Of course, I don't ever read much poetry," she went on; "but you used to, didn't you, Jim?"

"Don read it to me most of the time, I guess," he said glumly.

"I'll see that you read more, Isabel," threatened Don as he took the book from her. Then he told her that poetry was the only art that hadn't yet degenerated in the world. Because it was so personal, it resisted the influence of advertising and money. "Which is easy," he added, "because it never makes any money these days. But that won't last long. Then poetry, too, will get flabby. They'll find some way to make it help man to fool himself. Listen to this, though."

While he read one of the poems, Jim seemed to grow taut. A shoulder twitched, and he stretched out his arm. As if hearing a far-off voice that puzzled and fascinated him, he watched them wistfully.

When Don finished, Isabel stood up. "How about some cake and coffee?" she asked. "It won't take long."

Don agreed enthusiastically, but Jim mumbled that she shouldn't bother for him. "I better go," he said dejectedly.

"No, you've got to stay for the coffee," she commanded.

Closing the door behind her, she wondered why she always said the polite thing even when she didn't want to. But then, she did feel sorry for Jim. Though he wasn't lying about his loneliness, she wished he wouldn't bring it to her house, spreading it about in his silence, his unhappy eyes, his uneasiness, until it invaded her and spoiled her evening with Don. Already that had happened; and as she prepared the coffee in the kitchen, she felt the loneliness of her life emphasized again in her home.

All of the long years, the many dates, the few men she had been close to, had withdrawn and left no human warmth in which to lose herself. Only the vicarious warmth of books and music, memories and travel was left to take the place of a man's companionship and understanding and love. She insisted again and again that these interests were more enduring than most marriages and that few of the men she had known would have shared them with her; but all the time she knew that it was rationalization. She wanted a husband, although the companionship were lacking, or the understanding, or—yes, or even the love. She felt an unaccountable shame never to have had a man propose to her, to have let the possibilities slip away from her to other girls, and she couldn't understand why it happened that way. It was dreary to contemplate the future, now feeling the loneliness that Jim evoked; it was desperate to try to plan, unless she embraced that last plan of flight into the arms of some transient love in a distant city. Either that, or . . .

She roused herself from staring at the spouting coffee under the glass dome of the percolator, consciously, from fear of considering what Don might mean or do to her life, how his actions might influence her decision. Taking a fruitcake from a tin box she sliced off wedges onto a plate. On a tray, she spread a cloth and arranged the silver coffeepot, cups, plates, sugar and spoons. Then she pushed open the swinging kitchen door and, guilty at her curiosity, listened for voices. Perhaps they were talking too low for her to hear; perhaps they were silent.

With a gesture of resignation, she brushed her hand across the hair at her temple. When the coffee was made and poured into the pot, she carried the tray into the living room. The phonograph was playing again, as if their silence had been intolerable. Don and Jim seemed hardly to have moved.

"Now, it didn't take long, did it?" she asked cheerfully, as she filled the cups.

Don handed one to Jim, who sat more stiffly in his chair. Then he returned to the sofa beside Isabel. "The sugar and cream," she reminded him.

"Oh, let him come get it, if he wants any," said Don.

"Never mind," said Jim quietly. "I don't want any." He broke off pieces of cake on the plate under his cup and ate thoughtfully.

"Are you tired of the music, Jim?" Isabel inquired. "We can turn it off."

"Why . . ." he hesitated. "If you turn it off, I'll have to talk. Or go home." He grinned understandingly.

And when he had finished his coffee and cake, Jim said he must leave. Isabel urged more on him, but he refused and moved unwillingly toward the door. As she rose to accompany him, Jim held out his hand to Don as if they had met for the first time, and said, "Good night, Don. Be seeing you."

There was something impregnable about Don's nature, Isabel thought, turning slowly away from the front door and listening to Jim's car grind into gear and drive off. Even to an old friend like Jim, he was now distant and enclosed in a shell. He didn't ask completion of his life from anyone outside himself; it was strange, and it made her angry. She must know, if she herself were ever to be at peace for many years, what had shaped him in that way; for she must begin to understand the seeds of her own failure and learn to be reconciled.

"Jim isn't very happy, is he?" she remarked when she returned to the living room.

"No, he isn't," Don agreed.

"You don't do much to cheer him up."

"No, I don't."

She stopped the phonograph. She closed the lid and leaned back against the machine. "I'm not either," she said apprehensively. "Not really."

He sat relaxed and meditative, and she knew that this was the moment when she ought to be there on the sofa beside him; but she couldn't move toward him. Something told her she must stay there, at the opposite wall, tracing his features and movements with her eyes, and come to know him through words, those inadequate sounds that tried to bind mankind in understanding, rather than know him ultimately through action. "Are you—happy?" she asked.

He stiffened and looked defiantly at her. Her fingers gripped the ledge at her back. She shouldn't have been so inquisitive.

"No," he said, and lowered his eyes.

In the silence, Isabel sought new words, a new topic, a joke. What had she done, innocently and yet desperately out of her own need, that touched this guarded spot in Don? She stood motionless, thinking that tears would rise up and overflow her eyes. Gradually Don lifted his head and looked almost hypnotically toward the chair where Jim had sat. After a moment he rose to his feet. A quick heat emptied and twisted Isabel's senses. Don walked to the green chair, picked up the plate and saucer beside it and came back. He set the dishes on the tray and, turning to Isabel, pulled out a pack of cigarettes.

"Want to smoke?" he asked.

Now she could move. Her limbs tightened and she was moving awkwardly toward him. She took the cigarette and sank down in the corner of the sofa. He lighted hers and his own.

"I don't know what I'd like to do, Isabel," he was saying. "We all want some place to land, some one single center that's everything we want. But what, and where?" He sat down and leaned his elbows on his knees. The ashes from his cigarette fell on the plates.

"You don't want to stay in Ashton, do you?" asked Isabel gently.

"I guess not, really. I'd like to mean something here, but I'm afraid I don't. I never will. The town wouldn't let me. I'll have to get out sooner or later."

"Oh, nonsense, Don. You don't know what you're talking about."

He laughed a dry, mirthless sound. "And neither do you." After a moment he continued. "I've got to look out just for my own self. I've got to be my own little world, somehow, and try to make it work without contact with Ashton or anything like it. That's why I ought to sink away in a big city. Little personal worlds are no good in this big world."

"If you make them fit, they are," said Isabel. She drew up her legs onto the cushion and, tucking her heels under her, stretched a hand along the back of the sofa and picked at the fibers.

"But I don't think I fit. I'm sure I don't."

"I can't see why you feel that way. You have so much to give to Ashton, and working on the *Herald* you can do it."

"It's not what you have to give," he said; "it's what people are willing to take. I don't belong here."

"Would you like to belong?"

"Maybe." He dropped his cigarette into a cup where it sizzed in the cold coffee. "Yes, I think I would." He leaned back on the sofa, his hands folded in his lap and turned his face to her. "Big cities are excuses for people like me. I don't like them. I like . . . I like . . ."

His eyes filmed with incoherence, puzzlement and then tenderness. He shifted them gradually away from her. When she spoke, Isabel was rather surprised at what she said, since it had no relation to their conversation. Perhaps because she was so intently studying his features while he stared at the green chair, her own mind wandered off into private suggestions. (Or perhaps the minute acts of others announced to us the truth that they always concealed and we always ignored.)

"We all have memories we like to keep," she said.

Their voices had grown soft. Isabel bent over the coffee table and put out her cigarette. As she straightened, Don's head rolled again toward her and she paused briefly when she saw the expression of gentle humor in his eyes and the faint smile on his lips. Then she leaned further back, with her hand following again along the molding, and her fingers touched his hair. She brushed across the waves of it and spread her fingers through it, and Don looked at her, still smiling as if he knew her thoughts, and she glanced away.

Her fingers burned, her arms quivered. She must take away her hand. Her throat was pounding. She felt all her strength and will clattering carelessly away like noisy children running out of a school building. But she wasn't ashamed for having shown her feelings, and when she looked again at him, still smiling, she saw his hand hovering over her free arm. It closed around her wrist and pulled her toward him. Her face, questioning, urging, hung before his, and her arm slid between the sofa and his shoulders and pressed tightly around him. Then the smile on his lips sank away. His chin lifted slightly, and their mouths touched tentatively, then firmly.

For some time they remained with her head on his shoulder. They did not talk. He held her hand and she brushed her forehead against the light beard on his cheeks. Then he released her and got up.

"I think I'd better go, Isabel," he said wearily.

"Oh, Don. It's early yet." A cry of despair wailed inside her. Again it was to be failure; again she wouldn't quite be loved.

"Well, mother's home alone tonight," he said. "Aunt Marny's gone to the movies." He was edging to the door, not looking at her. "I'll call you tomorrow."

And he was gone. Although he promised, even a second time going down the steps, she felt sure he was gone from her inner life forever. To him it had meant nothing—as casual as walking out of the drugstore after a soda and saying, "Charge it." She hadn't penetrated that opaque shell that enclosed his personal world, but had deluded herself into thinking they were on the verge of understanding.

Never again could she put her hand on him without the guilty consciousness that he was thinking she wanted to be kissed. Southern gallantry! She closed her eyes for a moment. Then slowly she made the circuit of the living room and put out the lights.

8

To travelers passing through on the afternoon train the town of Ashton must have seemed very inactive—so dead that they would lean toward each other with frowns and say, "Wouldn't you hate to live here?" The day was overcast and cold, and few people walked along the streets. There was little business around the stores since the holiday season was past. Along the three blocks of the main street which paralleled the railroad, the buildings rose like ragged, soggy lichens on a seam of wood bark. The meeting and passing of two automobiles emphasized the loneliness that hung over the community.

In the living room of Doris's house on Mulberry Street, Bea flipped the pages of a fashion magazine, while Doris studied another. She hadn't wanted to come here to dinner, but as Doris put it over the phone, they were both golf widows—or rather, hunting widows—with their husbands gone to the Delta, and they might as well keep each other company. Now that the meal was over, Doris seemed at a loss about entertaining her. For some time they had been exchanging comments on the new styles, showing each other the pictures of dresses they admired.

Doris yawned behind the magazine. "Let's go lie down a while, Bea," she said, tossing the magazine away. "I always feel drowsy after eating."

No wonder, thought Bea, with the house so overheated. "Sure, if you like."

"Come on into my bedroom."

There was something oppressively schoolgirlish about the ruffled, pinkish room, something never even touched, much less violated, by a man. How strange that a woman like Doris should be bearing a child.

"You've decorated it so beautifully," exclaimed Bea politely. "You know, I haven't been in here since you and Jim were first married. Remember that tea you had after the honeymoon?"

"Is it that long?" asked Doris. "I haven't entertained in ages, I know. After all, with a house like this— But when the baby is born, I'm going to start having lots of parties."

"Does Jim like the room this way?" asked Bea. "I'd think . . ."

"James sleeps in the front room," Doris replied casually. "I fixed it up for him like a man's room."

"Well," Bea remarked, rather ineptly, "it is more comfortable this way, I guess."

"Yes, James likes it better. He snores anyway, so I don't mind. And it's just as well, now . . ." Doris studied her stomach while she drew off her blouse and dropped it on the foot of the bed.

Bea was surprised that Doris, in her condition, would be immodest enough to take off her clothes before a friend. She refused to appear in public and hardly ever went outside the house. Having spread her dress on a chair, Bea moved toward the bed. They both sank on the mattress and stretched beside each other.

"I think this is such fun," said Doris with a sigh. "It's like Mother and I used to do back in Oakville. . . . Why don't you come over and see me more often these days, Bea? Never going out, I get lonesome. I can't even drive the car now, damn it."

"But you could if you wanted to, couldn't you?"

"Yes, I suppose so. But I wouldn't want to take a chance of having to get out downtown."

"Why, that's silly, Doris."

"Oh no," she said seriously. "You just don't know all the nasty things men say about you—when you're like this."

"But don't you go down to Dr. Everett's office for examinations?"

"Certainly not. He comes up here. I told him he'd have to. Oh, it's awful, Bea. It's awful. Don't ever have a baby." She sounded like a child warning another of something her mother would punish.

"But don't you want one?" asked Bea.

"Why, yes, of course," Doris said curtly. "It brings us all so much closer together. Mr. and Mrs. Furlow, you know. They were sort of on the outside until now. But with a grandchild they feel closer to us."

"It must bring you closer to Jim, too," said Bea.

"Yes."

The little conceited bitch, thought Bea; selfish, cold bitch. How could all of them have been taken in by her beauty and her protested delicate sensitiveness? How could she think that they would believe her contradictory words and actions? It must be because she knew that her only point of relation to anyone in Ashton was Jim, and Jim was a helpless, acquiescent confirmation of her position.

"I wish I could have a baby," said Bea. "We can't ever have one."

"Oh, Bea, you're lucky." Doris put her hand on Bea's arm and patted it.

"I don't know why."

"Look how ugly I am. It may spoil my figure for life. And I'll always be slaving for the child now. The whole thing is repulsive. . . . I hate it. I hope it dies." Her voice was musing and impersonal.

"Doris! How can you say such things?" cried Bea, rising on her elbow to stare in horror at Doris's impassive face. "You know you don't mean it."

The blonde face, now fatter around the cheeks and eyes, twisted toward her and smiled. "No, I don't mean it really. The baby will keep me and James—*make* us closer together. You know, Bea," murmured Doris, "a woman in my condition has strange ideas sometimes—does wild things. Dr. Everett told me so. That's why—women do funny things they don't mean. You mustn't ever trust what a pregnant woman does. She's not herself." The blonde face turned upward to fix its blue eyes on Bea with a gleam of triumphant conspiracy, as if in the exchanged glances a secret of womanhood had been shared.

With some surprise at the implication of candor in Doris's expression, Bea let her gaze slowly drift down the body beside her. The breasts seemed too small, almost too vestigial, to feed a baby; they barely raised the thin pale silk of the slip. But Doris's middle rose proudly, to her, with the mysterious mechanism of fertile woman. It was not beauty, as she supposed men were accustomed and trained to think of beauty, and she couldn't imagine that a man would want to sleep with a pregnant woman; but in its own deeper scheme of life, its symbol of endurance, bearing, suffering through love, its bondage of two people (but she was always thinking of herself and Tray), it was beautiful, and she envied Doris.

"Can you feel it move?" she asked.

"Yes, I sure can." Doris's voice was surly. Then she shuddered and gasped, "Ugh! I feel like I've got a horrible parasite on me, sucking my blood, killing me!"

"Oh, Doris, Doris," soothed Bea, unable to conceal her envy in her distaste. "Let me feel it move. Does it kick often?" She put her hand out gingerly, waiting for Doris to object to the intimacy of her touch, and then laid her palm on Doris's body.

Without a word, Doris covered the hand with her own, moved it slightly to a better position and held it there. Her face grew calm and the lids drooped over her eyes, as if she were recalling the pleasure of a similar experience. "It may be a little while," she said. "I hope it will be a girl. I hope it will be a beautiful girl."

"I'd want a boy, I think," Bea answered dreamily.

"I'm going home to mother's to have it. Mother can look after me. Maybe I'll stay a long time there. Maybe I'll let her bring up the baby. I don't want James to have anything to do with it. He'd only ruin it."

Then Bea felt a delicate inquisitive movement under her hand. Her skin covered with goose-pimples and an eager wondrous light came into her eyes. "Oh," she breathed, forgetting the unnatural mood in Doris, "it kicked. I felt it." Tears rose up in her eyes as she looked at the blonde face, the blonde body which bore life in its womb and was so lifeless. If that furtive gesture toward the world had only been made inside her own empty loins, that would never know life, though her body loved so much, wanted so much and in its silent way prayed so much for birth. But her love for Tray would never reach forward from its present time and with them would die. It was Doris who was blessed, whose love had never once put out its hand to another.

I, whose love, fretted Isabel, lying on the bed in her room across town, whose love had time and time again put out its hand, only to have it shaken, man-fashion, or kissed mockingly or waved at cheerfully; never to have it held tightly as if time or man might come between the clasp, never to have it imprisoned between their two breasts, inescapably bound there by their own knowledge of belonging, never to hold love and have her love held . . . unless . . .

She placed face down beside her the book that told of loving and living happily ever after. Reading was the poorest substitute for life that anyone could fall upon, and she much preferred at this moment to feel her own personal wounds and cherish her remembered pleasures than conceal her reality behind the vicarious suffering and joy of best-seller characters. At least she could know that she was living and could search for strength in her problems and not ignore her actual being, as so many people did, in the haze of sentimental fiction.

It was strange that all the things that had brought her and Don together, the books and music and pictures, now loomed in her mind as her only residue from their contact. As if Don hadn't existed at all except as a fictional character who entered her life from a book bringing certain congenialities of taste, he was now vanishing from an imagined reality at the end and when she once closed the cover he would be gone forever into the shadowy life of memory. She would be left again with her solitary interests, lonely in her house, alone in her body and spirit.

The same loneliness she sensed in many people all about her, the unfulfilled urge, at least of the body, and the hungering quest of the personality. Miss Rosa Walker at the drugstore, daringly reaching to Dr. Everett; Miss Julia, the accountant, and Miss McKinney, the stenographer, defeatedly clinging to each other; Alice Barnette and Anita Leffingwell, despairingly making their last feeble attempts. And there were the men, too—Horace Saxon, the widower Judge Dorn—lonely and no doubt puzzled, as far as she knew, longing for the union which would help them to express their lives. But why had all these been forsaken, what had happened to their little world that marriage had become more difficult, not only to achieve, but to sustain? For both husbands and wives seemed to revolt from its demands, as if it were an outmoded custom to which neither wanted to conform more than for preliminary requirements. All around her and in all the news she saw the same two facets of life—loneliness and unhappiness, either in or out of marriage. What had happened to the people of their world?

She shoved the book to the foot of the bed and rolled on her side. Staring at the diagonal splashes of foliage on the wallpaper, she thought of forests and of Don and Jim and Tray out hunting. Perhaps men could adjust themselves more satisfactorily to a lonely life; it had been their privilege from the beginning to hunt not only game for food but one woman, or another and another. But women could not, without some effects of strain, enjoy such a life. They wanted, she felt sure, stability and a home. They wanted to be taken possession of.

She did. Bit by bit and in long stories that she told over drinks, she had offered to Don her past life, exposing her weaknesses and, she hoped, her strength; throwing it all to him in a forlorn desire to have it assume the concrete form of the gift of herself, and spread like nets over his emotions, so that in this token of giving herself she might require that he take her and make her belong to him, and she would thus also possess him. But he remained merely interested and polite and did not offer to return his own life or to be bound in the meshes of hers. He had in some way betrayed her into confidences which he possibly regarded with amusement. She had been subtly robbed.

On the paper around the walls of the bedroom, the clumped leaves staggered up in heavy diagonals. Outside, in the winter, the leaves, brown and soggy on the ground, lay heavy. In the winter forest, Don was hunting on a Delta lake. And she hunted through her mind, her life, for an answer. To him, she had given herself in her inner dedication, as she had never even offered herself to any other man, in the cheerful, fashionable courtships of her youth; and she wanted his arms around her and his lips on hers. Oh Don, Don, she murmured into the pillow, what is arranged wrong, what cards are stacked against me, what more can I give you that I do not now know?

9

In the raw January morning, the flat Delta land unrolled endlessly its fallow brown fields, its always receding horizon of trees and its scattered cabins under veils of smoke. When they turned off the highway onto a dirt road toward the swamp, Don was excited by the wildness of the trip. The car swayed and bounced through mudholes, with Josh grumbling that the jolts were breaking his back and Andy McGill squealing that they'd never get back out if it rained again. Jim had little to say; without any reaction, he watched the muddy water splash out on both sides and streak the side glasses. Tray plunged on, winding expertly between crowding trees, and cursed when the springs crashed heavily against the axles.

About ten o'clock, they reached the cabin. Standing on the small stoop, Cy Baudry waved a greeting. He was a short, blondish man, with a broad face sagging and dirty from neglect. "Bring it all in here," he commanded, as he turned back into the cabin. "Ain't but one big room, but there's plenty of beds."

Two big logs were burning in the fireplace and the cabin was filled with the odor of food. At one end of the room eight folding cots were lined against the wall and at the other stood a large crude table and many cane-bottomed chairs. Adjoining this section was a small kitchen.

"The john's down that path a ways," he announced, pointing out one of the windows. "And this here's where you wash up." It was an old-fashioned washstand, with a china bowl sunk into the surface, a huge flowered pitcher at its side and a slop pail beneath.

The five hunters threw their baggage on the cots they chose as their own. After poking the mattresses and grunting their dismay, they began to wander aimlessly around the room. They warmed their hands at the fire, muttered about drafts, admired the smell of food and stared out the windows.

"Anybody want a drink?" asked Josh.

"Oh for God's sake," said Tray. "That eternal echo."

Cy stuck his head out of the kitchen and said sadly, "The glasses are already on the table."

"I thought we came out here to shoot ducks," remarked Don.

"Later on," Tray explained. "Dawn and sunset—when they feed."

During the afternoon, they lay on the cots and talked casually. Bored with the inactivity, Tray suggested a poker game. While the others settled down at the table, Don walked out into the boggy woods.

Toward sundown, when he had returned, Cy prompted them to get ready to go to the blinds. Don quietly moved beside Tray and whispered, "Let me go with you."

Pulling his hunting coat about his shoulders, Tray nodded, smiled and winked.

"You promised to show me how to shoot," Don went on uneasily.

"Get your gun over there," said Tray. "I know the way. Cy'll show Jim and Andy where their blind is."

Along with Josh, Don followed Tray through the woods. On reaching the blind of dead branches stuck thickly in the ground, they sat down on heavy wooden boxes that Cy had provided. While they waited, Tray explained to Don how to aim and fire the gun. They talked softly and fitfully, and smoked. The sun sank lower in the hazy sky. The air grew sharp and cold. During the silence, the limbs of trees could be heard scraping mournfully in the wind.

But Don was not uncomfortable from the weather nor saddened by the atmosphere. There was something pleasantly unalterable about the whole trip; he could control nothing here, yet he liked being swept along with the others. It was like an ocean of contentment that nestled him with the independence, the isolation, that he longed for, though he knew he had neither. The silence of the forest, the impossibility of interruption, the distance from the insistence of the world, most of all the oneness of the group, even if Josh and Andy were present, even if it were only for two days, filled him with a strange peace and satisfaction.

A distant birdcall drifted over the lake. He didn't care whether any ducks flew over or not.

That evening after supper, Josh and Andy continued drinking at one end of the big table while Don played double solitaire with Tray at the other. Jim stretched on a rug before the fire and stared into the popping, hissing fire. Don's attention constantly wandered from his cards to the outstretched figure.

"What you dreaming about, Jim?" called Tray.

"Just thinking," he answered without stirring.

"Leave him alone," said Don.

"Well, you wanted to know, didn't you?"

With boisterous shouts, Josh summoned them all to have a drink together. They were just finishing to the sing-song of one of Josh's toasts, when Cy appeared in the kitchen door.

"I'm going to hit the hay," he said. "I'm calling you at five for breakfast."

"Are we too rowdy?" asked Don, who was nearest the kitchen.

"Same as all the others," sighed the hunter. "I see lots of peculiar characters out here, but the worst are husbands." He withdrew into the dim kitchen, where his cot was made to avoid his guests, and closed the door.

"Think I'll turn in, too," said Jim.

"Me too," said Don.

Josh and Andy objected loudly and tried to force them back to the array of glasses and bottles. "Just one more," they urged. "Just a nightcap." But they broke through, and Jim went to the door which he opened on the sharp night.

"Christ," he moaned, "do I have to walk all that way?"

"Just do it in the bushes," said Tray.

Don turned down the covers of his cot. Laughter came in waves from the other side of the room. With the dying fire, the air was growing chilly, and he shivered as he unbuttoned his shirt.

Tray was moving undecidedly about the open center space and glancing curiously at him. Then he came close and said in a low voice, "You want to take my cot—next to Jim's?"

Don dropped his shirt and turned with puzzled outrage.

The ingenious light of conspiracy in Tray's eyes faded out swiftly. His brows puckered and his mouth seemed to gasp for words. He gestured helplessly, as if to explain what he couldn't speak. Then abruptly he walked away to the hearth where he stood abjectly with his hands in his pockets.

Hurriedly pulling off his trousers, Don got under the covers and lay still, listening to the pounding of his heart. The cold bedclothes made him shiver and his anger made him tremble. He had not yet relaxed when he heard footsteps.

Tray was leaning over, holding out a lighted cigarette. When he didn't bring his hand up to take it, Tray sank onto the edge of the cot and put it between Don's lips.

"I—didn't mean it that way, Don," Tray said softly and with difficulty. "It's because of Jim. He's different out here—that's what I was thinking of—the times when he always had fun. And he's having fun now. I didn't mean to hurt you."

With trembling fingers, Don took the cigarette from his mouth and blew out the smoke. Although he didn't want to look at Tray, feeling a surge of antagonism and fear for him, he knew what Tray was trying to explain. Tray had meant to be kind; but the crudeness of his kindness hurt him, seemed to flatter him by insult, to insult him by understanding, and to understand nothing by helping in this fashion. Don couldn't answer him.

"Ah . . . don't be mad, Don," said Tray. "I get things all wrong, I know. I remember when I was a kid . . . but beyond that, I don't know. I don't see how it could mean more than . . . friendship."

"Bastard," Don whispered hoarsely. His teeth clenched behind his quivering lips.

A look of anguish came over Tray's face, suddenly wiping the softness from his eyes, shadowed from the lamplight. He drew in fiercely on his cigarette, threw the butt to the floor and stamped it. Then he rose quickly, crossed to the table and took a drink.

Don lay quite still, the cigarette beginning to burn down to his fingers, and closed his eyes. He dropped the butt carelessly on the floor and hoped he would stop shaking. At length, he heard the door closing, and then Jim's voice through the noise of Josh's raucous singing. Shortly after, he heard it near the cots and Tray's voice with it, and the sounds of going to bed.

"Is Don asleep?" Jim asked.

"Maybe," said Tray.

The joints of the cots creaked. There was a thrashing of blankets and a sigh.

"I don't ever want to go home," Jim murmured. "Unless it gets too cold."

Don sensed a sudden stillness near him. His eyelids flickered open. Tray was sitting across from him, smoking and grinning like a mischievous boy.

"Shake?" Tray whispered and held out his hand a short way.

When Don reached to it, Tray stood up quickly, pressing his hand; and then scuffled Don's hair, blowing smoke down at him, and crawled briskly under his covers. A sense of relief spread over Don as he lay watching the darting streaks of firelight on the brown ceiling.

"Gosh," Jim was saying softly, "this is wonderful. . . . Just us out here . . . and no one to bother."

When they had finished their subdued breakfast by lamplight, they gathered their hunting gear. Outside the cabin in the shivery darkness just before dawn, the party divided again into two groups. This time Don went with Jim, stumbling together uncertainly through the woods, saying little until they settled down on the boxes in the blind.

Before them the shallow lake, unrippled and cold, stretched like a huge strip of dirty cellophane. Through the scrawny branches shielding their position, they watched the water quietly catching the first touch of light from the east.

Thin clouds rising before the sun were almost transparent for a moment and then a light yellow. They could see the fog of their breath, gray and close to their faces, but they saw each other only as huddled, bulky shapes.

"I don't think there're many ducks this season," said Jim. His voice, though soft, sounded rude in the still dawn.

"Tray and Josh got some yesterday," answered Don. He pulled the khaki hunting cap closer to his ears. Beyond the blind the little fleet of Cy's hand-carved decoys floated becalmed. He picked up an acorn, threw it over the blind and gazed at the rhythmic swelling circles that spread where it sank. The decoys nodded.

"I'm not much of a hunter, anyway," murmured Jim, pressing his fingers about the stock of his gun. "No more than you, even if I have made some cracks about it."

A line of mottled red streaked the sky at the horizon. In the increasing light a few gaunt, bare trees, standing in the shallows of the lake, detached themselves from the dark background and threw their reflections on the brightening water.

Don and Jim were silent for some time. The sun began to show above the treetops. Don could see Jim clearly now, sitting slightly hunched, with a placid, contented expression on his face.

"I don't like to kill things," Jim said.

"Neither do I," replied Don. "But all animals kill—nearly all—for food."

"But we've made it a sport."

"Man has made almost everything a sport."

"Mankind," corrected Jim. "Women, too."

Faintly Don smiled in agreement but said nothing. The satisfying silence enclosed them again while they waited, forcibly bound to that one place by the convention that they should shoot at ducks. The dark color of the landscape emerged in the daylight, and the smooth gray lake changed to undulant tan in the wind and the sun. Waiting in the cold tranquility of the woods, they expected nothing, actually not even a formation of ducks. They required nothing.

After a while, Don noticed that Jim was smiling at him and raised his head questioningly.

"It's the weather," Jim explained.

"The weather?"

"It's different," said Jim. "It's the only important thing that is different."

"From what?"

"That picnic at Cadman's Bluff on the Tallahatchie," murmured Jim. "Years ago. Remember?"

"The deserted town," said Don flatly.

"It was like this, except it was spring. I mean it felt like this feels. A kind of unity—nothing to come in, nothing to go out, no relation to anything or anybody—just this."

A kind of unity—no relation? thought Don. But something does come in, and it ends, just as it ended that time: A large group of them on the high bluffs above the yellow river, with pale green willows waving below their feet, and in the midst of undergrowth and woods and ancient apple trees and irises gone wild, no sign of the former town except two crumbling chimneys, an overgrown well and a graveyard. After the picnic lunch, Jim whispered to Don, "Let's take a walk," and Don followed him. They disappeared through the woods and found the graveyard, its mottled, stained stones rising above the deep grasses and bushes, and under four cedar trees they sat on a broad slab. Only the breathing of the wind, the clicking and buzzing of insects reached their ears. It seemed free, because it seemed hermetic, as if the spirits of the dead had drawn a magic, impenetrable curtain around them, and they didn't need to talk but only to catch each other's eyes. For a long time they sat there; they didn't want to move. But they heard voices calling through the woods. The curtain of the dead was not strong enough; they moved through it sadly and rejoined their friends.

"You've lost it, Jim," said Don quietly. "I've always kept it." Just as when they sat on the gravestone, their eyes met and lingered. And then Jim turned away.

Shifting the gun across his knees, Jim stretched his legs and surveyed the lake attentively. He rubbed his hands together briskly. Every time Don glanced at him in the silence that followed, Jim returned a sudden smile, as if he were pleased with being noticed. Perhaps Jim was thinking that he was troubled by their being again alone together in the woods. The smile seemed to invite some response which Don could not summon.

"You ought to get married, Don," said Jim at last. "All men should. It's a fine thing—the only way to be happy."

For a long time, Don said nothing. He sat with elbows on his knees, breaking twigs torn from the branches of the blind. He ran them under his fingernails, grouped them in twos and threes and broke them again. The nervous motions of Jim's body, the false urgency of his voice convinced him that Jim didn't believe his own words.

"I think I will get married someday," he said. "Soon, maybe. I might as well belong, too." He scattered the twigs on the ground and pressed them into the mud with his feet. Expecting a burst of derision, he looked defiantly at Jim; but Jim's face grew sad and his eyes filled with a solemn, helpless yearning. Then he drooped his head to stare at the gun on his lap, and Don wondered why he should suddenly lose the sly cheerfulness he had shown earlier.

"I could've married Isabel once," Jim said with a forced breath. "She always liked me."

Don sat very still. In Jim's tone was that same acid undercurrent that characterized his manner in town. It hadn't been evident on the hunting trip, but now, somehow irresistibly, it welled out of him. Why should he want to bring up Isabel, and in such a manner as to recall their evenings with her long ago, all their young pastimes and relations which now existed on such different bases? Jim's tenuous bridge to the graveyard at Cadman's Bluff had faded away, the curtain of the dead was broken again by the living.

"I knew her too well, though," Jim resumed harshly. "I just didn't feel like I wanted to love her. Even if she did want me. She was after me all the time, but I couldn't be bothered."

So much of what he said was true, but not in the sense that his tone and viewpoint implied. Don knew that Isabel had made no overt attempt to win Jim's love, for he had seen virtually all of their meetings. If Jim was trying to make him angry, what could his reason be? He sounded both jealous and vindictive. With tightly pressed lips, Don rose slowly from the box where he sat.

"She's still trying to get a man," Jim said loudly and crisply. "Why don't *you* take her? You can have her. I—I give her to you. Nobody else wants her."

"How are you the one to give her?" asked Don tightly. He stared down at Jim with contempt for his condescension and offensiveness. He raised his gun slowly to his waist and held it tensely in both hands.

Jim met his glare with a hard, almost cunning smile. His shoulders jerked and he laughed abruptly and briefly. He began to beat the palms of his hands hypnotically on his knees. A flash of frenzy passed across his face, distorting his mouth and widening his eyes. He breathed in quick gasps.

"I give you to her!" Jim cried. "I give you—I—" His voice died away in shame. A vein throbbed visibly in his neck.

Don's arms clamped taut against his sides and he whirled around. The desperate eyes implored and yet challenged him.

Low and furiously Jim spoke again. "Go on and shoot me!"

Neither of them moved. Then Jim swept his gun from his lap to the muddy ground. "There's always accidents—on hunting trips. Go on."

Don raised the butt of the gun. Jim's face relaxed into serenity. The mania seemed to vanish. "Today—for a little while," he stammered wistfully, "I've been happy. . . . First time in years." Then his shoulders lifted erect, his breathing grew regular and he closed his eyes.

Lifting the gun to his shoulder, Don turned away and aimed not at Jim but out over the blind where a flight of ducks had risen over the trees. The noise of the explosion shattered the tension, but its residue lay heavy inside him. He let the gun slide down to his feet and, bowing his head over his chest, clutched the dead branches before him.

"Of course you couldn't," sneered Jim. "You haven't the nerve."

PART FOUR

1

Warm spring twilight moved gently through the open windows. A foliage-scented breeze puffed out the lace curtains in intermittent billows. Deepening shadow sank over all the furnishings of the living room, but Jim did not rise to switch on a light. He remained stretched full length on the sofa and, while he listened to the ticking of the clock, inspected minutely the patterns in the dust on the rough plaster ceiling. His cigarette lay on the ashtray, burning out against the metal.

The baby had been born a week before; he was a father now. He had his child; except that now this child would never mean anything to him. For Doris, having never wanted it, had taken possession of it. It became a symbol and instrument of her power, and maintained the balance of their sterility.

She had insisted on going to Oakville where her mother could be with her during birth. "And father's a doctor, too, so it's all for the best this way," she pointed out. "You can come down after the baby's born."

"It looks strange, Doris," he protested. "They have good doctors here. Dr. Everett will think it's mighty odd, after caring for you so far. Our friends will think it's funny for you to go running off home."

"Nothing funny about it. You just want me to be here so they can all tell you how wonderful you are because you're a father." She drew the comb through her bright hair and watched it in the mirror dropping strand by strand to her head. "You've done everything you could to make me miserable. I think I have a right to say what's best for me now."

"I thought you didn't want to have a child."

"I didn't. I don't now. I wish it would be born dead."

"Doris, you're talking crazy."

As the hair rose and fell through the teeth of the comb, she smiled at her face, smiling back at her from the mirror. She looked deprecatingly at her eyes, rather puffed around the lids, and at the unusual fatness about her cheeks and chin. "I'm not talking crazy," she said dispassionately. "I'm simply being honest about it. While I'm in labor, you'll be up here having a fine time."

He plead with her, but she only grew more bitter. She was taking the train for Oakville tomorrow. Peachy could cook for him and take care of him, "Unless, of course," she added, "you want to ask in some of the women who find you so fascinating."

"Doris, how can you think such things? You know I'll be worrying about you and the baby. Let me go down to Oakville too."

"Fiddlesticks, James! I've already told you you can't. Mother wouldn't like it." She put the comb down on the vanity dresser and turned her blue and bitterly cold eyes toward him. "You know perfectly well you won't worry. You know you never really wanted a baby. It's obvious from the way you act—the way you've been acting all the time. You know it was just to hurt me that you insisted. You wanted to insult me, to make me suffer, to make me ugly, to tie me down like a slave. You know it's true—"

He slapped her and with a look of horror and loathing, both for her and for himself, walked out of the room. But he knew that in one respect she had been almost right. He didn't any longer want the child, for all the pride and pleasure he might have anticipated in it was now shriveled in the fire and ice of her hatred.

Doris left for Oakville the following day. If she would only die in childbirth, he thought; and thought Yes, it's not Christian to wish such things, but I do, almost. I think of it as a fortunate possibility; I don't wish it, I don't pray for it. If she would only die . . . and the child, too, which I'm dragging into this world to hate its parents. Then, if that were to happen, I could go back to my room at home, where college pennants once flared on the walls, where my books and pictures and dreams, now splintered, all lived with me. But he'd never be able to revive the room as it was five years ago, no more than he could revive the tenderness and tingling desire he had felt for Doris's beautiful body when they married.

During the week before the child was born, he sat alone in the house, trying to read, trying to listen to the radio, trying to think. But no thoughts came to him. Only fragments of the past, disorganized, meaningless and mocking, floated through his brain like visions in clouds.

He couldn't bear calling any of his friends. He recoiled at the idea of going to a movie where acquaintances would whisper and wonder why Doris was gone and he at home alone. He hated to meet anyone on the street. A wretched, frantic, gasping dullness settled over him. His father commented on it at the office: "Worried over Doris? It'll be all right." But he hadn't expected his father to understand his distraction since he had kept its origin a secret from him. "Go home and relax, Jim. It'll do you good."

There was no rest at home. He was surrounded with death in the suggestion of each room; the dreary living room, the separate bedrooms, the spareness of his own and the ruffly pinkness of hers. He never left the office until the usual closing time. Once at home, he began to drink slowly and with faint self-commiseration, sitting in the kitchen because it was cold and white and hard and impersonal. It seemed to smell now a little of Peachy, who always left him a supper in the refrigerator, and he was rather glad to have her odor around instead of his own or Doris's.

One night while he drank and watched the cinema of cloud visions, he seemed to become dead inside with the poison of the present, and he walked deliberately into Doris's bedroom and ripped every ruffle from the dressing table, the chairs and the windows. He piled them on the bed and, staring as if they were a warm nude woman or an enemy, he spat on them. He knew it was insane.

A long distance call came for him at the office. It was her father telling him about the child. "When was it born?" asked Jim dazedly.

"Day before yesterday"—softly, as if apologizing.

Jim couldn't force any words out; he was trying to think.

"Come on down here, son," said Doris's father.

"Did Doris say anything . . . about . . ."

What was there in the voice that touched Jim like an echoed tone? "No, nothing," it said. "Come on. See your baby. I'll meet you at the afternoon train."

"I'll drive," said Jim.

When he walked into Doris's room in her family home, she looked up at him scornfully and defiantly. Her mother sat beside the bed; she did not move from her place, as if by keeping it, she protected her daughter from the world. Doris did not hold out her arms, and he did not offer to kiss her. He leaned toward the round face showing above the covers of the crib beside her bed.

"It's a girl," said Doris, "just as I hoped."

Why, he asked himself, had he wished to bring this child into the world; above all into their lives? What could he or she ever make of it, or give it of love? What monster would this child, in their world, turn out to be? But instinctively he put his hands into the crib and drew back the covers.

"Don't touch her!" cried Doris. Her mother rose now and circled the bed. "You're never to touch her—not as long as she lives." Her mother stood at the crib and pulled up the covers till only the ancient, sleeping face was visible. A wadded hand pushed up to its mouth.

"That will be hard to manage," said Jim.

"No, James, it won't."

He looked at the sweet features of her mother, sitting again in her senti-
nel chair, and the gentle eyes looked calmly back at him. "If we go on living
together," he suggested.

"We will," she said placidly. "We can't separate now. We owe it to the child to
give her a home." Her lips spread slowly in a smile and she smoothed her hair.
"But I'll not stand for you to train her your way. You'd be teaching her your
selfish traits before she was grown."

Her soft, almost casual tone deafened him. He swallowed noisily and his
fingers trembled. There was a long silence while they fixed their eyes on each
other, as silent and as separate as aquarium fish on each side of a glass partition,
motionless, glaring, impotent. When does a man—why don't more men—think
of murder, he wondered. In thinking of their own death too often, selfishly,
they are turned aside from planning the death of others. He wanted his own
to come, he had thought, on the hunting trip, for he could foresee nothing
better in his life than those two days; at least he would have been spared this.
But Don was not capable, and God was not thoughtful. He didn't know how
long he stood there transfixed, but he finally realized that Doris's mother was
fanning her with a palm leaf.

"When are you coming home?" he asked hoarsely with anger at the dismal
sound of his words.

"I'll let you know."

His fingers found the doorknob and he wandered blindly downstairs. He
thought he remembered seeing her father and feeling a handshake, but that
was all.

His right hand, dangling off the sofa cushion to the living-room floor, waved
in the air as if trying to summon again the lost actions of those last minutes in
Oakville. But nothing more came; it was blotted out by the pain that burst in
lightning flashes inside him when he thought of Doris, and his hand sought
delicately and sightlessly for the glass of whiskey which sat somewhere near
the legs of the coffee table. In such a little glass was contained the wistful sum-
mary of the only times in his life he could remember as free, uncomplicated
and happy. Times of adolescence, yes—his fingers touched the glass and he
brought it swiveling before his eyes, held at arm's length above his head—but
a time of unabashed (no, he hadn't been)—well—daring, frank, free awareness.
No, it hadn't been awareness; it hadn't been frank, at least he hadn't really been
so. Then what? Whatever it was, it was something different from now. This now,
this age of acting an adult, was nothing more than a denial of the knowledge
of adolescence and a stifling of what mankind knew with fright was its only

liberty. The simplicity must be trussed up like an enemy by the adult and tangled with delusions that were meant to mean maturity. What simplicity, he asked himself doubtfully; what delusions? Returning through that time, he could find the simplicity in his vision; he could feel the ease and comfortable warmth, the inexplicable joyousness of merely being there, young and unresponsible to anyone but himself. He moved the glass slowly, ritually toward his lips and without raising his head, tipped it. Some of the liquor ran out the sides and trickled down each jawbone onto his neck. He didn't wipe it off, but returned the empty glass to the floor.

Although two weeks had gone by since the child's birth, Doris hadn't returned home. Dissembling for his family and for the tediously congratulating friends the distress in himself, he passed through the days in a terrible and constricting dream. Uncertainty and impotence swarmed through his thoughts. There was no rest, no calm for him in the world, except in his retreat to the past; and his whole nature, battered now and smarting, withdrew through whiskey from the intricate web of his marriage into the welcome aura of his youth. But that aura could welcome him only in its former perfected time; none existed in the present for he had stubbornly thrust it away from him.

Another drink, his mind whispered; and he sat up on the sofa and then walked with the glass, somnambulistically, to the kitchen. The hazed kaleidoscope of visions, dissolving and evolving, was more sedative than the whiskey, but whiskey was the instrument which shaped and colored it now....

In those springtimes the willows, at first luminous yellow in flower, shone greener than any that had budded since, and their feathery branches undulated with more grace above the shallow creek than any willows today. They swayed against the deep sky and its voluptuous clouds, and under their faintly metallic rustling the water in the creek flowed clear, cold against the warm sun, about their ankles sinking in the yellow sand. Their paper boats, behind which they waded, rocked up and down where the stream crossed over a serrated bar and lay becalmed where a pool was washed out at a bend. Then they would push them on with long sticks as they walked on the bank around the pool, for the edges of the pools were all of quicksand. If they approached too close, they sometimes sank to their knees. In the dark depths, against the grassy bank, they could see minnows darting out and they hoped someday to spy a catfish lost after floodtime on a foolish adventure up from the O'Tuckalofa River. There were cylindrical towers on the banks down which occasional crawfish shrank and there were narrows where they tried to build a dam of sand from bank to bank. Far to the south of town, in the pastures alongside the creek, where cattle grazed in the distance, they built a fire and boiled eggs as if they were explorers, and wandered deep into the hills in the west where they thought no man had ever been.

There, in the great smooth notches of a beech tree overhanging a terracing bluff, surrounded by thick, crowding foliage of the woods, they hid from the world and played at jungle life. Don was Tarzan, swinging for the branches and standing upright where they were broad enough, and Jim, crouching and gibbering, was Kala, his ape foster mother. And there, walking barefoot one day along a limb without holding to those above his head, Don slipped. Jim saw his right leg scrape to the groin while the torso swung in an arc and Don crashed through the leaves to the porous moss and mold on the bluff. While he scrambled in an agony of dread and love down the tree, he glimpsed Don rolling spasmodically to the bottom of the bluff, just as men did in the movies; and suddenly he knew, running after him, that their play acting had come true. He was now truly Tarzan's foster mother, racing to save him. The old serials would have announced: "To Be Continued"; but Don lay below and he couldn't wait. In a spray of dirt and dead leaves he slid to his side and hugged him close, whispering, "Don, Don, are you hurt? Don?" When Don groaned something indistinct, he felt relieved. Then Don moved his hand toward his thigh. "My leg . . . oh . . ."—and added in a shaking voice—"It knocked the breath out of me." Jim tried to roll up the trousers but they were too tight, and he opened them and drew them down to show the wide scrape on the inside of the leg. He wiped it awkwardly with his shirttail where the blood was oozing. "I—I thought you were killed," he said. "I'll carry you back. You mustn't walk on it." "Ah, shucks, sure I can." And Don got up stiffly to go. . . .

Jim stretched out again on the sofa, watching the pictures unreel on the rough ceiling. All that was childhood, of course; but it was the beginning, the mutual possession then so unconsidered that later must be shattered for humanity. But it had not been completely shattered; it was still not shattered, but only thrust into an attic among old-fashioned clothes. It had grown a more conscious bond in college and had become a private, unadmitted dedication, living beneath the masquerade with which society gradually veiled their conduct. . . .

Returning one night across the campus from the girls' dormitory where he had left his date after a few kisses, he recognized Don's figure standing in the darkness under the trees. "It was a nice dance, wasn't it?" Jim said as he joined Don. "Yes, lots of fun," answered Don. And Jim asked, "What you been doing? The dance has been over a long time, and you didn't have a date." "Just walking around. The moonlight . . ." They moved away, with no more words, through a grove far from the class buildings and found an open space circled by the dark pillars of trees where the moon shot its light sadly around them. They sat down in the silence and watched the thin white clouds hanging translucent in the sky, imperceptibly moving or given an appearance of movement by the moon's passage, and then they lay on their backs and stared up at the hypnotic, dark-fringed iris of the sky. Finally they talked in low voices, as if the other's words were his own and each talked to himself, but made a unity of words that was neither of them; and nothing was said of the late hour or duties or weariness. They talked of things that are gently laughed at by older people as sophomoric, but they were seriously fumbling toward a key to their lives; and whatever they did talk about on such nights seemed now more profound than any of the platitudes of the older people they and their friends had become. That first positing of themselves against the world seemed healthy and honest. It had none of the adult suffocation of doubt in honor of a decaying standard of money and esteem. It rose before Jim at this time with the excitement of forgotten truth and abandoned happiness that he might in some way recover.

For during all those years he was conscious of growth in his mind and peace in his spirit. He felt that shielding sphere about the two of them. Inside it was the only unselfish tenderness he had ever known; and the sphere did not close the world away from them but rather brought it to them more acutely and comprehensibly. He was penetrated with calm as he lay after a swim, on the sand of the deserted lake in the forest and listened to Don reading from the books he had brought along. Don read Hart Crane aloud and the words wound mysteriously inside of Jim. Although he didn't know what to make of it, he was silent, ashamed for his own deficient reaction, and was grateful for having heard the poems, for Don had given them to him by his reading. Then Don picked up a copy of *transition* and read something by Gertrude Stein, and a Dada poem at which they both burst into laughter, and a page of Joyce which stopped them both. "No," said Jim. "It won't work." "But it can be done," argued Don. "We just don't have the right minds—we've got defunct mass brains. Human brains are becoming vestigial. They're just instinctive agents, like the antenna on an insect." "Well, I'm an antenna," said Jim. "Read something easier." Don changed to E. E. Cummings and read, "Pity this busy monster manunkind Not . . ."

And when they went to the lake with girls, it seemed hardly any different. They would swim more for each other than for their companions. They would horse about in the water, with the girls squealing, half wanting to be engaged in the roughness and half glad not to be, until they gradually came to feel, self-consciously, that they had ignored their dates. Then, they would splash them and duck them. But later on, in a canoe with the two girls in front while they paddled at the stern, they shared the secret pleasure—Don more than either of them must have felt it—of their physical closeness; shoulders, thighs, arms brushing together as they pushed through the water.

Jim couldn't understand to what compulsion he had yielded that made him forsake the so close perfection of those days for marriage with Doris. As he grew older, he feared the town or himself; he doubted the endurance of this adolescent happiness which dragged on into young manhood. He forced himself to scoff at it. But now he feverishly returned to it each night of his loneliness, plunging deeper and deeper into its drugging space, and thought despairingly of the emptiness of his choice. Even if his were an exceptionally poor marriage, he would never again, with it dissolved, venture on another. He wouldn't allow himself to be tortured by another wife, but would choose lonely bachelorhood and let the world consider him undutiful and ungrateful. He had really been kept a bachelor in his marriage, so that he couldn't see the world's point unless something were involved that really had nothing to do with love. But for him there was no way to freedom, for he had tied himself more securely by his own insistence on having a child. He had never won Doris; he had lost his child to her; and of course, he had lost Don.

But perhaps not irretrievably; perhaps only in his own insensitivity. During all those early years of their friendship he was aware that the greater dependence, the stronger emotion, the more trying restraint was in Don; and that awareness was largely responsible for his own calm happiness, because he was not required to declare himself in word or action and he knew that Don would not demand it. Between disguised rejection and mute acceptance, their relationship had stayed in balance. Jim always felt that his control over Don lay in his own evasiveness; and he always knew how Don felt toward him. Even as recently as the duck hunt, sitting in the blinds at dawn, Don had reassured him: "I've never lost it." So then, neither had Jim lost Don; he still belonged to him.

With sudden resolution, he rose from the sofa and took a step. But his resolve faded and he stopped. Puzzled and frightened, he searched about the room. Then, again determinedly, he went into the kitchen. Although he had forgotten his glass, he didn't take another from the cabinet; he held the bottle to his mouth and drank. It was a big swallow and he lighted a cigarette to use as a chaser rather than water. His eyes glared uneasily about the white wood and porcelain and tile. He turned up the bottle again and then inhaled quickly on the cigarette.

"Fright. Fright," he said to himself. "Always fright. That's what it's been, all the time, all my life. . . ." He didn't know whether whiskey would help or not, but he did know that he could hardly do anything to make more of a mess of his life. He drank again, set the bottle noisily on the table and went quickly out of the house.

2

The sun, sinking slowly down the April sky, produced one of those lingering pale dusks that would reappear each day through the summer. There was a cool brightness outside, but in Mrs. Mason's bedroom, shut off from the world by both the porch roof and the starched lace curtains at the windows, it was dim and oppressive. Don lighted the lamp on the center table and pulled off his light jacket.

"Did you have a nice day, Donald?" asked Mrs. Mason.

Lying in that eternal attitude of forbearance and abnegation, his mother always suggested to him a vulgar modern statue of a maternal saint. Once more he wondered why something didn't compel her to get guiltily out of her bed or die decently in it. Her eyes trailed hungrily on his every movement, imploring some sign of devotion, and from time to time her hands raised indecisively toward him as if to hold him at the bedside. Unenthusiastically he related a few incidents of the day's work. From the kitchen came the noises of Aunt Marny's supper preparations. His mother repeated questions of many days past and he again answered them grudgingly. She told him again bits of petty local news which she had told the day before. Their talk lagged and expired; and he sat patiently in the rocker by the table and glanced over the daily Jackson paper.

At length Aunt Marny entered with a cloth and service to lay on the center table at the foot of the bed. After he had helped her set their places, he arranged the pillows behind his mother's back. Then Aunt Marny put the supper tray across her legs. They began to eat in silence. Toward the end of the meal his mother inquired, "You're not going out again tonight, are you, Donald?"

"Yes, I have a date," he answered wearily.

"Over—there?"

"Yes."

"Wouldn't it be nice if you stayed home with me some evening?" she asked in the abject voice in which she always pronounced this nightly catechism. "You're gone all the time—to work, to the movies, to a party or to her house. Don't you ever think of my happiness?"

"It might be better," he said, "if I didn't have to leave home to see Isabel." He didn't look up at either of the women, but he could sense the incredulous horror in their stares. They weren't eating any longer. Their knives and forks were poised, motionless, and their short breaths were audible.

"Donald," his mother said at last, "you mean . . ."

"She could be here," explained Don mechanically. "In—the family."

Aunt Marny's fork clattered on her plate. "You know you can't possibly think of such a thing," she said sharply.

"Another woman in my house, Donald?" whimpered Mrs. Mason.

Although he wasn't eating, either, he had been making a pretense of it by stirring his food about on the plate and breaking up the bread. Now he abandoned that and turned to his mother. "If I'm going to stay in Ashton all my life, Mother," he said, "I want—"

"You're not thinking of leaving me here to die alone?" she interrupted in alarm. "You're not going to run away?"

"Donald, Donald," reproached Aunt Marny.

"I can't go away, don't worry about that. But I want a home, I think."

"But you have my home, Donald. It's our home. Why would you want to leave it?" In fright and dejection Mrs. Mason fumbled with the dishes on her lap and stroked the sheet.

"I want my own—" He hesitated. "I want home life. It isn't here now. All these rooms empty and unused. There could be friends here and parties and . . ." Again his voice sighed into silence and the words choked somewhere in his brain.

"How can you be so thoughtless—so cruel?" whispered Aunt Marny angrily.

"I always knew she'd trap you," moaned Mrs. Mason. "I knew she'd drag you away from me."

"She's done no such thing, Mother," Don said sternly. "She'd understand you and be patient with you."

"Yes, Donald, yes, I know. But there's something else I can't seem to make clear. Isn't all this—just us in our own house—good enough for you?"

"You don't understand either, Mother. There's an emptiness—like all these rooms of ours—a dullness inside. . . . Incompleteness."

"Oh, Donald, take away this tray," his mother broke in. "It's hurting my legs."

He removed the dishes to the dresser. "I have a feeling of not using," he went on in the same pensive tone; "of waste somewhere."

"You used to be happy here," said his mother, "before you went to New York."

"Yes, I was." He stood thoughtfully, with his hand on the back of the chair where he had been sitting. "But what once makes you happy later on deserts you. It doesn't have the same power any more. I like Isabel. I want to . . ." He walked to the chair where his jacket lay. "I want to . . ." With a fretful movement, he caught up the jacket and went toward the hall door. "I better dress," he said. "Don't worry, Mother. You'll be taken care of, no matter what."

"Oh, Donald, my baby boy," Mrs. Mason sighed, with her lips twitching and distorting the sounds.

In his own room, Don began to bathe and change his clothes. He was buttoning his trousers when he heard Aunt Marny's voice in the hall below. "Why, yes, he's upstairs dressing." He pulled the belt through its buckle and fastened it. "Go on up." The sound of footsteps on the stairway and then the closing of a door below came to him. He picked up the tie he had decided to wear, but dropped it on the dresser and went to the head of the stairs.

"Oh, hello, Jim." Don backed confusedly into his room, surprised to see Jim's upturned face moving up toward him. Then he added, "Come in."

"Are you going out somewhere?" asked Jim.

"Over to Isabel's. Sit down. There's no hurry."

Jim's eyes fixed first on one corner of the room and then on another; then they moved fearfully to the open door as if his escape might quietly have been shut off from him. He walked to the dresser and, with a shaking hand, put out his cigarette in the ashtray.

"You look all shot," said Don. "What have you been doing? Besides drinking, I mean."

"Nothing much." Jim sat down in a wicker chair near the dormer window. His head bent slightly forward. "I'm pretty messed up, I guess," he murmured; "pretty miserable."

"Well, don't go to pieces, Jim. Doris and the baby will come back soon. You're just lonely, that's all."

"Yes, just lonely . . . I'm lonely when she's there." His voice had a toneless, automatic quality that brought a frown to Don's face. His movements were distracted, but taut with restraint. "I don't want her to come back."

"You don't mean that." Don sat on the edge of his bed and wondered with exasperated tenderness what he could say or do that would help Jim to conquer his troubled mind. He wanted to help him, to wipe out his anxiety, to restore him to what he used to be; for now Jim's wretchedness passed sympathetically into Don's own nature and filled him with unhappiness. Tonight, when he and Jim for the second time since his return were completely alone, he felt it more keenly and considered briefly whether they both were not wrong in resisting each other for so long. No doubt he owed Jim, as Tray had tried to explain, the loyalty of an old friend to stand by when difficulties arose. But he couldn't think of any way to help.

"I do mean it," groaned Jim in ludicrous anguish. "I do mean it. I want to be free of them." He drew in a deep breath and leaned back in the chair. In the silence that followed he seemed to wait for Don to confirm his rightness. But Don had no comment to make, and finally Jim turned to him and asked, almost tearfully, "Have you got any whiskey?"

"No, I haven't," he said. "Drinking doesn't do any good, does it, Jim?"

"Yes. Sometimes I think it does." He leaned toward Don with his arms on the broad woven arm of the chair. "Are you going to stay here in Ashton for good, Don? You're really planning to get away, aren't you?"

"I don't know, exactly. I can't leave right now. There're lots of things."

"But couldn't you do better in some city—almost anywhere else? Wouldn't you be happier?"

The urgency in his voice puzzled Don. He remembered their first meeting at the Daltons' when Jim had made him feel that he would be relieved if Don didn't stay in town. Then it was for his own benefit that Jim had plead; now it seemed to be for Don's. "Would you be happier if I left?" he asked, joking half-heartedly.

"Yes," Jim whispered. Then painfully, forcibly: "If I went with you."

Don's fingers closed around the edge of the mattress. In the long quiet that eddied around them Jim lowered the lids over his eyes and slowly sank back in the chair. The whirlpool of silence continued on and on, but it could drown neither of them now, no matter how much each for his own reasons might wish it. After endless minutes, Don broke through.

"What do you mean?" And he hoped he wouldn't be told; yet he hoped he would, but hoped most of all that he hadn't heard.

"I know I'm drunk, Don. But it's not because I'm drunk. I had to be able to—" Jim stopped suddenly as if his throat had closed over and stifled the words. He linked his fingers together and pressed so that the knuckles and interlocked joints went white. "I can't stand to live here any more. It's been hell—all of it—and it'll keep on being. Seems like the only times I can remember being happy were— with you, Don." His fingers broke apart and, grasping the chair arm, he turned again toward Don. "And I'm not ashamed of it. My marriage—my wife—are what I'm ashamed of. There's been nothing honest or decent in them, and if I was at fault—if I didn't—" With a convulsive movement, he crashed his elbows on his knees and his head into his hands. His words quavered. "I tried. I tried."

Rising bewildered from the bed, Don kept saying over and over to himself: Why didn't he go to Tray? Why didn't he go to someone—anyone else? He stood in the center of the room, looking with terror and pity at Jim, and then began to focus on objects around the walls as if in hope that they would clarify his mind and give him a basis for decision. "You're out of your mind, Jim," he said gently. "Let's forget it. Let's go get a drink and go see Isabel."

Jim sprang from his chair and confronted him angrily. "No!" Then the anger faded away and his arms raised slightly, possibly imploringly, and he shook his head sadly. "No," he repeated in a quiet tone. "You're not being honest. You're trying to avoid me, Don, just when I need you most. You know what you've always said to me, what you told me again on the hunting trip. You know you've always made it plain to me."

"And you always understood, didn't you?" There was a kind of proud defeat in the way he said it.

"In a way, I did. Now I know I do." When Jim walked slowly toward him, Don stood as if paralyzed, watching both destruction and love approaching; and all the room around blurred out so that nothing remained before his eyes except Jim's figure haloed darkly like his childhood view through the front door's oval lace border, now sullied with age, in which he had expected the image of his escape and happiness to appear. "Let's go away together, Don. You've always wanted to. You still do. Let's be together, in some other town, in some city. We can both be happy then. We can't either of us ever be happy here."

"You have a wife and a child, Jim," said Don.

"Damn them!" Jim's hands wavered before his chest and then lifted awkwardly and spread on Don's shoulders. "Maybe I've never been honest with you—about this. But Don, I am now. I want never to see them again. I want to be with you, like we were years ago, like I remember us, like you want us to be." His hands pulled Don closer to him.

The strength which Don never expected came, and with his eyes moist with anger and resistance, he wrenched away from Jim's clasp. "We can't do it," he said. He leaned his hands on the foot of the bed and bowed his head.

"We can."

Don took a deep breath and stood erect. Facing Jim defiantly, he spoke. "*I* can't do it."

"You're afraid to."

"That's not it." He came close before Jim, this time with no distrust of his control. "Now I'll be honest, Jim. You're the coward." At first his voice was crisp and metallic, but it softened into a tenderness and regret that made it difficult for him to speak the words he knew he must say.

"No one in the world has ever meant more to me than you did, Jim—and still do. Maybe no one ever will. During all those years behind us, I loved you. But you always threw it away, because you could always be sure it was there." He looked straight at Jim and saw the flicker of his eyes. "Maybe there would never have been in it what you wanted. Maybe I would have found out the same thing. But it lasted, for me—a special thing which seemed to give a meaning to my life. Now it's too late. Too late for both of us. What you should have offered of your own free will, years ago, you're now offering like some kind of desperate bribe. I won't take it. I won't spoil what I've kept so close inside me, just so you can patch up the mess of your own mistakes. You've been a coward all the way. You're a worse coward for coming to me now."

"You're not making sense, Don," muttered Jim. "I'm not a coward to offer to go away with you. It would take a lot of courage."

"You never offered such a thing when you could have made a choice. You were a coward when we were young, a coward when you married. And now, when you can't face your marriage, you want me to rescue you." His muscles twisted in torment as he talked, his heart hurt in its pounding, his lungs could hardly expand for air. If only, in his conscience, he could say yes to Jim; or if only somewhere far back in those years his emotion had actually burned away into a feeble, laughable ash. "It's a dirty trick, Jim, to say this to me so late. Because you know I'll have to live here in Ashton with Mother. You know I've thought of marrying—Isabel. And you know I'm trying to find some way to be happy, since I couldn't find it the way I first expected to. But you were confident, I guess—of what I felt and what I'd answer."

"So you want to 'belong' too," sneered Jim, "to 'qualify.'"

"Yes." They were staring directly at each other. "But I've chosen it consciously—sensibly, I think. And I think I've chosen the right kind of partner. I expect to live up to my choice."

For a long time they looked seriously at each other—the last time, probably, that any understanding would ever flame between them, that any regret or tenderness or compassion would ever meet in their eyes. And while they stood face to face, the sound of Aunt Marny's rocker in the room below seeped through the floor. But neither heard anything more than the retreating winds of a distant, aged forest in their minds, that brushed across the alleys and coves and ravines of their youth and, as the landscape dissolved, died mournfully away. The expression of disbelief on Jim's face at length broke. A hysterical, bonelike laugh burst from his lips.

"You fool," he wheezed; "you God damn silly fool!" And he swerved, almost toppling to the floor, and stumbled down the stairs.

Don walked quickly to the dormer window and, trembling violently, leaned on the sill. Below him, Jim's shadowy figure veered deliriously across the lawn and down the sidewalk under the street light. The door to his mother's room opened and Aunt Marny called up to ask what was the matter.

"Nothing," he answered; "it's all right."

"Aren't you going out?" she asked.

"Yes, in a few minutes." He stopped at the dresser and picked up his tie. Then he dropped it listlessly and went back to the dormer window. He sat on the stool in the alcove and fed his eyes on the night.

Perhaps he was a fool to refuse Jim; or a fool to think of marriage; a fool to stay in Ashton; a fool to run away, a fool to ever have thought so of Jim. It was a world of fools, for there were none but fools to guide them. He felt unable to move from this little cave which looked out on a darkened world. From here, through the rounding fringe of trees, he watched on the first evening of his return last summer the solitary man walking up the midnight street. With an effort he rose, finished dressing and went downstairs to forestall any further curiosity on the part of his mother and his aunt. After a hurried good night to them, he left the house and walked slowly toward the main street.

In Callahan's Café he telephoned Isabel that he wouldn't be able to come over tonight. "Some extra work on the paper," he said unconvincingly. "I'll call you." Then he walked across the railroad tracks and into an untidy dwelling district where no one would readily recognize him.

He walked and walked, plunging into the dim tunnel of tree boughs and sidewalk, until the sidewalk ended and the paving ended and he was on a gravel road leading into the country. He walked on and on. Finally he climbed a low bank at the roadside and sat down. Leaning against a rough fence post, he raised his head and looked into the sky.

After that night, as the days passed slowly about his increasing sense of loneliness, he began to reconstruct the interview with Jim and, adding various endings to it, to pursue the imaginary life they might have brought him. He was surprised and discontented to find that none of the other endings, if he followed their results far enough, offered any more happiness than the one he had chosen.

He did not, of course, really choose it any more than Jim chose his part in it; it sprang out of him in reaction. And sometimes, while he walked at night past Jim's house and pictured him sitting inside with Doris, shriveling with all sorts of hates, now that he had added one more, Don almost wished he had consented. He felt that he still wished to do so, that he would like to burst into the house and shout excitedly, "Let's go—let's get away from here!" And then the long, long dream that had curled inside him all his remembered life would come true. And he would stand beside a hedge in the dark, looking at the house, and dream the dream, with its succeeding images spreading over the shadows before him; and a great longing and frustration would tighten about him, lasting for days, even after his consciousness of their cause was gone.

Then one morning, in the office, he would suddenly realize that his attitude was childish and he was no longer in a child's world. He could almost laugh at the folly, the real insanity of Jim's proposal and his desire to accept it. He would wallow in a bath of pity for Jim and his desperate ruse to escape. But later on, the dream would return, slyly steaming up in his mind until it was all filled with clouds; and he did not want to see Isabel.

At last he told himself that he was actually watching an old dream die. I'm using artificial respiration, he thought, to keep it alive. It was a dream whose possible materialization was long past, whose blood was now sentimentality, whose future was transformation. Its life as a dream obviously depended on its not becoming real; and because it had never been allowed to be real, it had lived long. "The old Grecian urn business," he whispered, seeing himself and Jim in college, listening to a professor in a classroom when they wanted to be outside among the green leaves of spring. Now it could die out slowly over the years, and perhaps he should feel thankful to Jim for killing it. But Jim had killed something of himself with it, and Don would always be trying to revive the older Jim he had known. And through that effort, he was afraid, some of the dream might take shape again and grow and overwhelm him.

3

Along the grassplot, separating the railroad tracks from the main street, horses were tethered to the iron fence. The worn wagons to whose tongues they were still harnessed shielded them from the traffic behind. With lowered heads tossing fretfully at flies, with brandishing tails and twitching skin they waited in the summer sun for their masters to finish the Saturday trading. The farmers and their families sauntered stiffly down the sidewalks or clustered patiently at the curb and against store fronts.

Winding tediously through the crowds, Tray walked with Jim down the street from the drugstore where they had retreated from the heat. Over their coke and cigarette, Jim had betrayed more openly the anxiety that had grown constantly more pervasive in his conduct. His nervous lips, the haggard pouches under his eyes, the brown stain of nicotine on his fingers told Tray all he needed to know of Jim's state of mind. The odd thing, though, was that now Jim wasn't worried over Doris, as he used to be, but over Don and Isabel.

"What makes you think they wouldn't?" Tray asked, stepping wide to avoid the dung on the pavement as they crossed a side street. "To hear people talk, they've been as good as married for months."

"What I mean is," said Jim peevishly, "do you actually know anything? You see them more than I do."

"That's your own fault. I don't see why you're so interested."

"I just don't think Don's the type. Has he said anything definite that sounded like—?"

"Why should he?" Tray interrupted, annoyed at the cautious approach to the knowledge of Don that each of them guarded. "Has he said anything to you?"

"No." Jim waved listlessly to a clerk in the open doors of a farm implement store. "I just feel that Isabel's fooling herself—or else she's put an idea into his head."

"Well, somebody's got to put it there. The whole town's been trying to, ever since he came back. Why should you care?"

"I don't. I don't care. It's none of my business."

"You don't sound that way."

"It's just not right, that's all."

"Is there any reason it's not?" Tray was pretty much fed up with this bickering, especially after Jim's long, resisting silence on his own worries; but because of that, he supposed he could overlook Jim's present distracted attitude. Perhaps Jim was coming out of his personal depressed state and trying to concern himself over someone else. But if Jim so much as hinted at what was in his mind, Tray would let him know straight out how cheap it was. He almost wished he hadn't tested Jim's honor with the question.

Jim walked more slowly, as if considering possible reasons against the marriage. "No," he said finally, "I don't know any." But his slackening pace showed an irresolution that denied his answer. They passed the hotel and the furniture store beside it. The crowds were beginning to thin. "You mean you'd stand by him?"

"Sure, why not?" replied Tray in a cold, steadfast voice. "He's a good friend and so's Isabel. I'd like to see them marry. But it's their affair whether they do or not."

"And me?" Jim asked almost piteously. His unblinking eyes were trained far down the sidewalk.

Tray pushed Jim's shoulder in rough affection and laughed uneasily. "Where do you get these ideas, anyway? We're old friends, too, Jim. We all live here, we grew up together. If we turn away from each other, where can we go? There's nobody else to turn to. We're—habits to each other, I guess." He took Jim's arm in a tight grip and shook it. "Don't be a fool, Jim. You're just lonely because Doris is away. But all of us—"

"Oh, no," said Jim hastily. "No, it's not that at all. She's coming back." He pulled away from Tray with a slight lift of his shoulder. "I don't believe Don really loves her," he blurted out.

"How would *you* know?" asked Tray scornfully.

Jim answered him vaguely and abstractedly. Eventually he lapsed into a moody silence, as if his mind were on some complex problem. At length, when they reached the quiet section of the street where filling stations and warehouses began to mingle with the stores, Jim faltered and said indecisively that he must go back to his office.

Somewhere in Tray's mind, disunited and indistinct, the causes of Jim's prolonged disturbance floated, touching each other gingerly and flashing apart, and gradually approached closer and closer to the surface. If Jim weren't married, he'd almost think it was jealousy eating at him. Well, in a way it probably was, because Jim had once dated Isabel. It was envy too, because he had lost her—some way—and to see her marry Don would only emphasize his loss. But that was no reason for Jim to argue against the marriage unless he hated for Don to be happy. Unless what? But Jim couldn't blame Don for anything. Good God, what an idea! Jim just didn't realize what he was saying—what it could mean. Of course, he was really trying to protect Isabel from unhappiness.

From time to time after that, Tray found himself wondering why he himself, who was just as aware as Jim of possible objections, had never opposed Don's marriage. Like everyone else, he had merely accepted it as a fact that Don would marry Isabel. No question of right or wrong for either of them had ever arisen; it was always considered right for a man and a woman to marry.

Then several days later, as he sat in his office wondering if after all Jim wasn't right to want to protect Isabel, his phone rang. Isabel spoke from the receiver.

"Tray—I wonder how much trade-in I could get on my car?"

He made an offhand quotation and explained that he'd have to look it up to be definite. Before he had finished, she told him she wasn't concerned so much about the cost as how soon she could get a new one.

"You want it right away, you mean?" He picked up a pencil and began to scribble figures on a desk pad.

"Well . . . yes, I think so. . . ." Her voice became uncertain and faded slightly.

"I've got two here, Isabel. But what's the hurry?" Jim's conversation about her marriage speared up in his mind. So then, she and Don were going to marry and they wanted a new car for the honeymoon.

"I thought I might go away," she said.

"Alone?" he asked mischievously. Not until after he had spoken did he notice the frail sound of despondency in her tone.

"Yes." There was a long pause as if she couldn't say any more.

And Tray, baffled at her unexpected answer, couldn't speak for a moment. "Hello?" he began in a gruff voice. "Isabel?"

"I'm here."

"You mean a vacation." He was drawing lines and letters on the pad and digging his pencil into the paper.

"Maybe so. I don't have anyone to go with, though." Now she seemed to be suddenly lighthearted and casual. "But maybe I won't come back."

"Won't come back?"

"I thought I might go to New Orleans or somewhere like that and look for a job. Do you think I could get one?"

As the recollections and ideas of the past months slowly combined and emerged in his mind, he spoke hesitantly and gently. "Is something—wrong, Isabel?"

With a laugh she said, "Why, no." But he was sure she was lying, perhaps with the intention that he should know it.

"What's the matter, then?"

"Nothing, Tray. Don't be silly."

He waited a moment in a tumult of thinking. Twisting the pencil in his fingers he at last forced out the words. "Is Don—coming this evening?" He broke the lead point with his thumb and pressed down the wooden splinters where it fell out.

"I don't think so," she said soberly.

"I'll come by," he said, "and talk to you. About the car—and the job."

There was the briefest silence before her voice came in a whisper, a sighing sound of gratitude and relief that formed the word "Yes." And then another silence while Tray waited for something more, until he heard her receiver click and he hung up.

Leaning back in his swivel chair he stretched his legs wearily. Then Jim had actually done something to keep Don back—to keep Isabel from Don. Or maybe Don himself had been unable to escape finally from his loyalty to Jim. Whatever it was, Tray knew that Isabel was at the decisive point of two lives. Once more he had jumped into something he wasn't prepared to discuss; once more he had yielded to his impulse to help, to protect. Only this time it was going to be worse than ever because it was a woman. "I can't reason, I can't figure things out," he scolded himself, with a kick at the wastebasket. "I can only feel. I just know people ought to be happy. They're never fair to each other. Never honest."

None of his nervousness had vanished by the time he rang her bell. She let him in at once, as if she had heard his car and was already at the door.

"All alone?" he inquired brusquely.

"Of course."

He followed her into the living room. When they sat down side by side on the sofa, he saw a smile on her lips—something of a trusting smile—but he saw too an uneasiness that matched his own and a strain of determination. His fingers twisted about each other in slow indecisive coiling. A large tray with glasses, ice, soda, and a bottle of whiskey sat on the coffee table.

"Let's have a drink," suggested Isabel petulantly.

"It'd be better."

She mixed them and handed him one.

"Why do you want to go away, Isabel?"

"You don't have to ask me that, do you, Tray?" she countered with mild disappointment. "I don't want to grow old sitting here, doing nothing, having nothing—nothing important, I mean."

"But you do have something important, don't you?"

"Do you think so?" She shook her head. "Not really. If I have to turn into another Miss Julia or Miss McKinney, I'd rather do it in a place where nobody would know much about me. I could be alone and have something to fight against. Fight to make a success in my work, with new friends. Here I have nothing to fight against—only inaction."

"Seems to me you're rushing a little." Tray waited for her to reply, but she continued to stare into her glass. "Aren't you, Isabel?" Still no answer; and Tray felt inside himself that breathless excitement and pity that always came to him when he tried to say something he didn't want to and was afraid shouldn't be said. I can say things right out to men, he thought; I don't have to worry about delicacy. But to tell Isabel something she wants to hear is a hard thing to do. And it might be the wrong thing; it might show her what a big fool I am. He drank, and set his glass on the table and studied her now patient, submissive face. Whatever he might say, she wanted him to say it; it might hurt her, but it would also hurt him.

"You want to get married." He had meant it to be a question, spoken gently, but it came out a harsh, flat direction.

She lifted her eyes slowly to his. "Yes, Tray."

"Is that why you're running away, then?"

"In a way it is." Her eyes, imploring above the thin, rigid smile on her lips, stirred in him the same helpless anxiety he had felt for Jim during the last year. "I hoped it might—force the answer—force something—anything—to happen. I can't bear this waiting and waiting for all my life. It's gone on for years, and the years have piled up behind me, empty. Years and years. It doesn't seem possible anyone could go on waiting that way for the one simple thing that's going to mean life. And we do it by the thousands."

He couldn't face her any longer. He got up and crossed the room. Beside the phonograph he stopped and brushed his fingers over the petals of Cape Jessamines in a vase on the top.

"And now I still wait," Isabel went on quietly; "but it's waiting for a definite thing, not the vague, abstract idea to come true. But still it's endless, it seems. There's to be no end, no answer no matter how patient I am. Months and months—a year now— And the hope I had—and it seemed so happy, so just about to happen and be true—well, that's faded away too, just like all the months and years. It's as if life were moving away from me instead of toward me, into me. I can't ever again let myself be—hurt—by hopes like that. I don't want to any more. There's nothing left of me to hold out for anyone to hurt now. So now I—want to know—if you can tell me—Tray, is there any—"

He didn't let her finish. "Why didn't you go to Jim?" His voice was deep with irritation. "He's a closer friend than I am. Why did you come to me?"

But even as the words were pouring from him, he realized the answer. She was jealous of Jim and hadn't admitted it to herself; she had admitted nothing that subconsciously she already knew. Like most people, she wanted to put on someone else the burden of making suspicions real through the magic of words. He came back to the sofa and stood before her, listening to her hesitant voice saying, "Because there's something—good about you."

With both anger and tenderness he looked down at her. "You know, Isabel," he said severely. "Why do you want me to say what you already know?"

"I don't know, Tray, I don't." Her eyes begged piteously. "I don't know that I know." She stood up, rising close before him, catching his arms in her hands, and whispered, "Say it."

For a long time he stared at her and gradually knew that she did want said whatever final, however horrible thing he could tell her, so long as it supplied the answer. But he lowered his head, shook it despairingly and turned away out of her clasp. "I'm such a fool," he muttered. He sat again on the sofa and hunched over his knees. "Don is a fine boy—if that's what you want to know."

"I know that, Tray." Then her voice sank to an almost tearful, humiliated gasp. "I'd like to—marry him." She stood rigid in shame.

"Then do it," said Tray.

She waited silently, motionless, until Tray thought he could not bear it any longer and would have to rush out of the house. It was much worse, surprisingly more painful, than he had bargained for. When he reached for his drink, the tinkle of the ice seemed to arouse Isabel. She spoke then more calmly.

"He's slipping away. . . . Things have changed."

"Lots of times things that are supposed to change don't."

The stiffness of her features vanished, and with arms slowly reaching toward him, she sat at his side. "What do you mean?"

"Don't you understand, Isabel? Don't you remember?"

She searched in his face for the answer he didn't want to give. Then she shook her head in defeat.

"When you used to have dates with Jim—" Tray hesitated and swallowed, but he had to blunder on, for he had trapped himself and all of them. "Maybe you were jealous of Don." While he paused, her shoulders drew together with a sharp constriction. "Because—" Hearing the voiceless sigh that escaped her lips, he knew he didn't have to go on.

They sat awhile in painful silence.

"That's—dreadful," she said in bewilderment.

"No, Isabel, don't look at it that way." Tray took both her hands between his. "It may only be jealousy in you. But understand, understand."

In her face there was no sign of relenting, only an aching sorrow. "But I've known Don so long."

"The person we know isn't identical with what the person is. We know the character and so don't suspect the secrets."

"It's not true," she said dully. "Tray, tell me it's not true."

"Isabel," he said urgingly, "I love Jim myself, and because of that I love Don too. There's ways of loving—degrees—but I guess at bottom it's all the same thing."

And now, during her prolonged silence, Tray's sentences were breathed out with difficulty, spaced by periods of inner turmoil in which he could separate no words from the whirlpool of thoughts that filled him. "People today are ashamed of love, I think—of real love. There's more than just the physical." Her hands were cold and though relaxed seemed to tremble in his fingers. He didn't know if she really heard him or not. "I've begun to see the two parts—the two double parts. I never thought about it till I realized Jim—But things hang on, they come back. Just understand, Isabel; just try." There was no response in her expression or movement. Leaning uncomfortably toward him, with her lips parted in shock, she uttered a barely audible sound. "Help Don," said Tray. "He may never marry unless—unless you—"

He could say no more. Misery for his clumsiness, and fear that he had acted with dishonor toward Don swept over him. He sat watching her almost cataleptic trance. The smell of Cape Jessamines drifted heavily across the room, a smell of nights of love and rooms of death; and the sound of leaves in the summer wind came through the open windows. Then without a word he released her hands and got up.

Isabel's body jerked, her arms moved outward and she rose and followed him. He stopped for a moment, and her outstretched hands reached him and held to his again. She looked desperately and beseechingly at him until he turned away. And her hands, quivering unwillingly, as if resisting a cloud that was beginning to sink around her, slipped away from his as he went out the door.

4

When Don rounded the landing of the stairway, the Ashton Hotel lobby spread below him in glaring, compressed barrenness. The two ceiling fans licked noisily at the sultry air and cast languid chopping shadows on the tile floor. Their breeze cooled only Alice Barnette, who drooped over a love-story magazine at the desk, and the Negro porter who squatted with a newspaper on his shoeshine box. The stiff chairs were empty, the glazed walls neutral and repellant.

A small boy pointed a short stick over the stair rail above him and aimed along the imaginary gun. In a gruesome soprano voice he said, "I'm a dangerous man!"

Don smiled at him and continued to mount the steps to the third floor. Both he and the boy, in their facetious make-believe, represented the truth. The boy was honest, of course, but the nature of his danger, which must later be cured by society, was still secret. Don's own danger—to himself and to the world—was now crystallized, never having emerged, and could no longer be a threat.

But if that were so, there was no reason to visit Horace Saxon to discover where his danger might lead him. Why shouldn't he relax quietly in the comforting notion that, now that he had been shaped in childhood and confirmed in youth, nothing could change or help or save him from his involuntary course? His inborn stubbornness refused to accept either revolt or code. Even though he could never shake off the chrysalis of youth, he wouldn't make it an excuse for avoiding decision. He must see how Saxon lived, how an old bachelor filled his hours and his life, how he himself in years to come might be laboring to make his existence signify something.

He walked down the hall on the third floor, reading the chipped, faded numbers in the dim light. The shabby wallpaper puffed in blisters from the walls. The runners carpeting the steps and the corridors were dusty and frayed. When he found the right number and knocked, the door swung partly open as if the latch were broken.

Beside a round table between the corner windows, Horace Saxon sat in a massive, leather-cushioned chair. He lowered his magazine as Don moved through the opening. "First time you've ever called on me," he said with unconcealed surprise.

"You've never asked me," Don replied, sitting in the rocking chair that flanked the other side of the table.

"I used to ask a few people up," mumbled Saxon, "but I got tired of being refused. Never bother with them now."

"It must be sort of lonely." There was more plaintive questioning than sympathetic comment in Don's words.

In a casual manner which he hoped would fool Saxon he examined the room. The walls must have been papered fairly recently as a concession to the editor's long residence. They were decorated with daguerreotypes of the Saxon family between which were tacked cluttering pictures of landscapes and people: Pershing and Wilson, a college group, Alice Joyce, Mae Murray and even a cover from *La Vie Parisienne*. A tilting armoire revealed through its constantly sagging doors the extent of Saxon's wardrobe. Its top was piled with papers; the table and the dresser were jungles of toilet articles, clothing, books, tobacco and ashes, fresh fruit, cartons of crackers and cookies, pencils and tumblers. The room, for all its informality, seemed comfortless and confining.

Saxon touched his reading glasses to settle them more firmly on the bridge of his nose. When he moved his thin face, the light glittered minutely in the gray stubble on his chin. "Yes, it's lonely," he said after a pause. "You wouldn't like it."

It was almost as if Saxon had said, You have your answer; now you can go. But the old man smiled shrewdly and went on. "Have you quarreled with Isabel?" he asked.

Don couldn't expect to deceive a man like him about everything. But that Saxon should enter at once into his private thoughts; in fact, leap beyond his admitted purpose to the real heart of his confusion, was unnerving. "You missed on that one," he replied lightly. "Why should we quarrel?"

"Then I'll say have you quarreled with her inside yourself?"

"I haven't seen her very much lately."

"That's what I mean."

"Maybe I have—disagreed," said Don resentfully. He got up abruptly and moved about the room, striving to draw out the essence of its kind of life.

"Everyone expects you to marry her." Strangely enough, the caustic tone and the brusque manner that Saxon, outside his room, cast protectively about him was almost absent tonight. He seemed to have assumed the role of Don's confessor.

Don halted before the window overlooking the quiet town. "I don't like the idea of being tied to someone."

"To her."

"To anyone."

"You're a liar, Don." If Saxon had expected him to whirl about angrily, he was mistaken. Don continued to watch the sparse cars passing on the dark street below. "You know it. You know the tie works both ways. Everybody wants that kind of possession. It doesn't affect your freedom any more than being a bachelor. Look—" He made a short gesture that included the room and himself.

"What bothers me is the way you're possessed," said Don.

"Well, yes. That has changed. Women—if that's what you're thinking about—no longer possess by anything closer to love than sex. When its power fails they turn to law. For two thousand years they've had marriage—and before that just force and emotion—and now they want something to take the place of marriage. They don't know what; but they still want to keep what they're giving up—respect, moral control, sexual attraction."

"That's not what I want to know," Don exclaimed impatiently, and was immediately chagrined that he had spoken out his need of advice.

"Of course it isn't," answered Saxon. "You're just like the women. You don't want to know what you do want to know. Women today destroy marriage because they destroy their own share in it. And constantly they destroy man's share without his knowing it."

"Then how do *you* know it?" asked Don.

"The same way you do," Saxon said. "Not being married, I can see without the prejudice of a solitary experience. We now have a world no sensible man ever dreamed of, and all our morals and philosophies are pretty much useless. But nobody yet has discovered a system by which man can live in it. As human beings we are supposed to be rational, and yet we've lost the intelligence of the animals. And the family is dying out."

"You mean it's silly for a man to marry?"

"For a man like you, it is."

Don considered for a moment, and then he asked, "Why?"

"Because you revolt against this new world and also against the old world at the core." As Saxon talked, Don walked slowly from the window to the rocking chair beside the cluttered table. "Everyone does, actually. Our industrial world demands the end of the family; our traditional world demands its support. Nature demands merely sex; but the spirit demands love—marriage. We're all caught—men and women—between the two. But women betray their tradition. What the man might seek, the woman has let be destroyed for the sake of industry—progress."

"Well, have you got any answer for it?" asked Don.

"Yes, but it's not very cheerful, I guess. When a woman can give a man the companionship he gives up in his friends and also, along with it, the physical love his friends may be too reticent to offer, then marriage can succeed. But women have become untaught—commercialized. More and more they believe that two large lumps on their chest and a crevice at the base of their torso is all that's necessary to a man's happiness. What fools!"

In his confusion, Don could only think What tommy-rot! The haphazard rubble of articles on the table made as much sense as Saxon's words.

"I simply want personal happiness," he said defensively. "That sounds stupid, too, I guess; idealistic. To begin with, I want to get away from this town, away from people I've always known, who expect definite things of me. I want to be alone and not belong to anyone."

"That's the modern temper, too, Don," Saxon spoke softly, with an affectionate glance at him. "Then go away from Ashton. Have your search—your lifelong, futile search."

"I can't as long as Mother lives."

"Then stay. And dribble away your energy with the years—fabricate excuses for not doing what you'd like people to think you could have done. And when your mother's finally dead, you'll live alone, friendless and filled with recriminations."

"Recriminations?" Don looked at the jumbled dresser and the pictures on the walls, anywhere but at his accuser.

"You'll be alone. It will be natural to have them."

"If I stay, I'd have to marry."

"Then go away."

With a pleasant sensation of alarm, Don thought he had wanted to hear those words at that particular moment, but he also thought that Saxon was a bitter, lonely old man who now expressed only cynicism. He said nothing to the repeated command.

"There is no reason these days for marriage," Saxon mused. "Most women aren't—can't be wives any more."

Saxon was playing with him, much as a scholar might with an upstart student. He was trying to shock him with cheap iconoclastic ideas, even though the ideas echoed agreeably in his own mind where they seemed neither cheap nor iconoclastic. It was a warped revenge, nursed in the old editor's breast for many years. Don had blindly walked into his trap.

"A man feels an urge toward belonging—toward sharing his life, even if it's only with a friend," he said haltingly.

"I once had a friend, Don. I once had a sweetheart." Saxon's eyes lifted furtively toward a patchwork of photographs beside the dresser. "The world no longer believes in friendship; you may have to murder your friend for your own advantage. So it can no longer believe in love either, except romantically— vicariously. Most of love is friendship."

Don did not speak. He was thinking that perhaps he would have wished for his father to talk to him as seriously as Saxon now did. But it might be that no father could express to a son or even formulate such ideas as Saxon had uttered. In spite of the warmth of the words, they couldn't have been spoken without the background of his misused, shriveled life. They were the rationalization of a defeated old bachelor.

"I am old now, Don. Few people have ever brought me what I wanted to find in them. I know what I'm going to say isn't sensible, but such things never are. You have been, like a quiet revived dream inside of me, my friend who was killed at Verdun; who stayed truer to me longer than my sweetheart. You've been the son the sweetheart might have borne me if she hadn't preferred to run off to Memphis with a cotton broker. I've kept all this to myself, making it live in my thoughts and feelings, because I knew it couldn't live in reality. And I've wanted to do for you what I would have done for them—leave you, when I'm dead, my love, my business and whatever of my experience could help you. I couldn't now give you the advice I would have given them. My advice is sour, warped, sterile. I've lived in this room, worked in that office down the street, and I've grown old. Life for you is more complex than it was then for me. I can only say that you should go away. Live alone. But be strong about it."

For a long time Don was silent, touched by Saxon's speech and puzzled by his intentions. Then he said, "I can't go away."

"That's part of the strength you'll need. You must. You'll never be happy in Ashton. You'll never be happy married. Even to Isabel."

The cluttered futility of the restricting room, the ugly furniture and aging memories imbedded in the objects about him swelled monstrously before Don. He saw himself down the coming years with his home, his friends, his possessions gradually dwindling away as he shrank into a life of loneliness, into this one room with its assortment of trinkets and pictures which would hold the remains of his young expectant days. Rising, he walked toward the mirror on the dresser. It didn't have to be this way for Saxon; it need not for me, he told himself. Nor need it be so in marriage. 'Whatever of my experience could help you,' the old man had said. Don turned from the mirror to the room which symbolized the fruit of Saxon's experience.

"I can," he said hoarsely. "I will." He looked straight into Saxon's eyes, but he knew nothing more to say.

After a while Saxon, without blinking or turning away, reached out toward the table and picked up his magazine. He brought it before him, opened the pages and, lowering his head without a word, began to read.

Don waited, but nothing more was said. He leaned against the dresser. The hint of a thin smile wavered on Saxon's lips. Don crossed to his chair and put his hand nervously on the top of it. He wondered if he should speak and if Saxon were angry. Finally, unable to bear the strange silence and unable to break it, he walked quietly to the door.

"Good night, Don," said Saxon sadly. But he did not look up.

Behind Don, the door closed noiselessly. Then the faulty latch clicked and the door slipped open again.

5

In her first despair after the interview with Tray opened her eyes to her own knowledge, Isabel thrashed about in a helpless state of disbelief. What she knew couldn't be true. It was a nightmare springing from her anxious uncertainty, but she couldn't drive it away. Not until the following morning when she began to think about her girl friends, herself and her early courtships in school, did any glimmer of calmness open before her. For in surveying her buried perceptions, she lay back coverings that hadn't been disturbed in her consciousness for many years. No one was more childish about such things than grownups who should know better.

After all, it was quite obvious that Don liked her and during the past year had spent more time with her than anyone else in town. If he was slipping away now, it wasn't the fault of Don but of herself, who should, as Tray had suggested, do something about it; perhaps frankly talk to Don and save them both. Would it save them, she wondered? So few were really saved these days; marriage was more and more a temporary affair. What had gone out of it? she asked herself; what has gone out of me?

But she easily answered the last question. All of herself she had given to Don; in words, she had thrust on him her whole life and thoughts and hopes. And she never felt that she had lost anything, but rather that she had enriched herself by giving—until Tray made her feel that she had wasted herself and her love on Don. She couldn't help it that at the time he didn't mean her to feel that. And now she was glad, for she knew she loved him in spite of what else she knew.

But for many days she was relieved that Don did no more than call occasionally to chat listlessly over the phone and offer vague excuses for not coming to see her. She couldn't avoid the feeling, identical with what she felt the night she kissed him, but less intense now, that he felt that she expected something of him. It was an attitude not peculiar to Don alone; she had noticed it from time to time in other men. They hid under politeness their discomfort at the obligations of women; and their discomfort ranged from the requirement of holding a woman's handbag or opening a car door to the degrading necessity of making love if the woman chose. She was ashamed that she had been guilty, in her desperation (which she knew wasn't shared with the most guilty and aggressive young women), of forcing Don to kiss her. Her excuse, which couldn't be theirs, was that her chances of marriage were almost gone. Although she knew now that Don would never choose a wife, she thought also that women had robbed men of the privilege of choice and thereby robbed themselves of the virtue of desirability.

For herself there could be no other course, unless she wished to wait in fast-dwindling hopes that someone else would come along; and she didn't consider that very likely. She knew that she loved Don; and she knew it more deeply than ever before since Tray had talked to her and made her understand what Don's life had been in the hidden corners of his heart. Slowly, as she denied and fought against her knowledge, she came to see what Tray had tried to make her see—that a man's life is not a story-book life and the vices that weave through it may not be really vices, but secrets common to all; that they can and must be forgiven, and on that forgiveness will rest whatever love mankind can foster.

She let a week go by while testing the stability of her decision, and when she was sure that it didn't waver and that no recurring horror flooded her, she called Don at the office of the Ashton *Herald*. At the sound of Charlie Ann's voice answering the phone she remembered her disapproval of aggressive women, but assured herself, with Tray's implicit support, that in this instance it was necessary. Then Don spoke over the wire.

"Oh—uh," he stammered, "Isabel. How are you?"

"Same as ever."

"I've been meaning to call you," he put in hastily and, she imagined, guiltily. "What have—what are you doing?"

"Nothing in particular, Don." What a dreadful distance the telephone put between them; but what a convenience to hide her own embarrassment. "I thought maybe we might get together this afternoon when you quit work. I wanted to—" She hesitated, because it would sound too blunt. "The summer's almost gone, and none of us has had a picnic yet. What do you think about it?"

"Well, is it a ritual every year?" he asked with a laugh.

"No, of course not. But there's really so little to do here. It's nice sometimes to get out in the country."

"When would you like to go?"

"This afternoon, if you can." She waited, trembling, and wondered what his silence meant. She heard a word, but not a word so much as a vague sound, and then she went on. "I'm having Dulcy fix up some food. It'll be cool and pleasant in the late afternoon. . . . If you're not busy."

"Why, no, I'm not." But there was little enthusiasm in his words. "Who else is going?"

Now she was silent, hurt at the thought that he expected someone besides themselves. But she told herself that she must seem casual, and she said, "No one," as brightly as she could.

"Oh, just us."

"Do you want anyone else? I could try to get—"

"No," he interrupted. "No, Isabel."

Something plaintive in the tone of his last words touched her and she hoped that Tray was right. She couldn't speak for a moment, and then she asked when he would be finished.

"Come by about five," he said. "We'll have at least two hours of daylight."

The afternoon was still warm when they drove out on the country road. They didn't talk much, but watched the empty road, swept occasionally by shadows of clouds, as it wound between fields and trees.

"Where are we going?" Don asked at last.

"The old Winthrop place. You remember it, don't you?" Isabel's heart beat faster each time she had to speak. She was afraid she would rush confusedly into the confession she wanted to make, or that she would stumble on words and never be able to say what she meant.

"It's years since I was out there. The plantation's all chopped into little farms now, isn't it?"

"Yes. Not like it was. But the little grove of trees around the chapel has been kept the same. The people who built where the old house was didn't want to destroy that."

Isabel drove on swiftly, rounding the curves firmly with a whirring of the tires and the rattle of gravel under the fenders, and at length slowed and turned off on a dirt lane that led between a gap of the wire fence. At the left they could see the low chapel, with its steep roof and pinkish walls of slave-labor brick, hunched dark and lonely under the heavy trees. The ground about it had been kept free of bushes, and the car wound between the tree trunks and stopped on a sparsely sodded clearing. They both got out and carried the baskets of food and drink from the car.

"Where shall we sit?" asked Isabel.

"Anywhere, I suppose," answered Don, "as long as a breeze comes through."

Isabel stood deliberating at the base of a huge oak tree. She looked about at the scene, thinking it was somewhat more shadowed than she had remembered, and wished there were a brook near by. There was something about water that relaxed and released the mind. "Is this all right?"

"Sure. Good as any." He let the baskets drop to the ground.

Isabel sat disconsolately on a big root that spangled out from the tree, and crossed her arms over her knees. She shouldn't have dared this picnic; it was going to end badly. Don was in a strange mood, indifferent, lifeless, reticent, and as she looked up at him she imagined that an inextinguishable dislike of her was welling up in him. She had exceeded her privilege; and to him it would be more distasteful than to most other men. But all she could think of was how much she loved him, how little she cared about his secret, how she wanted to hold him in her arms as if she were a mother and he her child, although she wanted him to be her lover too. And as she thought that, she grew more depressed at what it suddenly meant to her. With a sad snicker at the tinges of her own miserable emotions, she lowered her head to her folded arms.

Don's hand touched her shoulder and she started. In her worry over the theory, she had forgotten the reality of their meeting. He was sitting beside her, quite close, and he looked seriously into her eyes. She tried to think of something frivolous to say.

"Why did you want us to come out here?" Don asked before she could speak.

So then she hadn't been able to hide her disturbance. "Must there be a special reason?" she countered. "We always used to do things just because we wanted to."

"You didn't really want to this time, did you?"

"Why do you ask that? Why should you think so?" The words jostled almost on top of each other coming from her mouth.

"Because you don't look or act as if you 'just wanted to.' You look like you're driving yourself—being forced—and you don't like it. Do you?"

She shook her head one time slowly. Her vexation at his first questions faded through her mind in the rising tide of gratitude that he had at least partly understood.

"I'm glad you—planned it, though," he went on. She saw him turn slightly from her. "Somehow, lately I haven't felt like—haven't been able to find any time to see you. I've been trying to decide something. If Mother weren't living, I'd have gone away." He was gazing through the fading light under the branches. His voice was soft, mournful. She wanted to touch his hair. "I'd have gone away," he repeated. "I think I would have. It's the dream of all young people, you know—to go away from where they are, to hope that they'll be someone else in some other place. But I'm too old for that now; I can't be anyone else. I can't change." To her his voice seemed to have an intensity that only she would have noticed; only she, or Tray, would have sensed the emphasis which removed his meaning from the dream of going away on which he hung it. "But something has changed. I've had to make myself know it was gone from me and I was alone, even inside myself, in my thoughts and dreams—free, but alone."

The light around the grove was ruddy from the setting sun. The trees enclosed them in a darkening chrysalis. The windows of the chapel caught the colors of the western sky, and by contrast to the slashes of light the building seemed blacker. At the edge of the grove, where cedar trees merged with the oaks, the chalky gravestones in the small burial ground were turning yellow.

"I've thought of going away too," said Isabel. "Something changed for me too."

In their difficult silence, she heard the wind running through the leaves and the first katydids cricking and a tree frog barking. After a while Don put his hand on hers and said, "I'm sorry, Isabel."

She slowly moved her arm, and then stood up to avoid the burning under his hand. Her courage seemed to have fluttered away; she couldn't face him with her knowledge. "Have you ever been in the chapel?" she asked nervously. "You could see it before it's too dark."

"The chapel?"

"Of course, there's nothing in it now. I suppose there's no reason to go."

Then, as she looked down at him, a faint grimace spread on his face—a kind of pitying but inverted smile—and she said, "What are you smiling at?"

"Nothing," he replied. "Not at you anyway. Just remembering something. An empty church."

"That's a strange thing to be amused at."

"Yes, I suppose it is. I'd tell you about it, but you might not think it funny. The circumstances were different then." He tilted his head and studied her face. "It sprang up in my mind. An incident suddenly coming back after all that time—Jim was with me." Don's eyes slowly moved from her face and fixed on the dark shape of the chapel. The light was fading now, with the sun hanging hugely on the horizon.

A bewildered impotence filled Isabel as she wondered what she should do or say. She struggled against surrender to the impossibility of ever coming close to him, or to anyone in the world. She almost sobbed at the silly notion that she ought to mention the food. Then harshly determined to seem casual, she sat down on the thick root beside Don. He turned from the chapel to her.

"Don," she said. Her throat began to tighten. "I know—about you and Jim."

Without a movement or a change of expression he met her eyes. Gradually a frown of earnest questioning spread over his face. His lips parted as if he meant to speak, but then slowly and firmly closed. He turned slightly away from her, toward the dim panels and columns of the graveyard. A hard, but surely also sentimental, smile broke over his mouth. He must be wondering who told her or slyly hinted to her, but he refused to ask and she was glad of it.

"It doesn't matter," she said. "I think I understand now."

She wanted to put her arms comfortingly around him, but this was not the time. She must not touch him at all. Perhaps he would hate her, just as people often hate those who know their deepest hidden secret, and the rest of their lives in Ashton would be miserable with suspicions of each other. If he would only answer her, and not stare so hypnotically at the little burial ground.

"I'm glad I know, Don. Because I know you better. You would never have told me—as I told you." She waited for some response from him, but none came. "Why do you keep looking at the graveyard? What is there?"

Then he spoke quietly, as if he hadn't been affected at all by what she had been saying. "One time in high school, were you on a picnic with a crowd of us at the forsaken town on the river bluff? There was Jim, and me and—" Suddenly he seemed to relax and his head drooped toward the ground beside him. "Picnics—and graveyards," he murmured. "I was sort of saying good-by to something I've already said good-by to in a—a bitter way. This time it was kinder—sweeter, because I found again, there in the twilight on a grave slab, the memory of its best part. The worst is gone now, Isabel. Dead. That was what happened to me. I'm glad the best of it comes back."

"Don—" But she couldn't go on; she was baffled by his words. They seemed to mean more than they said; or not as much as she supposed.

"It's over," said Don. "Me and Jim."

"I'm sorry."

He stretched an arm over her drawn-up legs and laid his forehead and cheek against her knees. In the gray light of the grove, still vibrant with reflections from the yellow western sky, she looked down at him with his eyes closed and his lips pressed tightly together. Her hands, which hovered briefly over his hair, she clasped in her lap.

The windows of the chapel faded to broad colorless streaks on the gloomy walls. The trees were black around them. The graveyard seemed a blur of gray under the cedars. Isabel didn't want to move or speak, for it would break the little sphere of this most intimate moment; but it must end soon, and it might be in the wrong way.

"Don, have you ever thought about us—together?" she asked.

"Yes, I have."

Shaking with uncertainty, her hands went up to her cheeks. "Did you ever think we—might marry each other?"

"Yes, Isabel."

But he did not move. Her fingers pressed on her temples and raked through her hair.

"We could be happy together," she whispered rapidly in order not to choke on the words.

"We have been. It could go on."

"Don—" Suddenly she thought she might become hysterical, but just as suddenly she grew very calm. "Will you marry me?"

He raised his head from her knees. "In spite of—?"

"Not so much 'in spite of' as because of," she said. "Because I love you, Don; and my love hasn't been hurt by knowing you loved Jim."

"But maybe, someday—" He hesitated, and then caught her hands. "I'm not worth it, Isabel. You couldn't ever be sure. I couldn't promise anything."

"I won't be jealous of what I don't know." Impetuously she wrenched her hands loose from his for fear she would return the pressure which she knew was a plea and not a caress. "It's silly for us to talk this way about it. We're not talking about children. We're talking about us."

"Yes," he said. "You're very sensible, Isabel. I'm not. Not about myself, anyway."

"I think you are. But you're afraid to deny yourself anything."

"That's right."

"Then you mustn't deny yourself this, Don. I certainly am not perfect, but for you—I think, now, I should be your wife. I know this is terrible, saying such things. I shouldn't try to convince you. But we have been happy together. We can go on that way. I've told you I love you. I don't ask much more than—than—"

"You see?" he said softly, accusingly. "The doubt hangs on. The little hidden question is there—always—isn't it?"

"No!" she said angrily. "No, Don. Not the question of you, because I know the answer. I can't be surprised; and that can't ever come between us. I was questioning me—my own honesty, I suppose. It will be very difficult for us both. But I want to try. I want you to marry me."

A sense of shame in laying herself thus open to him pressed more and more heavily over her. In an awful moment, when with a quick movement he got to his feet and stood above her, she fought back the growing idea that she didn't really love him but was saying so because he was her last chance, and that he realized her strategy. To what degree, she wondered, could the mere wish to marry transform a vague emotion, perhaps even verging on dislike, into a conception of love? She hated herself and wished she were alone in her house where she could cry and think of finding work in a faraway city.

"Look," said Don. "It's dark already. It's easy to say things in the dark, isn't it?"

She didn't lift a hand to wipe away the tears that slid down to each corner of her mouth. If she could only go home now and never see Don again! Soon he leaned over her and said, "We *could* make a marriage go—couldn't we?" When she didn't speak, he sat on his heels at her side.

"Isabel!" He put his fingers to her cheek. "Are you crying?"

With a hand at each of her shoulders he rose, bringing her up with him, and circled her with his arms. Rigid with mistrust and delight, she felt herself pulled close to him and his face, blurred in the night, descending on hers. Their lips touched. She stood against him, her arms dangling foolishly, still unable quite to believe that he had just then come to her, caught her in his arms and kissed her. He kissed her again and then on the cheeks and he brushed back her hair with one hand.

"You're salty with tears," he said after a while.

She laughed, almost with a sob. "Oh Don, you're a fool." She leaned her face on his shoulder.

"Yes, I am."

They stood, each now with arms around the other, as if neither wished to surrender the meaning of those few minutes.

"I would have come to you sooner or later, Isabel," said Don finally. "Last month was an awful time. I needed you, but I couldn't turn to you for help. I need you now. But I didn't know until tonight how much you could bring me that most men don't get—how much understanding, I guess. Faith, love—call it anything. At first, after you told me you knew about Jim, I didn't think you meant what you said about marrying. But I didn't know what to think, either."

"I began to wonder if I meant it, too," she said. "But I was sure before I came out here. And I'm sure again now. I think I'll always be sure of it."

"Let's make it very soon. Let's not wait a long time."

"A month—two. Whatever you say."

"One month."

"Then let's—" She pushed back from his arms. "Oh! I started to say, 'Let's eat,' but I don't think we can." She began to laugh. "We could have a moonlight picnic, but the moon isn't up yet."

"Maybe we can't even find the food—who knows?"

They held hands and crept about the tree trunk, stooping over to search out the dim shape of the baskets. Isabel stumbled on a root, but Don caught her quickly enough around the waist.

"Here it is," he said, taking up the two baskets.

"We'll have to spread the supper at home," Isabel murmured. "Dulcy will think we're crazy."

"Old Negro women are mighty wise," said Don as he opened the car door. "Let's go. I'm hungry."

The lights flashed across the chapel walls when they turned through the trees. Then the empty road unwound before them, a tunnel through the dark night, leading them home.

6

Night after night, after coming back from her mother, Doris sat in the fusty living room wondering what to say to James; rocking the baby back and forth, listening to the radio and straining against boredom. With no appreciation of her concession in returning, James restlessly paced the rooms or sprawled on the sofa. Sometimes he pretended to read, but more often he smoked with a preoccupied air and ignored her. He no longer bothered to leave the house for his drunken sprees, but staggered about before her with a glazed look while he emptied glass after glass of whiskey until he was in a sullen stupor.

And night after night when he was about to pass out, hateful and resigned, she would lug him to his bed. Sometimes out of pity bordering on annoyance, she would undress him, but usually she let him lie in his clothes, looked at him in his ridiculous defeat and wondered what in the world had happened to their marriage. Then the baby would whimper and she would tiptoe to the door of her room.

When she tried to sleep she was awakened by crying from the bassinet beside her bed. Her temper grew quick to bursting, but she controlled it and with a more reconciled attitude than she expected, went on with her job of motherhood. During the day Peachy helped her, so that she could get out of the house and call on friends, or shop or drive around in the Lincoln. But at night, when James was home, the nursing was all hers—the feeding, the bottles, the diapers, the quieting. For if the baby screamed too long, James would break into curses and, glaring bitterly and trembling, confront her as if she were the cause of it all.

His disposition was worse—stranger and more unreasonable than before the baby was born. The first night his parents came to see the child, he left the house before they arrived. "He'll be back soon," she told them; "he just went down to the drugstore for me." But she knew that he wouldn't return until they left. His mother gave her a quiet, sympathetic glance, as much as to say she understood more than Doris did.

And so it wasn't a complete surprise when Mrs. Furlow, on a morning call, brought up the subject of James's conduct. They were sitting in the living room—Mrs. Furlow cradling the baby and tickling her chin and Doris sipping a coke—and about them was that easy intimacy that blankets women alone in a house. With a cautious look to see that the kitchen door was closed on Peachy, Mrs. Furlow said, "We've been hearing rumors about Jim drinking, Doris. Have you—"

"Why, yes. He does—quite a lot," replied Doris with humiliation.

"Mr. Furlow and I simply couldn't believe it at first. It's not like Jim. Wandering around at night drunk, and all that. I—I hate to bring it up, Doris, but we wondered if you knew any reason—"

"No, I don't, Mrs. Furlow. I've been terribly upset. I can't imagine why he does it. We're perfectly happy—except for that. He wanted a child, but now he doesn't seem to care a thing about it."

"I'm afraid something bad might happen. We can't talk to him, Mr. Furlow and I. We want to, but he'd think it was meddling. But we've got to get him out of this somehow, Doris. Isn't there anything you can do?"

Doris finished the coke and put the glass on the rug beside her chair. "I don't know why he does it, Mrs. Furlow. It worries me all the time. It's a—a threat to our home. He might—"

A film of anxious tears lined the edges of the older woman's eyelids. "I know you're just as sweet and kind as can be, Doris. You don't deserve to have something like this right when you have the baby to think about. If we can help any way, just tell us."

"I talk to him about it," said Doris, "but it doesn't do any good. I feel helpless. If we'd quarreled or anything like that, I could understand. But there's no reason for him not to be happy. I—I just hope he'll stop it and settle down. I think he will, don't you, Mrs. Furlow? When he sees the baby growing, and realizes what he owes us—his home?"

"Oh, he must, Doris. He must." Mrs. Furlow drew the cover about the sleeping baby's head. "Every wife has to face something like this some time or other. We'll just have to be patient, and trust in God."

After that morning they had many quiet, anxious talks, but could reach no conclusion about why James continued to lead such a dissipated life. Somewhere very deep, Doris felt twinges of guilt for his condition and almost admitted the first slight intuition that she could, if she would, do something to help him. But she kept insisting, over and over, it wasn't her fault, because she had to believe that. In time he would calm down, relax in their quiet home, assume his family responsibilities as all men do in the long run, and seldom again relapse into such a long period of foolishness. She was patient, as Mrs. Furlow had said all wives must be; she could wait.

With the news of Don's approaching marriage to Isabel, James became more peevish than ever. He wouldn't let her talk about it without storming for no reason at all, and she got no satisfaction out of relaying the gossip she heard. In the stores, at morning coke parties and over the telephone, all the details of the wedding were announced before the Ashton *Herald* could print the formal notice. The ceremony was to be held in Don's house, the stories went, because his mother was an invalid. A few people whispered their suspicions that he was marrying Isabel for her money. Isabel was to rent her house and Don was going to remodel his mother's cottage. And so on. As fast as pieces of news could be garnered, they were spread over town.

One morning Doris met Alice Barnette on the street and they suggested at the same time having a coke at Herring's drugstore. It wasn't long, naturally, before Alice was talking about the wedding with an envious excitement that made Doris rather sad.

"Have you heard the latest?" asked Alice in a carefully lowered voice. "Don has asked Gus Traywick to be his best man. You'd think he'd—"

"Now isn't that peculiar?" Doris remarked.

"Not half as peculiar as Isabel, though," said Alice. "Isabel has asked Bea Traywick—a married woman—to be the maid of honor!"

"Why, I never heard of such a thing."

"Just what you might expect of Isabel, I guess," whispered Alice. "First, the wedding in the groom's house, and now this. She probably won't even wear a veil, so she can shock everybody."

"It just shows a lack of taste, that's all," said Doris.

Possibly James knew of this already and hadn't told her. At any rate, it would account for his being so touchy about the wedding, for he'd naturally have supposed that Don would ask him to be best man. When she mentioned it that night, he cut her short.

"What the hell do I care?" he growled and secluded himself in his bedroom until she called him to supper.

During the week before the wedding several parties were given for Isabel: a "shower" at Bea Traywick's, a luncheon at Madge's. And Tray planned a stag supper for Don. But on the night before Tray's party, James called and told him he couldn't come; he had to go out of town.

"That's a stupid thing to do, James," Doris said, as he hung up the receiver. "They'll all find out you told a lie."

Without answering or looking at her, he sat down and reached for the drink he had left on the table.

"Of course," she went on, "I think it's stupid too for Don not to ask you to be best man. After all, you've been best friends all your lives. I don't understand it."

"You don't have to," he shouted.

"You don't have to scream at me, James. You'll wake up the baby and I'll have to nurse her back to sleep. You'd have a much better disposition if you'd stop drinking. You're going to ruin your health and your business."

"I drink when I want to," he said, emptying the glass.

"Well, I don't see how we can ever have a home and a decent place for a girl to grow up in."

"Does it make much difference?"

"Yes, it does. How can you talk like that? You don't seem to care at all for our child or me or anything."

"You don't seem to want me to have any friends." He got up and wandered unsteadily through the dining room to the kitchen.

"Why, James, I *want* you to have friends," she said in an injured tone. "Men friends, I mean. I certainly don't want you making a fool of both of us with—" (she raised her voice so he could hear) "—with Madge Dalton and such women. But look how you treat your old friends."

"Will you shut up about that?" he cried, striding heavily back into the living room. "We're not friends. We never were. I wouldn't raise a finger to help him." His words were husky and uncertain when he finished.

"You've changed such a lot since we married," she mused.

"So have you."

"I don't make myself the talk of the town wandering around drunk in the car. Your father and mother are worried about it."

"Oh, they are? I guess you told them."

"No, I didn't. Everybody's talking about it. But your mother and I have had some long talks. She thinks it's strange too that Don didn't ask you—"

"Stop harping on that. It's nothing to me. I'd have refused anyway. He knew better than to ask me."

"What's got into you, James? We have a home to think of. We have a child. You wanted a child, but you're destroying our—"

"We still don't have any love, do we?"

"That's not the point. Lord knows, I try to get you not to drink, but what can I do?"

"Nothing, now. It's too late."

"No, it's not too late. You're just depressed about something." She moved close to him and touched his shoulder. "Whatever it is, James, please get over it. Think of me and our child—our home. That's the important thing. We don't want it to go to pieces."

"Oh, baloney!" He shrugged away from her and leaned over to turn on the radio.

"Then think of your family—your respect in town. You want to preserve that. I know you'll quit this drinking soon. You've been under a strain, maybe. But we'll work it out together. Won't we, James?"

She must have patience, she must control herself right up to the point where everything became unbearable. Otherwise she'd never be able to control James or her home. She couldn't go out into the world alone with her child; she couldn't even face her own parents with the admission that her marriage had been shattered. Sooner or later James would realize how much he owed to her and would take hold of himself. Then they could enter that calm security of the home every woman dreamed of having: dusk, with father in slippers and smoking jacket before the gas log; the child playing on the new rug; mother returning from a social gathering in a fur jacket and prompting the servant about dinner; and old friends dropping in later to admire the new radio, the new silver service, the new furniture. And no worries, no quarrels, no emotional outbursts. She could see it plainly in her mind almost as if she were remembering something already seen—some scene in a magazine or a movie—and she knew that eventually they would both achieve that state. But for the time being, she would have to be very understanding and patient. Men were such children.

7

In front of the Mason cottage, men and women in light summer clothes passed up the sidewalk, converged at the gate between the clipped lygustrums and crossed the green lawn to the crowded porch. The low hum of voices reached Jim as the motor of the Lincoln died, and a tremor of dismay flashed over him. The sound of treacly piano music spilled from the open windows.

"I don't think—I can talk to anyone," he whispered, almost in a gasp.

"What's the matter?" Doris asked. She was waiting at the wheel for him to come around and open the door for her.

With bewildered annoyance, he shook his head. "I don't know. I don't know."

"You'll be all right," she consoled. "It's probably jitters from too much liquor." Fussily, she got out of the car and opened the door beside him. "Come on, James. Don't hold a grudge."

As in a nightmare, he walked with her to the porch and among the guests who chattered in hushed voices. There, coming out of the house, was Horace Saxon grinning as never before, and behind him Dr. and Mrs. Everett. Isabel's sister, who had come from Missouri for the occasion, met them at the door. Gesturing with her hand, she told them they could find Mrs. Mason in the parlor.

Fern, smilax and flowers littered the room in all available places. Against the windows opposite the hall door, a bower of foliage was flanked with light frames that imitated cathedral candelabra. Before it a lectern rose from an undergrowth of ferns. In the rows of chairs that filled the rest of the room a few guests were already seated.

At the left of the lectern, Mrs. Mason was stationed in a wheel chair. In a new dress, with her face lightly made up and her hair carefully arranged, she looked surprisingly healthy. As he shook hands, Jim, hoping to avoid any reminiscences, could bring out no more than the barest of formalities. But Doris launched into a stream of compliments.

"Oh, it's a special dress," laughed Mrs. Mason, "ordered just for the wedding. The chair, too. They rented it so I wouldn't have to try to walk."

"I know you're awfully happy today," said Doris.

"Well, in a way I am." Mrs. Mason's cheerfulness clouded with sad fortitude and she twisted a handkerchief in her fingers. "I hate to lose Donald, of course, but then I tell myself I'm not losing my son but gaining a daughter."

"That's such a sweet way to look at it," murmured Doris.

"Go in and look at all the presents," invited Mrs. Mason. "In my room, right across there."

As they passed through the hall, the Daltons halloed gaily from the porch— Jim couldn't stand to listen to Josh making jokes today—and there, with Judge Dorn hovering over, was Charlie Ann Davis scribbling on a pad and peering at the decorations and the dresses. At the bedroom door Aunt Marny took them in hand, and wedged them through the crowd toward the tables so she could point out the prize gifts.

"And look at this!" she cried, holding up an envelope. "Mr. Saxon just brought it."

"Hundred-dollar bills?" asked Doris facetiously.

"No," said Aunt Marny, extracting an official-looking paper; "a deed to half-interest in the *Herald* and its property."

"Oh, how wonderful!" Doris exclaimed. "Isn't it wonderful, James? Then Don will be editor some day."

His skin burned as he stood there unable to focus on the vases, candlesticks, plates and linen on the tables. To prompt him, Doris nudged his arm. "Yes, that's fine," he managed to say. He wanted to rush through the admiring group, out of the house and into the silent, dim countryside.

Isabel's sister appeared at the door and announced that the ceremony was about to begin and they must all find seats. A contralto voice was singing, "I Love You Truly."

In the hall, Jim halted by the stairway while the people moved sluggishly past him toward the parlor. "I'll stand here by the door and look in," he said. "There's not enough seats."

"You certainly won't," said Doris. "You're going to sit with me." She pushed him along toward the entrance, where all the voices sank into the muted speech that precedes a ritual.

Isabel's sister rushed up and grabbed a chair that Jim was shoving aside. "Don't move that," she said. "It's for Dulcy. Come on, Dulcy," she called over her shoulder; "here's your place."

With a grateful, fearful smile, the old Negro woman inched timidly toward the seat and waited till the crush about the door had moved inside.

"More of Isabel's pranks," whispered Doris when they had gone through the door. "But I bet she'll settle down soon enough."

The Wedding March began, ringing thinly from the piano, and Jim clenched his fingers. The minister came from a door on the right. When it opened again slightly, he knew that Tray was behind it, with Don at his side, ready to walk before him. Bea was advancing slowly down the center aisle, with the bouquet in her hands quivering at each restrained step.

He lowered his eyelids till he could hardly see and let his head droop—not much, because someone might notice it—and held himself rigid. From the wave of pious gasps he knew that Isabel had appeared at the hall door. It seemed to take her forever to go down the aisle, and all the faces in front of him were turned in his direction to watch her and murmur how beautiful she was. And there was Don now—Don, gone from him forever—standing beside the minister, and then Isabel. What fools they were—what fools they all were!

Doris stirred in her seat and pulled a handkerchief from her bag to dab at her nose.

Tears tickled at the rim of his eyes. Silently he asked, against the monotone of the ritual in the minister's mouth, What have I done to myself? What have I done? He was sinking through a hot dark buzzing—his sense of touch vanished, his sight shut off, his mind reduced to a pinpoint of query. Then at last it was over and the piano triumphantly clanged for the two couples to march out.

With the upsurge of voices and the clatter of scraping chairs around him and the blurred vision of the ceremony—Don's final renunciation, thrusting him back into an empty, cold life—vibrating in his mind, he could hardly find the will to rise from his chair. Doris linked her arm through his and he let her lead him, jostled by other friends, to the front door.

At the end of the long porch, Don and Isabel stood with the Traywicks to receive congratulations from the line of guests that had formed. As the first of the people returned, two Negro maids served plates of cake, and ice cream molded into hearts with an imprinted bride and groom.

Jim looked in dread down the line ahead of Doris. Everyone seemed to be jabbering gaily, twisting about, and those in front of the bride and groom were vigorously shaking hands, tripping and fluttering over ecstatic words and joking about kissing the bride. He couldn't escape; he must face this before he could have peace.

The line before him was growing shorter. He could see the stiffness of the smiles on Don's and Isabel's faces, and hear their weary, repetitious answers. Doris was talking to Bea and Tray, and then she passed on, leaving him before them powerless to speak. But he said something—he thought he did—and made a grimace which he hoped was a smile. Perhaps under the bubbling of Doris's chatter no one would notice his behavior.

Now he was there, in front of Don and Isabel, face to face with the man who might have helped him, but refused. Suddenly, remembering the history of the offerings which each had made, he was overwhelmed with the guilt and selfishness of his resentment; and once more he wanted to hide from himself and the world. He looked at the floor between their feet.

The familiar, stirring voice came, saying "Jim" tenderly, and Don's hand was held out to him. He raised his eyes. Don was no longer smiling the fixed smile; his gaze searched deeply and forgivingly into him. He took Don's hand, and his head sank forward. It had passed in a few seconds, though it seemed interminable. No one could have noticed anything unusual.

"Jim!" broke in Isabel, "you must kiss the bride!" She caught his arm and pulled him to her and he put his lips on hers. "Come and see us when we get back," she said softly. "Will you? We want you to."

He smiled quickly like a scared child. "Yes," he said, "yes." But when would he be able to endure seeing them happy in their own home? How long would it take him to readjust himself to the life he would have to lead so that they could all be friends again—rather, so that he could feel natural about their being friends? Isabel seemed to sweep away with those few earnest words a great deal of his despair. He felt momentarily that in years to come he and Don would laugh over their cigars and drinks about the past years. But now that the line of guests had pushed him forward and he was gone from her warmth and Don's tenderness, he was enveloped again in dismay.

Uneasily he wound through the crowd toward the front steps. One of the maids offered him a plate of refreshment but he couldn't think of eating. While Doris was talking with the McGills, he slipped by unnoticed and edged quickly through the door into the hall. But the hall, too, was thick with people. The bedroom with the display of wedding presents was filled and among the disordered chairs in the parlor a few groups sat eating and talking to Mrs. Mason. When Josh and Madge Dalton got up to leave the old woman, Jim ran up the stairs.

No one was on the top landing. Now that he didn't have to pretend any longer, he began to tremble. He went through the open door of Don's room and sat down. Clothing was scattered on bed and chairs, and two suitcases were set near the door. He stared at each piece of furniture, deliberately and painfully, just as if he recognized them from a bad dream rather than from his days of school and summer idleness with Don. So little in a piece of furniture changes, he thought, and yet it gathers about it so much of the life it has merely accommodated.

After how long he didn't know, he heard footsteps on the stairs. He didn't move. The sounds stopped abruptly in the doorway. When he heard his name he turned his head.

"Oh—Jim. You here?" Tray came to him and dropped his hand lightly at the middle of his shoulder while he scanned the room much in the same way that Jim had, as if he dimly understood and sympathized.

"They're leaving in a minute," said Tray as he picked up the bags. "Isabel's changing now. Come on down and see them off." He waited a moment at the door.

"I think I'll stay here," said Jim with an effort at lightness. "I can see them better from the window."

"But they'd want to see *you*."

"Well—I'll come on down," he mumbled.

When Tray had gone, Jim got up as if hypnotized by his own words and went to the dormer window. In the yard below, a few couples strolled or stood talking, and sometimes disappeared under the eave of the porch to be replaced by others. The summer dresses made senseless patterns of bright movement against the grass. Tray carried the suitcases down the walk and put them into the car. Then all the people vanished as if on a summons, and shortly after, while the vacant lawn heaved almost dizzily below him, there was a shout of many voices. Isabel must have tossed her bouquet to the girls; they would be coming out now.

He stepped back from the window protectively. In their presence he weakened, he repented and yearned toward them; but here, at a distance, able to look down in judgment on their foreshortened figures, he was filled with revulsion not only for Don, but also for Isabel who took him, and for the marriage which bound him to her.

Aimlessly he paced with slow steps about the room, touching a chair, drawing his fingers along the foot of the bed, picking up and smelling the brushes Don had left behind on the dresser. At the wide bookcase, he stooped to read the titles that flashed with a cluster of allied experiences in his memory. He hadn't meant to stop there, but from some unsensed compulsion he sat on the floor and pulled out the book that fixed his attention. The title danced before his eyes and at last wavered away while the words of a poem, "Pity this busy monster manunkind Not . . ." wriggled across his brain as if written in water. And beside the water he lay with Don, wet from swimming, hot in the sun on the yellow sand; and Don reading to him, and the quiet of the woods all around.

Through the dream he heard more cries from below, the sound of running feet on the pavement, squeals and shrieks, a slamming car door and tinkling sprays of rice against the car and "Good-by! Good-by!" as a motor raced down the street.

At the touch of a hand on his shoulder, he whirled about furiously and glared up at Tray. For a moment neither said a word. Then he asked hoarsely, "Why did you come back?"

"Doris is waiting downstairs," Tray said quietly.

Jim scrambled to his feet and walked across the room. "She's got the car. She can go on home." He waved the book of poems as if to dismiss Doris and Tray both.

"Bea and I want you to have dinner at our house and celebrate."

Jim snorted and turned his back. He opened the book again and pretended to read.

"Don asked me to say good-by for him," said Tray, after a pause. "He—hoped you'd wish them happiness."

"That's a lie," he said sharply, facing Tray.

"Yes, it's a lie," replied Tray, as he walked toward Jim. "You want to know what he really said?" The same expression of pleading and pity that he had seen on Don now softened Tray's features.

"Sure."

"He said . . . 'Take care of Jim.'"

His face contorted into conflicting grimaces of astonishment, amusement and anger. "Well, of all—" He took a deep breath. "The damned little fairy!"

Tray's hand smashed against his cheek and he swayed against the foot of the bed.

"Shut up!" said Tray.

Jim held shakily to the bedpost, his eyes fixed in hatred on Tray. Then he wheeled about to sink down on the mattress; and his eyes flickered, and wavered from Tray to the floor.

"At least let him try to be happy," Tray said softly.

With a shuddering expiration of breath, Jim clutched the book of poems between his interlaced fingers and pressed his legs tight against them. His shoulders drooped forward and he began to cry.

"You're a damn coward, Jim." Tray spoke gently and moved in front of him to sit on the bed at his side. "You're selfish, too. You've never tried, deep down, to be happy, I guess. You always want somebody else to bring it to you."

Tray pulled Jim's shoulders upright. Then he found the tears shining on Jim's cheeks, and heard the caught breath, the little choked moan of a child. "Jim," he whispered, "Jim . . . don't do that. Please."

But Jim couldn't stop. He could only shake his head hopelessly and turn the book over and over in his hands.

With his fists clenched as if to strike out at some unknown danger, Tray watched, bewildered, and begged him to hush. Finally, he put both arms around him and pulled him awkwardly against his chest, with Jim's face sniffling on his sleeve, and held him there, swaying gently as if he were a mother rocking her child.

"Jim . . . Jim . . ." he whispered; and then he became silent, waiting hopefully for the end of this distress. After a long time he spoke, but the voice sounded strange, not his own, as if he had not expected to say anything.

"If only people could forgive each other for loving."

And Tray, never having been taught how to be good, nor having felt any guilt for his lack of this knowledge, wondered for a moment what his own words meant.

ABOUT THE AUTHOR

Hubert Creekmore (1907–1966) was an American poet and author from Water Valley, Mississippi. He is author of *Personal Sun, the Early Poems of Hubert Creekmore*; *The Stone Ants*; *The Fingers of the Night*; *The Long Reprieve and Other Poems of New Caledonia*; *Formula*; *The Chain in the Heart*; *Lyrics of the Middle Ages*; and *Daffodils Are Dangerous*, among other publications.

ABOUT THE CONTRIBUTOR

Phillip "Pip" Gordon is the author of *Gay Faulkner: Uncovering a Homosexual Presence in Yoknapatawpha and Beyond* as well as numerous essays on William Faulkner, the Queer South, and LGBTQ+ Young Adult literature. A native West Tennessean, he holds degrees from the University of Tennessee-Martin and the University of Mississippi. He currently lives and works in Wisconsin, where he teaches writing, literature, and LGBTQ+ studies.